THE DARK FOREST

CIXIN LIU

TRANSLATED BY JOEL MARTINSEN

HEAD
ZEUS

Originally published as 黑暗森林 in 2008 by Chongqing Publishing Group in
Chongqing, China. First published in the United States of America in 2015
by Tom Doherty Associates LLC.

First published in the UK in 2015 by Head of Zeus Ltd.
This paperback edition first published in 2016 by Head of Zeus Ltd.

Translation by Joel Martinsen

9 7 5 4 6 8

A catalogue record for this book is available from the British Library.

Paperback ISBN 9781784971618
Ebook ISBN 9781784971588

Typeset by Adrian McLaughlin
Printed and bound by CPI Group (UK) Ltd, Croydon, CR0 4YY

Head of Zeus Ltd
First Floor East
5–8 Hardwick Street
London EC1R 4RG

WWW.HEADOFZEUS.COM

RUSSIAN SYNTAX

RUSSIAN SYNTAX

Aspects of Modern Russian
Syntax and Vocabulary

F. M. BORRAS
University of Leeds

AND

R. F. CHRISTIAN
University of Birmingham

OXFORD
AT THE CLARENDON PRESS

Oxford University Press, Ely House, London W.1

GLASGOW   NEW YORK   TORONTO   MELBOURNE   WELLINGTON
CAPE TOWN   SALISBURY   IBADAN   NAIROBI   LUSAKA   ADDIS ABABA
BOMBAY   CALCUTTA   MADRAS   KARACHI   LAHORE   DACCA
KUALA LUMPUR   HONG KONG   TOKYO

EO 016870

FIRST PUBLISHED 1959

REPRINTED LITHOGRAPHICALLY IN GREAT BRITAIN
AT THE UNIVERSITY PRESS, OXFORD
FROM CORRECTED SHEETS OF THE FIRST EDITION
1961, 1963, 1968

PREFACE

This book does not contain all that would normally be found in a work on Russian syntax. It does not, for example, attempt to classify the various types of sentence. At the same time, it includes lexical material which does not come within the scope of syntax. For these reasons the title *Russian Syntax* has been qualified in the sub-title by the words *Aspects of Modern Russian Syntax and Vocabulary*.

Our principal object in writing this book has been to help English-speaking students with a good knowledge of Russian grammar to overcome some of the difficulties of writing consecutive Russian prose. While keeping this object in view, we have tried to bring out some of the essential characteristics of the Russian language as an instrument of expression. The choice of material, especially lexical material, may in places appear arbitrary, but it has been governed largely by a consideration of our own difficulties in learning to write Russian, and by the observation of difficulties experienced by English students. We hope that this book, based on such an approach, may contribute within its limits to putting the study of Russian in English-speaking countries on a comparable footing to the study of other European languages.

Examples to illustrate the text have been drawn from Soviet literature and the Soviet press, as well as from nineteenth-century authors. Much valuable help has been obtained from the Soviet Academy of Sciences' Грамматика русского языка, vol. ii, Moscow, 1954, and also from standard Russian dictionaries, notably that edited by Ushakov (Толковый словарь русского языка, Moscow, 1935–40), and the volumes so far published of the current Academy Dictionary (Словарь современного русского литературного языка, Moscow–Leningrad, 1950–). Sections on the translation of certain common English words have been appended to four of the eight chapters, and word-order is dealt with briefly in the final chapter. The Table of Contents is comprehensive, but a separate English–Russian index and an index of Russian words have also been included. These indexes do not include words listed alphabetically in the vocabulary sections, which can easily be located.

The book was read in manuscript by Professor Unbegaun and Mrs. Arian, to both of whom we are indebted for suggestions and improvements. Other native Russian speakers have given valuable assistance on occasions, notably Mrs. Birkett, Mr. Zekulin, and Dr. Inna Baykov. We wish to acknowledge our gratitude to all the people mentioned, and also to Professor Jopson, who saw and commented on part of the work in its early stages. We would also like to thank the Delegates of the Clarendon Press for the attractive presentation of the volume.

F. M. B. and R. F. C.

CONTENTS

CONTENTS

V. THE PRONOUN AND PRONOMINAL WORDS

VI. THE PREPOSITION

I

THE NOUN

1. In this chapter we shall deal mainly with problems related to gender, number, and the use of cases. The question of diminutive nouns will also be treated, and a final section will be devoted to the translation of individual words which in our experience have given difficulty to students.

GENDER

2. With the exception of nouns ending in a soft sign in the nominative case, the determination of gender in Russian is quite straightforward. Nevertheless there are some difficulties related to gender which are worth commenting on.

3. (i) Generally speaking the gender of declinable foreign words taken over by Russian is determined by their endings and not by their gender in the language from which they are borrowed. Thus до́гма is feminine, though neuter in Greek; аква́риум is masculine though neuter in Latin.

(ii) If the borrowed noun is not declined in Russian and refers to an inanimate object (e.g. такси́), it is always neuter regardless of ending, with the exception of ко́фе which is masculine (*black coffee* чёрный ко́фе). Even ко́фе, however, is sometimes regarded as neuter colloquially: *this coffee is not nice* э́то ко́фе не вку́сно (as well as э́то невку́сный ко́фе).

(iii) If the borrowed noun is not declined and refers to a human being it takes its gender from the sex of that being. Thus ле́ди is feminine.

(iv) Borrowed indeclinable nouns denoting animals (e.g. шимпанзе́) are generally masculine regardless of sex, except when unmistakable reference is made to the female.

(v) The principle followed with foreign indeclinable nouns denoting rivers, towns, and newspapers is for the noun to take the same gender as the generic words река́, го́род, and газе́та:

Down the wide Missouri   Вниз по широ́кой Миссу́ри

4. As a general rule the gender of a diminutive or augmentative noun is the same as that of the parent word. Hence the final vowel gives no indication of gender (but it does indicate the *type* of declension). For example, the augmentative suffix -ищ- has an -e ending for masculine as well as neuter nouns: огро́мный доми́ще (gen. огро́много доми́ща) 'huge house'. The pejorative suffix -ишк- has an -a ending for masculine nouns denoting persons and animals, and an -o ending for inanimate masculines: ужа́сный хвастуни́шка (gen. ужа́сного хвастуни́шки) 'awful little braggart'; жа́лкий доми́шко (gen. жа́лкого доми́шка) 'squalid little house'. The augmentative (and often pejorative) suffix -ин-a is hardly ever used except after masculine nouns, and adjectives in agreement are normally (though not invariably) masculine: сти́льный доми́на (gen. сти́льного доми́ны) 'period house'.

5. To the masculine gender belongs a group of nouns denoting male persons such as дя́дя *uncle*, ю́ноша *youth*, слуга́ *servant*. They are declined as feminine nouns, while adjectives in agreement with them have masculine endings:

I see your uncle   Я ви́жу ва́шего дя́дю
I do not see your uncle   Я не ви́жу ва́шего дя́ди

Such nouns denote male persons only, although an exception must now be made for судья́ *judge* which in the Soviet Union can be used of a woman judge. In this use it is still regarded as masculine and adjectives in agreement with it have masculine endings:

She is a people's judge   Она́ наро́дный судья́

6. Not to be confused with the examples in paragraph **5** are nouns with the conventional feminine final vowels -a, or -я, which can be applied to either sex. When adjectives qualify these nouns of *common* gender, they are declined with masculine or feminine endings according to whether the noun denotes a man or a woman (in contrast to судья above):

This girl has no mother or father	Эта девочка — круглая сирота
This boy has no mother or father	Этот мальчик — круглый сирота

Many such words have a pejorative meaning, e.g. невежа *ignoramus*, неряха *sloven*, обжора *glutton*, лежебока *sluggard*, пьяница *drunkard*, убийца *murderer*. (N.B. the current colloquialism стиляга 'teddy-boy'.) Those which are not disparaging often express suffering or deprivation, e.g. бедняга *poor fellow/girl*, калека *cripple*, сирота *orphan*, and possibly in the same category may be included левша *left-handed person*, i.e. a departure from the norm. But notice too умница *clever person* and работяга *hard worker*.

7. Nouns with masculine endings which, by virtue of their meaning, can be applied to both sexes, e.g. человек *person*, друг *friend*, товарищ *comrade*, and nouns denoting membership of a profession open to both sexes such as педагог *teacher*, have adjectives in agreement with them declined in the masculine even when they refer to women:

Sonya is a nice person and a very good teacher	Соня — милый человек и очень хороший педагог

8. (i) There are many masculine nouns denoting persons which have corresponding feminine forms with characteristic suffixes. We are accustomed in English to such pairs as *conductor, conductress*; *Englishman, Englishwoman*; *hero, heroine*, and therefore to the Russian кондуктор, кондукторша; англичанин, англичанка; герой, героиня. But in Russian the range of feminine suffixes is wider than in English and the appropriate feminine form more widely used. It is important therefore to observe pairs like студент, студентка, *student*; певе́ц, певи́ца, *singer*; крестья́нин, крестья́нка, *peasant*; касси́р, касси́рша, *cashier*; уча́стник, уча́стница, *participant*; коммуни́ст, коммуни́стка, *communist*; рабо́тник, рабо́тница, *worker* where English uses one form for both sexes.

(ii) With the participation of women in almost all trades and professions in Russia the number of specifically feminine forms began to increase, e.g. уда́рница, *shock worker*. As against this, however, a tendency can be observed to revert to the masculine form, especially, curiously enough, when women exceed men in a particular occupation and this modifies to a slight extent what has been said in the previous paragraph. Thus in towns where all tram conductors are women, the basic term конду́ктор has again become common usage, and учи́тель is often applied to a woman teacher, especially in a predicative context:

His sister is a mathematics teacher	Его́ сестра́ — учи́тель матема́тики

(iii) Слуга́ is a *male servant*, служа́нка a *female servant*, прислу́га either a *female servant* or a collective word for *the servants*.

(iv) Князь *prince*, has two feminine forms where English has one: княги́ня *princess*, means *a prince's wife*; княжна́ *princess*, means *a prince's daughter*.

9. There are a few nouns in -ша still in colloquial use which may mean either a woman of a particular occupation as opposed to a man, or else the wife of a man of that occupation. Библиоте́карша can only mean *a woman librarian*. On the other hand, инжене́рша is only accepted as correct usage in the meaning of *an engineer's wife*. Examples of both до́кторша and профе́ссорша may be found in either meaning, although in practice nowadays до́ктор and профе́ссор are almost invariably used of both sexes, and до́кторша and профе́ссорша, when met in colloquial speech, will mean *doctor's wife* and *professor's wife* respectively.

10. (i) Russian is more observant of gender distinctions with animals than English now is. Both languages share such pairs as лев, льви́ца, *lion, lioness* or тигр, тигри́ца, *tiger, tigress*, but Russian has separate words for the male and the female *bear* (медве́дь, медве́дица), *eagle* (орёл, орли́ца), *hare* (за́яц, зайчи́ха), and several other animals and birds.

(ii) *Cat* and *dog* are usually translated by the feminine nouns ко́шка and соба́ка unless specific reference is made to the sex of the animal. In this case the pairs are кот, ко́шка, *tom-cat, she-cat*; and кобе́ль, су́ка, *dog, bitch*. Пёс, which suggests *hound*, is colloquial and often vulgar.

(iii) Ло́шадь is the normal word for *horse*. Конь is used of a cavalry horse, and it often corresponds to *steed* in poetic or rhetorical contexts. When specific reference is made to the sex, the pair is жеребе́ц, кобы́ла, *stallion, mare*.

11. Ту́фля *slipper*, зал *hall*, роя́ль (masc.) *piano*, and жира́ф *giraffe* are accepted as correct modern usage; ту́фель (masc.), за́ла, роя́ль (fem.), and жира́фа are colloquial or archaic. But скирд and скирда́ *haystack*, and ста́вень and ста́вня *shutter* are equally permissible alternative forms.

ANIMATE AND INANIMATE CATEGORIES

12. Next to gender may be considered the question of the animate and inanimate object. This distinction is encountered very early in the study of Russian but mistakes are often made because of the apparent reluctance to regard animals, birds, and insects as animate beings:

I heard a lark	Я слы́шал жа́воронка
He found a bug in the bed	Он нашёл клопа́ в посте́ли

13. The following irregularities or illogicalities in the system of assigning to all nouns not only a specific gender but also an animate or inanimate label should be noticed:

(i) Trees, plants, and vegetables are not regarded as

animate objects although they are alive. On the other hand покойник *the deceased* and мертвец *a corpse* are animates.

(ii) A few neuter adjectives or participles used as nouns such as насекомое *insect,* животное *animal,* пресмыкающееся *reptile,* and млекопитающее *mammal,* and also the neuter nouns дитя *child* and лицо *person,* are animate as their meaning would suggest, but it is only in the plural that their accusative and genitive cases coincide. In the singular their accusative is the same as their nominative form.

(iii) Sometimes a normally inanimate noun is used figuratively to designate a living person. Then it becomes animate:

Do you know this old simple- ton?	Знаете вы этого старого колпака?

Колпак which normally means *a tall cap* is here colloquially used to mean *dunce* or *dunderhead.* Similarly too with кумир *idol*:

In the Soviet Union at the moment the Russian leaders are removing their old idol, Stalin, from his pedestal	Теперь в Советском Союзе русские вожди развенчивают своего давнишнего кумира, Сталина

(iv) Sometimes a normally animate noun is used in an inanimate context, as in the title of a book. It then retains its animate character:

To read the 'Brothers Kara- mazov'	Читать „Братьев Карамазовых"

Alternatively one says: Читать роман „Братья Карамазовы". Compare too:

They were watching the sculp- tor model a horse	Они смотрели, как скульптор лепил коня

(v) Technical terms in certain games illustrate some curious uses of the animate genitive. The logic behind сбро́сить короля́ *to discard a king* is clear enough. Perhaps too снять туза́ *to cut an ace* is understandable since туз was once applied figuratively to an important person, although this use is now archaic. Положи́ть ша́ра в лу́зу *to pot a billiard ball* remains curious, but the accusative шар is also widely found in this expression nowadays.

(vi) Тип in the colloquial sense of *a type, a person*, has ти́па for its accusative:

To meet an interesting type	Встре́тить интере́сного ти́па

(vii) Collective nouns referring to a group of animate objects are as a rule inanimate:

You must love the people	Наро́д на́до люби́ть

Compare too то́лпы *crowds*, отря́д *detachment*.

NUMBER

14. Many Russian nouns which have only plural forms (pluralia tantum) have parallels in English: очки́ *spectacles*, но́жницы *scissors*, брю́ки *trousers*. Among the more common pluralia tantum where English has a singular noun are: черни́ла *ink*, де́ньги *money*, сли́вки *cream*, обо́и *wallpaper*, часы́ *watch*, счёты *abacus*, су́мерки *twilight*, ро́ды *childbirth*, крести́ны *christening*, по́хороны *funeral*, щи *cabbage soup*, са́ни *sledge*, хло́поты *fuss, trouble*. Some of these nouns admit of a singular or plural meaning, i.e. часы́ can mean both *watch* and *watches*, са́ни can mean both *sledge* and *sledges*. Compare:

I have only one watch	У меня́ то́лько одни́ часы́
I have two watches	У меня́ дво́е часо́в

15. (i) Nouns used only in the singular give no difficulty with the possible exception of the names for various fruits and vegetables, and for some precious stones. Карто́фель means *potatoes*, not simply *a potato*; крыжо́вник *gooseberries*; морко́вь *carrots*; горо́х *peas*; зе́лень *vegetables*; же́мчуг *pearls*; and there are other common examples.

(ii) To express one potato, carrot, pea, pearl, &c., a suffix is usually employed, e.g. картофелина, морковка, горошина, жемчужина. (But N.B. a *gooseberry* ягода крыжовника.) Notice also солома *straw*, соломина *a straw*.

(iii) Other useful singular collective nouns are провизия (no plural) *provisions* and лучина *sticks, matchwood* (plural not used collectively).

16. Ложь *a lie, lies* is a singular noun and has no plural (one may use выдумки *fabrications*). Зло *evil* has only one form in the plural, namely the genitive зол.

It's a pack of lies	Это всё ложь
The lesser of two evils	Меньшее из двух зол

17. In the case of homonyms, difference in meaning may be shown by different plural endings:

(i) Plurals in -ы (-и) and -á (-я):

Орден   (*a*) *order* (monastic, architectural), plural ордены
              (*b*) *order* (decoration), plural ордена

Образ   (*a*) *shape, form*, plural образы
              (*b*) *icon*, plural образа

Хлеб   (*a*) *loaf of bread*, plural хлебы
              (*b*) *corn, cereal crops*, plural хлеба

Тон   (*a*) *tone* (of sound), plural тоны
              (*b*) *shade* (of colour), plural тона

Пропуск   (*a*) *omission*, plural пропуски
              (*b*) *permit, pass-word*, plural пропуска

Мех   (*a*) *bellows*, plural мехи
         Note that both singular and plural can denote a pair of bellows: эти мехи *these bellows*, кузнечный мех *a blacksmith's bellows*.
         (*b*) *fur*, plural меха

Счёт	(*a*) *abacus, counting machine*: счёты (no singular)
	(*b*) *bill, account*, plural счета́
	But N.B. своди́ть (свести́) счёты с *to settle accounts (settle up) with.*
Цвет	(*a*) *flowers*: цветы́ (singular *a flower*: цвето́к)
	(*b*) *colour*, plural цвета́

(ii) Plurals in -ы (-и) and -ья:

Зуб	(*a*) *tooth*, plural зу́бы
	(*b*) *tooth* (of a saw, machine, or other implement), plural зу́бья
Лист	(*a*) *sheet* (of paper, metal), plural листы́
	(*b*) *leaf* (of a plant), plural ли́стья
По́вод	(*a*) *pretext*, plural по́воды
	(*b*) *rein*, plural пово́дья
Ко́рень	(*a*) *root*, plural ко́рни
	(*b*) *spices*: коре́нья (no singular)

(iii) Сын may have two plural forms. The usual plural is сыновья́, but сыны́ is used in a figurative, rhetorical context such as сла́вные сыны́ сла́вной ро́дины *glorious sons of a glorious motherland* (cf. the use of дитя́ for ребёнок in a few stock expressions of a figurative nature, e.g. он дитя́ своего́ ве́ка *he is a child of his time*).

(iv) Notice the difference in meaning between гла́зки *little eyes* and глазки́ *buds* (i.e. for grafting). The singular in both cases is глазо́к.

18. Коле́но has three possible plural forms:

(i) *knees*: коле́ни, коле́ней, коле́ням . . . ;

(ii) *sections* or *stretches* between two bends (e.g. of a river, an instrument, a stem or stalk of a plant) or the bends themselves: in these meanings both коле́нья, коле́ньев, коле́ньям . . . and коле́на, коле́н, коле́нам . . . are used;

(iii) *branches* of a genealogical tree, and in a biblical context *tribes* (двена́дцать коле́н Изра́илевых *the twelve tribes of Israel*). In this meaning, which is generally archaic, only колéна, колéн, колéнам . . . are used.

19. Some general semantic observations on singulars and plurals:

(i) Долг which means both *debt* and *duty* in the singular, only means *debts* in the plural (*duties* is обязанности).

(ii) Пóле *field* can, in the plural only, mean the brim of a hat:

A hat with no brim	Шляпа без полéй

It is also used commonly in the plural, where English uses a singular, to mean the margin of a book, &c.:

To write in the margin	Писáть на полях

but the singular form is used to emphasize one particular margin:

In the left margin	На лéвом пóле

(iii) The plural form холодá can mean *a cold spell*. Жары in the sense of *a hot spell* is seldom, if ever, used now.

(iv) Compare красотá *beauty*, красóты *beauty spots*; длиннотá *length*, длиннóты *diffuseness*. (N.B. длинá is the usual translation of 'length'—see para. **89.**)

THE CASES

Nominative

20. The construction что за with the nominative case should be noted. This is used in both interrogative and exclamatory senses, compare German *was für*. . . .

What sort of man is Smith?	Что за человéк Смит?
What weather! (i.e. *What awful weather!*)	Что за погóда!
Whatever do you want to write novels for?	Что тебé за охóта писáть ромáны?

21. It is often difficult to choose between the nominative and instrumental case to translate a predicative noun after

the verb *to be* (whether or not быть is actually expressed in Russian). Two sets of circumstances may be considered:
(i) When there is no verbal link. Here the predicate will normally go in the nominative:

I am an engineer	Я инженер
The main aim is justice	Главная цель — справедливость
Your aunt is a beautiful woman	Ваша тётя — красивая женщина

Sometimes, however, the predicate appears in the instrumental case:

(*a*) with вина *fault*, причина *reason* and порука *token*:

Your laziness is to blame for it all	Всему виной — ваша лень

(*b*) idiomatically, as an alternative to the nominative, when it denotes certain occupations or professions, *and* when the predicative noun is qualified or restricted by an adjunct:

His father is a teacher here	Его отец здесь учителем

(*c*) when the same noun is used both as subject and predicate and the clause followed by an adversative statement introduced by 'a':

Business may be business, but love is love	Дело делом, а любовь любовью (Kazakevich)

(ii) When subject and predicate are linked by some part of быть:

(*a*) With the *present* tense of быть (есть, and occasionally суть) a nominative predicate is always used:

Business is business (cf. (*c*) above)	Дело есть дело
The history of the C.P.S.U. (b) is the history of three revolutions	История ВКП(б) есть история трёх революций (Press)

(*b*) With the *future* tense of быть a nominative predicate is very rare in modern Russian (though not in the 19th century) and the instrumental can be regarded as standard usage:

I shall be an engineer	Я бу́ду инжене́ром

(*c*) With the *past* tense of быть, both nominative and instrumental noun predicates are found. In general the choice is determined by whether the predicate denotes a temporary state or property, or a characteristic related to a particular moment in time (instrumental), or a more or less static or permanent characteristic unrelated to any particular moment in time (nominative):

At the time I was a student at Oxford	В то вре́мя я был студе́нтом Оксфо́рдского университе́та
My governess was Swedish	Моя́ гуверна́нтка была́ шве́дка

22. (i) Noun predicates following the imperative or subjunctive moods of быть are almost invariably in the instrumental in modern Russian:

I don't want you to be a doctor	Я не хочу́, что́бы вы бы́ли до́ктором

(ii) A noun predicate may appear in the instrumental when the past tense of быть is not expressed, but is implied:

Even as a boy I loved music	Ещё ма́льчиком я люби́л му́зыку

where ма́льчиком = когда́ я был ма́льчиком.

23. The difficulty of agreement of verbs (gender and number), linking subject and predicate is most apparent when numerals and numeral words form the subject and predicate of a sentence. This will be considered in the chapter on the numeral (paras **763** ff). Here it may be noted that in combinations of nominal or pronominal subject, with verb and nominal or pronominal predicate, if the subject and predicate are of different gender or number, the verb agrees in gender and number with the subject. As a guiding rule the subject is the more particular or specific word, the predicate the more general or abstract:

The professor (subject) *was a sympathetic soul* (predicate)	Профе́ссор был душа́ — челове́к
It seemed to him that the cause (predicate) *of the war was the intrigues* (subject) *of Britain*	Ему́ каза́лось, что причи́ной войны́ бы́ли интри́ги А́нглии
Somebody entered the room. It (predicate) *was the doctor's wife* (subject)	Кто-то вошёл в ко́мнату. Э́то была́ жена́ до́ктора

24. (i) While not strictly relevant to the nominative case of nouns, the idiomatic translation of an English multiple subject, not by two or more nominatives, but by a nominative coupled with one or more instrumentals after the preposition **c,** may conveniently be considered here.

My brother and sister and I	Мы с бра́том и сестро́й
You and Peter must work harder	Вы с Петро́м должны́ (ты с Петро́м до́лжен) бо́льше рабо́тать
My grandfather and grandmother went into the kitchen	В ку́хню вошли́ де́душка с ба́бушкой

This idiomatic construction may be used of all persons, (1st, 2nd, and 3rd) where a combination of noun and pronoun forms the subject of the sentence, and also where there are combinations of two or more nouns or two or more pronouns as plural subjects. It is very common with nouns referring to members of the family circle and with words such as това́рищ (*comrade*) or друг (*friend*) which border on the family circle. The 1st person plural мы с бра́том construction (which is always followed by a plural verb) may be replaced by the somewhat less common я с бра́том (with a *1st person singular verb*). Я и брат (plural verb) is also occasionally found.

(ii) When the construction is used, as it sometimes is, with inanimate objects, the two nouns involved are always closely linked together, the first as the main and the second as the subsidiary object. Thus ча́шка с блю́дцем *cup and saucer*, самова́р с ча́йником *samovar and tea-pot*, where in both cases the nouns are intimately associated in daily use as parts of a whole unit.

(iii) The construction may also be used in an oblique case:

Did you see her and her mother?	Ви́дели вы её с ма́терью?
That was a stroke of luck for us both	Э́то нам с тобо́й повезло́

Vocative

25. Although this case is quite obsolete there are two common survivals in modern Russian as popular interjections: Бо́же мой! Го́споди! *good heavens! good Lord!*

Accusative

26. Apart from its obvious function of expressing the direct object of a transitive verb, the accusative case is used:

(i) To express *time during which*, the implication being that the action of the verb occupies the whole time referred to (cf. the accusative in Latin and Greek in the same sense):

All the time she was looking at me with curiosity	Всё вре́мя она́ смотре́ла на меня́ с любопы́т-ством (Chekhov)

(ii) To express *space over which, extent*:

He ran two kilometres	Он бежа́л два киломе́тра
He slept the whole journey	Он проспа́л всю доро́гу

The latter example may, of course, be regarded as duration of time. Notice however the translation of *wide* or *broad*:

Ten miles wide	Ширино́й в де́сять миль

or less commonly:

	Де́сять миль ширино́й

(iii) To express repetition, with раз:

I've told you a thousand times Я вам тысячу раз говорил

(iv) To express *time when*, an archaic usage superseded now for the most part by в and the accusative. Сию минуту *this minute, at once*, survives, the adjective сей (этот) betraying the archaic form, as also in сейчас *now*.

(v) Both the accusative and the genitive case are used after жаль. Followed by the accusative it means *be sorry for*; by the genitive *grudge*:

I am sorry for your sister Мне жаль вашу сестру
I grudge the time Мне жаль времени

(vi) The predicative должен in the sense of *owe* is treated as a transitive verb and is followed by a direct accusative:

I owe you a thousand roubles Я вам должен тысячу рублей

27. Notice the use of the nominative/accusative, not the genitive/accusative form of animate nouns denoting members of a class, social rank, trade, profession, &c., when used after the preposition в and a verb indicating entering, being promoted to or becoming a member of such classes or occupations:

He became a waiter Он поступил в официанты

To get on in the world Выйти в люди

Genitive

28. Genitive case after nouns

There is no need to dwell on the more obvious uses of the genitive after nouns which can signify 'possession' (*the boy's book* книга мальчика, and N.B. *this house is not mine but Meshkov's* этот дом не мой, а Мешкова), 'definition' (*a man of outstanding valour* человек выдающегося мужества), 'the subject' (*the tsar's decree* указ царя), 'the object' (*the capture of Berlin* взя́тие Берли́на), and several minor properties which are sometimes called 'aggregation' (*a pile of stones* гру́да камне́й), 'relation' (*the manager of a factory* дире́ктор заво́да) and others. In all these examples a comparison with the English *of* or the apostrophe *s* makes the Russian construction quite comprehensible. An obvious difference between English and Russian usage, however, is the translation of *the city of Moscow* (and other similar constructions) by two nouns in apposition—го́род Москва́. (In oblique cases the two nouns usually remain in apposition, but as well as the normal в го́роде Москве́ one also meets в го́роде Москва́.)

29. Notice:

(i) nouns followed by a genitive case in Russian but by a preposition other than *of* in English:

Khrushchev's visit to London	Посеще́ние Хрущёвым Ло́ндона
My plan for producing Boris Godunov	Мой план постано́вки „Бори́са Годуно́ва"

(ii) nouns followed by *of* in English, but by a prepositional construction in Russian (see paras. **604, 667**):

A work of 250 pages	Рабо́та в 250 страни́ц
A view of the lake	Вид на о́зеро
A bag of ferrets	Мешо́к с хорька́ми

Compare:

He received a sack of flour in payment (i.e. a sackful)	Взаме́н пла́ты он получи́л мешо́к муки́
He is dragging a sack of flour (i.e. containing, but not necessarily full of, flour)	Он та́щит мешо́к с муко́й

30. A Russian noun, or adjective and noun, in the genitive case may idiomatically render an English adjective or adjectival expression:

The chair was early 18th century	Стул был начáла 18-ого вéка
My sister is very robust	Моя́ сестрá óчень крéпкого здорóвья
At that point a middle-aged gentleman entered the room	Тут вошёл в кóмнату срéдних лет господи́н
What colour are the flowers? They are blue	Какóго цвéта цветы́? Они́ си́него цвéта

Genitive case in -у (-ю)

31. (i) Probably the chief difficulty students have with the genitive case concerns the -а/-у, -я/-ю alternation in certain masculine nouns. The difficulty is to know which nouns may take -у (-ю) in the genitive singular, and under what circumstances. Two general observations may be made first of all. In the first place there is not a single masculine noun which cannot form its genitive singular in -а (-я), while the parallel forms in -у (-ю) are losing ground all the time. In the second place the use of -у (-ю) in the genitive singular is most common in colloquial and familiar speech forms and dialects, proverbs, fables, and certain stock expressions.

(ii) There are a small number of masculine nouns referring to *concrete material substances* or *objects in the mass* which show a genitive in -у (-ю) *in certain constructions only*. Their number is limited by the fact that they are all nouns which cannot be combined with numerals; that is to say, they are all aggregative or quantitative nouns, and not nouns denoting single objects. Some Russian grammars give a comprehensive list of these words, including many where a genitive in -а (-я) is far more usual nowadays than one in -у (-ю). The list below, on the other hand, is small and includes only those words which are expressly shown in Ushakov's dictionary as having alternative genitive forms: виногрáд *grapes*, горóх *peas*, клей *glue*, лёд *ice*, мёд *honey*, мел *chalk*, миндáль *almonds*, нарóд (= лю́ди) *people*, песóк *sand*, сáхар *sugar*, сор *dirt*, товáр *goods*, чай *tea*. These words only show a genitive in -у (-ю) after:

(*a*) A very limited number of nouns expressing quantity, measurement, or weight of which the commonest include: фунт *pound*, килó *kilogramme*, стакáн *glass*, чáшка *cup*, кýча *heap*, кусóк *piece*, бáнка *jar*. It is perhaps best to try to remember them in combination with one of these nouns with which they are commonly associated, e.g. *a cup of tea* чáшка чáю, *a piece of chalk* кусóк мéлу, *a jar of honey* бáнка мёду. When there is no quantitative meaning present, the noun takes the normal genitive in -а (-я), e.g. *the taste of sugar* вкус сáхара. Similarly if an adjective qualifies the noun in the genitive, the -а (-я) ending is normally used: *a cup of strong tea* чáшка крéпкого чáя.

(*b*) Adverbial expressions of quantity such as мнóго *a lot*, немнóго *a little*, and the negative нет *there is not*. Note, however, that мнóго нарóду in the sense of мнóго людéй *many people*, is colloquial.

(*c*) Verbs such as the following, after which the -у (-ю) ending of the noun is partitive and suggests *some*:

To take some sugar	Взять сáхару
Give me some more tea, please	Дáйте мне, пожáлуйста, ещё чáю

Also *buy* покупáть (купúть) and *get* доставáть (достáть).

(iii) There are also several *abstract nouns* which in the above partitive or quantitative senses, often after мнóго, мáло, немнóго, may form their genitive singular in -у (-ю), notably вздор *nonsense*, толк *sense*, шум *noise*. However, in modern Russian, the genitive in -а (-я) is probably just as common with these nouns.

(iv) There are a considerable number of nouns which, in conjunction with certain prepositions only (без, из, от, с) take -у (-ю) in the genitive singular, often in expressions of place, cause, or manner.

(*a*) Sometimes the prepositions have become merged

with the nouns to form new adverbs (e.g. све́рху *from above*, сни́зу *from below*, сбо́ку *from the side*).

(*b*) Alternatively the prepositions and nouns may remain separate, but form an invariable combination which is virtually an adverb:

Of/from laughter	Со сме́ху
At a run	С разбе́гу
In alarm	С испу́гу
Indiscriminately	Без разбо́ру

Compare:

He ran away from home	Он убежа́л и́з дому
He ran out of the house	Он вы́бежал из до́ма

(*c*) In other cases the preposition-noun combinations are not fully adverbialized, and besides the -y (-ю) genitive one will also find the normal genitive in -a (-я):

Out of the wood	И́з лесу (or из ле́са)
To pick up off the floor	Поднима́ть (подня́ть) с по́лу (or с по́ла)
To lose sight of	Упуска́ть (упусти́ть) и́з виду (or из ви́да)

It often happens that the preposition is accented when the noun following takes its genitive in -y (-ю).

(*d*) There are quite a number of stereotyped expressions involving a noun with an -y (-ю) genitive ending with or without a preposition which one meets frequently in spoken Russian:

There's no doubt about it	Спо́ру нет
With all the power of one's arm	Со всего́ разма́ху
To talk non-stop	Говори́ть без у́молку
To confuse (disconcert) *somebody*	Сбива́ть (сбить) с то́лку кого́-нибудь
There's no news of him at all	Нет о нём ни слу́ху ни ду́ху

| *Any moment* (of something imminent) | С ча́су на ча́с |
| *Tête à tête* | С гла́зу на гла́з |

It is better to regard the examples in section (iv) of this paragraph as idioms, rather than to think of смех, разбе́г, &c., as having alternative genitive singulars in -y.

Genitive case after verbs

32. Verbs requiring an object in the genitive case to indicate *desire, request, aim,* or *achievement* of aim may be divided into two categories:

(i) The following verbs only govern the genitive case:

Жа́ждать

| *The country craves for peace* | Страна́ жа́ждет ми́ра |

Добива́ться

| *We must strive for better results* | Нам на́до добива́ться лу́чших результа́тов (Press) |

(The perfective aspect доби́ться does not mean *to strive*, but only *to attain*.)

Достига́ть (дости́гнуть)

| *Your mother has attained fame* | Ва́ша ма́тушка дости́гла изве́стности (Panova) |

Каса́ться (косну́ться)

| *As far as mother is concerned* | Что каса́ется ма́тери |

(каса́ться до is archaic)

Держа́ться

| *Keep to the left side of the street* | Держи́тесь ле́вой стороны́ у́лицы |

Придéрживаться
The ship hugged the coast   Корáбль придéрживался
бéрега

(ii) After the following verbs either the genitive or the accusative case may be used according to circumstances: искáть, просúть (попросúть), спрáшивать (спросúть), трéбовать (потрéбовать), ждать, желáть, and хотéть:

(*a*) The accusative is almost always used if the object of the verb is a person or animate object:

I am waiting (looking) *for my sister*   Я жду (ищý) сестрý
I want a daughter   Я хочý дочь

(With masculine animate objects, of course, the accusative/ genitive is used.) Occasionally a feminine noun denoting a person is found in the genitive after искáть, as in the following sentence from Sologub:

Everyone knew that Volodin   Всем извéстно бы́ло, что
was looking for a bride with   Волóдин искáл невéсты
a dowry ...   с придáным ...

but невéсту would be correct in this context and indeed more likely in modern Russian.

(*b*) With inanimate objects, there is undoubtedly some confusion of usage in modern Russian. For example, there is no apparent difference between Толстóй úщет нóвые литератýрные фóрмы... для выражéния своегó зáмысла (Bychkov) *Tolstoy is seeking new literary forms to express his intention*; and Толстóй искáл нóвых приёмов сопоставлéния и противопоставлéния (Vinogradov) *Tolstoy was seeking new methods of comparison and antithesis ...* However, the following general principle may be laid down. The accusative case is used if the object is individualized or particularized (most commonly with concrete nouns which are much more readily particularized than abstract nouns), while the genitive is used if the object is not particularized (most commonly with abstract nouns), or if the object, although concrete, is used figuratively. Compare:

He is looking for the brief-case he has lost (concrete and specific)	Он и́щет поте́рянный портфе́ль
I was looking for a chance to have a quiet read (abstract)	Я иска́л слу́чая споко́йно почита́ть
Ask your neighbour for his pencil (concrete and specific)	Спроси́те каранда́ш у сосе́да
To ask for advice (abstract)	Спра́шивать сове́та
She asked for an entry visa for the U.S.S.R. (concrete and specific)	Она́ попроси́ла ви́зу на въезд в СССР (Press)
I have come to ask for your daughter's hand (figurative)	Я прие́хал проси́ть руки́ ва́шей до́чери (Chekhov)
This worker is demanding his wages (concrete and specific)	Э́тот рабо́чий тре́бует зарпла́ту
My client demands an explanation (abstract)	Мой клие́нт тре́бует объясне́ния

The idiom *to cry halves* may be translated either by тре́бовать свою́ до́лю or тре́бовать свое́й до́ли.

(c) As a general principle, the accusative case is used when the object in question is known to both speaker and hearer, or reader and writer, i.e. when it has already been talked about or referred to before. The following example is from a letter written by Gor'ky:

Much excited by your news and eagerly await the manuscript	О́чень взволно́ван ва́шим сообще́нием и жду ру́копись нетерпели́во

(the manuscript has already been referred to in the letter to which Gor'ky is replying).

But:

I am waiting for a train	Я жду по́езда

With this may be conveniently contrasted:

| *What train are you waiting for?* | Како́й по́езд вы ждёте? |
| *I am waiting for the passenger train which leaves at 7 o'clock* | Я жду пассажи́рский по́езд, кото́рый отхо́дит в 7 часо́в |

(N.B. The use of the accusative here is a feature of spoken, rather than of written Russian.)

(*d*) With хоте́ть and жела́ть, although the genitive is still normal usage with abstract nouns, что is much more common than чего́ in the spoken language:

| *What do you want?* | Что вы хоти́те? |
| *The shops sell everything you want* | В магази́нах продаётся всё, что хоти́те |

33. Verbs requiring a genitive to indicate movement away from an object, avoidance, flight, revulsion, fear, deprivation. There are many parallels with the Greek genitive and Latin ablative of separation. In English the prepositions *of* or *from* prepare the way for the genitive:

Боя́ться, пуга́ться (испуга́ться)

| *He replied that all three had been frightened by the noise and the firing* | Он отве́тил, что все тро́е испуга́лись шу́ма и стрельбы́ (Fedin) |

Стыди́ться (постыди́ться)

| *I am ashamed of my appearance* | Я стыжу́сь своего́ ви́да |

Сторони́ться, чужда́ться

| *He began to shun* (keep clear of) *his old friends* | Он стал сторони́ться свои́х ста́рых друзе́й |

Стесня́ться (постесня́ться)

| *The little boy is shy of girls* | Ма́льчик стесня́ется де́вочек |

Избега́ть (избежа́ть and избе́гнуть)

She always avoided (kept clear of) *the company of unpleasant people*	Она́ всегда́ избега́ла о́бщества неприя́тных люде́й

Лиша́ть (лиши́ть)

To deprive someone of civil rights	Лиша́ть кого́-нибудь гражда́нских прав

Some verbs which would once have come into this category are now constructed with от, e.g. удаля́ться (удали́ться) от *to move away from, withdraw from*, where a simple genitive would be archaic.

34. Verbs requiring a genitive to indicate *value*:

Заслу́живать

This suggestion merits serious attention	Э́го предложе́ние заслу́живает серьёзного внима́ния

Compare the perfective verb заслужи́ть (no imperfective) which means *to earn* in the sense of *to receive* (often praise or blame), *to obtain, to win*. Заслужи́ть is followed by the accusative case:

He won the confidence of his chief	Он заслужи́л дове́рие своего́ нача́льника

Сто́ить

With сто́ить the genitive implies the meaning *to be worth*, the accusative—*to cost* (a sum of money):

One hour in the morning is worth two in the evening	Час у́тром сто́ит двух часо́в ве́чером
The book is worth three roubles	Кни́га сто́ит трёх рубле́й
The book costs three roubles	Кни́га сто́ит три рубля́

The genitive case may also translate *to cost* in the sense of *to need, to require*

It cost me a great deal of effort	Мне сто́ило большо́го труда́

Notice that the distinction between cost and value can also be expressed with the noun цена́ but with the genitive and dative cases respectively:

The price (cost) of this book is high	Цена́ э́той кни́ги высока́
The author of 'Oblomov' knows the true value of this milieu	А́втор „Обло́мова" зна́ет по́длинную це́ну э́той среде́ (Tseitlin)

35. Some verbs require a genitive case when a partitive meaning is to be conveyed, the object following them being divisible. *To give, to take*, and cognate verbs are common examples. Compare:

Give me some bread	Да́йте мне хле́ба
Pass me the loaf	Переда́йте мне хлеб

Here, as elsewhere in Russian, the precise use of cases can compensate for the lack of an article. Notice also the partitive genitive in the idiom:

To add fuel to the flames	Подлива́ть (подли́ть) ма́сла в ого́нь

36. The verbs наеда́ться (нае́сться) and напива́ться (напи́ться) which, in the perfective aspect, mean to satisfy one's hunger or thirst, both require the genitive case:

He had his fill of strong beer	Он напи́лся кре́пкого пи́ва

This sense of sufficiency (and the genitive case to express it) is evident in хвата́ть (хвати́ть). The opposite sense of inadequacy, deficiency, is conveyed by the genitive case after недостава́ть (недоста́ть). Compare the genitives in Latin and Greek with verbs of filling and lacking, and see para. **302.**

37. Genitive case after negatives

There is considerable confusion in modern Russian over the use of the genitive and accusative cases after negative verbs. The broad distinction between abstract object (genitive) and concrete object (accusative) is a useful working one, but does not go far enough.

(i) The accusative is always used after a negative verb when the object is qualified by an instrumental predicate:

I do not find Russian very difficult	Я не нахожу русский язык очень трудным

(ii) The accusative is very frequently used after a negative imperative:

Do not hang your hat on this hook	Не вешайте вашу шляпу на этот крючок

(iii) It is also usual with feminine nouns (and masculines of the дядя type) which refer to persons, and especially with proper names:

We had not seen Nadya for a long time	Мы давно не видали Надю

(iv) The accusative will be preferred to the genitive:
(*a*) when the object precedes the verb:

He remembers the last war, but the First World War he no longer remembers	Он помнит прошлую войну, но первую мировую войну он уже не помнит

(*b*) when the object is a concrete noun denoting a part of the body or a common object in everyday use. This is especially true if such a noun is qualified by an adjective or pronoun:

I have not yet read today's newspaper	Я ещё не читал сегодняшнюю газету

(*c*) when the verb is emphatic, but the negation is unemphatic:

I don't read books nowadays, I only skim through them	Я не *читаю* книги теперь, только их перелистываю

(*d*) with the combinations чуть не, едва́ ли не:

I have been practically right round the globe   Я чуть не объе́хал весь земно́й шар

(*e*) when for stylistic reasons it is desired to avoid a series of genitives:

Nobody set any limit to the conference agenda   Никто́ не ограни́чивал пове́стку дня совеща́ния (Press)

(v) Both accusative and genitive cases will commonly be found after infinitives dependent on negative verbs, although it is probably true to say that with concrete nouns especially the accusative is generally preferred in modern Russian:

Little boys do not like to wash their hands   Ма́льчики не лю́бят мыть ру́ки (rather than рук)

(vi) The genitive, and not the accusative case is almost invariably used after a negative in certain stock expressions where noun and verb are very closely associated with each other. Common examples are *not to take part* не принима́ть (приня́ть) уча́стия, *not to pay attention* не обраща́ть (обрати́ть) внима́ния, *not to make an impression* не производи́ть (произвести́) впечатле́ния.

38. The simple genitive case with no preposition is used to express the date:

On the first of May   Пе́рвого ма́я

(Cf. too сего́дня, from сей день.)

It is also used to express age (at the age of):

I started smoking at sixteen   Я на́чал кури́ть (закури́л) шестна́дцати лет

39. Dative

The use of the dative case presents some difficulties owing to the various possible ways of rendering in Russian the English preposition *to*:

I gave the book to the teacher   Я дал кни́гу учи́телю
I walked to the window   Я пошёл к окну́

We are going to school today	Сего́дня мы идём в шко́лу
We are going to the Caucasus today	Сего́дня мы е́дем на Кавка́з
Two (tickets) to the terminus	Два до конца́

In the first sentence the simple dative, in its most obvious construction, translates the indirect object after a verb like *give, send, show, write, tell,* &c. (N.B. писа́ть may also be followed by к and the dative, but a simple dative with no preposition is usual in modern Russian.) The translation of *to* in the other sentences will be dealt with in the chapter on the preposition.

40. There are many verbs which are followed in Russian by a dative case without any preposition. The example given in paragraph **39** is an obvious one, but the following verbs need special care.

41. Verbs which may be transitive in English and which in Russian require a simple dative case. Common examples may be divided for the sake of convenience into three groups :-

(i) Verbs used widely of both persons and things:

Ве́рить
I don't believe you	Я вам не ве́рю
To believe one's own eyes	Ве́рить со́бственным глаза́м

(But ве́рить в + accusative *to believe in*; *I believe in God* я ве́рю в Бо́га.)

N.B. *Belief in the rightness of our cause*	Ве́ра в правоту́ на́шего де́ла

Зави́довать (позави́довать)
Everyone envies him	Все зави́дуют ему́
She envied his free life	Она́ зави́довала его́ свобо́дной жи́зни

Russian cannot express a double object after зави́довать,

and to translate a sentence such as 'I envy you your wife' some periphrasis is necessary, e.g. мне зави́дно, что у вас така́я жена́.

N.B. *Envy of* . . . За́висть к . . .

Льстить (польсти́ть)

Don't flatter me Не льсти́те мне
Her attention flattered his vanity Её внима́ние льсти́ло его́ самолю́бию
N.B. *Flattery of* . . . Лесть к . . .

Вреди́ть (повреди́ть)

This doesn't hurt me Э́то мне не вреди́т
Smoking harms the lungs Куре́ние вреди́т лёгким

Подража́ть

It is impossible to imitate Shakespeare Шекспи́ру невозмо́жно подража́ть
It is impossible to imitate Shakespeare's style Невозмо́жно подража́ть сти́лю Шекспи́ра
N.B. *Imitations of the classics* Подража́ния кла́ссикам

Противоре́чить

He frequently contradicts himself Он ча́сто сам себе́ противоре́чит
Your second remark patently contradicts the first Ва́ше второ́е замеча́ние я́вно противоре́чит пе́рвому

Аплоди́ровать

The public warmly applauded the actors Пу́блика горячо́ аплоди́ровала актёрам
All to a man applauded Lenin's speech Все до одного́ аплоди́ровали ре́чи Ле́нина

Служи́ть

Honourably to serve king and country Че́стно служи́ть царю́ и оте́честву
N.B. *The honourable service of the people* Благоро́дное служе́ние наро́ду

Изменя́ть (измени́ть)

She betrayed both her husband and her native land	Она́ измени́ла и му́жу и родно́й стране́
N.B. *Betrayal of one's country*	Изме́на ро́дине

Помога́ть (помо́чь)

He would always help a man in trouble, he said	Он сказа́л, что всегда́ помо́жет челове́ку в беде́
The wide discussion of this book will help to remove defects	Широ́кое обсужде́ние э́той кни́ги помо́жет устране́нию недочётов (Press)

Меша́ть (помеша́ть)

I am not disturbing you, am I?	Я вам не меша́ю?
These two occupations did not interfere with each other	Э́ти два заня́тия не меша́ли друг дру́гу

Compare the cognate verb препя́тствовать (воспрепя́тствовать):

It was necessary to impede the flow (of capital) abroad	На́до бы́ло воспрепя́тствовать уте́чке (капита́ла) за рубежи́ (Fedin)

Грози́ть

Misfortune threatens us	Нам грози́т беда́
Disaster threatened the town (See para. **47** (ii))	Катастро́фа грози́ла го́роду

(ii) Verbs used widely of persons, but only occasionally, if at all, followed by the dative of things:

Сове́товать (посове́товать)

I advise you not to work	Я вам сове́тую не рабо́тать

But

The doctor advises a trip to the Caucasus	До́ктор сове́тует пое́здку на Кавка́з

Позволять (позво́лить)
Allow me to introduce . . .   Позво́льте мне предста́-
                                   вить . . .

Запреща́ть (запрети́ть)
I forbid you to smoke   Я запреща́ю вам кури́ть

Мстить (отомсти́ть)
I avenged myself on him for   Я отомсти́л ему́ за э́ти
  these insults   оби́ды

Угожда́ть (угоди́ть)
It is easy to please him   Ему́ легко́ угоди́ть
(Also на + accusative)

Досажда́ть (досади́ть)
The pupil annoyed his teacher   Учени́к досади́л учи́телю
  by his questions   свои́ми вопро́сами

Подходи́ть (подойти́)
I hope my terms will suit you   Я наде́юсь, что мой усло́-
  (i.e. be convenient, agree-   вия вам подойду́т
  able)

Compare подходи́ть к + dative:

They suit each other (i.e. are   Они́ подхо́дят друг к
  a good match)   дру́гу

(iii) Verbs used of things only:

Равня́ться
Twice three equals six   Два́жды три равня́ется
                                   шести́

Удовлетворя́ть (удовлетвори́ть)
  (*a*) Although удовлетворя́ть is, of course, used of persons,
it will then always govern the accusative/genitive case.
  (*b*) Удовлетворя́ть is followed by both dative and

accusative of the thing with a fine distinction of meaning. Compare:

Not all shops satisfy the customers' need for tinned goods	Не все магазины удовлетворяют потребность покупателей в консервах

Here the verb means to satisfy or meet a need.

This wallpaper does not satisfy my taste	Эти обои не удовлетворяют моему вкусу (or мне не по вкусу)

Here the verb means to measure up to the standards of, to be in accordance with.

Учиться

To study singing	Учиться пению
N.B. *He is studying to be a doctor*	Он учится на доктора

42. Verbs which are intransitive in English and are followed by a preposition, and which in Russian take a simple dative case, both of persons and things:

Принадлежать

To whom does the North Pole belong? (i.e. who owns it?)	Кому принадлежит северный полюс?

N.B. принадлежать к + dative *to be a member of, be included among.*

Tolstoy's novels belong among the best in world literature	Романы Толстого принадлежат к лучшим в мировой литературе

Радоваться (обрадоваться)

It was so clear to Anna that nobody had anything to be glad about . . .	Анне было так ясно, что никому нечему было радоваться . . . (L. N. Tolstoy)

Сочу́вствовать

I can't help sympathizing with your intentions	Я не могу́ не сочу́вствовать ва́шим наме́рениям
N.B. *Sympathy for a friend*	Сочу́вствие дру́гу

Улыба́ться (улыбну́ться)

Don't smile at my ignorance	Не улыба́йтесь моему́ неве́жеству

Смея́ться

In the meaning of *to make fun of* смея́ться is no longer followed by the dative case in modern Russian, but only by над and the instrumental case. Смея́ться, however, is followed by the dative in the meaning of 'to laugh at' (something funny):

All the others laughed at his anecdotes	Все остальны́е смея́лись его́ анекдо́там (Panova)

Удивля́ться (удиви́ться)

When the object is a thing, удивля́ться is always followed by the dative case. When a person is the object, it is common to invert the sentence:

I am surprised at you	Вы меня́ удивля́ете
N.B. *Surprise at the student's rapid progress*	Удивле́ние бы́стрым успе́хам ученика́

43. The verbs учи́ть, надоеда́ть, and напомина́ть:

Учи́ть

He teaches the children grammar	Он у́чит дете́й грамма́тике

(accusative of person, dative of thing)

Надоеда́ть (надое́сть)

I'm sick of work	Рабо́та мне надое́ла

Надоéсть, a resultative perfective, is found in the past tense, where English uses the present to mean *to be sick of*. The present tense of надоедáть suggests *to plague* or *pester*:

He keeps pestering me with his questions	Он всё надоедáет мне свои́ми вопрóсами

Напоминáть (напóмнить)

This city reminds me of Rome	Этот гóрод напоминáет мне Рим

44. The dative case is found as well as the genitive:

(i) with примéр and доказáтельство:

One curious fact may serve as evidence of this	Доказáтельством э́тому мóжет служи́ть оди́н любопы́тный факт (Press)

(ii) with вина́ and причи́на, especially when these nouns are themselves in the instrumental case:

My continual rashness is to blame for everything	Всемý винóй — моя́ вéчная необдýманность (Turgenev)

(iii) with some stock expressions in which a noun closely associated with a verb *may* be followed by another noun in the dative case. The noun in the dative case in Russian is in effect the indirect object of the verb, the direct object of which is the noun in the accusative case:

An essay summing up the author's researches over many years	Очерк, подводя́щий ито́ги многолéтним исслéдованиям а́втора (Press)
But compare The results of his researches	Ито́ги егó исслéдований

To give a proper appreciation of a work of literature	Дать пра́вильную оце́нку литерату́рному произ-веде́нию (Press)
But compare *The evaluation of property*	Оце́нка иму́щества
To shake the soldier's hand	Пожима́ть (пожа́ть) ру́ку солда́ту

Notice the colloquial рознь used predicatively with the same noun in both nominative and dative cases to indicate dissimilarity:

| *There are contradictions and contradictions* | Противоре́чия противо-ре́чиям рознь |

45. The dative case is used after the adjective рад:

| *I am glad of the opportunity* | Я рад слу́чаю |

and rather colloquially:

| *I was glad to get your letter* | Рад был ва́шему письму́ |

Instrumental

46. Apart from its obvious use to denote the instrument or agent by which an action is performed, the instrumental case is commonly found in expressions of time, manner, route, and extent or measurement:

(i) **Time**

(*a*) Such forms as у́тром *in the morning*, ле́том *in summer*, ве́чером *in the evening*, are in effect temporal adverbs, although their instrumental endings indicate their origin. With them it is not the whole period of time which is envisaged (all the morning, all summer); it is the action, qualified by the adverb, which is thought of as taking place at some time in the morning, in the summer, &c. Compare *I start school in winter* (зимо́й) and *I attended school all winter* (всю зи́му). Such adverbialized instrumentals may be qualified by adjectives: глубо́кой но́чью *at dead of night*; ра́нним у́тром *early in the morning*; по́здней о́сенью *late in autumn*. Notice too with the seasons:

The house was finished last spring	Дом был зако́нчен про́шлой весно́й (весно́й про́шлого го́да)
The house will be finished next summer	Дом бу́дет зако́нчен бу́дущим ле́том (ле́том бу́дущего го́да)

But: *this morning* сего́дня у́тром (not э́тим у́тром); *last night* вчера́ ве́чером; next *morning* на сле́дующее у́тро. N.B. Combinations with a noun as the main word: рабо́та вечера́ми утомля́ет меня́ *evening work tires me*.

(*b*) The instrumental case is sometimes used to indicate duration of time, or to translate *on end*:

For hours on end	Це́лыми часа́ми

(ii) Manner

To sing tenor	Петь те́нором
To sleep soundly	Спать кре́пким сном
To speak in a whisper	Говори́ть шо́потом
To weep bitter tears	Пла́кать го́рькими слеза́ми
The articles came out as a separate book (in book form)	Статьи́ вы́шли отде́льной кни́гой

Under this heading may be included the instrumental case denoting comparison:

To die like a hero	Умира́ть (умере́ть) геро́ем

N.B. Combinations with a noun as the main word: пе́ние ба́сом *bass singing*.

(iii) Route

He was returning home through the forest	Он возвраща́лся домо́й ле́сом

To walk across the field (along the bank)	Идти́ по́лем (бе́регом)
To travel by land (sea)	Путеше́ствовать сухи́м путём (мо́рем)

N.B. Combinations with a noun as the main word: пое́здка трамва́ем *a tram journey*.

(iv) **Extent or measurement**

The instrumental is sometimes used with comparatives to express the extent or degree of comparison:

He is a year older than his sister	Он го́дом ста́рше сестры́

(but more commonly, на́ год)

A page later he writes just the opposite	Страни́цей да́льше он пи́шет как раз обра́тное

47. The following common verbs which are transitive in English require the English object to be expressed in the instrumental case in Russian:

(i) A number of verbs which may be grouped together as having a cognate meaning of *authority over*, e.g. *rule, guide, manage, direct, own*, &c. These verbs, which express essentially durative actions, have no perfective aspects:

To govern a country	Управля́ть страно́й
To drive (steer) a car	Управля́ть (пра́вить) маши́ной

N.B. The most usual expression now is води́ть (вести́) маши́ну.

To own one's own house	Владе́ть до́мом
To possess an acute mind	Облада́ть о́стрым умо́м
To possess (have available) the first printed edition	Располага́ть пе́рвым печа́тным изда́нием
To command a division	Кома́ндовать диви́зией
To lead the masses	Руководи́ть ма́ссами

To run (be in charge of) a department (e.g. at a university)	Заве́довать ка́федрой

Nouns formed from some of these verbs may themselves govern other nouns in the instrumental case:

In full possession of one's powers	В по́лном облада́нии свои́ми си́лами
Leadership of the masses	Руково́дство ма́ссами
Management of a factory	Управле́ние заво́дом

(And *manager of a factory* is управля́ющий заво́дом.)

If it is further desired to express the agent (e.g. *the management of the factory by the director . . .*) the theoretically possible translation управле́ние заво́дом дире́ктором . . . would be avoided because of its obvious clumsiness, and the phrase управле́ние дире́ктора заво́дом . . . may be used. In the spoken language of an educated Russian one may nowadays even hear управле́ние заво́да дире́ктором . . .

(ii) With the following verbs this sense of authority is not present:

Обме́ниваться (обменя́ться)

After the battle both sides exchanged prisoners	По́сле би́твы о́бе сто́роны обменя́лись пле́нными

N.B. *Exchange of prisoners* may be translated both by обме́н пле́нными and обме́н пле́нных.

Награжда́ть (награди́ть)

He was awarded the Order of the Red Banner	Его́ награди́ли о́рденом Кра́сного Зна́мени
N.B. *The conferment of a decoration*	Награжде́ние о́рденом

To express both donor and recipient would involve a cumbersome series of nouns in Russian, e.g. *Stalin's conferment of the Order of Lenin on Malenkov surprised nobody* награжде́ние Ста́линым Маленко́ва о́рденом Ле́нина не удиви́ло никого. Such a heavy nominal construction would be avoided by using some such translation as то, что Ста́лин награди́л Маленко́ва о́рденом Ле́нина не удиви́ло никого́.

Любова́ться (полюбова́ться)

You cannot help admiring her beauty	Вы не мо́жете не любова́ться её красото́й

N.B. (*a*) любова́ться means *to look with pleasure at, enjoy looking at,* and not *admire* in the sense of *respect, esteem.* (*b*) Любова́ться may also be followed by на and the accusative, especially with persons and concrete or specific objects:

To admire oneself in the glass	Любова́ться на себя́ в зе́ркало

Же́ртвовать (поже́ртвовать)

Out of love for him she sacrificed all	Из любви́ к нему́ она́ всем поже́ртвовала

N.B. Же́ртвовать is followed by the accusative when it means *to donate, to contribute*:

To contribute money to the upkeep of the church	Же́ртвовать де́ньги на содержа́ние це́ркви

Дорожи́ть

The Russian people values its heritage	Ру́сский наро́д дорожи́т свои́м насле́дием

Злоупотребля́ть (злоупотреби́ть)

You are taking unfair advantage of his kindness	Вы злоупотребля́ете его́ добото́й
N.B. *Abuse of power*	Злоупотребле́ние вла́стью

Наслажда́ться (наслади́ться)

The travellers were enjoying the scenery	Путеше́ственники наслажда́лись пейза́жем
N.B. *Enjoyment of the scenery*	Наслажде́ние пейза́жем

Вертéть

She can twist him round her little finger	Онá вéртит им, как хóчет

N.B. In this figurative sense only the instrumental is used, but an accusative may follow вертéть in its literal meaning of *to twist, to turn.*

Пренебрегáть (пренебрéчь)

He spurned the lawyer's advice	Он пренебрёг совéтом юрúста
N.B. *Disregard for wealth*	Пренебрежéние богáтством

Again the use of the instrumental to express the subject (e.g. *Tolstoy's disregard for wealth is well known*), though theoretically possible, would in practice be avoided. A Russian might say пренебрежéние Толстóго богáтством ... or use a periphrasis of the sort всем извéстно, что Толстóй пренебрегáл богáтством.

Рисковáть (semelfactive рискнýть)

It's not worth risking your life	Не стóит рисковáть жúзнью

Щеголя́ть (semelfactive щегольнýть)

The peacock loves to parade its feathers	Павлúн лю́бит щеголя́ть своúми пéрьями

Занимáться (заня́ться)

This question needs to be studied	Нáдо заня́ться э́тим вопрóсом

Делúться (поделúться)

They exchanged impressions of the books they had read	Онú делúлись впечатлéниями о прочúтанных кнúгах

Грозúть

An event which threatened serious complications	Собы́тие, грозúвшее большúми осложнéниями

> *The tower threatened to col-* Ба́шня грози́ла паде́нием
> *lapse*

Contrast this with the use of грози́ть and the dative case (para. **41**). Here the instrumental expresses the misfortune which is likely to happen. The dative (para. **41**) expresses the person or thing to which the misfortune happens, the misfortune itself being the subject of the sentence.

48. The following verbs constructed with a preposition in English are followed by a simple instrumental case in Russian:

Увлека́ться (увле́чься)

They are absorbed in their studies	Они́ увлека́ются свои́ми заня́тиями
N.B. *Pushkin's passion for the theatre*	Увлече́ние Пу́шкина теа́тром

Бре́дить

He simply raves about music	Он так и бре́дит му́зыкой

Интересова́ться

Are you interested in art?	Интересу́етесь ли вы иску́сством?
N.B. *Interest in art*	Интере́с к иску́сству

Горди́ться, хва́статься (похва́статься)

I am proud of you although I never boast of your achievements	Я горжу́сь ва́ми, хотя́ я никогда́ не хва́стаюсь ва́шими достиже́ниями

По́льзоваться (воспо́льзоваться)

We must make use of this opportunity	Нам на́до воспо́льзоваться э́тим слу́чаем
N.B. *In using quotations*	При по́льзовании цита́тами

Торгова́ть

This merchant trades mainly in ready-made goods — Э́тот купе́ц торгу́ет гла́вным о́бразом гото́выми изде́лиями

N.B. *Trade in ready-made goods* — Торго́вля гото́выми изде́лиями

Восхища́ться (восхити́ться)

The girls were delighted with the pretty frocks — Де́вушки восхища́лись краси́выми пла́тьями

N.B. *Admiration of her beauty* — Восхище́ние её красото́й

Ограни́чиваться (ограни́читься)

The director confined himself to a brief report — Дире́ктор ограни́чился кра́тким докла́дом

49. The following verbs have this in common that they all express scent or smell:

Дыша́ть (подыша́ть)

I want to get a breath of fresh air — Я хочу́ подыша́ть све́жим во́здухом

Па́хнуть

There is a smell of burning — Па́хнет га́рью

Ве́ять

Spring is in the air (there is a breath of spring) — Ве́ет весно́й

Тяну́ть

A smell of hay wafted through the window — В окно́ тяну́ло за́пахом се́на

50. Страда́ть and боле́ть may be followed both by an instrumental case and by от and the genitive. In the context of disease or illness, the distinction is between a chronic state of illness (instrumental) and a temporary ache or pain, mental or physical (от and the genitive):

Compare:

He has got consumption	Он боле́ет чахо́ткой
He is suffering from toothache	Он страда́ет от зубно́й бо́ли

In other contexts the instrumental suggests *to possess some negative characteristic*; the genitive after от *to be suffering as a result of*:

Compare:

The town suffers from a short-age of parks	Го́род страда́ет недоста́т-ком па́рков
The east coast is suffering from floods	Восто́чное побере́жье страда́ет от наводне́-ний

51. The following verbs which all govern an instrumental case have this in common that they all denote movements involving different parts of the body:

To throw stones	Броса́ть (бро́сить) камн-я́ми
To hurl stones	Швыря́ть (швырну́ть) ка-мня́ми

(But in both cases the accusative ка́мни is commonly found.)

To wave one's arms	Маха́ть (махну́ть) рука́-ми
To brandish a sword	Разма́хивать мечо́м
To shrug one's shoulders	Пожима́ть (пожа́ть) пле-ча́ми
To move (twiddle) one's fingers	Дви́гать (дви́нуть), шеве-ли́ть (шевельну́ть) па́льцами
To bang the door to	Гро́мко хло́пать (хло́п-нуть) две́рью
To nod one's head	Кива́ть (кивну́ть) голо-во́й

To wink an eye	Мига́ть (мигну́ть) гла́зом
To wag the tail	Виля́ть (вильну́ть) хвосто́м
To gnash one's teeth	Скрежета́ть (проскрежета́ть) зуба́ми
He didn't bat an eyelid (colloq.)	Он и бро́вью не повёл

52. The alternative use of the nominative and instrumental cases after the verb *to be* has been discussed above (para. **21**). Here we shall merely list common verbs which are nowadays virtually always followed by a predicate in the instrumental case:

(i) Synonyms of *to be*	Явля́ться, находи́ться, состоя́ть
To become	Станови́ться (стать), де́латься (сде́латься)

(ii) Verbs after which *to be* is explicit or implicit:

To be considered (*to be*)	Счита́ться (also за + accusative)
To be reputed (*to be*)	Слыть (also за + accusative)
To seem (*to be*)	Каза́ться (показа́ться)
To prove (*to be*), *turn out* (*to be*)	Ока́зываться (оказа́ться)
To pretend (*to be*)	Притворя́ться (притвори́ться)
e.g. *He is pretending to be ill*	Он притворя́ется больны́м
To elect (*someone to be*)	Выбира́ть (вы́брать)
To appoint (*someone to be*)	Назнача́ть (назна́чить)
e.g. *The youngest candidate was appointed professor*	Профе́ссором назна́чили са́мого мла́дшего кандида́та

(iii) Verbs after which *to be* is not explicit or implicit:

To be called	Называ́ться (назва́ться)

To part	Pасставáться (расстáть-ся)
To remain	Оставáться (остáться)
e.g. *I am just the same as I always was*	Каки́м я был, таки́м остáлся
To serve (as)	Служи́ть
To be born, to live	Роди́ться, жить
e.g. *He was born a gentleman and led the life of a gentleman*	Он роди́лся бáрином и жил бáрской жи́знью

Notice that with place names which are nouns the instrumental case is normally used after называ́ться:

| *The little town was called Elton* | Городи́шко называ́лся Эльтоном (Simonov) |

But if the place name is a substantivized adjective, it normally appears in the nominative:

| *Our village is called Pokrovskoe* | Háше селó называ́ется Покрóвское |

If the predicate is in inverted commas, the nominative is also normally used:

| *This collective farm is called 'Red Star'* | Этот колхóз называ́ется „Крáсная звездá" |

53. (i) The adjectives довóльный *satisfied with*, богáтый *rich in*, оби́льный *abounding in*, all govern the instrumental case.

(ii) Зáнят, the short form of зáнятый, is followed by the instrumental (= *busy with*), and in conjunction with a verbal noun translates the English *busy* and a present participle in the following examples:

| *He is busy reading (playing chess, building a house)* | Он зáнят чтéнием (игрóй в шáхматы, пострóйкой дóма) |

(iii) Пóлный *full of* is more frequently followed by the genitive than by the instrumental.

54. The function of the so-called limiting accusative in Latin and Greek is sometimes assumed in Russian by the instrumental, especially after adjectives:

> *Weak-spirited* (weak as to the spirit)   Слáбый дýхом
>
> *He resembles me facially*   Он похóж на меня́ лицóм

Here the adjective is limited to a particular quality, feature, or attribute.

Prepositional

55. Since this case can only be used after prepositions, most of our material will be included in the chapter on the preposition (Chapter VI).

56. Some masculine nouns have stressed -ý (-ю́) in the prepositional singular, as well as the normal endings in -e. These are for the most part inanimate, monosyllabic, and accented on the stem in the singular. For purposes of convenience, common examples may be classified as follows:

(i) Parts of the body: лоб *forehead*, нос *nose*, глаз *eye*, рот *mouth*.

(ii) Localities or surfaces: лес *forest*, луг *meadow*, сад *garden*, пруд *pond*, мост *bridge*, бéрег *bank*, порт *port*, борт *side (of ship)* (на бортý *on board*), край *edge*, бок *side*, круг *circle*, ýгол *corner*, пол *floor*, шкаф *cupboard*, бал *ball*, рай *heaven*.

(iii) Collective substances: мёд *honey*, лёд *ice*, мох *moss*, мех *fur*, клей *glue*, сок *juice*, снег *snow*, пот *sweat*.

(iv) Temporal expressions: год *year*, век *age, lifetime*, óтпуск *leave*.

(v) Place names: Дон *Don*, Крым *Crimea*.

(vi) Military expressions: полк *regiment*, бой *battle*, строй *rank, line*, плен *captivity*.

(vii) Miscellaneous: вéтер *wind*, долг *debt*, ряд *row*.

57. (i) The form in -ý (-ю́) is only used after the prepositions в and на (except полкý which may be used after any preposition), and then only in a restricted locative or concrete sense:

Although he lived in the forest, he never spoke about the forest	Хотя́ он жил в лесу́, он никогда́ не говори́л о ле́се

And compare:

To play the main part in the 'Cherry Orchard'	Игра́ть гла́вную роль в „Вишнёвом са́де"
To play in the cherry orchard	Игра́ть в вишнёвом саду́
He was covered in sweat	Он был весь в поту́
To work in the sweat of one's brow	Труди́ться в по́те лица́

(ii) Sometimes there is a clear semantic difference between the two forms:

To sit in the second row	Сиде́ть во второ́м ряду́
In a series of experiments	В ря́де о́пытов
To stand in the corner	Стоя́ть в углу́
In a right angle there are 90°	В прямо́м угле́ 90°

(iii) The -ý (-ю́) ending is found with a few masculine nouns (including nouns not listed above) in stock expressions, mainly with an adverbial sense of time, place, or means of action:

At what time?	В кото́ром часу́?
In one's lifetime	На своём веку́
In flight, in motion	На лету́, на ходу́
An article in great demand	Това́р в большо́м ходу́
In bloom (of flowers)	В цвету́

Compare the figurative:

At the height of one's powers	В(о) цве́те сил

(iv) While these expressions are invariable, there is some confusion between -е and -ý (-ю́) in the case of a few of the above mentioned nouns when used after в and на. Thus one finds both в пру́де and в пруду́ *in the pond*, and в о́тпуске and в отпуску́ *on leave*. Generally speaking when

this confusion exists, the -ý (-ю́) form is the more colloquial
(and in some cases professional jargon), the -e form is the
more literary.

DIMINUTIVES

58. (i) Broadly speaking there are two functions of the
diminutive noun: to indicate size and to indicate shades of
emotion. In the second case one has to consider not simply
the mood of the speaker, whether one of approbation or of
contempt, but also, and this is very important, the type of
audience addressed. Among one's family and intimate
friends and relations, one's language is more emotionally
charged; affection, annoyance, and playfulness are more
readily shown than among casual friends and acquain-
tances. In Russian too the situation and the company must
be considered—to a greater extent than in English—and
in conversation within the family circle, a wide range of
diminutive forms may be used. This is especially true of
conversation among children or between adults and children, as for example a doctor addressing a child: покажи́
язычо́к *let me see your tongue.* In a wider context, the 'emotional' diminutive may be used to convey politeness in
making a request: нет ли у вас огонька́? *have you a light?*
(cf. the English *have you such a thing as a light?*)

(ii) Obviously there will be confusion between shades of
size and shades of emotion, since to say that a thing is
small can be to imply that it is dainty and therefore attractive. Pushkin uses но́жки to mean *pretty little feet,* where the
feet are pretty simply because they are little. The distinction between size and affectionate regard (and here we
ignore the other shades of emotion such as contempt which
can be expressed by diminutives) is at best an ill-defined
one. There are few diminutives where the suffix conveys
size alone and not emotion. Nor are there many like
со́лнышко from со́лнце, the use of which is purely emotional and has nothing to do with size. But there are very
many where both size and emotion are suggested by the

same word in different contexts. The difficulty is to know when to use a diminutive form simply to indicate smallness, without the overtones of familiarity. Take for example дом and до́мик in the following sentences:

(a)	*They live in a small house near London*	Они́ живу́т в ма́леньком до́ме вблизи́ от Ло́ндона
(b)	*They have a cottage near London*	У них есть до́мик вблизи́ от Ло́ндона
(c)	*When I am sixty I shall buy a little house in the country*	Когда́ мне бу́дет 60 лет, я куплю́ (ма́ленький) до́мик в дере́вне
(d)	*What a nice little house, mummy*	Како́й ми́ленький до́мик, ма́ма
(e)	*The children were building a house of cards*	Де́ти стро́или ка́рточный до́мик

Example (a) is a simple factual statement: the house is small. In (b) до́мик stands for a special type of small house —a cottage or villa. До́мик suggests in (c) that the house will not only be small but will be pleasant to look forward to; in (d) the language of a child; in (e) a special, technical meaning which, as we shall see below, is often associated with diminutives.

Or take the pair го́род, городо́к:

(a)	*He lives in a little provincial town on the Volga*	Он живёт в провинциа́льном городке́ (в ма́леньком провинциа́льном го́роде) на Во́лге
(b)	*Oh, little town of Samara!*	Ах, Сама́ра, городо́к (Russian song)

In (a) городо́к has no emotional association and may be readily replaced by ма́ленький го́род. In (b) there is a definite note of endearment in the exclamation.

(iii) No definite rules can be formulated here, and observation of Russian usage is the only real aid; but (for the purposes of Russian prose composition) the following general principles may be useful:

(*a*) Many diminutives in Russian are highly colloquial and therefore outside the scope of narrative prose.

(*b*) Many diminutives common in the literary language are met with in writing mainly in dialogue passages, and are used of and by members of the family or close friends.

(*c*) A diminutive with no emotional overtones may just as well be replaced by its original noun, qualified by an adjective like ма́ленький or небольшо́й. (These adjectives, incidentally, will often be met with diminutive forms in what are apparently tautological combinations, e.g. небольшо́й городо́к, небольша́я карти́нка.)

(*d*) The diminutive forms which are most necessary to the student are those which have an additional, specialized meaning such as the ones given in the following paragraph, and which, in that meaning have no corresponding non-diminutive forms.

59.	*Noun*	*Diminutive*	*Additional meaning*
Hand	Рука́	Ру́чка	*Handle* (e.g. door-handle); *pen* (as opposed to nib)
Leg	Нога́	Но́жка	*Leg* of furniture (e.g. table-leg)
Back	Спина́	Спи́нка	*Chair back, back* of a garment
Head	Голова́	Голо́вка	*Head* of a match, nail or screw; in plural, *uppers* of a shoe
Hair	Во́лос	Волосо́к	*Thread, hair spring* of watch, *filament* of lamp
Nose	Нос	Носо́к	*Toe* of shoe or stocking
		Но́сик	*Spout* of jug or pot
Star	Звезда́	Звёздочка	*Asterisk*
Book	Кни́га	Кни́жка	*Card* or *book*, of official documents, e.g. (Post-Office) *savings book*: сберега́-тельная кни́жка

	Noun	Diminutive	Additional meaning
Paper	Бумага	Бумажка	*Note* (paper money)
Circle	Круг	Кружок	*Group* of people, *study group*
Fire	Огонь	Огонёк	*Flair*; артистический огонёк *flair for art*
Pipe	Труба	Трубка	*Telephone receiver, tobacco-pipe*
Horse	Конь	Конёк	*Hobby* (cf. English *hobby-horse*)
Stick	Палка	Палочка	*Baton*
Throat	Горло	Горлышко	*Neck* of a bottle
Dish	Блюдо	Блюдце	*Saucer*
Arrow	Стрела	Стрелка	*Pointer, hand* of a watch, *needle* of a compass
Bubble	Пузырь	Пузырёк	*Phial*

60. Notice the translation of the following words into Russian and the semantic difference conveyed by the diminutive form:

Hammer: молот is a large instrument for cutting metals or breaking stone; молоток is the ordinary household hammer.

Curtain: занавес is a large curtain, e.g. on a theatre stage; занавеска is a window curtain.

Bag: сумка is a shopping bag; сумочка is a handbag.

Table: столик is used of a restaurant table.

Window: окошко is used of a cash desk window.

Door: дверца is used of a vehicle door or cupboard door.

Bell: колокол is a church bell; колокольчик a hand bell.

61. Diminutive forms will be commonly found in idioms, popular sayings, and proverbs:

To make eyes	Делать глазки
I am all ears	У меня ушки на макушке
A drowning man clutches at a straw	Утопающий хватается за соломинку

62. A word of warning should be given about the numerous diminutive forms that some Russian nouns have acquired, and which would not be considered marks of a good prose style. For example, река, besides речка, also has ре́ченька and ре́чушка, both common to popular poetry and folk-song, and also речо́нка and речу́шка, both implying contempt (*a wretched little stream*).These latter pejorative diminutives (N.B. also лошадёнка *a miserable little horse*) are invariably colloquial in use and, like the few nouns in Russian with an augmentative suffix (e.g. доми́ще *huge house*), need not concern the student here.

SOME COMMON NOUNS AND THEIR TRANSLATION

63. Accident, Chance. Слу́чай means *incident, occurrence, opportunity*. Случа́йность is *chance*: *mere chance* пуста́я случа́йность; *by chance, by accident* случа́йно. *Accident* in the loose sense of *mishap* is несча́стный слу́чай: *accident insurance* страхова́ние от несча́стных слу́чаев. A specific accident involving a motor vehicle, ship, train, aircraft, &c., is ава́рия, and more catastrophically круше́ние or катастро́фа.

64. Afternoon. *In the afternoon* is most commonly rendered by по́сле за́втрака, обе́да (*after lunch, dinner*) or по́сле полу́дня (пополу́дни). There is, however, no single noun for *afternoon*, despite Pisemsky's ка́ждое по́сле-обе́да 'every afternoon'. Thus a sentence such as *the afternoon is the most pleasant part of the day* will usually be expressed by послеобе́денное вре́мя са́мая прия́тная часть дня. N.B. A common rendering of *L'après-midi d'un faune* is фавн по́сле полу́дня.

65. Age. *What age, how old is he?* Ско́лько ему́ лет? This expects a definite answer in years. Во́зраст is a stage in one's life. Како́го он во́зраста? would not expect a definite answer in years, but a general statement, e.g. он сре́днего во́зраста *he is middle-aged*. Век is the usual word for a prehistoric or historical period; *the Stone Age* ка́менный век; *the Middle Ages* сре́дние века́ (or средневеко́вье). Пери́од is usual for primarily geological periods; *the Ice Age* ледни́ковый пери́од.

They had not seen each other   Они́ не вида́лись це́лую
for ages and ages   ве́чность

66. Attack. In the widest sense нападе́ние. Наступле́ние is commonly used in a military context to mean *offensive*. Напа́дки (singular rare) are *critical attacks, accusations*. Ата́ка is often used of a military or aerial attack. Набе́г is *a raid*, вы́лазка *a sortie*. Припа́док is *a sudden attack* of an illness, *a fit*: *heart attack* серде́чный припа́док. При́ступ has the meaning both of a military attack (ата́ка) and an attack of an illness (припа́док).

67. Breadth, Latitude. As a concrete measurement of distance, opposed to length, ширина́. Широта́ is used in an abstract sense, e.g. breadth of view, outlook. It is also the geographical term for *latitude*. Ширь (fem., no plural) is sometimes used of wide open spaces and in the expression во всю ширь: на́до разверну́ть рабо́ту во всю ширь *work must be developed to the utmost extent.*

68. Building. The most general word for a building is зда́ние. Помеще́ние refers to the inside of a building, a room, premises, &c. Постро́йка may be a building site, a building under construction, or a building which has been completed. Сооруже́ние suggests a vast or imposing construction. Строе́ние corresponds most nearly to *structure.*

The act of building is постро́йка or строи́тельство. Often строи́тельство is used in a wide sense (шко́льное строи́тельство *building of schools*); постро́йка in a narrower sense (постро́йка до́ма *building a house*).

In the less tangible sense of the construction of a sentence, proposition, or theorem построе́ние is used. It can be used, too, of the building of a political system: построе́ние социали́зма *the building of socialism*, in which meaning, however, строи́тельство is also commonly used.

69. Change, Exchange. There are numerous nouns formed from the -мен root. Измене́ние means *change* in the sense of alteration, making different (not to be confused with измена *infidelity, treason*). Переме́на means *change* in the sense of replacing one thing by another similar thing, e.g. change of residence, occupation, climate, &c.

Разме́н and обме́н are closely allied in the meaning of *exchange*. Обме́н is the more versatile, and often corresponds to *interchange*: обме́н о́пытом *interchange of experience*; обме́н мне́ний *interchange of opinions*. Both the genitive and instrumental case are used after обме́н, e.g. обме́н пле́нных, обме́н пле́нными *exchange of prisoners*. Разме́н is used primarily of changing money.

Сме́на is most commonly used to mean *a replacement, a shift*: сме́на карау́ла *changing of the guard*; у́тренняя сме́на *the morning shift*. Заме́на means *substitution*. Notice the idiom: ме́на — не грабёж *exchange is no robbery*.

70. Character. О́браз, тип, and персона́ж are all commonly used of characters in a novel or play: *Dostoyevsky's women characters* же́нские ти́пы (о́бразы) у Достое́вского. The *dramatis personae* are де́йствующие ли́ца.

Хара́ктер is used of a person's moral character, and also means *character* in the sense of *characteristic, nature, property*. Прав is *disposition*. *A character* in the colloquial sense of *a person* is челове́к, not хара́ктер: *he's an interesting character* он интере́сный челове́к. (*A queer character* чуда́к.)

71. Colour. Notice that масть (fem.) and not цвет is used for the colour of animals (especially horses). It also means *a suit* of cards (*to follow suit* ходи́ть в масть). *Couleur locale* is ме́стный колори́т.

72. Communication. Compare обще́ние and сообще́ние. Пути́ сообще́ния are *means of communication* in the sense of rivers, roads, railways, &c.; in the phrase язы́к — сре́дство обще́ния (*language is a means of communication*), обще́ния means social intercourse.

73. Country, Land. Страна́ is one of the countries of the world. The use of сторона́ (*side, part, locality*) in the above sense has a poetical or popular flavour. *Native country* is ро́дина (*motherland*). Отчи́зна (*fatherland*) is archaic. Оте́чество (*fatherland*), however, is used, often in a patriotic context, to impart dignity and glory. The two greatest Russian struggles for survival in 1812 and 1941–5 have been honoured with the names Оте́чественная война́ and Вели́кая Оте́чественная война́. Ро́дина conjures up thoughts of hearth and home; оте́чество of honour and glory.

Besides its use to denote an administrative territory in the U.S.S.R., край is quite commonly found as a rather patriotic or sentimental alternative to страна́: наш сове́тский край *our Soviet land*; край родно́й *native land*.

Земля́ in the sense of страна́ is now archaic.[1] It signifies the earth (the planet), the land as opposed to the sea, land in the sense of the soil, the ground, the land belonging to a man. Су́ша means specifically *dry land*. *To travel by land* путеше́ствовать сухи́м путём.

Country as opposed to *town* is дере́вня. *To drive into the country* (for a day's excursion, &c.) е́хать за́ город (lit. *out of town*). *Broken country* (*terrain*) пересечённая ме́стность.

Mainland, continent матери́к.

74. Dream. Мечта́ has no genitive plural. Мечта́ний, genitive plural of мечта́ние, is used instead.

To have pipe dreams   Ви́деть волше́бные сны

75. Education. In the general sense образова́ние: *public education* наро́дное образова́ние. With образова́ние the emphasis is generally on the education, given and received, rather than on the actual process of imparting or imbibing knowledge, i.e. instruction. Обуче́ние is *instruction* or education in the narrower sense of teaching or imparting knowledge, *tuition*: compare *co-education* совме́стное обуче́ние, where the actual process of teaching and learning, not the academic or cultural content of the education, is envisaged.

Воспита́ние is *breeding* or *upbringing*. Воспита́тельный рома́н *Bildungsroman*. Физи́ческое воспита́ние (not

[1] But figuratively обетова́нная земля́ *the Promised Land* (bibl.).

образова́ние) is *physical education* (and cf. the new term физкульту́ра).

Просвеще́ние is wider than образова́ние, embracing culture as well as scholarship: эпо́ха Просвеще́ния *the Age of Enlightenment*. The Soviet educational system includes both Министе́рства просвеще́ния (Ministries) and a Министе́рство вы́сшего образова́ния.

76. End. Коне́ц and оконча́ние are often interchangeable, with оконча́ние having the more literary flavour—*ending, conclusion*: оконча́ние сле́дует *to be concluded*. But the use of оконча́ние instead of коне́ц may have verbal force. Compare:

Коне́ц ле́та	*The end of the summer*
Что вы собира́етесь де́лать по оконча́нии университе́та?	*What are you going to do when you have finished at the University?*

Similarly, notice the shade of difference between

Он не досиде́л до конца́ спекта́кля	*He did not wait till the end of the play*
Он ушёл, не дожда́вшись оконча́ния спекта́кля	*He went off without waiting for the play to end*

Кончи́на is a rhetorical synonym for *death*. *On end* (= *in succession*) подря́д.

77. Enemy. Враг is the strongest word, used of the enemy in war (when it has a more literary flavour than неприя́тель—cf. English 'foe'), and of a class or ideological enemy (кла́ссовый враг). Both неприя́тель and проти́вник are also used of the enemy in war (in the singular that is the only meaning of неприя́тель) and, indeed, неприя́тельские войска́ is the usual expression for the enemy forces. But generally speaking неприя́тели are merely people inimically disposed towards one, but not likely to do physical harm. Проти́вник has the general meaning of an adversary or opponent in games and sports, habits, and ideas.

78. Fall. Падéние is generally used of a drastic or irreparable event, the fall of a city or a government; понижéние of a controlled reduction. Compare падéние цен *fall in prices*, падéние нрáвов *fall in morals*, and понижéние цен *reduction in prices*, понижéние гóлоса *lowering of the voice*.

The usual translation of *The History of the Decline and Fall of the Roman Empire* is Истóрия упáдка и разрушéния Ρимской импéрии. *The Fall* in the Biblical sense is Грехопадéние. *A heavy fall of rain* проливнóй дождь, ли́вень.

| *To ride for a fall* | Самомý себé я́му рыть. |

79. Farm. Фéрма in Russia now is a specialized farm or branch of farming: *dairy-farm* молóчная фéрма. With reference to foreign countries, however, it means any farm. In Russia, *farm* will usually be колхóз (*collective farm*) unless reference is specifically made to a *state farm* (совхóз). Хýтор is mainly confined to the south of Russia (but notice the title of a recent Russian translation of Orwell's *Animal Farm*—,,Скóтский Хýтор").

80. Fire. Огóнь is the fire in the grate. Ками́н is the fire in the sense of the grate or stove itself. *To light the fire* топи́ть печь.

Пожáр is an outbreak of fire. Жар is the heat of the fire. (N.B. жар-пти́ца *fire-bird*.) Костёр means *camp fire, bonfire, stake*.

81. Friend. The degree of intimacy (greatest to least) is друг, прия́тель, знакóмый in that order. Подрýга is a close friend, who is at the same time a woman. *Girl friend* in the popular sense, *one's girl*, cannot be translated by подрýга, nor by возлю́бленная or невéста which are too strong. Дéвушка would be the popular translation (cf. *my girl*); прия́тельница a more formal rendering.

82. Gift. *Gift = present* is подáрок (in this sense дар is rather grandiloquent). *Gift = talent* is дар and даровáние.

83. Girl. Дéвочка is a young girl (i.e. before the age of puberty). Дéвушка is an unmarried girl of mature years,

a girl in her 'teens. Дѣ́ва is archaic and poetical for дѣ́вуш-
ка (cf. *maiden* and *girl*) but has also a derogatory meaning,
as has дѣ́вочка when applied to a woman (*prostitute*). Дѣ́ва
in the sense of дѣ́вушка is poetical, but *old maid* is always
translated ста́рая дѣ́ва.

84. Harvest. Урожа́й is the actual yield, the crops grown,
without reference to the harvesting processes: *last year's
harvest* урожа́й про́шлого го́да; *harvest festival* пра́здник
урожа́я. Жа́тва suggests the operation of the verb жать
(сжать), the cutting down or harvesting; it also means the
harvest itself before it is gathered in: жа́тва созрѣ́ла *the
harvest is ripe*. Убо́рка is the last operation in the cycle, the
garnering. Сбор may be used of picking fruit: сбор ман-
дари́нов *picking tangerines*; in the expression сбор урожа́я
зако́нчен *harvesting is finished*, it implies that every stage
including the убо́рка, or gathering in of the crops, has been
completed.

   To reap a harvest of praise   Пожина́ть (пожа́ть) сла́ву

85. Heart. Душа́ (*soul*) is used instead of, or as well as,
сѐрдце in some colloquial expressions where *heart* is used
in English: *with all my heart* от всей души́ (also от всего́
сѐрдца); *a heart to heart talk* разгово́р по душа́м; *in one's
heart of hearts* в глубинѣ́ души́.

By heart	Наизу́сть
The heart of the matter	Суть дѣ́ла
To take heart	Собира́ться (собра́ться) с ду́хом
To lose heart	Па́дать (пасть) ду́хом

86. Height. Высота́ is much more commonly used than
вышина́. Возвы́шенность means *high place* or *elevation*. For
the height of a person or animal, рост must be used.

The height of folly	Верх глу́пости
The gale was at its height	Шторм был в разга́ре

87. Holiday. Пра́здник is a day specially set apart as a
state or religious festival, a public holiday. О́тпуск is the
regular annual holiday or leave. Кани́кулы (Pl.) is con-

fined to school and university holidays. Выходно́й день means *day off*: *it's my day off today* у меня́ сего́дня выходно́й (colloq.), and more recently even я сего́дня выходно́й. О́тдых is leisure time, rest from one's normal job.

88. Law. Пра́во is *the law* in the sense of the aggregate of individual laws, rules, and regulations: *international law* междунаро́дное пра́во; *public law* госуда́рственное пра́во; *to study law* изуча́ть пра́во.

Зако́н is usually a specific law. In the sense of a body of laws (Иуде́йский зако́н *the Jewish Law*) it is archaic or has a religious flavour, e.g. зако́н бо́жий *scripture*. Пра́вило means *rule, regulation*.

Law and order	Правопоря́док
Martial law	Вое́нное положе́ние
To go to law	Начина́ть (нача́ть), возбужда́ть (возбуди́ть) суде́бный проце́сс

89. Length, Longitude. As a concrete measurement of distance, opposed to breadth, длина́. Длиннота́, in the singular, is more colloquial and less common. In the plural it has a literary flavour and means *tedious, prolix passages*. *Longitude* is долгота́.

Length of time, duration, is продолжи́тельность, and less commonly, дли́тельность. Notice too срок: *the length of the course in all universities is 5 years* срок обуче́ния во всех университе́тах — 5 лет.

90. Life. Житие́ in the sense of жизнь is now archaic. Its use is largely confined to the *life* of a saint, i.e. an account of his life. Житьё for жизнь is colloquial.

Быт is *a way of life, everyday life*. Бытие́ is archaic in the sense of *life*, but is used to mean *existence*. Бытьё for быт is archaic.

The colloquial житьё-бытьё (*life, way of life*) is still used.

91. Light, Lights. Свет translates *light* in almost every sense. *Lights* (of a ship, &c.) are огни́; *headlights* (of a car) фа́ры.

A light (i.e. something *burning* and giving light) is огóнь: *a light in the window* огóнь в óкнах. *Give me a light* (colloq.) дáйте закурить.

92. Line. Строкá of a number of words arranged in a line: *drop me a few lines* черкните мне нéсколько строк. Стихи are *lines of verse*. Линия can be used in virtually all other cases: e.g. *air-line* воздýшная линия; *party line* партийная линия. Чертá is a narrow or fine line on some surface, a boundary line, a feature or line on the face. (N.B. в чертé гóрода *within the city boundaries*.)

93. Marriage, Wedding. Женитьба is the act of marrying from the man's point of view, свáдьба the marriage ceremony. *After his marriage to Liza* пóсле егó женитьбы на Лизе; *silver wedding* (i.e. anniversary of ceremony) серéбряная свáдьба. Венчáние is the church expression for the ceremony. Брак is the state of married life, marriage: *marriages are made in heaven* брáки заключáются в небесáх (cf. безбрáчие *celibacy*). Other, somewhat archaic, words for *married life* are супрýжество, супрýжеская жизнь. Замýжество means *marriage* only from the woman's point of view.

Wedding ring обручáльное кольцó; *wedding dress* венчáльное плáтье.

94. Name. Имя is the *Christian name*; óтчество the *patronymic*; фамилия the *surname*.

What is his name? как егó зовýт? where the reply will generally be a Christian name; как егó фамилия? where a surname is required. Where no specific reference is made to either Christian name or surname, имя will be used, e.g. *your name was given me by Ivanov* Вáше имя я узнáл от Ивáнова.

The name of an object as opposed to a person is назвáние. The verb называть (назвáть) may be used of persons as well as things: *he goes by various names* егó называют по-рáзному.

Прóзвище is a *nickname*. Кличка is the name of an animal, a pet, as well as a nickname.

By name по имени. *In name only, nominally* только по имени. *In the name of . . .* от имени. *Named after* (in honour of) имени: *the Lenin Library* Библиотека имени Ленина.

95. News. Новости tends to be longer news with comment, известия to be shorter information without amplification. Последние известия may be the latest news, as broadcast on the wireless, or it may be stop-press in the newspapers. Весть (and the plural вести) means *a piece of news, tidings,* as in the proverb худые вести не лежат на месте *bad news travels fast.*

What news? что нового?, a colloquial greeting.

96. Night. The distinction between evening and night is more rigid than in English. *I am going to the pictures tonight* must be translated by сегодня вечером я иду в кино. Ночью would mean *during the night.*

97. Noise, Sound. Звук denotes a single or abrupt sound, very often the noise of a single action or instrument: *the sound of a trumpet* звук трубы; *the sound of a kiss* звук поцелуя.

Шум is a steady noise, the sound of rain falling continuously or of water generally, the hubbub of a town or crowded place. Compare звук голоса *the sound of a voice* with шум голосов *the noise of voices.*

Грохот is stronger than шум, the noise or rumble of gunfire; гул is used of a remote noise, hum, or rumble; звон—of a bell, a peal, metallic sound, tinkle; удар, раскат—of a clap, peal of thunder, стук—a knock at the door, rap; треск—a sharp, snapping sound, the crackle of twigs, or of a wood fire; топот—the clatter or stamping of hooves or feet; визг—a shrill, piercing, high-pitched often unpleasant sound, the squeak of a saw; свист—the whistle of the wind; шорох and лепет—the rustle of leaves, &c.; жужжанье—hum or buzz; журчание—the babble of a brook; лязг and бряцанье—the clang or clanking of metallic objects, chains.

98. Number. Количество is *quantity*; *a considerable number of people* значительное количество людей. Число can have the same meaning of quantity, as well as *number* as a grammatical concept or mathematical expression (*whole number*). Цифра is a *numeral*, the figures in a given number. Но́мер is a copy of a magazine or newspaper: *back number* ста́рый но́мер. Also a telephone number: *what's your number?* како́й у вас но́мер?; the number of a house and a numbered room, i.e. a hotel room.

99. Organ. Notice the difference between орга́н, a musical instrument, and о́рган, an organ in all other senses.

100. Part. Часть is *part* of a whole. Сто́роны may be *parts* in the sense of a district: *do you know those parts?* зна́ете вы те сто́роны? Also края́ in the same sense: *in our part of the world* в на́ших края́х.

Па́ртия is used musically of a solo part for voice or instrument: *the bass part* па́ртия ба́са.

For my part	Что каса́ется меня́
To play a part	Игра́ть роль
To take part in	Принима́ть (приня́ть) уча́стие в

101. Party. *Party* in the political sense is па́ртия; экску́рсия is an outing, sporting or recreational party; вечери́нка a social party; сторона́ a party to a suit, marriage, &c.

102. Payment. Упла́та is the action of paying: *payment of a debt* упла́та до́лга; пла́та is the actual fee: входна́я пла́та *entrance fee*. Зарпла́та (= за́работная пла́та) is a new term meaning *payment for work*, i.e. *wages*. Запла́та means *a patch* and NOT *payment*.

103. People. Наро́д may be regarded as applying to particular groups—*the* people—whether vast such as the nation, or smaller racial or social groups. Thus it may mean the nation, the entire population of a country, or it may mean the lower orders of society.

Лю́ди means people at large, without reference to groups or units. Compare *Our friends are interesting people* на́ши друзья́ — интере́сные лю́ди; *the Russians are an interesting people* ру́сские — интере́сный наро́д.

Many people мно́го люде́й. Мно́го наро́ду is also commonly used but is colloquial; compare *many folk, many people*. This colloquial sense of наро́д can be seen in such contexts as зде́шние уроже́нцы — хи́трый наро́д *the natives here are a crafty lot.*

In the genitive plural, люде́й is used after quantitative expressions, a few, a lot, &c.; челове́к after numerals (above four). *A few people* ма́ло люде́й; *ten people* де́сять челове́к.

People say . . .   Говоря́т . . .

104. Person. Челове́к is *a person*, without any qualifying attributes. Лицо́ also means *a person*, but often in a particular capacity, an official. *A very important person* о́чень ва́жное (значи́тельное) лицо́; *displaced persons* перемещённые ли́ца. Осо́ба *personage*, also suggests an exalted status, but is rather archaic. Персо́на too is used in a rather pompous sense as a personage of some note.

Ли́чность generally is *personality, individuality. Freedom of the person* (i.e. of the individual) свобо́да ли́чности; *the cult of the individual* культ ли́чности.

105. Performance. Of a play представле́ние, постано́вка; of a work of music исполне́ние.

106. Power. Власть means *authority*, especially political authority: *in power* of a government у вла́сти; вла́сти предержа́щие *the powers that be*. Си́ла generally means *physical power, strength*; also *force, validity, influence. The power of the printed word* си́ла печа́тного сло́ва; *to come into force* входи́ть (войти́) в си́лу; *eight horse-power* во́семь лошади́ных сил.

Эне́ргия often has a technical sense: электри́ческая эне́ргия *electric power*. Держа́ва is *a power*, i.e. a country or state: Вели́кие Держа́вы *the Great Powers*.

Powers = capabilities are спосо́бности, си́лы: *it is beyond his powers* э́то ему́ не по си́лам. *The power to express one's thoughts* спосо́бность выража́ть свои́ мы́сли. But *power = property* (of an *inanimate* object) is сво́йство: *this ring has the power to make you invisible* у э́того кольца́ есть сво́йство де́лать вас неви́димым.

107. Progress. Usually прогре́сс. Де́лать успе́хи is used of scholastic progress. Similarly успева́емость, a Soviet word, indicates the progress made or degree of success attained in one's studies.

Preparations are in progress	Веду́тся приготовле́ния

108. Scene. Пейза́ж is *landscape, scenery*. Сце́на is a *scene* in a play or novel. Зре́лище is *a sight* or *spectacle*.

The scene is laid in London	Де́йствие происхо́дит в Ло́ндоне
Behind the scenes	За кули́сами
The scene of the crime	Ме́сто преступле́ния
To make a scene	Устра́ивать (устро́ить) сце́ну, сканда́л

109. School.

We were at school together	Мы вме́сте учи́лись
What school did you go to?	Где вы учи́лись?

110. Service. In the widest sense слу́жба, including military service and church service. *Service — favour* is услу́га which is used, too, in the plural, of municipal services, gas, electricity, &c., provided for the householder. Служе́ние is the act of serving: служе́ние де́лу ми́ра *the service of the cause of peace*. Обслу́живание is *service* in a hotel, restaurant, &c. Cf. самообслу́живание *self-service*.

111. Ship, Boat. Парохо́д is the usual word for a passenger vessel, lit. *steamship*. Кора́бль, originally a sailing vessel (па́русное су́дно), may also be applied to a large ocean-going steamer, like парохо́д, and specifically to a naval vessel.

Ло́дка denotes a small boat, lifeboat, rowing-boat. Су́дно is *a vessel, a bottom*, and is usually qualified by an adjective, па́русное (*sailing-*), парово́е (*steam-*), &c.

112. Shop. Ла́вка commonly denotes a stall, or an open-air stand: *bookstall* кни́жная ла́вка; but it may also mean a small, covered shop. *The Old Curiosity Shop* is commonly translated into Russian as Ла́вка дре́вностей.

To go shopping   Идти́ (пойти́) по магази́нам (за поку́пками)

113. Side, Inside, Outside. *Side* generally is сторона́, but бок is used for the side of the body. Борт is the side of a ship. *Inside, interior* is вну́тренность: the *inside* or *reverse side* of a garment is оборо́тная сторона́, or изна́нка. (N.B. изна́нка жи́зни *the seamy side of life*.) *Outside, exterior* is нару́жность or вне́шность; the *outside* or *right side* of a garment is лицева́я сторона́.

114. Sight (*see* **View**). Зре́ние is the physical property of sight, *vision*. Взгляд may be used of a quick glance: *at first sight* на пе́рвый взгляд, с пе́рвого взгля́да. Вид is used to express being in, coming into or going out of the field of vision: *to disappear out of sight* скрыва́ться (скры́ться) из виду; *in sight of all* на виду́ у всех.

Спекта́кль is used only of a play, film, or other visual entertainment. Зре́лище is *a sight*, *spectacle* (something worth looking at). *The sights* достопримеча́тельности.

To know by sight   Знать в лицо́
To play at sight (of music)   Игра́ть с листа́
Out of sight, out of mind   С глаз доло́й, из се́рдца вон

115. Sorrow, Grief, Pain. Печа́ль is the primary word for unqualified sorrow, i.e. without reference to the intensity of the emotion. Го́ре is stronger and suggests profound sorrow. Беда́ often means *misfortune*, and is common in colloquial and proverbial usage. Грусть and го́ресть belong to poetic diction. Тоска́ is a weariness of the spirit which may be boredom or may be a nostalgic longing. Боль is used primarily of physical pain. Скорбь means *grief*.

116. Step. Basically шаг. Стопа́ in the sense of шаг is archaic or poetic, but is used in the idiom идти́ (пойти́) по стопа́м кого́-нибудь *to follow in someone's footsteps. To march in step with* идти́ (пойти́) в но́гу с + instrumental.

Поступь and походка both denote a way of walking, *gait, tread*: походка is the normal word, поступь the more poetic.

Крыльцо is *a flight of steps* (e.g. in front of a house)

Steps: приставная лестница is *a ladder*; складная лестница or стремянка *a pair of steps*. Ступенька is used of the step (stair) of a staircase; перекладина of the rung of a ladder. Подножка is the steps of a vehicle.

117. Student. Студент (студентка) is the general word. Вузовец (вузовка) is a popular Soviet coinage meaning a student at a *higher educational institution* (высшее учебное заведение), i.e. technical college, training college, university. Ученик often means *pupil, disciple*. Учащиеся is frequently used in the plural to denote the student body, a collective term for both sexes. *A student of Roman Law* изучающий римское право.

118. Thought. While there is overlapping between the words, a general distinction can be made between размышление, мышление, and мысль. Размышление is the process of thought, deliberation, reflection; мышление is the ability to think, the property of thought; мысль is the result of the thought process, a thought. Compare:

On second thoughts (i.e. after mature reflection)	По зрелом размышлении
Thought (i.e. thinking) *is the chief function of the brain*	Мышление — главная функция мозга
To collect one's thoughts	Собираться (собраться) с мыслями

Дума is now archaic or poetic as a synonym for *thought*.

119. Time. *What is the time?* который час? Час is confined to time by the clock; colloquially время may be substituted: сколько времени? = который час?

Время can mean *time, period, age, season* (also *tense* grammatically). Времена года *the seasons of the year*; летнее время *summer time, the summer season*. Сезон is used of a

theatre season or a social season; *the London season* лóндон-
ский сезóн, as well as of the appropriate time for carrying
out an action. *It's time to* is порá + the infinitive. Порá as
a noun in the same sense as врéмя is archaic, but still
occurs in such combinations as с тех пор *since*; до сих пор
up to now; в ту пóру *then*.

At my time of life	В мои гóды
It will last our time (lifetime)	Этого на наш век хвáтит

Time meaning *occasion* is раз: *time after time* раз за рáзом.
Nine times out of ten в девятú слýчаях из десятú.

Срок often is the date on which something has to be
completed or fulfilled; *the date for payment* срок платежá.
Also a definite, limited interval of time, a term of office:
twenty years is a long time двáдцать лет — большóй срок.

That was before my time	Это бы́ло ещё до меня

120. Today, Tomorrow, Yesterday. Both сегóдня and
зáвтра can be used as indeclinable nouns: *until tomorrow*
до зáвтра. This is not the case with вчерá: *since yesterday*
со вчерáшнего дня and not со вчерá.

121. Tree. Most names of trees are identical with the
names of their fruits; a few trees have their own form.
Among the commonest of the former are:

Pear and *pear tree* грýша
Plum and *plum tree* слúва
Cherry and *cherry tree* вúшня

of the latter:

Apple tree я́блоня; *apple* я́блоко
Orange tree апельсúнное дéрево; *orange* апельсúн

122. Truth. Прáвда and úстина are identical in this
meaning, but úстина survives in certain set expressions
and certain legal and religious formulae (cf. истéц *plain-
tiff*; во úстину *verily*). Common uses of úстина are гóлая
úстина *the naked truth* (and cf. чúстая прáвда); стáрая
úстина *an old truth*; гóрькая úстина *a home truth*; святáя
úстина *gospel truth*.

The somewhat solemn flavour of the English *verity* is contained in и́стина; compare also the translation of *in vino veritas* и́стина в вине́.

123. Turn. Connected with the во́рот root are: оборо́т which means a complete turn, the revolution of a wheel, a turn of speech, the reverse side of an object. Поворо́т means a movement to one side, a change in direction, a bend in a road. Notice поворо́т к лу́чшему *a change (turn) for the better* (поворо́т is the usual word for *turn, change* in fortunes, opinion, policies, &c.) *but* оборо́т in the idiom *things took a bad turn* дела́ при́няли дурно́й оборо́т. Переворо́т is an overturn, a sudden transformation, a revolution in a political sense. Отворо́т is something that turns over on a coat, &c., *lapels*. Изворо́тливость means quickness at turning and hence *resourcefulness*.

To wait one's turn	Ждать свое́й о́череди
At every turn	На ка́ждом шагу́
Turn of mind	Склад ума́
One good turn deserves another	Долг платежо́м кра́сен

124. View (*see* **Sight**). There are many nouns associated with the roots ви́д-еть, зр-еть (*to see*); смотр-е́ть, взгля́д-ывать (*to look*). Вид has the widest range of meanings and is the usual word for *view*: *a house with a view of the sea* дом с ви́дом на мо́ре; *to have in view* име́ть в виду́; *picture-postcard* откры́тка с ви́дом.

Зре́ние usually corresponds to *vision*, but N. B. то́чка зре́ния *point of view*. Обзо́р means *survey* or *precis*.

View = opinion is взгляд, which generally means the manner of looking at a thing, gaze, glance.

Connected with смотр-е́ть are осмо́тр *inspection* of luggage, *examination* of a patient; просмо́тр *viewing* of a film, *perusal* of a document; смотр a military *review, parade, inspection* of people.

View in the sense of a careful watch or observation is translated by наблюде́ние (cf. the archaic verb блюсти́ =

watch, preserve). *Viewpoint, observation point* is наблюда́тельный пункт. Надзо́р means *surveillance, supervision*.

125. Village. Дере́вня is smaller than село́, which in pre-revolutionary Russia signified a village with a church. Селе́ние is poetic and archaic. Посёлок, primarily a small settlement, is now used very widely to mean any place where people live, a village, or even a town which has recently sprung up.

126. Visit. *To pay a visit*: идти́ (пойти́) в го́сти, always has a pleasant connotation; посеща́ть (посети́ть) and посеще́ние not necessarily so. Навеща́ть (навести́ть) *to pay a visit* is colloquial and implies dropping in for a brief call, as does заходи́ть (зайти́) к. Визи́т suggests an official, ceremonial, or professional visit. *Visiting card* визи́тная ка́рточка.

127. Way, Road, Route. Доро́га and путь are in many contexts interchangeable. Both have the meaning of *journey* as well as *road* or *way* (figuratively): *Bon voyage!* счастли́вый путь! (счастли́вого пути́) or счастли́вой доро́ги! Путь is very commonly used now in such metaphorical expressions as путь к коммуни́зму *the road to communism*; сла́вный путь *a glorious path*. But *path* in a concrete sense is доро́жка (тропи́нка), and *road* in a concrete sense доро́га. *The high road* is больша́я доро́га.

Шоссе́ is a main, trunk road; магистра́ль a main line, main route (rail, river, &c.); алле́я *avenue*; у́лица, переу́лок *street, side-street*. Маршру́т means *route, itinerary*.

Way = means сре́дство, *= method* спо́соб.

To my way of thinking	По-мо́ему; на мой взгляд
To get one's own way	Доби́ться своего́; настоя́ть на своём

By the way = incidentally Кста́ти.

128. Work. Both труд and рабо́та can denote mental and physical work, with труд the more literary word stylistically, рабо́та the more colloquial.

Труд suggests labour, conscientious endeavour, industry, always implying expenditure of effort. Работа extends to a man's daily occupation which may or may not be laborious. Служба is the work of an official or professional man. Занятие, *an occupation*, often means academic studies in the plural: *we start work at the university in October* занятия в университете начинаются в октябре.

Дело is *a job of work, business*: *on business* по делам; *he's got some work* (a job) *on* он занят делом; *a moment's work* дело одной минуты.

An author's *works* may be произведения, сочинения, or, collectively in the singular, творчество. Творчество is creative power or creative work as a whole.

129. Worker. Рабочий is primarily a manual labourer, but in the Soviet period it is used in an appreciatory sense of all industrial and agricultural workers as distinct from professional people and intellectuals. Of the latter работник is used, especially of scientific and technical specialists and research workers in any field.

Трудящиеся refers indiscriminately to people actively employed.

The working class	Рабочий класс
A hard worker	Труженик, работяга and (slang) работящий
Office worker, white-collar worker	Служащий

130. World. Мир is more abstract (the universe, life, civilization), свет more concrete (the earth with its animal and vegetable life). Мы построим новый мир *we shall build a new world* (i.e. civilization); я живу в новом свете *I live in the new world* (i.e. America). *The ancient world* (implying a culture and a civilization, not a geographical area) античный мир.

The world of animals, sounds, colours, &c., is мир. The world as the aggregate of countries and oceans is свет. *A journey round the world* путешествие вокруг света (кругосветное путешествие).

Свет is also used of high society: *The fashionable set* мо́дный свет. *A man of the world* све́тский челове́к.

| *In this world; in the next world* | На э́том све́те; на том све́те. |
| *To get on in the world* | Вы́йти в лю́ди |

131. Writing. Письмо́ is the ability to write: *reading and writing* чте́ние и письмо́; *the art of writing* иску́сство письма́. Писа́ние is the act of writing: *your help in writing this book* ва́ша по́мощь при писа́нии э́той кни́ги. In a religious context писа́ние means *scripture*: свяще́нное писа́ние *holy writ, the scriptures.*

Гра́мота is the ability to read *and* write, i.e. literacy.

По́черк means *style of writing, handwriting, hand.*

132. Year. Лет and not годо́в is used as the genitive plural after the cardinal numerals five and upwards, and quantitative adverbs. Годо́в is used with ordinal numbers signifying decades: *before the thirties* до тридца́тых годо́в (see also para. **750**).

Лета́ (в лета́) are poetic or archaic for го́ды (в го́ды) in such expressions as в ва́ши лета́ *at your time of life,* в лета́ мое́й ю́ности *in the years of my youth* and the plural of год would normally be used in both these cases. But в лета́х is still used in speech as well as в года́х to mean *getting on in years.*

| *Leap year* | Високо́сный год |

133. Yesterday, *see* **Today, Tomorrow.**

134. Youth. The period of youth is мо́лодость and (more literary) ю́ность. But ю́ность is confined to the 'teens, while мо́лодость may refer to the 30's and 40's, up to middle age, in fact, and is also used in the expression втора́я мо́лодость.

Ю́ноша is *a youth*; молодёжь *the youth* (collectively). Молоде́ц! is a colloquial exclamation meaning *fine fellow!, well done!, nice work!*

II

THE ADJECTIVE

LONG AND SHORT FORMS

135. As a general statement, if an adjective has both long and short forms, the long form will be found most commonly in the attributive position, while the short form will be found only in the predicative. The use of the short form attributively is confined to a very few set expressions, e.g.

In broad daylight	Средь бела дня
Everyone regardless of age	От мала до велика
On one's bare feet	На босу ногу

N.B. not *barefoot* (босиком), but *with no socks or stockings on*: в калошах на босу ногу (L. N. Tolstoy) *wearing galoshes on his bare feet.*

136. (i) Рад is the only adjective in common literary use which exists *only in the short form* (cf. the attributive use of радостный).

(ii) There are a considerable number of relative and possessive adjectives, adjectives derived from verbs, and ordinal numbers which exist *only in the long form*. All adjectives in -ский[1] have the long form only, as have the vast majority in -ний (e.g. летний; N. B. the short forms of синий and древний are very rarely used), -шний (e.g. домашний), -яный, -янный, -аный, -анный (e.g. деревянный, кожаный) to mention only the most common.

(iii) Some adjectives in -ический which have no short forms have synonyms in -ичный which provide short forms. Common examples are трагический, трагичный *tragic*; комический, комичный *comic*; типический, типичный *typical*; драматический, драматичный *dramatic*.

(iv) Большой and маленький have as their short forms велик and мал respectively (see para. **163**).

---

[1] Except when the -с forms part of the root and not of the -ск- suffix —e.g. веский *weighty* which gives весок, etc.

137. When an adjective has two forms morphologically, there are certain contexts in which only the one form or the other is admissible as a predicative adjective.

(i) Sometimes the two forms have acquired different meanings, e.g. хоро́ший *good* and хоро́ш собо́й *handsome*; дурно́й *bad* and дурён собо́й *ugly*; плохо́й *bad* and плох *weak, ill*. In the meaning of *handsome, ugly,* or *ill* only the respective short forms may be used predicatively.

(ii) The short form only is used with a few adjectives to denote that the characteristic of the adjective is possessed in too great a degree:

| *This hat is too small* | Э́та шля́па мала́ |

Other common adjectives used in this way are дли́нен *too long*, ко́роток *too short*, вели́к *too big*, мо́лод *too young*; широ́к *too wide*, у́зок *too narrow*.

(iii) The short form only is used with the following adjectives which are followed by complements, which may be an infinitive, a noun or pronoun governed by a preposition, or a noun or pronoun in an oblique case:

(*a*) followed by an infinitive:

Free to	Во́лен, свобо́ден
e.g. *You are free to go where you like*	Вы свобо́дны идти́ куда́ уго́дно
Ready to	Гото́в
Bound to	До́лжен
Intending to	Наме́рен
Capable of	Спосо́бен
Agreeable to	Согла́сен
Inclined to	Скло́нен

(*b*) followed by a preposition:

Guilty before	Винова́т пе́ред
Far from	Далёк от
Similar, dissimilar to	Похо́ж, непохо́ж на
Inclined to	Скло́нен к

Deaf to	Глух к
Indifferent to	Равнодушен к
Agree with (agree to)	Согласен с (на)
N.B. *I agree with you*	Я согласен с вами
I agree to your conditions	Я согласен на ваши условия
Ready for	Готов к and на
N.B. *He is ready for the exams.* (i.e. he has made all the necessary preparations)	Он готов к экзаменам
He is ready for anything (i.e. he is reckless, foolhardy)	Он готов на всё

(*c*) followed by an oblique case of a noun or pronoun:

Worthy (unworthy) *of*	Достоин (недостоин) + genitive
Satisfied (*dissatisfied*) *with*	Доволен (недоволен) + instrumental
Rich in	Богат + instrumental
e.g. *The Russian language is rich in proverbs*	Русский язык богат пословицами

It will be noticed that an adjective in the short form followed by a preposition, or governing a noun or pronoun in an oblique case, may be identical in meaning with a verb formed from the same root:

I agree with him	Я согласен с ним = я соглашаюсь с ним
He is angry with me	Он сердит на меня = он сердится на меня

(iv) Nearly all the words given in (iii) can be used absolutely, without a complement. Other common adjectives used absolutely in the predicate, and only in the short form, are:

Right	Прав
Wrong	Неправ
Alive, vivid	Жив

e.g. *The events of the Second*   Собы́тия второ́й мирово́й
World War are still vividly   войны́ ещё жи́вы в
remembered by all (are alive   па́мяти всех
in everyone's memory)

(v) There are some adjectives which in their literal meaning have both long and short forms, but when used metaphorically have only the long form. Note especially глухо́й which in the literal meaning of *deaf* has both forms, but when used with the following meanings has only the long form: *blank wall* глуха́я стена́; *false window* глухо́е окно́; *remote province, backwater* глуха́я прови́нция; *voiceless consonant* глухо́й согла́сный. It is impossible to say э́тот согла́сный глух *this consonant is voiceless.*

(vi) (*a*) In some idioms and fixed expressions in Russian only the short predicative adjective is used:

My conscience is clear   Со́весть моя́ чиста́
He is more dead than alive   Он ни жив ни мёртв

(*b*) Conversely some idioms allow of only the long predicative adjective:

He was a lucky fellow   Рука́ у него́ была́ лёгкая
                                        (Turgenev)

138. Whereas the examples in para. **137** illustrate circumstances in which either one form or the other must be used, there are certain contexts besides in which one or other form is markedly predominant. The short form predominates:

(i) In generalized statements or definitions:

The earth is big and beautiful   Земля́ велика́ и прекра́с-
                                        на (Chekhov)
The soul, it is said, is im-   Говоря́т, что душа́ бес-
mortal   сме́ртна (L. N. Tolstoy)

(ii) When the *degree* of the quality expressed by the adjective is indicated, emphasized, or compared:

This 'blind man' is not as   Э́тот ,,слепо́й" не так
blind as I think   слеп, как мне ка́жется
                                        (Lermontov)

She thought that she was no longer young enough for me	Ей каза́лось, что она́ уже́ недоста́точно молода́ для меня́ (Chekhov)

(iii) The short form also tends to predominate when the subject is a part of the body and is accompanied by the personal pronouns его́, её, их:

Her face is pale	Лицо́ её бле́дно (Krymov)
Their eyes are bright and their faces shining . . . Their hearts are as soft as good soil	Глаза́ их я́сны, и ли́ца све́тлы . . . Сердца́ их мя́гки, как до́брая по́чва (Korolenko)

(iv) (*a*) The long form predominates in a context where in English the repetition of the noun in the subject as an indicator word is understood, or when the pronoun *one* (*ones*) is understood. This commonly occurs in English when the noun is *particularized* by the use of the definite article, a demonstrative adjective, a possessive pronoun, or an adverbial phrase:

Judging by all the rules the picture is a bad one	Судя́ по всем пра́вилам карти́на плоха́я (Press)
The part is an awful one	Роль ужа́сная
His servants are old	Слу́ги у него́ ста́рые
The play last night was wonderful	Вчера́шний вече́рний спекта́кль был замеча́тельный

(*b*) Contrast the predominant use of the short form, when the adjective is followed by a complement, or when it is qualified by an adverb of degree, or a comparative word:

He . . . is handsome in the old fashioned Russian style	Он . . . краси́в стари́нной ру́сской красото́й (Fadeyev)
This part is not important enough for her	Э́та роль не доста́точно значи́тельна для неё

The snow was as clean and smooth as a table-cloth	Снег был чист и гла́док, как ска́терть (Korolenko)

139. (i) In considering the above uses of the short and long forms of the adjective, it should be remembered that historically their functions were respectively defining and particularizing. The short form designated a quality without reference to any definite person or thing to which it belonged, whereas the long form attributed the quality to a definite person or thing. It is this emphasis of the short form upon the quality itself rather than identification of the quality with a definite person or thing that determines its use meaning *too* (big, small, &c.) and its use with adverbs of degree and comparison. Again the short form is used in such a generalization as *the soul is immortal* precisely because the sense is generalized—if the noun is particularized, the long form becomes possible:

. . . *the soul of this comely, stern woman is tender and true*	. . . душа́ у э́той стро́йной и стро́гой же́нщины не́жная и пряма́я (Kazakevich)

(cf. para. **138** (i) and (iv)). Such words as *earth* denote objects of which only one exists and therefore particularization is impossible (cf. the impossibility of saying in English *the earth is a big one*).

(ii) Although generally speaking the identification of the long form with particularizing constructions is clear, this does not mean that the short form is not also possible in Russian in particularized contexts, so long as the quality referred to is not a permanent one.

My sister's plaid is brand new	Се́стрин плед соверше́нно нов (но́вый)

There is no semantic difference between the use of the short and the long form in this sentence; the only difference is that the short form theoretically stresses the quality

of newness, whereas the long form theoretically identifies
the quality of newness with my sister's plaid [my sister's
plaid is (a) new (one)]. With certain adjectives, however,
this theoretical difference becomes a practical difference
and makes the replacement of one form by the other impossible. Compare:

Her mother is an invalid   Её мать больна́я
Her mother is always ill   Её мать всегда́ больна́

Here the complete identification of the adjective больна́я
with *her mother* is expressed in English by the use of the
noun *invalid* in the predicate, whereas the short form
больна́ simply states that proneness to illness is a fundamental characteristic of *her mother* without identifying the
two. Vinogradov states: 'long adjectives . . . denote that a
characteristic is present permanently in an object, that the
existence of this characteristic covers the whole period of
the existence of the object. Short adjectives on the other
hand express the fact that a characteristic is not permanent
in an object, but only the temporary condition of that
object.' This is another way of saying that the long adjective identifies a quality completely with an object or person, whereas the short adjective expresses only the quality
without identification. The long adjective will not therefore normally be used in explicitly temporary contexts
(e.g. *her mother was ill at the time*); the short adjective is
never found where the characteristic covers the whole
period of existence of a particularized object, but is used
to refer to permanent characteristics (земля́ — велика́)
when its function is defining and not identifying.

140. Predicative adjectives in Russian are used in the
instrumental case, as well as in the short form and the
nominative long form. The basic meaning of the instrumental form is a quality which is manifest at a given
moment or for a given time. In meaning, therefore, it is
similar to the short form. The only context in which it may
not be used is when there is no verbal link between sub-

ject and predicate. (See para. **21**: a *noun* predicate *can* be used in the instrumental case with no verbal link.) It is, for example, impossible to say её мать больно́й *her mother is ill*, but possible, and indeed usual, to say, for example, на́ша конститу́ция явля́ется наибо́лее демократи́ческой в ми́ре (Stalin) *our constitution is the most democratic in the world.*

Except in sentences where there is no verbal link, or except in sentences where the long or short nominative forms are for other grammatical or semantic reasons obligatory, the instrumental form is now widespread in modern Russian. In this respect there is a marked difference between nineteenth and twentieth century usage. The instrumental case is today almost invariable after a verb in the *present* tense, and nineteenth century constructions such as тепе́рь а́вгуст, вечера́ стано́вятся сы́ры (Goncharov) *it is now August, the evenings are getting damp* would not nowadays be used.

COMPARISON

141. Comparatives used predicatively

(i) These may be of two kinds: (*a*) where two persons or objects are expressly compared ('this is bigger than that'), and (*b*) where no object is mentioned as a standard of comparison. In both cases the simple form in -ee (-ей, -е) when it exists is much more common than the compound form бо́лее plus the adjective in the positive degree, which is sometimes considered *bookish*.

He is far taller than his brother	Он гора́здо вы́ше бра́та (чем брат)
Our friendship became stronger and more intimate	На́ша дру́жба ста́ла кре́пче и бли́же

The compound form, however, is commonly used with words of several syllables, although it cannot be said in Russian, as it can in English, that adjectives of three or more syllables take the compound and not the simple form of the comparative (e.g. *more difficult*, not *difficulter*).

(ii) With some adjectives only the compound form is possible, e.g. adjectives which have no short form (see para. **136** (ii)), adjectives in -овый (e.g. багро́вый *purple*), -истый (e.g. тени́стый *shady*), and various unclassified words including чёрствый *stale*, го́рдый *proud*, тя́жкий *heavy*, одино́кий *lonely* and generally speaking many adjectives with a -кий suffix.

Since all adjectives *may* take the compound form, while some may not take the simple, it will be advisable when in doubt to use the compound form even at the risk of *bookishness* and in spite of the known preference for the simple form when it exists.

(iii) The adjectives in -ический referred to in para. **136** (iii) which have synonyms in -ичный form predicative comparatives from these synonyms (e.g. траги́ческий, траги́чный, comparative траги́чнее):

I have never read anything more tragic than the life of Dostoevsky	Я никогда́ не чита́л ничего́ траги́чнее жи́зни Достое́вского

142. Comparatives used attributively

Here the simple form in -ee (-ей, -e) cannot be used:

The country is a healthier place than the town	Дере́вня бо́лее здоро́вое ме́сто чем го́род

But note that an English attributive comparative may be translated in Russian, especially colloquially, by a predicative comparative, often with the prefix по-:

Show me some cheaper frocks	Покажи́те мне пла́тья подеше́вле
I have seen worse houses in Moscow	В Москве́ я ви́дел доми́шки похýже (Erenburg)

143. (i) Where two forms exist for the comparative as with бо́льше, бо́лее; ме́ньше, ме́нее; да́льше, да́лее; до́льше, дóлее; it is the first form which is the comparative adjective, the second being only an adverb.

(ii) In the case of худóй, the two comparatives хýже and худéе are semantically different: хýже means *worse*, худéе *thinner*.

144. Superlatives

(i) The compound form, сáмый plus the positive form of the adjective, is by far the most common way of expressing the superlative in Russian, whether attributively or predicatively.

(ii) The suffix -ейший (-айший) is much less common. Relatively few adjectives can form their superlatives with it, and when it *is* used (in preference to the compound form with сáмый), it may sound *bookish*. It is found quite often in academic articles and in leaders in the Soviet press, although, of course, its use is largely a matter of individual taste. The following examples are taken from the same paragraph of a newspaper article:

The most careful check-up is required here	Тут необходи́ма тща́тельнейшая прове́рка
The matter requires the most careful investigation	Де́ло тре́бует са́мого тща́тельного рассле́дования

(iii) The -ейший (-айший) suffix will regularly be found in certain stereotyped formulas where linguistic convention has sanctioned it:

Down to the smallest details	До мельча́йших подро́бностей
There's not the slightest doubt	Нет ни мале́йшего сомне́ния
Sheer nonsense	Чисте́йший вздор
With the greatest of pleasure	С велича́йшим удово́льствием
His worst enemy	Его́ зле́йший враг
The prime duty	Перве́йший долг
In the shortest possible time	В кратча́йший срок

(iv) It may be noted that the use of -ейший (-айший) in a comparative sense, which is found in nineteenth-century literature, is now virtually obsolete. (But N. B. дальнéйший *further*, позднéйший *subsequent*.)

(v) The coupling of сáмый and an -ейший (-айший) suffix, though still met, is not considered good style.

(vi) Russian, like English, uses a comparative plus the words *than anyone* (всех), *than anything* (всего) to express a superlative meaning:

They were all rich, but Ivanov was the richest of all (lit. *richer than all*)	Онú все бы́ли богáтыми, но Ивáнов был богáче всех

(vii) The combination of the prefix наи- with the adjectival form in -ейший, -айший, -ший in a superlative meaning is generally considered *bookish*. Probably the most common examples in current use are наилýчший *best*, наибóльший *greatest*, наимéньший *least*:

With very best wishes from . . .	С наилýчшими пожелáниями от . . .

145. Comparatives/Superlatives in -ший:

There are a few pairs of adjectives which seem to hesitate between the comparative and superlative degrees. These pairs are (in the positive) in English: *big, small; good, bad; high, low; young, old*.

(i) бóльший, мéньший:

These are used only as comparatives meaning *greater*, *lesser*. Notice with бóльший that in some cases (i.e. instrumental singular and all cases in the plural) the form of the positive and the form in -ший are spelt the same but have different stresses.

With a great (greater) effort	С большúм (бóльшим) усúлием

(ii) Лу́чший, ху́дший:

These may be both comparatives and superlatives of
хоро́ший and худо́й (плохо́й), i.e. *better* or *best*; *worse* or
worst:

The critic is not a better, but a worse philosopher than the artist	Кри́тик не лу́чший, а ху́дший фило́соф, чем худо́жник ·
At best, at worst	В лу́чшем слу́чае, в ху́дшем слу́чае

(iii) Вы́сший, ни́зший:

These are primarily superlatives, their use as comparatives being already archaic:

In the highest degree	В вы́сшей сте́пени
The lowest temperature of the month	Ни́зшая температу́ра ме́сяца

It will be frequently noticed, however, that вы́сший and
(to a lesser extent) ни́зший are used in contexts where a
superlative is not used in English. Common examples are:

High command	Вы́сшее кома́ндование
High society	Вы́сшее о́бщество

Here вы́сший is no longer the superlative of высо́кий (one
cannot speak of a высо́кое кома́ндование). It has acquired
a special meaning. The fact that this meaning may correspond to a comparative or superlative form in English does
not mean that вы́сший expresses *degree of comparison* in
Russian, any more than *higher* would, in the same context,
in English. Вы́сшее образова́ние means 'higher education',
which cannot be compared to the impossible высо́кое
образова́ние or *high education*.

(iv) Мла́дший, ста́рший:

These too are virtually superlatives meaning first born
(ста́рший) and last born (мла́дший). However, when used

in relation to two people only, they correspond to English *elder* and *younger*:

My youngest brother (of many) Мой мла́дший брат
My younger brother (of two)

They also correspond to English *junior* and *senior*:

Junior officer Мла́дший офице́р
Senior assistant Ста́рший помо́щник

All the above adjectives in -ший may be combined with са́мый in a strong superlative sense. Hence вы́сший, itself a superlative, means *highest*; са́мый вы́сший *highest* or *very highest*. But the combination of са́мый with бо́льший and ме́ньший is virtually confined to the adverbial expressions са́мое бо́льшее *at most*, са́мое ме́ньшее *at least*.

POSSESSION

146. The English apostrophe *s* denoting possession is most commonly translated by the genitive case of the noun in Russian:

The policeman's boots Сапоги́ милиционе́ра

However, as some Russian nouns form their own possessive adjectives, we shall attempt here to classify them and note the range and limitations of their use.

147. Adjectives in -ов (-ев) and -ин (the latter especially from nouns in -а and -я). These may:

(i) Denote possession by one individual *specified by name*:

John Ива́н *John's house* Ива́нов дом
Jack (dim.) Ва́ня *Jack's house* Ва́нин дом
Barbara Варва́ра *Barbara's cat* Варва́рина ко́шка

Not all Christian names have these possessive adjectival forms and they are in any case most commonly associated with diminutives or nicknames: На́дин from На́дя, diminutive of Наде́жда; Та́нин from Та́ня (Татья́на). The form in -ов has obviously been instrumental in creating surnames, e.g. *John's son* Ива́нов сын has given Ива́нов (Johnson).

Such adjectives are generally speaking affectionate and used within the family circle. Exceptions are set expressions such as:

Adam's apple	Ада́мово я́блоко
Noah's ark	Но́ев ковче́г
Achilles' heel	Ахилле́сова пята́

(ii) Denote possession by one individual, *not specified by name, but by relationship within the family*:

The most common examples are:

Mother's	ма́мин, ма́терин	*Sister's*	се́стрин
Father's	па́пин, отцо́в	*Brother's*	бра́тнин
Wife's	же́нин	*Uncle's*	дя́дин
Husband's	му́жнин	*Aunt's*	тётин

These adjectives are essentially colloquial.

Observations: these -ов and -ин adjectives, which we can call 'specifying', may always be replaced by a noun in the genitive (except in set expressions such as the ones above). It is indeed felt nowadays that these adjectives, which are still used in the spoken language, are dying out in all branches of literature except fiction. With fiction, it is very much a question of individual style (many examples of possessive adjectives could be quoted, say, from Sholokhov). For the purposes of narrative prose composition, the student will have little need of them.

148. (i) Possessive adjectives in -ин and -ов are commonly lengthened by the addition of -ский, e.g. отцо́вский, матери́нский, се́стринский (*but* бра́тский). Their meaning may in this way be extended and some may cease to be possessive adjectives at all. Никола́евская шине́ль does not mean Nicholas's greatcoat, but a greatcoat of the time of Nicholas I. Матери́нская любо́вь is not the love of one mother, but motherly or maternal love. Бра́тский приве́т means *fraternal greetings*. Ги́тлеровская Герма́ния, the Russian for *Hitler(ite) Germany*, does not suggest that Germany was Hitler's own property, and the adjective may be called *classifying* as opposed to *specifying*.

(ii) It would, however, be wrong to think that a line can be drawn between -ов and -ин as referring specifically to one individual, and -овский and -инский as referring to a whole community or genus. The latter endings are taking the place of the former as 'specifying' suffixes (отцо́вский дом is certainly more common than отцо́в дом), although the former endings cannot be applied to 'classifying' adjectives (*maternal love* cannot be translated by ма́терина любо́вь).

(iii) To form adjectives from surnames the suffix -ский (not -овский, -инский) is used when the name already ends in -ов or -ин, e.g. ста́линский, крыло́вский, пу́шкинский. These adjectives do not denote personal possession by Stalin, Krylov, Pushkin. (*Stalin's car* would be маши́на Ста́лина, not ста́линская маши́на.) They suggest that the object they describe is similar to, modelled after, named after, Stalin, Krylov, Pushkin. Пу́шкинский дом is not *Pushkin's house* but *Pushkin House*. Ста́линская эпо́ха is *the Stalin age*. They may also express the fact that the object is written, created, or initiated, by the person concerned. Thus крыло́вские ба́сни *Krylov's fables*, ста́линская конститу́ция *the Stalin Constitution*.

149. There is quite a numerous group of possessive adjectives ending in -ий and -иный, formed from the names of animals with or without a consonant change in the stem. These are important for the student, for while one can avoid the use of, say, отцо́в and отцо́вский, one can only translate the idiom *a dog's life* by соба́чья жизнь. The fact that several such adjectives occur among the 5,000 or so most common Russian words confirms their importance. The following are common examples:

(i) Adjectives in -ий, -ья, -ье:

	Noun	*Adjective*		
Cow	Коро́ва	Коро́вий	*Cow's milk*	Коро́вье молоко́
Sheep	Овца́	Ове́чий	*Wolf in sheep's clothing*	Волк в ове́чьей шку́ре
Ram	Бара́н	Бара́ний	*Sheepskin cap*	Бара́нья ша́пка

	Noun	Adjective		
Wolf	Волк	Во́лчий	Wolf's den	Во́лчье ло́гово
Bear	Медве́дь	Медве́жий	Bear's paw	Медве́жья ла́па
Fox	Лиса́	Ли́сий	Fox's fur	Ли́сий мех
Bird	Пти́ца	Пти́чий	Bird's nest	Пти́чье гнездо́
Peacock	Павли́н	Павли́ний	Peacock's feathers	Павли́ньи пе́рья
Fish	Ры́ба	Ры́бий	Fish's tail	Ры́бий хвост
Cat	Ко́шка	Коша́чий	Cat's eyes	Коша́чьи глаза́

With young animals the possessive adjective is formed from the plural root, e.g. телёнок *calf*; plural теля́та; possessive adjective теля́чий.

(ii) Adjectives in -иный, -иная, -иное:

	Noun	Adjective		
Horse	Ло́шадь	Лошади́ный	Horse power	Лошади́ная си́ла
Lion	Лев	Льви́ный	Lion's share	Льви́ная до́ля
Swan	Ле́бедь	Лебеди́ный	Swan song	Лебеди́ная пе́сня
Hen	Ку́рица (dialect ку́ра)	Кури́ный	Chicken broth	Кури́ный бульо́н
Eagle	Орёл	Орли́ный	Aquiline nose	Орли́ный нос

It will be seen that these adjectives, besides denoting possession, may also show the property or characteristics of a species, origin (коро́вье молоко́), or comparison (орли́ный нос).

150. Another useful group of possessive adjectives with the suffix -ий derives from the names of people engaged in some profession or occupation:

	Noun	Adjective		
Shepherd	Пасту́х	Пасту́ший	Shepherd's horn	Пасту́ший рог
Fisherman	Рыба́к	Рыба́чий	Fishing smack	Рыба́чья ло́дка
Landowner	Поме́щик	Поме́щичий	Landowner's estate	Поме́щичья уса́дьба

151. The English apostrophe *s* denoting possession may sometimes be rendered in Russian by a *dative* case, under the direct influence of a verb:

To cut off a person's head Отруба́ть (отруби́ть) го́лову кому́-нибудь

| This fact must not blind the Americans to the real state of affairs (lit. shut the Americans' eyes) | Э́тот факт не до́лжен закрыва́ть Америка́нцам глаза́ на настоя́щее положе́ние дел (Press) |

RUSSIAN ADJECTIVE FOR ENGLISH NOUN IN THE GENITIVE

152. Attention may be drawn to some common examples of a Russian adjective translating an English noun in the genitive case:

(i) with titles. Where in English, to express royal titles or names of institutions, we say, for example, 'the Emperor of China' or 'the Bank of England', Russian uses an adjective derived from the place-name:

| The University of Liverpool | Ливерпу́льский университе́т |
| The King of England | Брита́нский коро́ль |

In these examples the Russian adjective precedes the noun. But with titles of the nobility, the adjective follows the noun:

| The Duke of Edinburgh | Ге́рцог Эдинбу́ргский |
| The Count of Paris | Граф Пари́жский |

(ii) with some expressions of time:

After a moment's silence	По́сле секу́ндного молча́ния
An hour's lecture	Часова́я ле́кция
A week's holiday	Неде́льный о́тпуск

ADJECTIVAL NOUNS

153. (i) Common examples such as столо́вая *dining-room*, вое́нный *soldier*, which the student meets at an early stage, give no difficulty. It is important, however, to distinguish between (*a*) words which can still be both adjectives and nouns, e.g. столо́вая *dining-room*; столо́вая ло́жка *table-*

spoon; and (*b*) words which are now only nouns, e.g. портной *tailor*.

(ii) Sometimes an adjective is used as a noun, when a noun from the same root and with the same meaning already exists; e.g. богáтый *a rich man* (богáч); бéдный *a poor man* (бедня́к); си́льный *a strong man* (силáч). A distinction can be made between the two by saying that the adjective (e.g. си́льный) suggests an abstract individual or a collective body (*the strong*), while the noun (e.g. силáч) often denotes a concrete individual, a real person:

The rich man sometimes forgets the poor	Богáтый иногдá забывáет бéдного
Stroganov is a rich man	Стрóганов — богáч

PARTICIPLES USED AS NOUNS

154. Many of these are identical in spelling and in stress whether used as participles or as nouns: e.g. дáнные *data*; учáщийся *student*; обвиня́емый *the accused*; начинáющий *a beginner*; ископáемые *minerals*. But notice рáненый *a wounded man*, but рáненный *having been wounded*; and учёный *a scholar* (no past participle passive).

PARTICIPLES USED AS ADJECTIVES

With no change in spelling or in stress

155. (i) There are many common examples of all the participial forms being used as adjectives. There is no change in spelling, but the adjective often acquires a wider, metaphorical meaning and becomes in effect a new word:

Present participle active:

Вызывáющий (part.)	*Challenging*
Вызывáющее поведéние (adj.)	*Provocative behaviour*
Блестя́щий (part.)	*Shining*
Блестя́щий учени́к (adj.)	*A brilliant pupil*

Past participle active:

Проше́дший (part.)	*Having gone by*
Проше́дшее вре́мя (adj.)	*Past tense*
Бы́вший (part.)	*Having been*
Бы́вший учи́тель (adj.)	*A former schoolteacher*

Present participle passive: (when used as an adjective, this is nearly always combined with the negative не—or with an adverb):

Выноси́мый (part.)	*Being tolerated*
Невыноси́мое оскорбле́ние (adj.)	*An intolerable insult*

Past participle passive:

Рассе́янный (part.)	*Having been scattered*
Рассе́янный вид (adj.)	*A distracted air*
Откры́тый (part.)	*Having been opened*
Откры́тый взгляд (adj.)	*A frank look*

(ii) There are a few examples of participles in -ся (present and past) serving as adjectives, e.g.

Выдаю́щийся учёный	*An outstanding scholar*
Вью́щиеся во́лосы	*Curly hair*
Опусти́вшийся челове́к	*A man gone to seed*

and with a negative prefix:

Неуда́вшийся а́втор	*An unsuccessful author*
Небью́щиеся игру́шки	*Unbreakable toys*

With change of spelling or stress

156. (i) There are a few adjectives of participial origin which closely resemble present participles active derived from the same root, e.g.

Ходя́чий (cf. ходя́щий)	*Mobile, current*
Ходя́чее выраже́ние	*A current expression*
Бродя́чий (cf. бродя́щий)	*Wandering, nomadic, stray*
Бродя́чий сюже́т	*A migrant theme* (folk-lore)
Летучий (cf. летя́щий)	*Flying, transitory, shifting*
Летучая мышь	*A bat*

Ползу́чий (cf. ползу́щий)	*Crawling*
Ползу́чие расте́ния	*Creepers*
Стоя́чий (cf. стоя́щий)	*In a standing position, stagnant*
Стоя́чая вода́	*Stagnant water*
Лежа́чий (cf. лежа́щий)	*In a lying position, recumbent*
Лежа́чее положе́ние	*A recumbent posture*
Сидя́чий (cf. сидя́щий)	*In a sitting position, sedentary*
Сидя́чий о́браз жи́зни	*A sedentary way of life*
Вися́чий (cf. вися́щий)	*Hanging*
Вися́чий мост	*A suspension bridge*
Паду́чий (cf. паду́щий)	*Falling*
Паду́чая боле́знь	*Epilepsy*

Other useful examples are: кипу́чий *intensive, feverish* (e.g. of work, activity), горю́чий *combustible*, жгу́чий *burning* (e.g. жгу́чий вопро́с), живу́чий *tenacious of life, viable* (он живу́ч, как ко́шка *he has as many lives as a cat*). Both теку́чий and теку́щий are used adjectivally. Теку́чий means *liquid, mobile, fluctuating* (теку́чие тела́ *liquid bodies*; теку́чая рабо́чая си́ла *fluctuating manpower*). Теку́щий means *current, present* (в теку́щем году́ *in the current year*; теку́щий счёт *current account*).

(ii) Some adjectives of participial origin have a -ный suffix while their related participles end in -нный:

Ры́ба, ва́ренная в кастрю́ле (part.)	*Fish boiled in a pan*
Варёная ры́ба (adj.)	*Boiled fish*
Солда́т, ра́ненный в ру́ку (part.)	*A soldier, wounded in the arm*
Ра́неный солда́т (adj.)	*A wounded soldier*

Compare also:

па́ренный (part.) and па́реный (adj.) *steamed*
со́ленный (part.) and солёный (adj.) *salted*
гру́женный (part.) and гружёный (adj.) *laden*
су́шенный (part.) and сушёный (adj.) *dried*
золочённый (part.) and золочёный (adj.) *gilded*

These participial forms, however, although given in Ushakov, are unlikely to be met, since a past participle passive is very rarely formed from an imperfective verb. Only the adjectival form жа́реный (*fried, roasted*) survives in modern Russian.

(iii) Occasionally there is a difference of stress, but no difference in spelling, between related adjectives and participles in -нный. Such differences were observed in the nineteenth century, but seldom are today. One still distinguishes between прибли́женный (part.) *having been brought near* and приближённый (adj.) *approximate*; and between совершённый (part.) *having been completed* and соверше́нный (adj.) *complete, perfect*—this now being rather a difference of spelling than of stress. But уни́женный (part.) *having been humiliated* is now also used as an adjective, as well as унижённый (adj.) *humiliated*; and заслу́женный *honoured* is now used both as adjective and participle to the exclusion of заслужённый (archaic).

(iv) Some adjectives of participial origin ending in -тый show a change of stress as compared with participles of the same spelling (stressed -ый becoming -о́й). Thus:

Сня́тый but снято́е молоко́	*Skimmed milk*
За́нятый but занято́й челове́к	*Busy man*
Ви́тый but вита́я ле́стница	*Spiral staircase*

157. Adjectives ending in -нный derived from past participles passive normally end in vowel + н (-ан, -ян, -ен) in their masculine singular short form. Thus:

Сде́ржанный	*restrained* has short form сде́ржан
Неожи́данный	*unexpected* has short form неожи́дан
Презре́нный	*contemptible* has short form презре́н
Рассе́янный	*absent-minded* has short form рассе́ян
Возвы́шенный	*lofty, exalted* has short form возвы́шен

But to quote the recent 'Совреме́нный ру́сский язы́к' (ed. Vinogradov, Moscow, 1952, p. 138): 'in the modern Russian literary language adjectives in -нный derived from participles show a tendency to make short forms in -нен: thus the use of two forms is now possible: презре́н and презре́нен, возвы́шен and возвы́шенен, неслы́хан, and неслы́ханен.'

'The forms in -нен in a number of cases become the characteristic feature of *adjectives* derived from participles, distinguishing them from the corresponding participles.'

As examples of this we may quote:

Он был возвы́шен в обще́ственном мне́нии (part.)	*He was exalted in the popular esteem*
Стиль его́ ре́чи возвы́шенен (adj.)	*He has an elevated style of speech*
Он был почтён за свои́ услу́ги (part.)	*He was honoured for his services*
Его́ по́двиг почте́нен (adj.)	*His heroic exploit is worthy of honour*
План был определён (part.)	*The plan was drawn up*
Его́ отве́т был определёнен (adj.)	*His answer was quite clear*

Note the spelling of the adjective in other genders:

Short form: определёнен, определённа, определённо

and compare the participle:

Short form: определён, определена́, определено́.

In view of the spread of this tendency in modern Russian, the student can only be referred to an authoritative up-to-date dictionary for guidance.

158. Those adjectives formed from past participles passive which do not show -нен in the short form masculine singular (e.g. рассе́ян, сде́ржан, неожи́дан) may duplicate the -н in other genders. Thus:

Рассе́янный (adj.) short form: рассе́ян, рассе́янна, рассе́янно

Сде́ржанный (adj.) short form: сде́ржан, сде́ржанна, сде́ржанно

Неожи́данный (adj.) short form: неожи́дан, неожи́данна, неожи́данно

Where, as in the first two cases, the form is still in use as a *participle* as well as an adjective, there will be a difference in spelling between the two parts of speech:

Вра́жеские войска́ бы́ли рассе́яны (part.)	*The enemy forces were dispersed*
Уча́щиеся бы́ли рассе́янны (adj.)	*The students were inattentive*

RUSSIAN ADVERB FOR ENGLISH ADJECTIVE

159. The presence of a predicative *adjective* in English will in certain contexts be the cue to use an *adverb* in Russian. Such adverbs are used with быть or a similar verb to describe the state in which an object happens to be at a given time, or to denote a person's mental or physical condition:

The sky was dull	На не́бе бы́ло па́смурно
The river is calm	На реке́ споко́йно
The bus was stuffy	В авто́бусе бы́ло ду́шно
He entered the room. It was noisy	Он вошёл в ко́мнату. В ней бы́ло шу́мно
She became sad	Ей ста́ло гру́стно
The poor boy grew happier at heart	На душе́ бе́дного ма́льчика ста́ло веселе́е
His mouth was dry	Во рту его́ бы́ло су́хо

It will be noticed in all cases that the state is a temporary one and not necessarily characteristic of the person or object. Some grammarians, indeed, postulate a special 'category of state' to include adverbs of this sort.

SIMILAR OR RELATED ADJECTIVES

160

Век:	Вековóй	*Ancient, very old*: вековóй вяз *age-old elm*
	Вéчный	*Eternal*: вéчная жизнь *eternal life*
Верх:	Вéрхний	*Upper* (from верх *top*): вéрхний этáж *upper story*
	Верховóй	*Riding* (from верхóм *on horse-back*): верховáя лóшадь *saddle-horse*
	Верхóвный	*Supreme*: Верхóвный Совéт *Supreme Soviet*
Вéтер:	Вéтреный	*Windy,* and in a figurative sense *empty-headed, flighty*
	Вéтряный	*Operated by the wind*: вéтряная мéльница *windmill*
Вкус:	Вкусовóй	*Pertaining to taste, flavour*: вкусовóе ощущéние *sense of taste*
	Вкýсный	*Tasty*: вкýсный суп *nice soup*
Водá:	Вóдный	*Applied to an expanse of water*: вóдный путь *waterway,* вóдное прострáнство *stretch of water*
	Водянóй	Used of things growing or living in water: водянáя лúлия *water-lily*; водянóй жук *water-beetle*; and of things operated by water водянáя мéльница *water-mill*
	Водянúстый	*Watery,* applied to things lacking in substance: водянúстый стиль *vapid style*

Де́рево:	Деревя́нный	*Wooden*: деревя́нный пол *wooden floor*
	Древе́сный	*Pertaining to trees*: древе́сный у́голь *charcoal*
Дух:	Духо́вный	*Spiritual*: духо́вная му́зыка *sacred music*
	Духово́й	*Operated by wind*: духово́й орке́стр *brass band*
Дым:	Ды́мный	*Filled with smoke, smoky*: ды́мная ко́мната *smoky room*
	Дымово́й	*Smoke-*: дымова́я труба́ *smoke-stack, chimney, funnel*; дымова́я заве́са *smoke-screen*
Здоро́вье:	Здоро́вый	*Healthy*
	Здра́вый	Has now lost this meaning, and is used only of mental processes, in combination with мысль, смысл, ум, &c.: здра́вый смысл *common sense*
Земля́:	Земно́й	*Terrestrial, of the planet earth*: земна́я ось *the earth's axis*
	Земляно́й	*Earthen*, to do with earth in the sense of soil: земляны́е рабо́ты *excavation*; земляно́й червь *earthworm*
	Земе́льный	*Pertaining to the land, property*: земе́льная рефо́рма *land reform*
	Земли́стый	*Earth-coloured*, of a complexion
	Зе́мский	*Pertaining to the* зе́мство
Зо́лото:	Золото́й	*Made of gold, golden-coloured*: N.B. золота́я середи́на (figurative) *the golden mean*

Зо́лото:	Золоти́стый	*Golden-coloured* (hair, corn, &c.), *like gold,* but not *made of gold* (золото́й)
	Золочёный	*Gilded, covered with gold*
Класс:	Кла́ссный	From класс meaning *school class, classroom*: кла́ссная доска́ *blackboard.* Also means *first class* in a sporting context: кла́ссный уда́р *good shot*
	Кла́ссовый	From класс meaning a social group: кла́ссовая борьба́ *the class struggle*
Ко́жа:	Ко́жаный	*Made of leather*: ко́жаный портфе́ль *leather briefcase*
	Коже́венный	*Relating to leather and its manufacture*: коже́венный заво́д *tannery*
Круг:	Кру́жный	*Devious, roundabout*: кру́жным путём *by a detour*
	Кругово́й	*Circular*: кругово́е движе́ние *circular motion*
Ложь:	Лжи́вый	*Mendacious, lying*: лжи́вый челове́к *liar*
	Ло́жный	*False, incorrect*: ло́жная трево́га *false alarm*
Мир:	Ми́рный	From мир meaning *peace*: ми́рная жизнь *peaceful life*
	Мирово́й	мирово́й судья́ *justice of the peace*
	Мирово́й	From мир meaning *world*: мирова́я война́ *world war*
	Мирско́й	*Secular, worldly* as opposed to *cloistered*: мирска́я суета́ *worldly vanity*

Молоко́:	Моло́чный	*Milky, made of milk, like milk*
	Мле́чный	Used only in the special sense of resembling milk, of the sap of certain plants and of the *Milky Way* Мле́чный путь
Ого́нь:	О́гненный and Огнево́й	Both mean *fiery* in a figurative sense, e.g. of words, eyes. О́гненный generally refers to the quality of fire, огнево́й to the action of fire: compare о́гненные языки́ *tongues of fire*; огнева́я су́шка плодо́в *drying fruit by fire*. Огнево́й is commonly used in technical and military contexts: огнево́е прикры́тие *covering fire*
Плод:	Плодо́вый (плодово́й)	*Bearing fruit*: плодо́вые дере́вья *fruit trees*
	Плодови́тый	*Fruitful, bearing much fruit*, e.g. of trees; *prolific* of an author
	Плодоро́дный	*Fruitful, fertile* of the land, soil
	Плодотво́рный	*Fruitful, favourable, auspicious, beneficial*: плодотво́рное начина́ние *auspicious undertaking*
Пух:	Пухово́й (пухо́вый)	*Made from down*: пухова́я поду́шка *feather cushion*
	Пуши́стый	*Covered with down, fluffy*: пуши́стый котёнок *fluffy kitten*

| Серебро́: | Сере́бряный and Серебри́стый | Only сере́бряный means *made of silver*. Both сере́бряный and серебри́стый are used metaphorically of melodious sounds. Серебри́стый especially denotes *silvery, silver-coloured*: серебри́стый то́поль *silver poplar* |

SOME COMMON ADJECTIVES AND THEIR TRANSLATION

161. Good. До́брый generally means *kind, generous, noble-hearted, honourable*. Хоро́ший means *nice, fine, proper, as it should be*. До́брый is used in polite requests: бу́дьте добры́ *be so good*; and in polite greetings: до́брый день *good day*. It is also used colloquially to mean *a good . . .* in the sense of *at least*: займёт до́брых два часа́ *it will take a good two hours*. *Good* of food is often вку́сный (*tasty*).

He is good at *sports*	Он спосо́бен к спо́рту
Apples are good for *one's health*	Я́блоки поле́зны для здоро́вья
It's a good job *you stayed at home*	Хорошо́ (вы хорошо́ сде́лали), что вы оста́лись до́ма
Good luck	В до́брый час!
Cape of Good Hope	Мыс До́брой Наде́жды

162. Bad. Плохо́й and дурно́й are often interchangeable, although дурно́й is the stronger in the sense of *foul* (дурно́й за́пах *a foul smell*), *wicked* (дурна́я же́нщина *an immoral woman*) or *ugly*. Дурно́й rather than плохо́й is often used in opposition to хоро́ший, especially with reference to moral behaviour: его́ дурны́е и хоро́шие привы́чки *his good and bad habits*.

163. Big (great) and Small. (i) Большо́й and вели́кий. In the attributive position большо́й is the more versatile, вел…кий more restricted and specialized in use. Вел…кий often suggests *great* or *grand* in solemn, laudatory, or rhetorical contexts:

The Great Patriotic War (i.e. 1941–5)	Вел…кая Отéчественная войнá
The Great Stalin	Вел…кий Стáлин
They knew all those simple but great truths . . .	Он… знáли все те прост…е, но вел…кие …стины . . .

It will translate *Grand* in formal titles such as *Grand Duke, Grand Inquisitor,* &c.

It will not correspond to *great* in the majority of cases, where *great* simply means *considerable* of time, size, standing, &c.:

They were great friends	Он… б…ли больш…ми друзья́ми
A girl of great promise	Дéвушка подаю́щая больш…е надéжды

In the predicative position (short form) the adjective вел…кий may be accented either вел…к, велика́, велико́ (meaning *big, too big*), or вел…к, вел…ка, вел…ко (meaning *outstanding, brilliant*). Compare:

This hat is too big for me	Э́та шля́па мне велика́
As a writer she is indisputably great	Как писáтельница, онá бесспóрно вел…ка

(ii) Мáленький and мáлый. The normal translation of *small* is мáленький (predicative мал). But мáлый is used in a few special expressions, notably in the sense of *lesser* as opposed to *greater* with proper names and titles: Мáлый теáтр (cf. Большóй теáтр) in Moscow; Мáлая Совéтская Энциклопéдия (cf. Большáя Совéтская Энциклопéдия) *the Small Soviet Encyclopaedia*; Мáлая Медвéдица *the Little Bear* (Ursa Minor); and with the names of plants and animals where in English we say *lesser*.

(iii) Крýпный and мéлкий. These words are common in

the general sense of *big* and *small*, but are more expressive
than большо́й and ма́ленький:

(*a*) *coarse/fine*:

Coarse sand (made up of big lumps)	Кру́пный песо́к
Fine rain	Ме́лкий дождь

N.B. the opposite is си́льный дождь *heavy rain*.

Berries, small fruit, eggs, precious stones, and substances
consisting of grains are commonly qualified by ме́лкий and
кру́пный:

These berries, though small, are nice	Э́ти я́годы, хотя́ ме́лкие, но вку́сные

(*b*) *large-scale/small-scale*

Used in this meaning of farms, undertakings, production,
&c.,

Large-scale agriculture	Кру́пное се́льское хозя́йство

(*c*) *important/trivial, petty, shallow*:

Major writer	Кру́пный писа́тель
Major defects	Кру́пные недоста́тки
Petty larceny	Ме́лкая кра́жа
Minor problems	Ме́лкие пробле́мы
Petty officialdom	Ме́лкое чино́вничество
Shallow water	Ме́лкая вода́

(*d*) with скот, по́черк, де́ньги:

Cattle	Кру́пный скот
He writes a small hand (of handwriting)	У него́ ме́лкий по́черк
Small change	Ме́лкие де́ньги

Idiomatically ме́лкая ры́ба or the somewhat archaic
ме́лкая со́шка is the equivalent of *small fry* (cf. больша́я
ши́шка *big shot*).

(iv) Си́льный may correspond to *big, very big*:

A big fire	Си́льный (большо́й) пожа́р

(v) *Big* (capital) and *small* letters of the alphabet are прописна́я бу́ква and строчна́я бу́ква respectively.

(vi) *Tall* and *small* of stature are often rendered by a genitive construction—*of tall height, not of tall height*, &c.:

Thereupon a small sunburnt peasant entered the room	Тут вошёл в ко́мнату невысо́кого ро́ста загоре́лый мужи́к

164. Old. Of the various words for old, дре́вний takes one back farthest into antiquity. It translates *ancient*, meaning belonging to the remote past:

Ancient Greece	Дре́вняя Гре́ция
Ancient monument	Дре́вний па́мятник

Ста́рый and стари́нный overlap to some extent. But N. B. (i) only ста́рый is used of animate nouns to mean having reached old age, (ii) стари́нный is used of things, especially customs, manners, *objets d'art*, to mean going back a long way in time. Compare стари́нный ча́йник *an antique teapot*; ста́рый ча́йник *an old* (i.e. much-used) *teapot*. Ве́тхий generally means *dilapidated, tumbledown*. But N. B. Ве́тхий Заве́т *Old Testament*; ве́тхий Ада́м *the Old Adam*.

Old boy (of a school)	Бы́вший учени́к
On the old side (*getting on in years*)	Пожило́й, в лета́х (or в года́х)

165. New. In some common expressions where English uses *new* Russian has *young* (молодо́й):

New moon	Молодо́й ме́сяц
New potatoes	Молодо́й карто́фель
New wine	Молодо́е вино́

166. Heavy and Light. In the widest senses тяжёлый and лёгкий (N.B. *light reading* лёгкое чте́ние). But notice:

Heavy losses	Больши́е поте́ри	*Light sleep*	Чу́ткий (неглубо́кий) сон
Heavy rain	Си́льный дождь		
Heavy cold	Си́льный на́сморк	*Light rain*	Ме́лкий дождь
Heavy sea	Бу́рное мо́ре		

167. Hard and Soft. In a physical, tangible sense твёрдый and мягкий. In a mental or intangible sense тяжёлый and нежный But notice:

Hard (3rd class) carriage	Жёсткий вагон
Soft (2nd class) carriage	Мягкий вагон
Hard water	Жёсткая вода
Soft water	Мягкая вода
Hard-boiled egg	Крутое яйцо (яйцо вкрутую)
Soft-boiled egg	Яйцо всмятку
Hard blow	Сильный удар
Hard master	Строгий хозяин
Hard worker	Усердный (прилежный) работник
Hard and fast rules	Твёрдые правила
Hard labour	Каторжные работы (note plural)
Hard climate	Суровый климат
Hard (stale) bread	Чёрствый хлеб

168. Long. Долгий refers almost always to time, and is hardly ever found in a purely spatial sense except in dialect use, and the popular saying: волос долог да ум короток, e.g. of an empty-headed woman.

Длинный which is generally associated with space (длинные волосы *long hair*, длинные руки *long arms*) may also be used in the temporal sense of lasting a long time, e.g. длинный рассказ *a long story*, where space and time cannot be separated. In the same way, долгий is used of journeys, where both space and time are involved, but obviously not of hair or arms. Notice долгий гласный *long vowel*; полная форма *long form* (of an adjective).

N.B. большой in the sense of *long*:

The journey from London to New York is a long one	Путь от Лондона до Нью-Йорка большой

A long time—see para. **434.**

169. Short. Коро́ткий is commonly applied to both space and time. Кра́ткий is rarer in either sense and has a *bookish* or technical flavour: thus кра́ткая фо́рма *short form* of an adjective; кра́ткий гла́сный *a short vowel*; кра́ткий курс *concise course.* Stylistically кра́ткий often seems to correspond to *brief*: не́сколько кра́тких слов *a few brief words*; кра́ткое объясне́ние *a brief explanation*.

170. Thick (Fat) and Thin (Lean). Of people: *fat* is то́лстый, ту́чный or, more polite, по́лный (*stout*); *thin* is то́нкий (*slim*) or худо́й, то́щий (*skinny*).

Of solid substances, material, &c., *thick* is то́лстый; *thin* то́нкий. Of liquids, густо́й and жи́дкий are used; of population пло́тный and ре́дкий (*dense* and *sparse*). Жи́рный and по́стный mean *fat* and *lean* of edible substances. Ча́стый лес is *a thick (dense) wood* (i.e. with *frequent* trees).

171. Bright and Clear. Both я́ркий and я́сный mean light-giving, but я́ркий emphasizes that the light is *bright* and shining, я́сный that it is *clear* and steady. In a figurative sense я́ркий can mean *outstanding* of ability, or *shining* of example; я́сный may mean *comprehensible, lucid, harmonious, fair*. *Clear* in the sense of *obvious, patent* is usually я́вный (я́вная ложь *a barefaced lie*).

Notice that прозра́чный (*transparent*) may have the applied meanings of я́сный (прозра́чный стиль *a lucid style*) and я́вный (прозра́чный намёк *an obvious hint*). *Brilliant*: блестя́щий is much more common than the somewhat archaic and poetic блиста́тельный.

172. Brave. There are numerous near synonyms in Russian as in English. Compare хра́брый, сме́лый *brave*; де́рзкий *bold, daring*; бесстра́шный *fearless*; неро́бкий *intrepid*; му́жественный *manly, courageous* and the rather elevated отва́жный *undaunted*.

173. Busy. Of persons, занято́й. Also занято́й день *a busy day* (i.e. one in which there is no time left for leisure—the basic meaning of занято́й). But not занято́й of, say, *a busy street* (оживлённая у́лица).

174. Different. Ра́зный and разли́чный are synonymous in the meanings of *differing* (у нас ра́зные [разли́чные] мне́ния *our opinions differ*) and *of different kinds* (стоя́ли блю́да с ра́зными [разли́чными] пирога́ми *there were dishes containing different kinds of tarts*). In both these cases there is a clear sense of *difference*. But if the meaning is one of *multiplicity* without difference, only ра́зный can be used (они́ живу́т в ра́зных дома́х *they live in different houses*—but one house might be exactly the same as the other). Note that отли́чный in the sense of разли́чный is archaic.

Because of their meaning ('differing', 'of different kinds', 'various'), ра́зный and разли́чный must apply to more than one person or thing—i.e. must have plural sense. But ра́зный is used in the singular in some common expressions which, despite their grammatical number, have plural meaning, e.g. ра́зное вре́мя 'at different times', ра́зного ро́да 'of different kinds'.

When 'different' is applied to one person or object—i.e. has singular sense ('not the same') it will normally be translated by друго́й, or its more literary equivalent ино́й: э́то — друго́е де́ло 'that's a different matter'; по́сле войны́ он стал друго́й 'after the war he became a different person'.

They are quite different from each other	Они́ соверше́нно непохо́жи друг на дру́га

175. Foreign. Иностра́нный is used in official contexts especially and in treaties and documents: Министе́рство иностра́нных дел *Foreign Office*; иностра́нная держа́ва *a foreign power*. Notice, too, иностра́нные языки́ *foreign languages*. Иноземный is an archaic synonym.

Заграни́чный is perhaps the most common translation of *foreign* and is widely applied to things produced, manufactured, or published abroad, and also to travel abroad generally: заграни́чный па́спорт *foreign passport*. Зарубе́жный in the same sense is a more literary word. Вне́шний means *external*, relating to or having dealings with foreign countries, especially commercial and political: внéшняя торгóвля *foreign* (external) *trade*; внéшняя полúтика (also инострáнная полúтика) *foreign policy*.

Чужóй means *belonging to somebody else, another's, a foreigner's*; егó ногá никогдá не ступáла на чужýю зéмлю *his foot had never trodden on foreign soil*; and also (with the dative or для and the genitive) *foreign to, alien to*. Чýждый also has the latter meaning, but is now archaic in the former sense.

176. Hot. Жáркий is commonly applied to intangible objects, a day, the weather, the climate, &c.; горячий to tangible objects, food, drink, and solid substances. But there is a wide margin in which both words are equally applicable, e.g. in the figurative sense of *heated* qualifying разговóр (*conversation*), спор (*quarrel*), &c., and in emotional contexts. Both words are used of the sun. Горячий can also mean *intensive, at a rapid tempo*; горячая рабóта *high-pressure work*.

177. Human and Humane. Человéческий and more colloquially человéчий mean *human*; человéчный *humane*.

178. Last. Послéдний generally means *ultimate, final*; прóшлый *the last one before the present*:

December 31st is the last day of the year	31 декабря — послéдний день гóда
Last time we were talking about Tolstoy	В прóшлый раз мы говорúли о Толстóм

But послéдний is also used in the above sense of прóшлый. Notice too the idiom за послéднее врéмя *very recently*, i.e. during the time immediately before the present.

Last but one позапрóшлый, i.e. the one before the previous one.

Penultimate предпослéдний, i.e. the one before the final one.

You're the last person I expected to see	Вот кого́ ме́ньше всего́ я ожида́л ви́деть

179. Latest. После́дний *last* may correspond to *latest* as in *latest news* после́дние но́вости; *latest fashion* после́дняя мо́да.

This is the latest thing in hats	Э́та шля́па — после́дний крик мо́ды (cf. *dernier cri*)

180. Mad. Of dogs бе́шеный. *Mad about* в восто́рге от, без па́мяти от.

181. Next. Of time, both сле́дующий and бу́дущий are used in reference to what has not yet taken place: *next week* на бу́дущей (сле́дующей) неде́ле. Only сле́дующий is used retrospectively:

I was born in 1917, and the next year the war ended	Я роди́лся в 1917 г. и в сле́дующем году́ война́ ко́нчилась
The next day	На друго́й (сле́дующий) день

Of space, distance, only сле́дующий is used: *next stop* сле́дующая остано́вка. *Next = adjacent*: both сосе́дний and сме́жный concretely, but only сме́жный figuratively: *adjacent fields of knowledge* сме́жные о́бласти зна́ния.

182. Sore. As an adjective applied to parts of the body, it is translated in Russian by a verb: *I have a sore finger* у меня́ боли́т па́лец. In this construction the noun commonly follows the verb.

183. Wrong. Notice the use of не тот, не туда́, &c., to translate *wrong*:

You have got the wrong number	Вы не туда́ попа́ли
He began at the wrong end	Он на́чал не с того́ конца́
The letter went to the wrong address	Письмо́ попа́ло не по а́дресу

184. The following expressions involving adjectives derived from the names of countries may be of interest:

Indian ink	Кита́йская тушь
India paper	Кита́йская бума́га
Indian summer	Ба́бье ле́то
Double Dutch	Кита́йская гра́мота
If he's a professor, I'm a Dutchman	Он тако́й же профе́ссор, как я кита́йский импера́тор
Safety pin	Англи́йская була́вка
Rickets	Англи́йская боле́знь
Working to rule	Италья́нская забасто́вка

There is no corresponding Russian idiom for *French leave*. Sometimes the French equivalent ('filer à l'anglaise') is translated literally and explained: Дми́трий Степа́нович ушёл по-англи́йски — не проща́ясь (A. N. Tolstoy).

III

THE VERB

ASPECT

Aspect and tense

185. The English verbal system is dominated by tense, the Russian by aspect. The imperfective aspect of a Russian verb describes an action in progress, or one which is frequentative or habitual, without reference to its completion or to its result. The perfective aspect, on the other hand, expresses the fact of its completion and draws attention to its result. The nature of each aspect determines the manner in which Russian aspectival forms express English tenses.

Simple Present

186. The English continuous present tense, expressing an action in progress at the moment of speaking, is rendered in Russian by the imperfective present:

I am washing the dishes   Я мо́ю посу́ду

The English continuous present, expressing an action projected in the near future, is also rendered by the imperfective present:

The ship is sailing this evening   Кора́бль отплыва́ет сего́дня ве́чером

187. (i) The English simple present tense, describing actions which are frequentative or habitual, is normally rendered in Russian by the imperfective present:

I wash the dishes every other day   Я мо́ю посу́ду че́рез день

(ii) Note, however, that the perfective present is often used, rather than the imperfective present, to describe habitual or frequentative actions which, in subordinate clauses introduced by such conjunctions as *when, as soon as, after,* are envisaged as completed before the actions described by the imperfective present in the main clause begin:

. . . whenever Germans or Englishmen get together, they talk about wool prices . . .	…когда́ сойду́тся не́мцы и́ли англича́не, то говоря́т о цена́х на шерсть.·. (Chekhov)
Every such attention occasioned Maslennikov the same delight as an affectionate dog feels when its master strokes it, ruffles its hair, tickles it behind the ears	Вся́кое тако́е внима́ние приводи́ло Ма́сленникова в тако́й-же восто́рг в кото́рый прихо́дит ла́сковая соба́ка по́сле того́, как хозя́ин погла́дит, потре́плет, почё́шет её за уша́ми (L. N. Tolstoy)

The reason for the use of the perfective present in such contexts is that, if both clauses contained an imperfective verb, the required meaning of one action being completed before the other begins would be obscured, since the fundamental function of the imperfective aspect, in clauses of relative time, is to describe one action occurring simultaneously with another:

In the morning, when the first grey light begins to show, we set off home	У́тром, чуть начина́ет сере́ть, отправля́емся домо́й (Kuprin)

When the verb in the subordinate clause describes a process, the perfective present must be used to avoid ambiguity:

In spring, when the earth thaws out, people also seem to become softer	Весно́й, когда́ земля́ отта́ет, лю́ди как бу́дто то́же стано́вятся мя́гче (Gor'ky)

If отта́ет were here replaced by отта́ивает, the primary

meaning of the clause would be *when the earth is thawing out*. The sense of one action following another is well illustrated in:

Spring, when she has completed her transformation, tarries a while, pauses to savour her victory	Весна́, когда́ она́ соверши́т перело́м, заде́рживается на како́е-то вре́мя, приостана́вливается, что́бы почу́вствовать свою́ побе́ду (Chukhovsky)

The sense of the perfective verb in these constructions is often that of an English perfect tense (resultative present):

Once a man is dead (i.e. has died), *his house should be burned*	Челове́к умрёт, так и дом на́до бы сжечь (Sologub) (как то́лько is understood)

Historic Present

188. Historic present constructions are much more common in Russian than in English. In such constructions Russian may use either the imperfective present or the perfective present.

189. Contrary to their normal usage, Russian verbs in the imperfective present, used as an historic present, may express single completed actions. This occurs:

(i) As in English, when the whole story is told in the present tense:

The tramp bares his head, . . . raises his eyes to heaven and crosses himself twice	Бродя́га обнажа́ет го́лову ...поднима́ет кве́рху глаза́ и осеня́ет себя́ два́жды кре́стным зна́мением (Chekhov)

(ii) When the narrative is placed in past time by the presence, in the same passage, of verbs in the perfective past. Because of their more strictly temporal meaning,

English verb-forms are not normally mixed in this manner:

The sisters bent over her and asked her what was wrong	Сёстры нагну́лись к ней, спра́шивают: что с тобо́й (Turgenev)
(He) comes up briskly, as if to make a report, straightens himself up, clicks his heels and salutes	[Он] подхо́дит чётким ша́гом, то́чно на докла́д, поровня́лся, щёлкнул в каблуки́, взял под козырёк (Furmanov)

(iii) When the narrative is placed in past time by the presence, in the same passage, of verbs in the imperfective past. The action described by these verbs (often concrete verbs of motion) is interrupted by the action depicted by the verbs in the imperfective present:

We were travelling through the wood when we heard something crackle	Éхали мы по́ лесу, слы́шим — трещи́т что́-то

190. The imperfective present, used as an historic present, may express, as well as single completed actions, frequentative or habitual actions of some duration which occurred in the past:

I remember, when my mother was still strong, she would work in the melon-field while I just lay there, on my back, looking at the sky	По́мню, когда́ мать ешё была́ здоро́вая, — она́ рабо́тает на башта́не а я — лежу́ себе на спине́ и гляжу́ высоко́ (Fadeyev)

Note that when the imperfective present is used in this way, the passage is often placed in past time through the use of the parenthetic word быва́ло (past neuter form of the iterative verb быва́ть *to be*):

I would sit like this alone with her in her bedroom . . .	Быва́ло, я одна́ с ней э́так сижу́ в её спа́льне (Turgenev)

191. Whereas the historic imperfective present describes habitual or frequentative actions of some duration, the historic perfective present depicts habitual or frequentative actions, each one of which was complete. This occurs:

(i) when the passage refers to a single occasion, upon which the same action was repeated several times, perhaps alternating with another:

He was clearly ill at ease. He would speak, fall silent, speak again	Он был я́вно смущён. Ска́жет, помолчи́т, опя́ть ска́жет (Maximov)

(ii) When the passage refers to repeated occasions, upon each one of which the same action or actions were performed:

. . . quite often, she herself spent the night in the garden, she would bring an armful of hay, spread it near my bed, lie down . . .	. . . нере́дко и сама́ она́ ночева́ла в саду́, принесёт оха́пку се́на, разбро́сает его́ о́коло моего́ ло́жа, ля́жет... (Gor'ky)

Быва́ло is often used in such passages, with the same function as when used with the imperfective present (see para. **190**). The following passage illustrates well the different uses of the imperfective and perfective present with быва́ло; the imperfective verbs describe durative habitual actions, the perfective verbs instantaneous habitual actions:

He would sit . . . gazing at Irina . . . and she would seem angry or bored, would get up, walk about the room, throw him a cold glance, shrug her shoulders	Быва́ло, сиди́т . . . и смо́трит на Ири́ну . . . а она́ как бу́дто се́рдится, как бу́дто скуча́ет, вста́нет, пройдётся по ко́мнате, хо́лодно посмо́трит на него́, пожмёт плечо́м (Turgenev)

192. As well as frequentative or habitual instantaneous actions, the historic perfective present may depict single, instantaneous actions as the climax or turning-point of a protracted action. The latter may be described by an imperfective past or imperfective present form, which is often repeated to express more clearly the protracted nature of the action:

He feels an irresistible urge: he fights it back, fights it back, but finally can restrain himself no longer	Бесёнок так и подмывáет егó: он крепúтся, крепúтся, наконéц не вúтерпит (Goncharov)

The perfective present, in such contexts, may be preceded by да как or да вдруг, to express the suddenness of the action it depicts:

Gerasim looked and looked, and suddenly laughed	Герáсим глядéл, глядéл, да как засмеётся вдруг (Turgenev)

Imperfect and Past Definite

193. (i) The continuous imperfect tense expressing an action in progress in the past is rendered in Russian by the imperfective past:

The town was becoming more and more unfamiliar and suspicious	Гóрод становúлся всё бóлее незнакóмым, подозрúтельным (Katayev)

(ii) The continuous imperfective past is often the best way of translating English constructions with *take* and expressions of time:

This collection took Alexei Maximovich many years to assemble	Эту коллéкцию Алексéй Максúмович собирáл дóлгие гóды (Nikulin)

Notice:

They took two hours to find us	Онú нас два часá не находúли

The use of искáли here, instead of не находи́ли, would mean simply *looked for* without necessarily finding; the use of the negative imperfective past gives the required meaning of the state of *not finding* lasting for only two hours (for negative expressions in general see para. **208**).

194. (i) The imperfect tense describing actions which were frequentative or habitual in the past is normally also expressed in Russian by the imperfective past:

. . . when, however, he read novels, told scabrous stories, went to see comic sketches at the French theatre . . . everyone praised and encouraged him	. . . когдá же он читáл ромáны, расскáзывал скабрёзные анекдóты, éздил во францýзский теáтр на смешны́е водеви́ли . . . все хвали́ли и поощря́ли егó (L. N. Tolstoy)

(ii) Note, however, that the perfective present may replace the imperfective past in frequentative constructions, in the same circumstances in which it replaces the imperfective present (para. **187** (ii)):

As soon as Peredonov awoke in the morning, he would think anxiously of Volodin	Ужé с утрá, как тóлько проснётся, Передóнов с тоскóю вспоминáл Волóдина (Sologub)

It is, once more (see para. **189** (ii)), the fact that Russian verb-forms have no strictly temporal meaning that makes possible this, to English ears, strange sequence of tenses.

195. The English past definite tense, depicting completed actions succeeding each other in narrative, is expressed by the Russian perfective past:

Mitrofan Il'ich threw himself to his knees and, with a trembling hand, seized the glistening object	Митрофáн Ильи́ч брóсился на колéни, дрожáщей рукóй схвати́л сверкáющий предмéт (Polevoy)

196. In the light of the remarks upon the use of the imperfective and perfective past made in the foregoing paragraphs, notice the use of both in:

... my grandmother would not, at first, agree to their marriage, but later gave her consent	... бáбушка сначáла не соглашáлась на их свáдьбу, а потóм согласúлась (S. Aksakov)

The consent was, at first, asked for and refused many times; finally, it was given only once. Notice English *would not* translating the Russian negative imperfective past. Notice also the same construction used not in a frequentative but in a durative sense:

He was asking Nesterov to let him have this object. Nesterov, for some reason, would not agree	Он просúл, чтóбы Нéстеров уступúл емý э́ту вещь. Нéстеров чтó-то не соглашáлся (Korin)

197. (i) If an action occurs several times, but the number of times is definitely stated, the verb expressing this action is translated into Russian by the perfective past:

Three mornings last week I got up at seven o'clock	На прóшлой недéле я три рáза встáл в семь часóв

Notice, however:

He suffered from over-eating about twice every week	Он рáза два в недéлю страдáл от обжóрства (Pushkin)

in which the meaning is habitual.

(ii) Verbs with the less definitely enumerative expressions, нéсколько раз (*several times*) and мнóго раз (*many times*), normally also in Russian stand in the perfective past:

Val'ko repeated Oleg's address several times until he had it by heart	Вáлько нéсколько раз повторúл áдрес Олéга, покá не затвердúл (Fadeyev)

With expressions like то и дело (*every now and then*), не раз (*time and again*), время от времени (*from time to time*), however, which emphasize the repetition of the action at intervals without enumerative sense, the imperfective past is used:

. . . *the side-horse in my troika . . . broke repeatedly into a sharp uneven trot*	. . . пристяжная в моей тройке . . . не раз попрыгивала неровным галопцем (L. N. Tolstoy)
Every now and then the convict gathered it (the cassock) up with the same motion as a priest	То и дело арестант подбирал её (рясу) жестом священника (Katayev)

198. (i) Worthy of attention is the predominantly stylistic use of the imperfective past where we might naturally expect the perfective because the verb describes a single completed action. Because the Russian verb is based on aspect, it is not always the fact of completion of an action which is important but sometimes the manner in which the writer regards and presents it. Compare the use of different aspects of the same verb in:

Near Chernigov they caught a White. The interrogation was carried out by Shor	Возле Чернигова они поймали Белого. Допрашивал его Шор (Erenburg)
A post-mortem was carried out on the 'dead body' on the day after the murder, and the district police-officer, Foma Fomich, interrogated the grooms	На другой день после убийства уже вскрыли ,,мёртвое тело" и становой, Фома Фомич, допросил конюхов (Ertel')

The effect of Erenburg's use of the imperfective verb above is summed up in Vinogradov's remark: 'The imperfective past does not move events. It is descriptive and pictorial.'

By slightly varying emphasis in the English translation, some approach to the Russian play of aspect has been achieved. Ertel' simply states in Russian that the interrogation took place as another link in the chain of events, whereas Erenburg halts the action and conjures up the scene of the interrogation.

(ii) The verbs есть and пить are commonly used in the imperfective past to describe completed actions because their perfective forms have marked resultative meaning. The corresponding perfective forms с'есть and вы́пить mean respectively *to eat up, to drink up.* Compare:

He dressed listlessly, drank some tea with distaste, and once, for some reason, even shouted rudely at Gainan . . .	Он вя́ло одева́лся, с отвраще́нием пил чай и да́же раз за что́-то гру́бо прикри́кнул на Гайна́на . . . (Kuprin)
He drank a pint of beer in six seconds	Он вы́пил пи́нту пи́ва за шесть секу́нд

(iii) The verbs ви́деть and слы́шать are commonly used in the imperfective past to describe completed actions because their perfective forms уви́деть and услы́шать have marked inceptive meaning—*to begin to see (catch sight of), to begin to hear (catch the sound of).* Compare:

I saw a fine film last night	Вчера́ ве́чером я ви́дел прекра́сный фильм
Straight in front of him, at the window, he saw a family so unlike the people around them that he could not take his eyes off them	Пря́мо пе́ред собо́й, у окна́, он уви́дел семе́йство, насто́лько непохо́жее на окружа́ющих люде́й, что он уже́ не мог оторва́ть от него́ взгля́да (Fedin)

(iv) The verbs писа́ть (написа́ть) and чита́ть (прочита́ть, проче́сть) are also commonly found in the imperfective past describing completed actions when the emphasis in the sentence is not on the results of writing and reading, but on the attendant circumstances. Compare:

. . . *aware that his days were numbered, Mozart in 1778 wrote to his father*	. . . зна́я, что его́ мину́ты сочтены́, Моца́рт пи-са́л отцу́ в 1778 году́ (Ogonyok)
He wrote three novels in six years	Он написа́л три рома́на за шесть лет

Just as писа́ть is commonly found, as above, in the imperfective past, so verbs describing the contents of what is written may appear in the imperfective form although they refer to one document written at one time:

Foma Fomich sent a note to Martin Lukyanich, in which he notified him that the preliminary investigation was complete	Фома́ Фоми́ч присла́л письмецо́ Марти́ну Лукья́нычу, в кото́ром извеща́л, что предвари́-тельное дозна́ние за-ко́нчено (Ertel')

(v) The imperfective past instead of the perfective is particularly common with verbs of motion when the latter imply 'a stay of short duration and subsequent return to the point of departure' (Forbes):

Wells came (to Russia) *for the first time in 1920*	В пе́рвый раз Уэ́ллс приезжа́л в 1920 году́ (Pavlenko)
A comrade dropped in on me just before you	Как раз пе́ред тобо́й ко мне заходи́л оди́н то-ва́рищ (Ignatov)

Future

199. The clearest indication of the predominance of aspect over tense in the Russian verbal system is furnished by the fact that, because the perfective aspect describes an action as completed, its present tense form cannot refer to an action in progress and cannot, therefore, have present meaning. The perfective present has acquired future meaning, because the completion of an action in progress can only occur in the future. To express an action in progress in the future, or one which is habitual, Russian employs a compound future, consisting of the future tense of быть and the imperfective infinitive of the verb concerned.

200. (i) The imperfective future is used, in general, to express the same kind of actions in future time as the imperfective past expresses in past time: the perfective future similarly corresponds to the perfective past. Since, however, actions in future time are only potential, their nature is not always as clear as those in past time. The difference between the imperfective and perfective future comes out most clearly when they are used in the same sentence:

Masha: *Imagine, I am already beginning to forget her face. People will not remember us either . . . we shall be forgotten*

Предста́вьте, я уже́ начина́ю забыва́ть её лицо́. Так и о нас не бу́дут по́мнить . . . забу́дут (Chekhov)

The imperfective future here describes a state which will embrace the whole future: the meaning of the perfective future is resultative.

The difference would be more marked in the past:

. . . people did not remember us . . . we were forgotten

. . . о нас не по́мнили . . . забы́ли

(ii) The imperfective future is used, like the imperfective past, to describe actions increasing in intensity with the passage of time:

Olga loves you and will love you more and more every day

О́льга тебя́ лю́бит и с ка́ждым днём бу́дет люби́ть сильне́е (Azhayev)

201. Both the imperfective and perfective future may be

used in Russian to translate an English future disguised as
a present:

Do you think I shall snivel or say nothing when they are beating me?	Ду́маешь, я бу́ду хны́кать и́ли молча́ть, когда́ меня́ бу́дут бить (Fadeyev)
I should like to meet you when you return to Moscow as an honoured citizen	Я хоте́л бы встре́титься с ва́ми, когда́ вы вернё-тесь в Москву́ заслу́-женным челове́ком (Trifonov)

Когда́, followed by the imperfective present, has frequentative, not future, meaning, . . . когда́ меня́ бьют *every time
they beat me.*

202. With verbs of motion, it is, of course, the frequentative or abstract form (see para. **284**) which is used in the
imperfective future, with frequentative meaning:

Along these streets streamlined buses will pass	По э́тим у́лицам бу́дут ходи́ть авто́бусы обте-ка́емой фо́рмы (Pano-va)

Referring to the actual course (not the resultant destina-
tion) of a single journey, the imperfective concrete verb is
used:

I shall drive fast and you will catch the train	Я бу́ду е́хать бы́стро и вы поспе́ете к по́езду

Perfect, Pluperfect, Future Perfect

203. (i) These tenses are taken together because they are
relative tenses and the Russian verb has no specific tense
forms to express relative time. The perfect and pluperfect
tenses are normally expressed in Russian by the perfective
past, in relation to the context or with the help of the adverbs уже́ and ещё; the future perfect, often disguised in
English as a perfect, is normally expressed by the perfective

present, also in relation to the context or with the help of the same adverbs:

You've read me like a book, Asyenka, he replied	Ты меня глубоко распознала, Асенька, ответил он (Fedin)
When the sound of his horse's hooves had died away, I went round on to the terrace and again began to look into the garden	Когда затих ужé тóпот егó лóшади, я пошла кругóм на террáсу и опять стáла смотрéть в сад (L. N. Tolstoy)
You will understand that when you have lived here a while longer	Вы это поймёте, когда проживёте здесь ещё нéсколько врéмени (Pushkin)

The inclusion of ужé is essential in the second example to give clear pluperfect sense to the verb затих, which might otherwise mean simply *died away*. For this reason ужé is often found in Russian where English, with its greater variety of temporal verb-forms, does not need to use *already*.

(ii) When two clauses in a complex sentence describe one state in relation to another, the Russian perfective past in relation to the present tense acquires perfect meaning, and in relation to the past tense, pluperfect meaning:

The sun has (had) just set and a crimson light lies (lay) on the green vines	Сóлнце тóлько что сéло и áлый свет лежит (лежáл) на зелёных лóзах

204. (i) When the English perfect and pluperfect tenses cover a certain period of time, they are normally translated by imperfective verbs:

Since poets have written and women have read them—how many times have they been called angels?	С тех пор, как поэты пишут и жéнщины их читáют, — их скóлько раз называли áнгелами? (Lermontov)

The past tense называ́ли has frequentative meaning. The present tenses пи́шут and чита́ют mean that the actions are still going on at the moment of speech. In corresponding pluperfect constructions, the imperfective past is used:

He had been living there two years when his father died	Он жил там уже́ два го́да, когда́ у́мер его́ оте́ц

In negative sentences both perfect and pluperfect are translated by the imperfective past:

'*Dmitri Korneevich*', *said Tosya quietly*, '*I haven't seen him for four years*'	'Дми́трий Корне́евич', сказа́ла То́ся ти́хо, 'Я его́ четы́ре го́да не ви́дела (Panova)
Almazova had not been to work for four days	Алма́зова уже́ пя́тый день не выходи́ла на рабо́ту (Panova)

(ii) The indefiniteness of an English question in the perfect tense often calls for the use of the imperfective past. The verbs ви́деть, слы́шать, and чита́ть (*to see, to hear, to read*) are particularly common in such questions and the answer with these verbs is also normally given in the imperfective past:

Have you not read in the newspapers about the officers' duel?	Вы не чита́ли в газе́тах об офице́рском пое-ди́нке?
No, but I have heard about it	Нет, не чита́л. Но слы́шал (Kuprin)

205. As well as by the temporal adverbs уже́ and ещё, relative time may, in certain contexts in Russian, be expressed by the use of the particle бы́ло. This particle is used almost exclusively with the perfective past and expresses the fact that the result which might naturally have been expected from a completed perfective action was frustrated. The action may actually have been begun or simply projected (English relative tenses *had begun to, was about to*) when it was interrupted by another action:

I was on the point of recovery and had begun to put on weight when suddenly . . .	Я бы́ло попра́вился и толсте́ть уже́ стал, да вдру́г... (A. Ostrovsky)
Tarant'ev had gone out into the hall but suddenly came back	Тара́нтьев ушёл бы́ло в пере́днюю, но вдру́г вороти́лся опя́ть (Goncharov)

In this example Tarant'ev had actually completed the action of going out into the hall but since he then returned, the logical outcome of his action—leaving the house—was frustrated. Similarly in:

She wrote Dasha a note but tore it up at once	Написа́ла бы́ло Да́ше коро́тенькое письмо́ но сейча́с же порва́ла (A. N. Tolstoy)

the note was written but the logical result of it having been written—its dispatch and receipt—was frustrated.

206. To express clearly the meaning that the action in the main clause was not begun, the expression совсе́м бы́ло may be used:

He also took hold of the spoon and was about to dip it in the soup, but straight away put it back on the table	Он то́же взя́лся за ло́жку и уже́ совсе́м бы́ло погрузи́л в суп, но сейча́с же опя́ть положи́л на стол (Shchedrin)

207. The English pluperfect expressions (*I*) *had meant to,* (*I*) *had intended to,* are often best translated into Russian by хоте́л бы́ло. Of the very few imperfective verbs which can be used with бы́ло, хоте́ть is the most common:

I had meant to tell you something romantic concerning myself but you, after all, are a geographer	Я хотéл бы́ло рассказáть вам нéчто романти́ческое меня́ касáющееся, но· ведь, вы — геóграф (Chekhov)

Notice also the phrase чуть не or чуть бы́ло не which means *almost*:

I almost fell	·Я чуть (бы́ло) не упáл

Compare чуть ли не which means *I think; if I am not mistaken*:

He died, I think, last year	Он у́мер чуть ли не в прóшлом году́

Negative constructions

208. In negative sentences, in general, in both past and future time, Russian shows a strong tendency to use the imperfective form of the verb because, very often, negation means a protracted omission to perform an action rather than momentary non-performance. The imperfective verb is particularly common in contexts where the actual period of non-performance of the action is mentioned:

The next morning I was already awake but had not *yet got up* . . .	На другóе у́тро я ужé проснýлся, но ещё не вставáл . . . (Turgenev)
But I have never *yet experienced such an intense access of delight* . . .	Но ещё ни рáзу до сих пор не испы́тывал я такóго си́льного наплы́ва востóрга (Kuprin)
The story of the three cards did not *leave his mind all night*	Анекдóт о трёх кáртах цéлую ночь не выходи́л из егó головы́ (Pushkin)

> *That night I did not sleep and did not undress*　В э́ту ночь я не спал и не раздева́лся (Pushkin)
>
> *We shall not dwell on this question here*　Мы здесь не бу́дем остана́вливаться на э́том вопро́се

Note, however, that when the verb describes a process, the perfective and imperfective forms have different meanings:

> *The sun had not yet warmed the earth when . . .*　Со́лнце ещё не согре́ло зе́млю, когда́ . . . (Furmanov)

The imperfective form согрева́ло here would mean *was not yet warming . . .*

Sequence of tenses

209. In reported speech in English, the tense of the verb in the subordinate clause is determined by that of the main verb, e.g. *he said that he would go*. In Russian, however, reported speech is expressed, independently of the main verb, in the tense in which the statement was originally made, or the question originally asked:

> *He said that he would go*　Он сказа́л, что пойдёт
>
> *I asked him if he was reading 'War and Peace'*　Я спроси́л его́, чита́ет ли он «Войну́ и мир»

The same construction is used after verbs of thinking, knowing, and feeling:

> *Ozyerov did not doubt that the commissar would bring important news*　О́зеров не сомнева́лся, что комисса́р принесёт ва́жные но́вости (Bubyonnov)

And after verbs of seeing and observing:

> *Bidenko . . . saw that the boy was asleep*　Биде́нко . . . уви́дел, что ма́льчик спит (Katayev)

Note especially that the same construction is used even

when no main verb is expressed in Russian but when one is implied:

Some of the fishermen were fishermen willy-nilly, waiting for work at the factory to turn up . . .	Часть рыбако́в занима́лась рыболо́вством понево́ле, пока́ не найдётся рабо́та на заво́де . . . (Azhayev)

Aspects in the non-temporal forms of the verb

Imperative

210. An imperfective command, in general, requires only the beginning and progress of the action concerned, a perfective command requires its completion and result. This difference, in certain circumstances, makes the perfective command more categorical than the imperfective, which is often rather a request or an invitation than an order. Thus certain formulas of polite social intercourse, where there is no question of the imposition of the will of the speaker upon the listener, are almost always found in the imperfective aspect:

Give him my regards	Кла́няйтесь ему́ от меня́
Take a seat, sit down	Сади́тесь

The perfective *ся́дьте* would be more appropriate on non-social occasions such as an invitation by a doctor or a dentist to sit down for examination. Its strict meaning is *adopt a sitting position*, although, of course, it cannot be expressed naturally in English except by *sit down*. Differences between the aspects of the imperative are, indeed, often felt by a Russian speaker or listener and cannot be translated into English. The use of the imperfective command, with its attenuated imperative sense, may simply imply an understanding between speaker and listener that the command will be obeyed. Thus many military commands are given in the imperfective.

211. Although more categorical, perfective commands are not necessarily, as is often stated, less polite than imperfective commands. Nor do they necessarily demand more immediate obedience. The slang English *get going* is far from polite although it is an imperfective command in the sense that the use of the present participle demands the progress of the action and not its completion and result. Russian, also, may use the imperfective aspect when immediate action is required, most typically after a perfective command which has not elicited ready obedience. This comes out clearly in the following passage:

> *'Get up, please', said someone's voice. I closed my eyes . . . and went to sleep. 'Come on, get up', repeated Dmitri, mercilessly shaking me by the shoulder*

> «Вста́ньте, пожа́луйста,» сказа́л чей-то го́лос. Я закры́л глаза́ . . . и засну́л. «Встава́йте же», повтори́л Дми́трий, безжа́лостно раска́чивая меня́ за плечо́ (L. N. Tolstoy, slightly adapted)

Nevertheless, unless accompanied by some such expression as пожа́луйста (*please*), a perfective command may, through its categorical nature, seem impolite and brusque. Such commands may be softened, as well as by пожа́луйста, by the addition to the imperative form of the particle -ка:

> *Please bring some wood*   Принеси́те-ка дров

212. An imperfective imperative is often found with clear durative sense followed by пока́ (*until*):

> *Drink . . . till you go black in the face*   Пей . . . пока́ почерне́ешь (Sholokhov)

It may also express the speaker's desire that the listener continue to do what he is doing:

> *Don't get up*   Сиди́те
> *Go on with your story*   Расска́зывайте

213. The two imperfective imperatives смотри́те *be careful*, and ступа́йте *be off with you*, have no corresponding perfective forms with the same meaning.

214. Negative commands in Russian, when they express prohibitions, are almost invariably expressed by the imperfective form. This is because a prohibition orders the listener to refrain from doing the action for some time or for ever, even though it may be inspired by a specific occasion:

Do not kill the dog   Не убива́йте соба́ку

When, however, a negative command expresses not a prohibition but a warning, the perfective form is normally used. This is because a warning does not usually request the non-performance of an action for some time or for ever but only at a given moment:

Be careful, do not break the   Смотри́те, не разбе́йте
plate   таре́лку

215. The perfective verb забы́ть (*to forget*, imperfective забыва́ть) is particularly common in negative imperative constructions. This is because the injunction *do not forget*, applied to a specific occasion, usually carries a note of warning:

Do not forget to buy some   Не забу́дьте купи́ть я́б-
apples when you go out   лок, когда́ вы́йдете

Notice that in such contexts не забу́дьте is followed by the perfective infinitive. When, however, *do not forget* is a request applied to a period of time, the imperfective imperative is used:

Do not forget me when you are   Не забыва́йте меня́, когда́
abroad   бу́дете за-грани́цей

216. First person imperatives are expressed by either the 1st person plural of the perfective present, or by бу́дем with the imperfective infinitive:

Let us buy this book   Ку́пим э́ту кни́гу
Let us read   Бу́дем чита́ть

The only imperfective verbs of which the 1st person plural
of the present tense may be used as an imperative are the
concrete verbs of motion (see para. **284**); the perfective
present may, of course, always be used as an alternative:

> *Let us go to the theatre*   Идём (пойдём) в теа́тр

When the command is addressed to more than one person,
or when it is desired to lend it the same note of politeness
as is possessed by the 2nd person plural of the present
tense, the ending -те is added to the first person forms:

> *Let us go to the theatre*   Идёмте в теа́тр

An alternative form of the imperfective imperative, common in spoken Russian, is the combination of the imperfective imperative forms дава́й, дава́йте, with the *imperfective* infinitive only:

> *Let us read Pushkin today*   Дава́й(те) чита́ть Пу́ш-
>   кина сего́дня

Occasionally дава́й, дава́йте are found together with the
future indicative and in this construction *both* the imperfective *and* the perfective future are admissible according
to the context:

> *Let us read Pushkin today*   Дава́й(те) бу́дем чита́ть
>   Пу́шкина сего́дня
> *Let us sit down*   Дава́й(те) ся́дем

217. The perfective imperative forms дай, да́йте, cannot
be used like дава́й, дава́йте to form compound imperative
forms. Both дай (-ка) and дава́й (-ка) (*not* да́йте, дава́йте)
may, however, be used in constructions with the 1st person
singular where the speaker expresses an inclination to do
something, often translated into English by *I think I'll* . . :

> *I think I'll call in on my neigh-*   Дай-ка зайду́ к сосе́ду
> *bour and see how he has*   взгляну́ть, как он уст-
> *settled down in his new place*   ро́ился на но́вом ме́сте
>   (Grin)

There is very little difference in meaning between дай and давáй in such constructions. Дай is more common.

218. Only the imperfective forms of 1st person imperatives are used in the negative:

Let us not exaggerate	Не бýдем преувеличивать

219. Third person imperatives are expressed by the combination of the particles пусть, пускáй, with the 3rd person singular and plural forms of the imperfective or perfective present: пусть and пускáй are used indiscriminately, aspectival differences being expressed by the following verb:

Let him have a good time if he wants	Пусть (пускáй) развлекáется, éсли хóчет
Let him read this book through	Пусть (пускáй) он прочтёт эту книгу

As with the 2nd person imperfective imperative (see para. **212**), the imperfective present after пусть or пускáй may be used when the speaker wishes to see an action already in progress continued:

Let them go on reading and we will work	Пусть они читáют, а мы бýдем занимáться

Infinitive

220. The choice of the imperfective or perfective infinitive is determined by the same general considerations as that of the imperfective or perfective aspect in finite forms of the verb. An imperfective infinitive expresses a durative or frequentative action, a perfective infinitive a completed action generally of short duration. Notice the manner in which English renders the aspectival difference in:

It's time to be leaving (It's time we were leaving)	Порá уходить
It's time to leave (It's time we left)	Порá уйти

The use of *we were leaving* and *we left* (contrast of durative and resultative sense) expresses exactly the Russian aspectival difference.

221. As with the imperative, many of the shades of meaning which inspire the use of one infinitive form or the other lie in the mood of the speaker and cannot be rendered at all in English or only through circumlocution. Since the use of the perfective infinitive evokes the notion of successful completion, often the presence in the speaker's mind of any factor which may make such completion uncertain or difficult calls for the use of the imperfective infinitive, even though the action concerned may be a single action of short duration. This explains the use of встречать in:

I am going to the station to meet him	Я иду́ на вокза́л встре-ча́ть его́

The speaker subconsciously takes into account the possibility that, for a number of reasons, he might miss the person he is going to meet. The imperfective infinitive is also used when the speaker emphasizes the duration of an action by describing his own reaction to it as it is going on. This is well illustrated in the following sentence, which Mazon quotes as the words of someone suffering from tuberculosis:

It is not death but the dying I fear	Мне умере́ть не стра́шно, а стра́шно умира́ть

222. Notice the change from the perfective present to the imperfective infinitive in:

'*He will kill you . . . Well, we'll see about that. What's that you say . . . kill you! He has no right to kill you, judge for yourself*'	„Убьёт . . . Ну э́то мы уви́-дим. Как э́то ты гово-ри́шь: убьёт! Ра́зве он име́ет пра́во тебя́ уби-ва́ть, посуди́ сама́" (Turgenev)

The perfective present refers to the killing of one person on one occasion: the imperfective infinitive expresses the killing of that person as a matter of principle at any time and in any place.

223. As with the imperfective aspect in general, the imperfective infinitive is used in negative constructions which emphasize the duration of the non-performance of the action:

Once I happened not to take up my pistol for a whole month	Одна́жды случи́лось мне це́лый ме́сяц не брать пистоле́та (Pushkin)

224. (i) After certain verbs which, by their very meaning, refer to the progress of an action—its beginning, continuation, or final stages—only the imperfective infinitive may be used. The simplest of these are:

To begin	Начина́ть (нача́ть), пуска́ться (пусти́ться), стать
To continue	Продолжа́ть
To remain	Остава́ться (оста́ться)
To finish, to stop	Перестава́ть (переста́ть), конча́ть (ко́нчить), броса́ть (бро́сить)

and all verbs of similar meaning:

The sailors who had remained sitting in the restaurant . . .	Матро́сы, оста́вшиеся сиде́ть в рестора́не... (Bunin)

Also after the impersonal expressions по́лно, бу́дет, дово́льно *enough*:

Stop crying	Бу́дет вам пла́кать

(ii) A number of verbs which refer in a broader sense than the above to the progress of an action must also be followed by the imperfective infinitive. Such are:

To learn	Учи́ться
To grow used to	Привыка́ть (привы́кнуть)
To forget how to	Разу́чиваться (Разучи́ться)
To lose the habit of	Отвыка́ть (отвы́кнуть)
To bore, to pall upon	Надоеда́ть (надое́сть)

| *I have got out of the habit of coming to this restaurant* | Я отвы́к ходи́ть в э́тот рестора́н |

225. Except in frequentative contexts, the verb успева́ть (успе́ть) *to have time to* must always be followed by the perfective infinitive because it naturally refers to a completed action:

| *Before I had time to look round . . .* | Не успе́л я огляну́ться, как . . . |

But notice (frequentative):

| *His son, Maxim, could hardly keep up with the typing of his father's numerous manuscripts* | Его́ сын Макси́м едва́ успева́л перепеча́тывать многочи́сленные ру́кописи отца́ (Chukovsky) |

Aspect and meaning

226. With certain verbs, the basic distinction between the aspects (action in progress/completed action) becomes a general contrast between an action attempted and an action carried to a successful conclusion. This is one of the most expressive functions of aspectival contrast based on the same verbal root. English can only make the same distinction by using different verbs or, sometimes, by the use of the verb *try* to translate the imperfective verb:

ENGLISH		RUSSIAN	
Imperfective	*Perfective*	*Imperfective*	*Perfective*
To chase	*To catch*	Лови́ть	Пойма́ть
To search for	*To find*	Оты́скивать	Отыска́ть
To urge	*To persuade*	Угова́ривать	Уговори́ть
To assure	*To convince*	Уверя́ть	Уве́рить
To entreat	*To prevail upon*	Упра́шивать	Упроси́ть
To contend	*To prove*	Дока́зывать	Доказа́ть
To seek comfort in	*To find comfort in*	Утеша́ться (че́м-нибудь)	Уте́шиться (че́м-нибудь)

Imperfective	Perfective	Imperfective	Perfective
To strive after	*To attain*	Добива́ться	Доби́ться
To discuss	*To decide*	Реша́ть	Реши́ть
To plead one's cause	*To vindicate oneself*	Опра́вды-ваться	Оправда́ться

Notice also заслу́живать (no perfective form) *to deserve* and заслужи́ть (no imperfective form) *to earn, to win* (praise, a reward).

227. Notice that whereas the perfective form of the above verbs may only have the meaning given, the imperfective forms (except заслу́живать), in frequentative or general statements, may acquire the meaning of the perfective form (for the contrast between the two Russian verbs is only aspectival and not semantic):

He always achieved his purpose	Он всегда́ добива́лся свое́й це́ли

228. The verbs given (and other less common verbs) are used with greatest effect in the same sentence:

She began to sing the tune of a song . . . which she had been trying to remember the whole way and had finally remembered	Она́ запе́ла моти́в пе́сни . . . кото́рый она́ лови́ла всю доро́гу и наконе́ц пойма́ла (L. N. Tolstoy)
We discussed for a long time what to do and finally decided to spend the night with a forester we knew	Мы до́лго реша́ли что де́лать, наконе́ц реши́ли переночева́ть у знако́мого лесника́

Either form may, of course, be used alone:

She shook him by the shoulder, kept at him, until he understood that he was wanted on the telephone	Она́ трясла́ его́ за плечо́, упра́шивала, пока́ он не по́нял, что его́ зову́т к телефо́ну (Mal'tsev)

Notice the interesting sentence:

She offered him tea but he refused it	Она́ угоща́ла его́ ча́ем, но он отказа́лся (Sologub)

229. The perfective present, expressing successful completion, contrasted with the imperfective present expressing endeavour, is often used with present, not future meaning:

Sleep never comes easily to me . . . I doze . . . lie and lie, and finally drop off	Мне никогда́ не спи́тся . . . я засыпа́ю . . . лежу́ лежу́, да и засну́ (Turgenev)

This may also occur when the imperfective and perfective forms are not of the same verb, but the essential meaning of gradual development and final result is present:

The sun gradually lights up one bush, then another, a roof, and suddenly floods the whole landscape with light	Со́лнце понемно́гу освеща́ет оди́н куст, друго́й, кро́влю и вдруг обольёт све́том це́лый пейза́ж (Goncharov)

Special perfective meanings

230. The case of идти́ (пойти́), an aspectival pair in which the perfective is formed from the imperfective verb by the addition of a prefix without specific meaning, is a comparatively rare one. Such prefixes, however, are sometimes added to imperfective verbs to form special perfective verbs related in meaning to the original imperfective verb but not forming an aspectival pair with it. The following paragraphs set out the commonest of these special perfective verbs.

231. По, added to certain imperfective verbs, may form perfective verbs meaning *to do for a while*:

The sentry stood for a while, then went away . . .	Часово́й постоя́л и ото- шёл . . . (A. N. Tolstoy)

Such verbs may correspond to the English *to have a . . ., to take a . . .*: поспа́ть *to take a nap*. They may also be translated by adding the phrase *a bit*:

His soft collar was a bit crumpled	Его́ мя́гкий воротни́к был помя́т (A. N. Tolstoy)

With verbs of motion по-, in this meaning, is attached to
the *abstract* verb (see para. **284**): полетáть на аэроплáне,
to do a bit of flying. But notice *to carry a bit* may be понестú:

Let me carry your bag a bit	Дай, я понесý ваш чемо-дáн

Поносúть means *to wear for a bit* as well as *to carry for a bit*:

Wear that coat a bit longer …	Поносúте то пальтó ещё немнóго …

232. По-, secondly, is added to certain *concrete* verbs of
motion to form perfective verbs meaning *to start, to set off*:

The horse set off at a walk	Лóшадь пошлá шáгом
It began to drizzle	Пошёл мéлкий дождь
Who will set the ball rolling?	Кто покáтит шар?

Also поéхать (*to set off*), полетéть (*to fly off*), поплы́ть (*to
sail off*). A small number of verbs, other than verbs of
motion, combine with по- in this meaning:

A wind blew up	Подýл вéтер
He fell in love with her	Он полюбúл её
His mouth began to water.	У негó слю́нки потеклú

233. За- prefixed to many imperfective verbs forms
special perfective verbs with inchoative meaning. Many of
these verbs describe noises and English may use the simple
verb, whereas the Russian verb makes it clear that the
beginning of the action is meant:

The thunder roared	Гром загремéл
The hooter sounded	Гудóк загудéл
The wolves howled	Вóлки завы́ли

234. Referring to the beginning of a state, за-verbs may
translate *to turn, to grow, to fall, to become, to go*:

The rye has begun to turn yellow	Рожь зажелтéла

The horse suddenly went lame	Лóшадь вдруг захромáла
He has grown idle	Он заленѝлся

Also задремáть (*to fall into a doze*), заболѐть (*to fall ill*).

235. За- verbs may also correspond to English verbs used with adverbs such as *up, down, out, off, in, away*:

The wind quietened down	Вѐтер затѝх
The lilac has come out	Сирѐнь зацвелá
They strode off to the public garden	Онѝ зашагáли к сквѐру (Panova)
The orchestra struck up a march	Оркѐстр заигрáл марш

Also заплáкать (*to burst into tears*), засмея́ться (*to burst out laughing*).

236. An idiomatic group of за-verbs are those formed from verbs of colour in -еть with the meaning of *to show white, red, green,* &c. The prefix gives these verbs the perfective meaning of *to come into view*:

Far ahead the red roofs of the houses came into view	Далекó впередѝ закраснѐли крýши домóв
Before me spread the green sun-drenched forests	Пѐредо мной зазеленѐли залѝтые сóлнцем лесá

If the colour expressed by the Russian verb is the natural colour of the object concerned (*blue sea*), it may translate an English construction with no mention of colour:

Ahead I caught sight of the sea	Пѐредо мной засинѐло мóре

237. За- with inchoative meaning makes special perfective verbs of motion only with the abstract verbs. Such perfective verbs retain the original indeterminate meaning of the abstract verb and are often translated with the help of the English adverb *about*:

We let the bird out of the cage and it began flying about the room	Мы вы́пустили птѝцу из клѐтки и онá залетáла по кóмнате

238. Note the meanings of закури́ть and запи́ть *to take to smoking, to take to drink*:

> *After his wife's death he took to drink* — По́сле сме́рти жены́, он запи́л

Закури́ть may also mean *to light up* (a cigarette). Note the imperfective form заку́ривать, which is not used in the meaning above:

> *. . . lighting one cigarette from another, he said gaily . . .* — ...заку́ривая от одно́й папиро́сы другу́ю, он сказа́л ве́село... (Fedin)

239. The verb зави́деть means *to catch sight of* from a distance:

> *The sun, going to meet the moon, does not see it and frowns; but as soon as it sees it at a distance, it beams* — Со́лнце идёт навстре́чу ме́сяцу и не ви́дит его́, так и хму́рится, а уж как зави́дит и́здали, так и просветле́ет (Goncharov)

240. На- forms special perfective verbs meaning *to do a lot of*:

> *To tell a lot of lies* — Налга́ть

The object of transitive verbs of this kind is naturally almost always a quantitative expression and appears, as such, in the partitive genitive:

> *To litter the floor with paper* — Наброса́ть бума́ги на полу́

Notice, however, the use of the accusative of quantity with a numeral complement after the verb налета́ть:

> *This airman has flown a thousand hours* — Э́тот лётчик налета́л ты́сячу часо́в

(abstract verb of motion signifying multiple direction).

N.B. Some of these perfective verbs with a на- prefix have corresponding imperfective forms:

> *Put plenty of jam on, it's nice* — Накла́дывайте варе́нья, оно́ вку́сно (Dudintsev)

241. Ha- prefixed to certain reflexive verbs forms perfective verbs meaning *to do something to the limit of one's desires or powers*:

I've worked myself out	Я наработался
I've read all the novels I ever want to read	Я начитался романов

In the negative these verbs translate *cannot enough*:

And then he goes once more to the window . . . after prison he cannot see enough of the world	А потом опять к окну . . . после тюрьмы-то, не наглядится (Korolenko)

242. От- forms special perfective verbs which may translate idiomatically *to finish*:

When we had finished supper	Когда мы отужинали
The thunder of war has died away, the first post-war year is almost over	Отгремела война, идёт к концу первый послевоенный год (Panova)

243. Whereas от- may give the sense of an action carried through to the end, the prefix про- may be used meaning an action carried on for some time:

You . . . spent the whole war driving about in an ambulance	Вы . . . всю войну проездили в санитарном автомобиле (Panova)

Notice also прокашлять всю ночь *to cough the whole night.*

244. Из- forms perfective verbs denoting that the action or state they describe covered the whole surface of an object or was carried through to completion:

Over the churned-up leaden sea fly broken clouds	Над изрытым свинцовым морем летят рваные тучи (A. N. Tolstoy)
The men's tattered clothing	Изорванная в клочья одежда мужчин (Tikhonov)

The house was in a state of   Дом изветшáл совсéм
    complete dilapidation

Semelfactive verbs

245. These verbs form a subdivision of the perfective aspect and, as their name implies, describe a single action once performed. Their distinguishing mark is the suffix -ну- and they are prefixless. They usually correspond to imperfective verbs which describe not only a durative but also a complex or repetitive action which the semelfactive verbs reduce to unity, e.g.:

To blink (a number of times)	Моргáть	*To blink* (once)	Моргнýть
To bite (a number of times)	Кусáть	*To take a bite*	Куснýть

Semantically, the semelfactive verbs may be compared with special perfectives formed with по- from the same imperfective verbs but denoting that, although the action was completed, it consisted of a number of small actions and lasted for a certain time:

The coach lurched once or twice *and stopped*	Вагóн покачáлся и стал на мéсто (A. N. Tolstoy)
The pendulum moved once *and stopped*	Мáятник двúнулся и остановúлся

Notice the difference in meaning between трóнуть *to touch once* and потрóгать *to feel* (i.e. to touch a few times):

He touched my arm	Он трóнул мою рýку
He smiled and felt my muscles	Он улыбнýлся, потрóгал мой мýшцы (Serafimovich)

Iterative verbs

246. These verbs form a subdivision of the imperfective aspect. Semantically, they are the exact opposite of the semelfactive verbs because they designate actions repeated many times with no indication of completion. They are marked by the suffix -ыва- (-ива-). It should be observed, however, that verbs containing this suffix and prefixed by any other prefix than по- or при-, although they may be used iteratively, are now used much more commonly with normal imperfective durative meaning. Verbs with the suffix -ыва (-ива-) and prefixes по- or при-, however, have exclusively iterative meaning and may translate idiomatically certain English turns of speech:

The telephone kept up a persistent, intermittent ringing	Телефо́н насто́йчиво позва́нивал вре́мя от вре́мени (Kazakevich)
My head aches on and off	Голова́ у меня́ поба́ливает

Verbs prefixed with по- very often, and verbs prefixed with при- almost always, denote a frequently repeated action taking place as the accompaniment to another action:

Nibbling his sparse beard, Akundin looked round the hall	Пощи́пывая ре́дкую бо́роду, Аку́ндин огляде́л зал (A. N. Tolstoy)
He went hopping (limping) along	Он шёл припля́сывая (прихра́мывая)

VOICE

Passive

247. Passive actions which are durative or frequentative and of which the subject is inanimate are expressed predominantly by the reflexive forms of imperfective verbs followed, where appropriate, by the instrumental of the agent:

The cliffs are washed by the sea	Утёсы омыва́ются мо́рем
The house will be painted every year	Дом бу́дет кра́ситься ка́ждый год

Animate subjects almost invariably give such verbs intransitive or reflexive, but not passive meaning:

All books are returned from here to the central library (Passive)	Все книги возвращаются отсюда в центральную библиотеку
The travellers are returning from abroad (Intransitive)	Путешественники возвращаются из-за границы
The dishes are washed by the servant (Passive)	Посуда моется служанкой
I wash in cold water (Reflexive)	Я моюсь холодной водой

No verb describing a physical action, with an animate subject, can be used reflexively with passive meaning; such English constructions are normally rendered in Russian by an active construction, with inverted subject and object:

The child is washed by the nurse	Ребёнка моет нянька

A very small number of verbs, however, describing non-physical actions, may be used reflexively with passive meaning, even though the subject is animate:

I am considered by everyone a generous man	Я считаюсь всеми щедрым человеком
People are changed by events	Люди изменяются событиями

248. An English past participle passive, describing a durative or frequentative action, in an adjectival or subordinate clause, may sometimes be rendered in Russian by the present participle passive:

The priest, preceded by the deacon, approached the church	Священник, предшествуемый дьяконом, приближался к церкви
Everyone attends the dinners given by the governor	Все присутствуют на обедах даваемых губернатором

The present participle passive in such contexts always expresses an action contemporaneous with the action described by the main verb. Its use is severely restricted by the fact that it can be formed from a comparatively small number of verbs only. Where the verb concerned lacks the present participle passive, a durative or frequentative action in a subordinate or adjectival clause may sometimes be expressed by the reflexive form of the imperfective present or past participle active:

The building under construction on this spot ...	Здáние, стрóящееся на э́том мéсте ...
The paper written by the student during the last month ...	Доклáд, писáвшийся студéнтом в прóшлом мéсяце ...

Occasionally, also, recourse may be had to the present participle passive formed from a synonymous prefixed verb:

The long-awaited day	Давнó ожидáемый день
The towns being burned by the enemy	Городá сжигáемые врагóм
The criminal accused of murder	Престýпник обвиня́емый в убúйстве

The prefixless verbs ждать, жечь, and винúть have no present participles passive.

249. When the subject is a quantitative expression, passive constructions may be rendered in Russian by the neuter short form of the past participle passive:

Many letters have been received here today	Здесь сегóдня полýчено мнóго пúсем

250. Single, completed passive actions are normally expressed in Russian by the past participle passive, combined with the past or future forms of быть, or standing alone where the English meaning is perfect:

A special stock-taking committee has been formed	Образóвана осóбая комúссия учёта (A. N. Tolstoy)

At a general meeting of the crew of the 'Derbent' the plan for the first Stakhanovite run was approved	На о́бщем собра́нии кома́нды „Дербе́нта", был утверждён план пе́рвого стаха́новского ре́йса (Krymov)
This play will be performed in London	Э́та пье́са бу́дет поста́влена в Ло́ндоне

Pluperfect meaning is expressed by the same construction as past definite meaning, often strengthened by a temporal adverb:

Very close to the town was the village of Torguevo. One half of it had been recently incorporated in the town, the other half remained a village	Под са́мым го́родом бы́ло село́ Торгу́ево. Одна́ полови́на его́ была́ неда́вно присоединена́ к го́роду, друга́я остава́лась село́м (Chekhov)

251. The past participle passive is formed almost exclusively from perfective verbs. Note, however, that the three verbs писа́ть, чита́ть, and петь, possess past participles passive which express the fact that, although completed, the action took some time to perform (see para. **198** (i)):

A picture painted by Rembrandt . . .	Карти́на, пи́санная Рембра́ндтом . . .

252. The English passive of state (cf. German *war* (state) and *wurde* (action)) may be expressed in Russian by either the past participle passive or by the perfective form of the reflexive verb; the English passive of state is, of course, fundamentally, a resultative construction:

The lost book has been found	Поте́рянная кни́га нашла́сь (найдена́)

It should be noted that the English passive of action expressing a single completed action in the past may not be expressed in Russian by the perfective form of the reflexive verb. It is incorrect to translate *the lost book was found by the librarian* потéрянная кнѝга нашлáсь библиотéкарем; the correct translation is потéрянная кнѝга былá нáйденá библиотéкарем or потéрянную кнѝгу нашёл библио-тéкарь. The use of the perfective reflexive precludes the naming of the agent. Such constructions as:

. . . *the edges of the (river) banks became covered with a golden-pink border*	. . . краяˊ береговˊ подёрну-лись золотóй с рóзо-вым каёмкой (M. Prish-vin)

are resultative and descriptive (note English *with* not *by*). When Gor'ky wrote to a young writer:

. . . *if you have anything written, send it here . . .*	. . . уж éсли чтó-то напи-сáлось, присылáйте сюдá . . .

he meant, literally, *if anything has got itself written*. The expression послы́шаться, often quoted as a passive *to be heard*, is not a true passive since the agent is named in the dative and not the instrumental case:

. . . *he heard the rattle of anchor chains*	. . . емуˊ послы́шался грóхот яˊкорных цепéй (Krymov)

253. Russian possesses a further idiomatic way of expressing, in special contexts, single completed passive actions. The action in this form of expression is always physical and the agent always inanimate. The inanimate agent is regarded as the instrument of the will of some external force. It is often a natural phenomenon. The verb in these constructions is impersonal thus expressing the absence of active intention in the agent. The noun naming the agent is placed in the instrumental case:

At dawn the land became en-veloped in fog	На рассвéте тумáнами затопѝло зéмлю (Bub-yonnov)

Kvashin's corpse was carried away by the river	Труп Квашина унесло́ реко́й (A. N. Tolstoy)
I saw a soldier killed by a cannon-ball	Я ви́дел, как ядро́м уби́ло солда́та (L. N. Tolstoy)
The idler-wheel was knocked off the tank by one shell, the turret was wedged by another	Одни́м снаря́дом у та́нка вы́било колесо́-лени́вец, други́м — закли́нило ба́шню (Bubyonnov)

To express such actions actively (e.g. грана́та уби́ла челове́ка *the grenade killed the man*), while possible, is unusual in Russian. The construction described may also be used when the agent is not named:

Chapaev was shot through the arm	Чапа́еву проби́ло ру́ку (Furmanov)
On the second day of Yuletide the ice broke up . . .	На второ́й день рождества́ взлома́ло лёд . . . (Sholokhov)

Transitive and Intransitive verbs

254. English often uses the same verb to express both a transitive and an intransitive action, Russian very seldom. One of the main functions of the reflexive suffix -ся in Russian is to form an intransitive from a transitive verb. The following are among the commonest of these pairs:

Transitive and Intransitive	*Transitive*	*Intransitive*
To spread	Распространя́ть (-ни́ть)	Распространя́ться (-ни́ться)
To stop	Остана́вливать (останови́ть)	Остана́вливаться (останови́ться)
To return	Возвраща́ть (-ти́ть)	Возвраща́ться (-ти́ться)
To continue	Продолжа́ть	Продолжа́ться
To dress	Одева́ть (оде́ть)	Одева́ться (оде́ться)
To wash	Мыть (помы́ть)	Мы́ться (помы́ться)

There are many other such pairs, especially corresponding to English verbs in -*en*:

Transitive and Intransitive	Transitive	Intransitive
To weaken	Ослабля́ть (осла́бить)	Ослабля́ться (-и́ться)
To soften	Смягча́ть (смягчи́ть)	Смягча́ться (-чи́ться)

255. Certain transitive verbs in Russian correspond to intransitive verbs formed from the same root. Common among such pairs are:

	Transitive	Intransitive
To hang	Ве́шать (пове́сить)	Висе́ть
To weigh	Взве́шивать (взве́сить)	Ве́сить
To grow	Выра́щивать (вы́растить) (цветы́) Отра́щивать (отрасти́ть) (бо́роду)	Расти́ (вы́расти)
To freeze	Замора́живать (заморо́зить)	Мёрзнуть (замёрзнуть)
To sink	Топи́ть (потопи́ть)	Тону́ть (потону́ть)
To drown	Топи́ть (утопи́ть)	Тону́ть (утону́ть)

(But он утону́л в кре́сле *he sank into the armchair*). Note also, formed from different roots:

To burn	Жечь (сжечь)	Горе́ть (сгоре́ть)

Other uses of Reflexive verbs

256. Reflexive verbs are used to describe certain actions which are permanent characteristics of the subject:

This dog bites	Э́та соба́ка куса́ется
This horse kicks	Э́та ло́шадь for ляга́ется
This cat scratches	Э́та ко́шка цара́пается
This wire bends	Э́та про́волока гнётся
This material will not tear	Э́та мате́рия не рвётся
These cups do not break	Э́ти ча́шки не бью́тся

To describe an action with a specific object, however, the non-reflexive form is used:

This dog does not bite children   Эта собáка не кусáет детéй

257. (i) Sometimes a reflexive and non-reflexive verb exist together to describe fundamentally the same action, but the reflexive verb expresses a different attitude to the action on the part of the doer:

To threaten	Грозúть (пригрозúть), грозúться (погрозúться)
To ring	Звонúть (позвонúть), звонúться (позвонúться)
To knock	Стучáть (постучáть), стучáться (постучáться)

The reflexive verb expresses the keen personal interest of the doer in the effect his action will produce. Грозúться, for example, may mean that a person is not serious in his threats but is only using them to achieve his ends:

He won't do that, he is only   Он э́того не сдéлает,
threatening   тóлько грозúтся

Стучáться and звонúться mean that the knocker or ringer hopes for an answer to his knocking or ringing, and in the context of knocking or ringing at a door these reflexive verbs are very widely used.

(ii) Notice also the verbs слýшать (*to listen*) and признавáть (признáть) (*to acknowledge*) which acquire different meanings when used reflexively. Слýшаться (послýшаться) means *to obey* and признавáться (признáться) *to confess*.

258. Certain reflexive verbs change in meaning when they lose the reflexive suffix -ся and take the full reflexive pronoun себя́ as a direct object:

To feel better   Чýвствовать (по-) себя́ лýчше

but чýвствуется means *is felt, one feels*:

One feels great talent in this Чýвствуется большóй та-
picture   лáнт в э́той картúне

To wonder (French *se demander*) спра́шивать (спроси́ть) себя́, but спра́шивается means *the question arises, one asks; one wonders*:

> If more students come to us, the question arises, where will they work ?   Е́сли к нам придёт бо́льше студе́нтов, то спра́шивается, где они́ бу́дут занима́ться?

To take one's own life лиша́ть (лиши́ть) себя́ жи́зни, but лиша́ться (лиши́ться) жи́зни means *to lose one's life*.

To maintain (keep) oneself содержа́ть себя́, but содержа́ться means *to be contained*:

> How much petrol does this can contain ?   Ско́лько бензи́на содержится в э́том бидо́не?

To behave well вести́ себя́ хорошо́, but вести́сь means *to date from*:

> This custom dates from ancient times   Э́тот обы́чай и́сстари ведётся

259. The dative reflexive pronoun себе́ may, in Russian, be used to make perfectly clear the translation of such English expressions as *he is having a house built*. This may be translated either он стро́ит дом or, more explicitly, он стро́ит себе́ дом. Compare он шьёт сы́ну костю́м *he is having a suit made for his son*.

MOOD

Subjunctive

260. The Russian subjunctive is the same in form as the conditional (see para. **407**). It has certain uses in common with the subjunctive in Western European languages although it is not used so widely as in those languages. For its use in concessive clauses see paras. **411–17**.

261. In main clauses the subjunctive is used to express the desirability of an action. Desirability may be objective; i. e. externally viewed, *it is desirable that someone should do*

(*should have done*), *ought to do* (*ought to have done*) *something*.
Notice that the subjunctive in such constructions may
refer to past, present, and future time:

You should have written to the landlord yesterday	Вы бы написа́ли вчера́ хозя́ину
You should write to the landlord today (*tomorrow*)	Вы бы написа́ли сего́дня (за́втра) хозя́ину

The desirability may also be subjective; i. e. internally
viewed, *I wish that, if only*. Here the subjunctive may be
accompanied by the conjunctions скоре́е, поскоре́й, хоть:

I wish I could read a bit longer	Я почита́л бы ещё немно́жко
If only they would start calling us up	Скоре́е бы на́чали вызыва́ть (Krymov)
If only he would come	Хоть бы он поскоре́й пришёл

In English and Russian such desires may sometimes be
expressed without a verb, but in Russian the particle бы
must not be omitted:

Just one sunny day and everyone would cheer up	Оди́н бы день со́лнца, всем ве́село бу́дет

262. Desirability, expressed by the subjunctive, may be
strong enough to take on mild imperative meaning:

Nina and I will unpack and you show your father your present	Мы с Ни́ной бу́дем распако́вываться, а ты показа́л бы отцу́ пода́рок

Notice that the subjunctive constructions in this use (and
when they express only desirability) consist of the protasis
of a conditional sentence.

263. In subordinate clauses, the Russian subjunctive is
used after verbs of wishing or endeavouring. Such verbs
are followed by the conjunction что, and the subjunctive

particle бы is joined to что, making one word чтобы (чтоб). Common verbs of this kind are:

To want	Хоте́ть (захоте́ть)
To demand	Тре́бовать (потре́бовать)
To try to bring it about (perf. to bring it about)	Добива́ться (доби́ться)
To wait	Ждать
To insist	Наста́ивать (настоя́ть)
To see to it	Смотре́ть, следи́ть

All of these verbs are followed by the construction чтобы кто́-нибудь сде́лал что́-нибудь (*that someone do something*) (see para. **390** for alternative constructions with ждать):

On Sunday Lida insisted that Pyrin take her with him into the town	В воскресе́нье Ли́да настоя́ла, чтобы Пы́рин взял её с собо́й в го́род (Popov)

264. The subjunctive with что is also used in Russian after verbs of commanding, permitting, persuading, warning. It should be noticed, however, that with these verbs the subjunctive construction is only an alternative to the use of the infinitive combined with the English direct object in the accusative/genitive or dative case:

To order	Веле́ть, прика́зывать (-каза́ть) кому́-нибудь
To ask	Проси́ть (по-) кого́-нибудь
To permit	Позволя́ть (позво́лить) кому́-нибудь
To forbid	Не веле́ть (кому́-нибудь)
To persuade	Угова́ривать (уговори́ть) кого́-нибудь
To warn	Предупрежда́ть (предупреди́ть) кого́-нибудь

Yulia Dmitrievna, the commanding officer has ordered you not to absent yourself anywhere	Ю́лия Дми́триевна, нача́льник веле́л, чтобы вы никуда́ не уходи́ли (Panova)

Alternative construction: . . . вам веле́л никуда́ не уходи́ть.

265. Verbs of fearing are followed either by что or как and the **negative** subjunctive, or by что and the perfective present. Such verbs are:

To fear	Боя́ться
To be uneasy	Беспоко́иться (о-)
To be apprehensive	Опаса́ться
To be frightened	Пуга́ться (ис-)
I was afraid that he would come	Я боя́лся, что́бы (как бы) он не пришёл
	Я боя́лся, что он придёт
I am afraid that he will come	Я бою́сь, что́бы (как бы) он не пришёл
	Я бою́сь, что он придёт

Notice that the same construction is used whether the verb of fearing is in the past or the present. Notice also that if the verb of fearing in English is followed by a negative construction, the negative perfective present (but not the subjunctive) is used in Russian whether the verb of fearing is in the past or the present tense:

I am afraid that he will not come	Я бою́сь, что он не придёт
I was afraid that he would not come	Я боя́лся, что он не придёт

For the use of the perfective present in the second example see para. **209.**

266. Verbs of doubting used affirmatively and verbs of saying or thinking used negatively, when they refer to the past or present, are also followed in Russian by что and the subjunctive:

To doubt whether	Сомнева́ться, что
Not to see that	Не ви́деть (уви́деть), что
Not to say that	Не говори́ть (сказа́ть), что
Not to hear that	Не слы́шать (услы́шать), что
Not to think that	Не ду́мать, что
Not to believe that	Не ве́рить, что

Not to suppose that	Не предполага́ть (пред-положи́ть), что
Not to imagine that	Не представля́ть (пред-ста́вить) себе́, что
Never, not even when he again took up with Aksinya, did he think that she would ever become a second mother to his children	Никогда́, да́же вновь сойдя́сь с Акси́ньей, он не ду́мал, что́бы она́ когда́-нибудь замени́ла мать его́ де́тям (Sholokhov)

When, however, such verbs refer to the future, they are followed by the imperfective or perfective future, the choice being governed by normal aspectival considerations:

I doubt whether he will be there (will come)	Я сомнева́юсь, бу́дет ли он там (придёт ли он)

267. The subjunctive is also used in Russian in subordinate clauses following a negative antecedent. The effect of the negative in the main clause is to make the statement in the subordinate clause contrary to fact. The subjunctive is used in the subordinate clause whether the verb in the main clause is past, present or future:

I do not know a single actor who found a part entrusted to him in one of Gor'ky's plays irksome	Я не зна́ю ни одного́ актёра, кото́рый тяго-ти́лся бы пору́ченной ему́ ро́лью в го́рьков-ских пье́сах (Skorobo-gatov)
They met no other persons whom Makar favoured with his special attention	Не встреча́лось бо́лее лиц, кото́рых Мака́р удосто́ил бы свои́м осо́бенным внима́нием (Korolenko)

This usage is paralleled in French and Spanish (cf. French *Je ne connais personne qui puisse vous répondre*, and Spanish *No he visto jamás un hombre que tuviera mayor atractivo*).

Perfective Present

268. The perfective present has a certain limited range of modal use. For the use of the perfective present in conditional and concessive clauses see paras. **402** and **411** respectively.

269. In main clauses the perfective present is used to express possibility or impossibility:

The horses will never be able to pull them	Лóшади их не повезýт (Azhayev)
I simply cannot find the time, Alexei Kuz'mich, honestly	Врéмени никáк не вýкрою, Алексéй Кузьмúч, чéстное слóво (Andreyev)
You cannot please everybody	На всех не угодúшь
Just look at the weather. You might lose your way altogether	Да вишь какáя погóда, как раз собьёшься с дорóги (Pushkin)
I want to note down Mr. Rudin's last sentence. If it is not noted down, it might easily be forgotten	Хочý записáть вот эту послéднюю фрáзу господúна Рýдина. Не записáв, позабýдешь, чегó дóброго (Turgenev)

Note the frequency with which the indefinite 2nd person singular, with general application, is used in these constructions.

270. With enumerative expressions, the meaning of possibility expressed by the perfective present approaches that of approximation:

With him you might make one component, without him ten	С ним сдéлаешь однý детáль, а без негó дéсять (Polevoy)

271. The perfective present may be used in a subordinate clause after an indefinite antecedent, in the same way as the subjunctive in Spanish (cf. Spanish 'No puedo confiar estas cosas al primero que llegue' *I cannot entrust these things to the first person to chance along*). In Russian the perfective present may follow a main verb either in the past or present (and of course, future):

The thieves were breaking into the house and taking whatever they fancied	Во́ры вла́мывались в дом, бра́ли всё, что пригля́нется (Fadeyev)
It is essential that a writer should portray and not narrate whatever comes into his head	Тре́буется, что́бы писа́тель изобража́л, а не расска́зывал что в го́лову ему́ придёт (Gor'ky)

Notice the indefinite English *whatever*.

Infinitive

272. The Russian infinitive has a very wide range of modal use, in which it sometimes appears with the particle бы, but more often without. Like the subjunctive (para. **261**), the infinitive with бы may express either objective desirability (*it is desirable that*), or subjective desirability (*if only*):

You ought to take some treatment	Вам бы полечи́ться (Gor'ky)
Rather than watching plays, you should take a look at yourselves more often	Вам не пье́сы смотре́ть, а смотре́ть бы поча́ще на сами́х себя́ (Chekhov)
I want to be an airman	Стать бы лётчиком!
Could we but see in time the beam in our own eye	То́лько бы во́-время успе́ть увида́ть бревно́ в своём глазу́ (L. N. Tolstoy)

A desire expressed by the infinitive is, in general, stronger and more emphatic than a desire expressed by the subjunctive.

273. The negative infinitive with бы expresses warning or apprehension:

Whatever you like, only mind you don't separate from him	Всё что хотите, но тóлько бы не разлучáться с ним! (L. N. Tolstoy)
Be careful you don't catch cold	Не простудиться бы вам

274. (i) The infinitive without бы is also used to express desirability. Desires so expressed are usually very strong:

You should be tied up and put in an asylum	Связáть тебя да в сумасшéдший дом (A. Ostrovsky)

(ii) Desirability expressed by the infinitive may, as in English, amount to an imperative:

Everyone to be in their places!	Всем быть на местáх!
Meet here in an hour	Чéрез час собрáться здесь (Trenev)

(iii) The infinitive is also used to express a downright command. Such commands are stronger than those expressed by the imperative. In such constructions no dative complement is possible with the infinitive:

Down oars!	Опустить вёсла!

As with the imperative, prohibitions expressed by the infinitive are normally expressed by the imperfective form:

Do not walk on the grass!	По травé не ходить!
No talking in the ranks!	В строю не разговáривать!

275. The infinitive with or without бы may express fitness, English *should, ought to*:

... it is not you that should be riding Mishka, but Mishka that should be riding you ...	... не тебé на Мишке éздить, а Мишке на тебé (Fadeyev)

> . . . (*Senya*) *at once began to ponder how he should approach her* . . .

> . . . (Сéня) срáзу нáчал соображáть, как бы подойти́ ему́ к ней (M. Prishvin)

276. The infinitive without бы may express a sense of duty or obligation, English *have to, must*:

> *I have still to water the horse, amuse yourself*

> Мне ещё коня́ пои́ть, гуля́й себé (Fadeyev)

Such constructions may be negatived to express English *not up to, not my duty to*:

> *So goodbye, Prince, it is not up to me to set you right*

> Итáк, прощáйте, князь, не мне вас выводи́ть из заблужде́ния (Lermontov)

277. (i) In interrogative constructions the infinitive without бы may translate *shall, should, will, are to*:

> '*Should I pour you some?*' *she added, taking up the tea-pot*

> ,,Нали́ть тебé,'' прибáвила онá, взя́вшись за чáйник (L. N. Tolstoy)

> *Wherever will my mother get so much money to pay for me?*

> Где мáтери стóлько де́нег взять за меня́ заплати́ть? (L. N. Tolstoy)

> '*How are we to manage?*' *I asked Ermolai*

> ,,Как нам быть?'', спроси́л я Ермолáя (Turgenev)

With бы, such constructions usually have the meaning *can*:

> '*How can I get rid of him, without offence?*', *thought Nekhlyudov*

> ,,Как бы отде́латься от негó, не оби́дев егó?'', дýмал Нехлю́дов (L. N. Tolstoy)

(ii) Infinitive constructions with где or кудá may be used to express incredulity or disinclination:

> *A fine actor he'll make!*

> Где емý быть актёром! (Turgenev)

What do I want to burden my-self with a wife and fuss over children for?	Куда́ мне обременя́ться жено́й, ня́нчиться с детьми́? (Pushkin)

278. Like the perfective present (see para. **269**) the infinitive without бы may express impossibility:

All over his face was written: 'I cheat you on every purchase but you will never fool me'	На его́ лице́ бы́ло напи́сано: ,,Ведь я же тебя́ надува́ю при вся́кой поку́пке, а уж тебе́ меня́ не провести́" (Herzen)
You will never be his wife, you might as well know it	Жено́й его́ тебе́ не быва́ть, так и знай (Sholokhov)

Without the negative such constructions acquire the meaning not of possibility but of inevitability:

Our countess was bound to marry a general, I always said so	Я вот всегда́ говори́ла, на́шей графи́не быть за генера́лом (Herzen)
There's trouble brewing, sir	Быть беде́, ба́рин (Chekhov)

279. A special emphatic form of infinitive construction may be used in Russian to express *all right* in such contexts as:

They spent the whole day firing their machine gun at their Führer and at night stole a scarecrow. They stole it all right but lost three men in the process	Це́лый день из пулемёта по своему́ Фю́реру стреля́ли, а но́чью у-кра́ли чу́чело. Укра́сть-то укра́ли но трёх челове́к всё-таки потеря́ли (V. Nekrasov)

In the negative such constructions mean *not exactly*:

He would smile . . . and say, 'I haven't exactly lost it, but I can't find it'	Он улыбнётся . . . ска́жет, ,,Потеря́ть не потеря́л, а найти́ не могу́" (Azhayev)

Imperative

280. The 2nd person singular form of the imperative has a certain limited range of modal use. For its use in conditional sentences see para. **410.**

281. A speaker may use the 2nd person singular imperative form to describe an unpleasant action or activity which he or another person must carry out. Often this activity is compared with the good time someone else is having:

They're off to a ball, but father has to run about, cap in hand	Им бал, а ба́тюшка таска́йся на покло́н (Griboyedov)

282. By using the imperative instead of the perfective past, a speaker may emphasize the suddenness or unexpectedness of an action which interrupts or frustrates another action:

He had hardly struck up the waltz when—snap went a string	Едва́ он заигра́л вальс как ло́пни струна́

Sometimes the expression возьми́ да is used in such constructions to strengthen the sense of unexpectedness:

He should have thrown himself to one side, but what did he do but run straight ahead	Ему́ бы в сто́рону бро́ситься, а он возьми́ да пря́мо и побеги́ (Turgenev)

283. The imperative singular form is used, finally, with a third person subject to translate the English *may* with optative sense:

May the Lord help him!	Помоги́ ему́ Госпо́дь!

VERBS OF MOTION

Abstract and concrete verbs

284. There are fourteen verbs of motion which have two different imperfective forms, one with abstract, the other with concrete meaning. These verbs are:

Abstract	*Concrete*	
Ходи́ть	Идти́	*To go, to walk*
Води́ть	Вести́	*To lead*
Е́здить	Е́хать	*To travel*
Носи́ть	Нести́	*To carry*
Бе́гать	Бежа́ть	*To run*
Пла́вать	Плыть	*To swim, to sail*
Лета́ть	Лете́ть	*To fly*
Вози́ть	Везти́	*To cart, to convey*
Ла́зить	Лезть	*To climb*
Броди́ть	Брести́	*To wander, to make one's way*
Гоня́ть	Гнать	*To drive*
Ката́ть	Кати́ть	*To roll*
По́лзать	Ползти́	*To crawl*
Таска́ть	Тащи́ть	*To drag*

285. The abstract verbs express the simple fact of movement without reference to time, purpose or direction. They are used therefore to describe movement as a permanent characteristic:

Fish swim	Ры́бы пла́вают

Their present participle active is used adjectivally:

Flying Fortress	Лета́ющая кре́пость
Climbing plants	Ла́зящие расте́ния

Compare the strictly verbal and temporal meaning of the present participle active of the concrete verb лете́ть in:

The aeroplane flying over the town is Russian	Самолёт, летя́щий над го́родом, ру́сский

286. The abstract verbs express movement as a physical action:

I am a slow walker	Я хожу́ ме́дленно
He was faced with the prospect of walking on crutches for the rest of his life	Оста́ток жи́зни ему́ предстоя́ло ходи́ть на костыля́х (Panova)
The seriously wounded were followed immediately from the barge by about fifteen of those who could still walk	Вслед за тяжело́ ра́неными с ба́ржи сошло́ деся́тка полтора́ тех, кто мог ещё ходи́ть (Simonov)

287. (i) A very characteristic function of the abstract verbs (but not in the present tense) is their use to express return journeys. The concrete verbs would be inappropriate in this use since they describe movement in one direction. Compare:

I lost my gloves when I went to the theatre	Я потеря́л перча́тки, когда́ ходи́л в теа́тр

(The gloves may have been lost at any time from the moment the speaker left home to the moment of his return.)

I lost my gloves while I was on my way to the theatre	Я потеря́л перча́тки, когда́ шёл в теа́тр

(The speaker means he lost them between his home and the theatre.) An abstract verb may express a series of return journeys:

The match-maker went back and forward for about two weeks	Неде́ли две ходи́ла сва́ха (Pushkin)

(i.e. between the homes of the prospective bride and bridegroom).

(ii) Perfective verbs with the meaning of making a return journey are formed from the commonest of the abstract verbs by the addition of the prefix c-, сходи́ть, своди́ть, сбе́гать, съе́здить, сноси́ть:

What sort of trip did you have? Как вы съе́здили?
(now that you're back)

Compare как вы дое́хали? also meaning *what sort of trip did you have?* but referring to the journey in one direction only. The perfective verbs with c- should not be confused with imperfective verbs of motion often spelt in the same way but with different meanings and possessing corresponding perfective forms. Сходи́ть (сойти́) means *to come down, to alight* (from a conveyance), *to land* (from a ship). Своди́ть (свести́) means *to bring down* or *to bring together*. Notice, however, the different stress in сбега́ть (imperfective) and сбе́гать (perfective); notice also съезжа́ть (not съе́здить), an imperfective verb (perfective form съе́хать) meaning *to go down* or *to move house*.

(iii) In the meaning of making a return journey the imperfective abstract verbs are often used where the perfective form might seem more natural (see para. **198**):

We went to France last year Мы в про́шлом году́ е́здили во Фра́нцию

But the perfective form must, of course, be used to express future meaning, referring to a single visit:

Then we shall pay a visit to the cinema, to the theatre or to the circus Пото́м в кино́, и́ли в теа́тр схо́дим, и́ли в цирк (Ketlinskaya)

288. Precise direction, with an underlying sense of purpose, is the characteristic which most often distinguishes the action in progress described by the concrete verb from that described by the abstract verb. Compare:

He was walking slowly along the street to the bank Он шёл ме́дленно по у́лице, направля́ясь в банк

(movement in a specified direction towards a definite goal)

He was walking slowly back and forward along the street Он ходи́л ме́дленно взад и вперёд по у́лице

(movement in more than one direction without a definite goal).

This link between the concrete verb and precise direction is so fundamental that a concrete verb may be used, even with frequentative or habitual meaning, if each action takes place in one direction and towards a definite goal:

. . . a good soldier does not think of death when he is advancing upon the enemy . . . хоро́ший солда́т не ду́мает о сме́рти, когда́ идёт на врага́ (Fedin)

Compare the use of concrete and abstract verbs in the following examples, all of which refer to habitual actions:

. . . she had a sister who went charring . . . у неё была́ сестра́ **ходи́вшая** на подённую рабо́ту (Chekhov)

. . . I settled down in the old flat from which in previous years I used to attend the scientific academy . . . я посели́лся на ста́рой кварти́ре, отку́да в пре́жние го́ды **ходи́л** в реа́льное учи́лище (Gladkov)

My foot no longer slips on its steep slope, when I am going down it in the morning on my way to work Нога́ уже́ не скользи́т бо́льше на его́ круто́м скло́не, когда́ я спуска́юсь по нему́ у́тром, **идя́** на рабо́ту (Grin)

I would help her to feed the cows and calves and we would go home to have breakfast Я помога́л ей зада́ть коро́вам и теля́там ко́рму и мы **шли** домо́й за́втракать (Grin)

The abstract verb in the first two examples states simply the fact of the habitual action, the concrete verb in the third and fourth examples stresses direction and purpose as well as stating the habitual action. Thus, true to their nature as imperfective verbs, the concrete verbs of motion may express habitual or frequentative actions, if each action is specific enough to be viewed individually instead of merely one in a series.

289. In negative sentences the abstract verbs express simply permanent absence of movement, the concrete verbs express either absence of movement on a single occasion or, if permanent, then for a definite reason. Compare:

> *In frosty weather the buses do not run*   При морóзной погóде автóбусы не хóдят

(this means that the authorities suspend the service),

> *In frosty weather the buses will not go*   При морóзной погóде автóбусы не идýт

(this means that the engine will not start). Notice the modal use of the concrete verb, expressed in English by *will not*:

> *If the weather is intolerable, the road wretched, the coachman stubborn and the horses will not pull—it is the station master who is to blame*   Погóда неснóсная, дорóга сквéрная, ямщúк упрямый, лóшади не везýт — а виновáт смотрúтель (Pushkin)

In a positive sentence the abstract verb would be used:

> *These horses pull well*   Э́ти лóшади вóзят хорошó

290. Where, in negative sentences generally, Russian uses the imperfective, in preference to the perfective verb (see paras. **208** and **214**), with verbs of motion the abstract imperfective form is used:

> *Don't go to this restaurant any more*   Не ходúте бóльше в э́тот ресторáн

The abstract form is used to express negative commands which are essentially prohibitions, but the concrete verb is used to express negative commands which are not prohibitions but warnings (see para. **215**):

Don't take the boy to the cinema tomorrow	Не води́те ма́льчика за́втра в кино́
Be careful not to walk among the nettles	Смотри́те, не иди́те по крапи́ве

291. When the meaning of a verb of motion is figurative and the sense of actual physical movement is lost, the concrete verb is used almost invariably:

Time flies	Вре́мя лети́т (бежи́т)
Negotiations are going on between the two ambassadors	Иду́т перегово́ры ме́жду двумя́ посла́ми
He keeps a diary	Он ведёт дневни́к

The concrete verb is used with figurative meaning even when the meaning is clearly frequentative or habitual:

When boxers are having no luck, they take off weight and fight in another category	Когда́ боксёрам не везёт, они́ сгоня́ют вес и выступа́ют в друго́й катего́рии (Tikonov)
A persistent rain began to fall, steady and quiet, such as goes on for a long time	Пошёл обложно́й дождь, равноме́рный и ти́хий, каки́е иду́т подо́лгу (Goncharov)

A participial adjective, with figurative meaning, is formed from the verb вести́:

The leading organs of the press	Веду́щие о́рганы печа́ти

(compare the adjectival use of the participles from abstract verbs with *literal* meaning in para. **285**).

292. Notice that the abstract verbs носи́ть and води́ть may be used figuratively, without the sense of actual physical movement, in the expressions носи́ть (not нести́) и́мя — хара́ктер — следы́ — отпеча́ток *to bear the name—the character—traces—the mark*, and води́ть (as well as вести́) дру́жбу с *to keep up a friendship with*. The expression води́ть за́ нос (not вести́) means *to make a fool of, to lead up the garden path*.

293. Certain abstract verbs have meanings not shared by the corresponding concrete verbs:

To wear (a blue hat)	Носи́ть (си́нюю шля́пу)
To look after (an invalid)	Ходи́ть (за больны́м)
To mangle (linen)	Ката́ть (бельё)
To roll (dough)	Ката́ть (те́сто)

Ходи́ть, идти́/е́здить, е́хать

294. These pairs of verbs are best distinguished by saying that ходи́ть, идти́ can never be used of any form of travel in a conveyance and е́здить, е́хать can never be used of motion on foot. Ходи́ть, идти́ are applied not only to motion on foot but to any form of motion where the moving object proceeds under its own power:

The train is travelling fast	По́езд идёт бы́стро
The car is travelling along the road	Маши́на идёт по доро́ге
One day in early spring we were sailing from Port Said to Batum	Одна́жды ра́нней весно́й шли мы в Бату́м из Порт-Саи́да (Bunin)

Of the passengers in these forms of transport, of course, е́здить, е́хать are used:

To travel by train	Е́хать по́ездом

Notice, however, that the verbs пла́вать, плыть (*to sail*) may be used of both ship and passengers:

The ship sailed from London to Leningrad	Кора́бль плыл из Ло́ндона в Ленингра́д
I sailed on that ship to Russia	Я плыл на том корабле́ в Росси́ю

295. Notice, also, that although, as explained above, ходи́ть, идти́ are always correct when used of vehicles proceeding under their own power, in present-day Russian е́здить and е́хать (or compound verbs) are sometimes found in this use, although still considered colloquial (cf.

the English use of *travel* for both conveyance and passengers):

A long column of vehicles goes past . . .	Мимо проезжает длинная колонна машин . . .
	(V. Nekrasov)

296. (i) Ходить, идти are used of very short journeys when it is not stated whether the person concerned went on foot or rode, even if (as, for example, with journeys within a city) transport is almost certainly used:.

We shall arrive at your house at six o'clock	Мы придём к вам в шесть часов

приехать would only be used here if the speaker wished to emphasize that he was not walking:

We will not walk but drive to your house	Мы не придём к вам пешком, а приедем

(ii) Notice the compound verbs заходить (зайти), заезжать (заехать) which, with the prepositions к and за mean respectively *to call upon, to call for,* while walking or driving past:

We shall call on you on our way to the University	Мы зайдём к вам по дороге в университет
We shall pick you up at six o'clock and drive together to London	Мы заедем за вами в шесть часов и поедем вместе в Лондон

297. Notice that with letters and goods, although these are conveyed, приходить (прийти) is used:

The letter arrived this morning	Письмо пришло сегодня утром

IMPERSONAL CONSTRUCTIONS

There is, there are

298. English *there is, there are,* with indefinite quantities or numbers, are normally translated into Russian by the indefinite expressions of quantity мно́го *many, much,* ма́ло *little, few,* дово́льно, доста́точно *enough,* не́сколько *several,* ско́лько *how many* (and others) or by the collective numerals дво́е, тро́е, че́тверо, &c., with the complement in the genitive case:

There are few good books in the library	В библиоте́ке ма́ло хоро́ших книг
There are three of us Englishmen in the hotel	Нас тро́е англича́н в гости́нице

With expressions of quantity, the complement may stand first for emphasis:

There are many learned men but few wise ones	Учёных мно́го, у́мных ма́ло

There is (are) not is translated by нет with, of course, a genitive complement:

There are no Russian books in the library	В библиоте́ке нет ру́сских книг

Нет may be strengthened by ни одного́ (одно́й) or ни еди́ного (еди́ной):

There is not a single theatre in the town	В го́роде нет ни одного́ (еди́ного) теа́тра

The complement may precede нет for emphasis:

There is no doubt at all that he is dead	Сомне́ния нет, что он у́мер

There was (were), there will be are, of course, translated by бы́ло and бу́дет:

There were many good books in the library	В библиоте́ке бы́ло мно́го хоро́ших книг

Notice that negative constructions with нет, не́ было, не бу́дет may correspond to English personal constructions with the verbs *to be, to have:*

Gerasim was no longer in the courtyard	Герáсима ужé нé было на дворé (Turgenev)
He had not the energy to intercede for Khlebnikov	У негó нé было сил заступи́ться за Хлéбникова (Kuprin)

299. (i) The English construction *there is—was—will be someone to do something* is translated into Russian by a special construction consisting of есть — бы́ло — бу́дет, accompanied by the infinitive of the action to be performed and комý, the dative form of the pronoun кто:

There is someone to intercede for us	Есть комý заступи́ться за нас

Interrogative meaning may be expressed by комý? or комý-нибудь?:

Is there anyone to intercede for us?	Есть ли комý(-нибудь) заступи́ться за нас?

Negative meaning by нéкому:

There was no one to intercede for us	Нéкому бы́ло заступи́ться за нас

(ii) If *someone* is not the subject but the object of the English clause, it is translated by кто, in the case required by the verb or, if necessary, governed by a preposition:

There is someone for her to talk to	У неё есть с кем говори́ть

Negative constructions are rendered with нéкого, in the appropriate case or with the appropriate preposition:

There will be no one, at least, for me to lament over	Нé на кого, по крáйней мéре, мне плáкаться бу́дет (A. Ostrovsky)

(iii) *Who is there to . . .?* is expressed by комý? and the infinitive:

For who is there to mourn her?	Да комý плáкать-то о ней? (A. Ostrovsky)

If *who?* is the object of the verb, кто is placed in the appropriate case or governed by the appropriate preposition:

Whom can she ask permission of? У кого́ ей спра́шиваться? (A. Ostrovsky)

300. If *anything*, *something*, or *nothing* is the object or complement of the verb, it is translated by что, не́чего in the appropriate case or with the appropriate preposition:

. . . she had something to relate	. . . ей бы́ло что порассказа́ть (Lermontov)
You are probably hungry and we have something to give you to eat	Вы вероя́тно го́лодны, а у нас есть чем угости́ть (Sholokhov)
In that hall there are all sorts of goods and chattels, there is something to sit on, something to sleep on, something in which to array oneself, something in which to look at oneself	В той пала́те мно́го добра́ и скарба вся́кого, есть на чём посиде́ть, поспа́ть, есть во что приоде́ться, есть во что посмотре́ться (S. Aksakov)
There is nothing here for us to read	Нам не́чего здесь чита́ть

301. Russian has also special constructions for translating *there is somewhere (nowhere)*, *there is reason (no reason)*, *there is no time* followed by the infinitive:

There is somewhere for us to pitch our camp	Нам есть где расположи́ться ла́герем
There's not room to swing a cat (i.e. *there is nowhere for an apple to fall*)	Не́где здесь я́блоку упа́сть
We have somewhere (nowhere) to go	Нам есть куда́ (не́куда) идти́
There was nowhere where Korostelyov could have got to know all that	Не́откуда Коростелёву бы́ло знать всё э́то (Panova)

There was no reason for you to say that	Вам не́зачем бы́ло говори́ть э́то
I fell silent and I had good reason to	Я замо́лк и мне бы́ло заче́м (Turgenev)
I have no time to see him	Мне не́когда его́ ви́деть

Когда́ is not used meaning *there is time* but ironically meaning *a lot of time*:

A lot of time I have for reading!	Мне есть когда́ чита́ть!

302. Special Russian impersonal verbs translate *there is* in expressions of sufficiency and insufficiency, presence and absence. These verbs are:

Хвата́ть (хвати́ть)	*There is enough*
Достава́ть (доста́ть)	„ „
Ста́ть (perfective)	„ „

(The imperfective става́ть is now archaic.)

Недостава́ть (недоста́ть) *There is lacking, missing*

These verbs take a complement in the genitive case:

The bread will last until the end of the week (i.e. *there will be enough bread until . . .*)	Хле́ба хва́тит (доста́нет, ста́нет) до конца́ неде́ли
. . . whiskers, each one of which would have made three beards	. . . бакенба́рды, из кото́рых ка́ждой ста́ло бы на три бороды́ (Goncharov)
That is the last straw (i.e. *there was only that lacking*)	Э́того ещё и недостава́ло
I cannot find words to express my gratitude	Мне недостаёт слов, что́бы вы́разить свою́ благода́рность
We missed you	Нам вас недостава́ло

303. Ви́дно and слы́шно are used in Russian meaning *there is visible* and *there is audible*. They are followed by a direct object which, if animate, follows the normal rules for animate objects. The negative forms не ви́дно, не слы́шно are followed by objects in the genitive case:

The song was audible even above the noise of the water	Пе́сню бы́ло слы́шно несмотря́ на шум воды́
At the end of the room we could see a tall man	В конце́ ко́мнаты нам ви́дно бы́ло высо́кого челове́ка
The train is not yet in sight	По́езда ещё не ви́дно

The auxiliary verb стать may be used with ви́дно and слы́шно with the meaning *to come into view, to become audible* and, with the negative forms, *to disappear from view, to become inaudible*:

Suddenly we heard the sound of the waterfall	Вдру́г нам слы́шно ста́ло шум водопа́да
The fog thickened and the town was lost to view	Сгусти́лся тума́н и города́ ста́ло не ви́дно

Ви́дно and слы́шно may also mean *one could see, one could hear*:

Even from the road one could see the many-coloured pansies among the stubble	Да́же с доро́ги бы́ло ви́дно, как в жнивье́ пестре́ли анютины гла́зки (Bubyonnov)
. . . one could hear the bombing near Vazuza	. . . бы́ло слы́шно, как шла бомбёжка близ Вазу́зы (Bubyonnov)

Notice the idiomatic use of ви́дно and слы́шно in:

He was not seen (heard of) for a year	Его́ не́ было ви́дно (о нём не́ было слы́шно) це́лый год

Impersonal constructions expressing obligation, possibility, fitness, chance

На́до and ну́жно *It is necessary* (French *il faut*)
Сле́дует *It is fitting*
Прихо́дится (придётся) *One has to, one has occasion to*

Возмо́жно, мо́жно *It is possible*
Невозмо́жно, нельзя́ *It is impossible*

304. (i) На́до (ну́жно) with a dative personal pronoun
means either *one must* or *one needs to*; in the sense of *one must*
some form of external necessity is implied:

I must go and see him this evening	Мне на́до пойти́ к нему́ сего́дня ве́чером
You need to read many more books about Tolstoy	Вам на́до чита́ть ещё мно́го книг о Толсто́м

На́до (ну́жно) *one must* may be toned down in meaning by
the addition of бы to *one ought to*:

I ought to go and see him this evening	Мне на́до бы пойти́ к нему́ сего́дня ве́чером

Бы added to на́до (ну́жно) in the sense of *one needs to* does
not change the meaning but simply reduces the force of
the statement:

You really ought to read more books about Tolstoy	Вам на́до бы чита́ть бо́льше книг о Толсто́м

In the past tense на́до (ну́жно) бы́ло means both *one had to*
and *one ought to have* (lit. *one needed to*):

I had to leave before six o'clock	Мне на́до бы́ло уе́хать до шести́ часо́в
You ought to have changed at Moscow	Вам на́до бы́ло пересе́сть в Москве́

Бы again simply reduces the force of the statement *you
really ought to have . . .*

(ii) На́до (ну́жно) meaning *is necessary* may take a direct
object:

A good interpreter is needed	На́до хоро́шего перево́дчика
I need a Russian grammar	Мне ну́жно ру́сскую грамма́тику

(iii) Прихо́дится (придётся) may be synonymous with

на́до (ну́жно) in the sense of *one must* but has also the special meaning of *one has occasion to*:

I frequently had occasion to see Hitler in a fury	Мне ча́сто приходи́лось ви́деть Ги́тлера в бе́шенстве

(iv) Сле́дует may be synonymous with на́до (ну́жно) in the sense of *one needs to, one should*, but has the additional meaning of *it is fitting that one should*:

That was to be expected (i.e. *one should have . . .*)	Э́того сле́довало (на́до бы́ло) ожида́ть
You should not say such things	Вам не сле́дует так говори́ть

In this sense of *it is fitting* сле́дует is often the best translation of English constructions with *proper*:

We applied to the proper quarter but received no reply	Мы обраща́лись куда́ сле́довало, но не получа́ли отве́та

305. The difference between возмо́жно and мо́жно is that мо́жно may mean either *it is possible, one can*, or *it is permitted, one may*, whereas возмо́жно may have only the first meaning, *it is possible, one can*:

May one smoke here?	Мо́жно кури́ть здесь?

In their common meaning мо́жно and возмо́жно mean *it is within the bounds of possibility*—both physically and mentally:

It is possible to drive from here to London in two hours	Возмо́жно (мо́жно) дое́хать отсю́да до Ло́ндона за два часа́
His words can be understood in two ways	Его́ слова́ возмо́жно (мо́жно) поня́ть двоя́ко

Only возмо́жно may mean *it is possible* in the sense of *it may happen*:

He may not come	Возмо́жно, что он не придёт

306. The opposite of возмо́жно is невозмо́жно, and the opposite of мо́жно is нельзя́. As the opposite of мо́жно, нельзя́ may mean either *one cannot* or *one may not*; it is, therefore, in certain meanings, synonymous with невозмо́жно:

It is impossible to knock him out	Нельзя́ (невозмо́жно) его́ нокаути́ровать
This problem cannot be solved in two hours	Эту зада́чу нельзя́ (невозмо́жно) реши́ть в два часа́

As the opposite of мо́жно, нельзя́ may also have modal meaning, unconnected with mental or physical impossibility—*one cannot, one must not*:

. . . he is a flighty person on whom one cannot rely	. . . он ве́треный челове́к на кото́рого нельзя́ положи́ться
We must not delay, not a day, not an hour	Ме́длить нельзя́, ни одного́ дня, ни одного́ ча́са

307. Although not an impersonal verb до́лжен (должна́–о́–ы́) should be noticed as a means of translating *one must, one ought to*, in certain contexts. Used with a personal subject, до́лжен implies a sense of moral compulsion on the part of the speaker, whereas на́до (ну́жно) imply compulsion from outside:

I must write to my father this very evening	Я до́лжен написа́ть отцу́ сего́дня же ве́чером

With the same subjective sense, до́лжен бы and до́лжен был бы mean *one ought to* and *one ought to have* respectively:

You ought to have written to your father earlier	Вы должны́ бы́ли бы написа́ть отцу́ ра́ньше

До́лжен may also mean *is due*:

The train is due to arrive at six o'clock	По́езд до́лжен прийти́ в шесть часо́в

The parenthetic expression до́лжно́ бы́ть means *must, must have* in a conjectural sense:

I expect you know that he is dead	Вы, должно́ быть, зна́ете, что он у́мер
He must have left two hours ago	Он, должно́ быть, уе́хал два часа́ наза́д

Note also очеви́дно and наве́рное:

He must be in the library at present	очеви́дно, он сейча́с в библиоте́ке
The expedition must now be reaching its objective	В настоя́щее вре́мя экспеди́ция, наве́рное, приближа́ется к це́ли

Impersonal constructions expressing the physical, mental, or emotional state of human beings

308. Several common impersonal verbs referring to the health or emotions are used in Russian with a direct object or with a complement governed by a preposition:

I am feverish, I feel shivery	Меня́ зноби́т
I feel sick	Меня́ тошни́т
He felt great relief	У него́ отлегло́ от се́рдца

309. Certain predicative adverbs may be used impersonally with a dative complement to describe a mental, emotional, or physical condition:

I enjoyed myself among you	Мне ве́село бы́ло среди́ вас
I am too lazy to move	Мне лень сдви́нуться с ме́ста

The predicative adverb жаль has two meanings. Followed by the accusative (or accusative/genitive) case it means *to be sorry for*:

I am sorry for your sister	Мне жаль ва́шу сестру́

Followed by the genitive case it means *to begrudge*:

I begrudge the time I have wasted on this problem	Мне жаль поте́рянного над э́той пробле́мой вре́мени

310. From almost all non-reflexive verbs, it is possible, by the addition of the reflexive particle -ся (-сь), to form impersonal verbs, taking a dative complement, which express predominantly disinclination or incapacity to perform an action. In this meaning such verbs are used only in the imperfective aspect and, of course, in the negative. More rarely the same verbs are used in the positive with the meaning of inclination towards the action, or with adverbs describing the manner of the action:

Litvinov took up a book, but he was somehow not in the mood for reading	Литви́нов взял кни́гу, но ему́ что́-то не чита́лось (Turgenev)
I can hardly wait to see you	Мне не те́рпится вас уви́деть
I went to bed early but could not sleep	Я лёг ра́но в посте́ль, но мне не спало́сь

Notice also мне не сиди́тся (не лежи́тся) *I cannot sit still (lie still)*

I shall write while I am in the mood for writing	Я бу́ду писа́ть, пока́ мне пи́шется
I fell into that special kind of sound sleep into which one sinks in moments of alarm	Я засну́л тем осо́бенным кре́пким сном, кото́рым спи́тся в мину́ты трево́ги (L. N. Tolstoy)
He finds life tedious. Nothing interests him	Ему́ живётся ску́чно. Ничто́ его́ не интересу́ет

Impersonal constructions expressing English passives

311. A number of verbs of decision, command, or purpose which, in active constructions, take an indirect object in the dative case, are used impersonally in passive constructions. Common among such verbs are:

Сказа́ть *To tell*   Позво́лить *To permit*

Веле́ть, приказа́ть *To order*   Суди́ть *To destine*
Не веле́ть *To forbid*   Отказа́ть *To refuse*
Поручи́ть *To entrust with the task*

In the Russian impersonal construction the past participle passive of these verbs, in the neuter short form, governs the subject of the passive construction standing in the dative case. (Since only the past participle passive of these verbs is relevant to this construction, only the perfective forms are given above.)

No one, not even Lenin, was told of the danger	Никому́, да́же Ле́нину, не́ было ска́зано об опа́сности (Andreyeva)
He is not allowed to go out	Ему́ не позво́лено выходи́ть
She, probably, as the best educated person in the household, was entrusted with the task of meeting and entertaining the doctor	Вероя́тно, ей, как са́мой образо́ванной в до́ме, бы́ло поручено́ встре́тить и приня́ть до́ктора (Chekhov)

Occasionally such verbs are used with a complement governed by a preposition:

The appeal will be rejected	В жа́лобе бу́дет отка́зано (L. N. Tolstoy)

It is impossible to use this construction when an animate agent is mentioned. If this occurs, then the passive construction must be translated into Russian by an active construction:

He was ordered by his colonel to return from leave	Полко́вник приказа́л ему́ верну́ться из о́тпуска

If, however, as rarely happens, the agent is inanimate, the impersonal construction is possible:

Here we are destined by nature to open a window on Europe	Приро́дой здесь нам суждено́, В Евро́пу проруби́ть окно́; (Pushkin)

312. English passive constructions, when the agent is not named, may also be translated into Russian by the use of the indefinite third person plural, similar, in this function, to indefinite *on* in French and *man* in German:

It was not until the spring of 1919 that Dibich was detailed for dispatch on a troop train . . .	То́лько весно́й 1919 го́да Ди́бича назна́чили к отпра́вке с эшело́ном . . . (Fedin)

Sometimes this construction may correspond to an English construction with indefinite *someone*:

Someone pushed him in the shoulder with the sharp edge of a soldier's kit-box	Его́ толкну́ли в плечо́ о́стрым ребро́м солда́тского похо́дного сундучка́ (Fedin)

PARTICIPLES AND GERUNDS

313. For participles used as adjectives see para. **155.**

314. For gerunds used as adverbs see para. **371.**

315. For the use of the present and past participles passive see under PASSIVE VOICE paras. **248, 249,** and **250.**

316. Present participles active can be formed only from imperfective verbs. When they replace relative clauses, they fulfil the same function as the present tense proper, referring to the moment of speech or making a general statement:

The man standing at the corner has just returned from France	Челове́к, стоя́щий на углу́, то́лько что верну́лся из Фра́нции
All soldiers who return to their home-land after two years of captivity will receive a gratuity of a hundred pounds	Все солда́ты, возвраща́ющиеся на ро́дину по́сле двух лет пле́на, полу́чат наградны́е в сто фу́нтов

317. Past participles active can be formed from both imperfective and perfective verbs. Those formed from imperfective verbs are used in the translation of English relative clauses to replace the imperfect tense:

> *The details of this incident, which engaged the attention of the whole of St. Petersburg, have slipped from my memory*
>
> Подробности этой занимавшей весь Петербург истории стёрлись у меня в памяти (L. N. Tolstoy)

When the main verb is in the past tense, either the present or past participle active may be used in Russian where English uses a present participle:

> *Next to me was sitting a man reading a Russian novel*
>
> Рядом со мной сидел человек, читавший (читающий) русский роман

The past participle active, formed from a perfective verb, has resultative sense and describes an action preceding that expressed by the verb in the main clause which may be past, present, or future:

> *I shall give this book to the first student who asks me*
>
> Я дам эту книгу первому студенту, спросившему её у меня

318. Gerunds in -a (-я), from imperfective verbs, designate an action coincident in time with the action described by the verb in the main clause, past, present, or future:

> *. . . Maslennikov, shouting something, again threw a grenade*
>
> . . . Масленников, что-то крича, снова бросил гранату (Simonov)

Many prefixless imperfective verbs lack the form of the gerund in -a (-я). When this is so, it is sometimes possible to overcome the deficiency by using the gerund from a related, prefixed verb. Note:

> *To send* слать   (no gerund) but use посылая
>
> *To wait* ждать   ,,   ,,   ожидая

To tear рвать	(no gerund) but use	разрыва́я
To press жать	,,	,,	пожима́я
To burn жечь	,,	,,	сжига́я
To sing петь	,,	,,	распева́я
To drink пить	,,	,,	выпива́я

319. Gerunds in -a (-я) may also be formed from certain perfective verbs. Such gerunds designate a secondary action, almost invariably preceding that described by the verb in the main clause:

Noticing (having noticed) the car, he ran across the street   Заме́тя маши́ну, он пере-бежа́л че́рез у́лицу

The gerund -a (-я) from perfective verbs is, however, normally secondary to the gerund in -ши or -в (-вши). Perfective verbs with the -a (-я) form as the more frequent are rare but include:

Having made a mistake	Ошибя́сь
Having gone past (gone in, arrived)	Пройдя́, войдя́, придя́
Having carried past	Пронеся́
Having read	Прочтя́
Having turned away	Отворотя́сь (от)
Having seized	Схватя́сь (за)

Perfective gerunds in -a (-я) are also found in a number of common idioms:

To sit doing nothing	Сиде́ть сложа́ ру́ки
To run headlong	Бежа́ть сломя́ го́лову
To stand gawking	Стоя́ть рази́ня рот
To do in a slipshod manner	Де́лать спустя́ рукава́

320. Gerunds in -ши, -в (-вши) may now only be formed, with one or two exceptions, from perfective verbs. Gerunds formed from imperfective verbs are found in 19th century authors, expressing simultaneity with the action described by the main verb, but they could only be used when the latter was in the past tense. Only е́вши and пи́вши are now in common use.

321. The gerund бу́дучи, from быть *to be*, can mean both *being* and *having been*:

Being unable to go, he sent his assistant	Не бу́дучи в состоя́нии пойти́, он посла́л помо́щника
But, once having been subdued, nature cannot be left uncoerced by man	Но, бу́дучи раз покорена́, приро́да не мо́жет остава́ться без челове́ческого возде́йствия

322. By far the commonest gerund forms from perfective verbs are those ending in -в (-вши) and -ши. Of the alternative forms in -в and -вши, that in -в is much the more common in contemporary literary usage. These gerunds most often describe an action preceding the action described by the main verb:

After passing his examinations, he left . . .	Сдав свои́ экза́мены, он уе́хал . . . (Gor'ky)

Like all perfective verb forms, they may have resultative meaning and are often used, with such meaning, with verbs of movement or state (especially ходи́ть, стоя́ть, лежа́ть, and сиде́ть) to complete the picture drawn by the author:

Grigori was lying with his legs spread out wide	Григо́рий лежа́л широко́ раски́нув но́ги (Sholokhov)
Dasha was sitting with her legs stretched out and her hands resting on her knees	Да́ша сиде́ла вы́тянув но́ги, урони́в ру́ки на коле́ни (A. N. Tolstoy)

Notice that, although a perfective form, the gerund in -в may be used with frequentative meaning:

When I had finished delivering the buns, I would go to bed	Ко́нчив разноси́ть бу́лки, я ложи́лся спать (Gor'ky)

323. Perfective gerund forms in -в may sometimes describe actions which do not precede but form one whole with the action described by the main verb:

Alexei approached Baimanova with the proposal that she sell him her house	Алексей обратился к Байма́новой, предложи́в ей прода́ть ему́ дом (Gor'ky)

The action described by the gerund may also be found to follow that described by the main verb, or to describe the result of the latter:

He threw his cigarette to the ground and crushed it with two excessively violent blows of his foot	Он бро́сил папиро́ску на зе́млю, растопта́в её двумя́ сли́шком си́льными уда́рами ноги́ (Gor'ky)
The sad news flew round the regiments and threw everyone into despondency	Тяжёлая весть облете́ла полки́, нагна́в на всех уны́ние (Furmanov)

THE TRANSLATION OF THE VERB 'TO BE'

324. Russian uses various devices to compensate for the fact that the verb *to be* быть has no present tense. The simplest of all is, of course, the complete omission of the verb:

Mercury is the nearest planet to the sun	Мерку́рий ближа́йшая к со́лнцу плане́та

If, however, the subject of the sentence is more strongly emphasized than in simple statements like the above, a dash may be used:

I like Turgenev and Dostoyevsky, but my favourite Russian author is Tolstoy	Мне нра́вятся Турге́нев и Достое́вский, но мой люби́мый ру́сский а́втор — Толсто́й

More emphasis still may be expressed by the use of the pronoun э́то and the dash:

It's an ugly word, Communism	Коммуни́зм — э́то некраси́вое сло́во

In speech a slight pause would correspond to the dash in writing.

325. (i) Есть and (theoretically) суть may be used if the English verb has a strong sense of definition. Суть for all practical purposes is now never used and есть is found, as a defining verb, with both singular and plural subjects and for all three persons. Even есть, however, is only obligatory when subject and complement are identical:

An order's an order, I'm off	Прика́з есть прика́з — е́ду

In other contexts, есть is only found with any degree of consistency in scientific and philosophical writings:

Everything you have lived and live by is falsehood . . .	Всё то, чем ты жил и живёшь, есть ложь . . . (L. N. Tolstoy)

(ii) There are, however, other circumstances in which the use of есть is desirable for stylistic reasons. Есть is often found in comparisons between *what is* and *what was*, or *what is* and *what should be*:

We should love people as they are and not as they ought to be	Ну́жно люби́ть люде́й как они́ есть, а не как они́ должны́ бы быть
Ivanov was your friend—he is still your friend	Ивано́в был вам друг — он и есть вам друг

Notice also *Go as you are* (i.e. *do not change*) иди́ как есть. Есть may also be used after the expression э́то и (э́то и есть), confirming a statement just made or identifying a person who suddenly appears:

That's life for you! (That's life, that is!)	Э́то и есть жизнь!
There's the man you are speaking about —	Вот челове́к, о кото́ром вы говори́те —
Yes, that's him, all right	Да, э́то он и есть

326. (i) *There is, there are* in the meaning of *there exist(s)* are often translated by есть:

| The earth is a large and splendid place, there are many wonderful people on it | Земля́ велика́ и прекра́сна, есть на ней мно́го чуде́сных люде́й |
| There is a God (God exists) | Бог есть |

Meaning *there is*, *there are*, есть is also commonly used with y and the genitive case, translating *to have*, especially in interrogative sentences:

| Have you any apples?—Yes, we have | Есть (есть-ли) у вас я́блоки? — Есть |

The same kind of question may be expressed more politely in the negative form:

| Have you any matches, please? | Нет-ли у вас спи́чек? |

Notice also the reflexive verb име́ться which may translate *there is (are)* meaning *there exist(s)*:

| There are books on all subjects in the library | В библиоте́ке име́ются кни́ги на все те́мы |

(ii) *To be* with frequentative or habitual meaning is normally translated into Russian by быва́ть, a verb with a normal present tense:

| He is in London every Tuesday | Он быва́ет в Ло́ндоне по вто́рникам |
| There is no smoke without fire | Без огня́ ды́ма не быва́ет |

(iii) Notice that быва́ть is used in negative sentences with indeterminate perfect or pluperfect meaning:

| I seemed never in my life to have been in such desolate places | Каза́лось, о́троду не быва́л я в таки́х пусты́х места́х (Turgenev) |
| Kalinych had once had a wife, whom he feared, but he had never had any children | У Кали́ныча была́ когда́-то жена́, кото́рой он боя́лся, а дете́й не быва́ло во́все (Turgenev) |

(iv) Notice the following idiomatic uses of бывáть:

Suddenly she remembered that the Khripaches, as they took their leave, had not invited them to visit *them*	Вдрýг онá вспóмнила, что Хрипачи́, прощáясь, не звáли их бывáть у себя́ (Sologub)
It sometimes happens *that books are not returned*	Бывáет, что кни́ги не возвращáются
Meetings are held *twice a month*	Заседáния бывáют два рáза в мéсяц

327. (i) The English verb *to be* often defines position or situation. In such expressions Russian uses verbs which are not merely substitutes for the missing parts of быть, but which satisfy the general tendency of the language to define position or situation concretely and precisely. When actual whereabouts is stressed, Russian uses the verb находи́ться (lit. *to be found*) in the same way as French uses *se trouver*:

Where is the inquiry office?	Где нахóдится спрáвочное бюрó?

Находи́ться is also used in abstract contexts when the meaning is literally *to find oneself*:

He is under suspicion of murder	Он нахóдится под подозрéнием в уби́йстве

(ii) Note also the occasional use of the past participle располóжен meaning *to be situated*:

The house is situated near the river	Дом располóжен у реки́

328. Russian frequently uses the three verbs стоя́ть, лежáть, and сидéть, to define position more exactly than English which makes do with the indeterminate *is* and *are*:

(i) Стоя́ть is used, in general, when the position of the object is upright:

The piano is against the wall	Роя́ль стои́т у стены́
The books are on the shelf	Кни́ги стоя́т на пóлке

It is used, also, of the position of ships at sea

The ship is at anchor (is lying at anchor)	Корáбль стои́т на я́коре
Near us lay a cruiser	Бли́зко от нас стоя́л крéйсер

(Note English 'lie' but Russian стоя́ть (lit. *stand*))

Стоя́ть is common, also, in expressions describing weather conditions:

The weather was settled	Погóда стоя́ла хорóшая
The heat was unbearable	Жарá стоя́ла невыноси́мая
There was a complete calm	Стоя́л пóлный штиль
Winter was well set in	Зимá стоя́ла давнó

Note the common expressions:

He was kneeling	Он стоя́л на колéнях
Prices are high	Цéны стоя́т высóкие
There are four routine matters on the agenda	На повéстке дня стоя́т четы́ре очередны́х вопрóса

(ii) Лежáть is used, in general, when the object is laid flat:

The letter is on the table	Письмó лежи́т на столé

Note that the same noun may be used with лежáть or стоя́ть depending upon the position described:

The books are on the floor	Кни́ги лежáт на полу́ (cf. стоя́т на пóлке)
The plates are in the cupboard	Тарéлки стоя́т (лежáт) в шкафу́

But only:

The knives, forks, and spoons are in the sideboard	Ножи́, ви́лки и лóжки лежáт в буфéте

Of a town either verb may be used:

Paris stands on the Seine	Пари́ж лежи́т (стои́т) на Céне

Лежáть is used with reference to illness:

He is in hospital	Он лежи́т в больни́це
He is down with influenza	Он лежи́т с гри́ппом

(iii) Сидѣть is used normally when the person or creature concerned is in a place which he cannot leave or does not wish to leave:

I was at home all day yesterday	Вчера́ я сиде́л до́ма це́лый день
He is in prison	Он сиди́т в тюрьме́
The elephant is in its cage	Слон сиди́т в кле́тке

329. The two verbs явля́ться (яви́ться) and представля́ть (предста́вить) собо́й are frequently used meaning *to be* in sentences where the complement defines the subject, in general terms:

The 'New Tale' which has come down to us in one copy only, and which is an anonymous letter written at the end of December 1610 or the beginning of January 1611 . . . is one of the most important works of the 'Time of Troubles'	„Но́вая По́весть", доше́дшая до нас в еди́нственном спи́ске и *представля́ющая собо́й* подмётное письмо́, напи́санное в конце́ декабря́ 1610 г. и́ли в нача́ле января́ 1611 г. ... *явля́ется* одни́м из значи́тельнейших произведе́ний вре́мени „Сму́ты" (Gudzy)

In many sentences явля́ться, представля́ть собо́й and the dash are interchangeable:

The whale is a large mammal	Кит — большо́е млекопита́ющее (явля́ется, представля́ет собо́й)

330. The verb состоя́ть is common in official language describing a person's occupation or position:

He is on the pay-roll	Он состои́т в спи́ске рабо́чих
He is a Member of Parliament	Он состои́т чле́ном парла́мента

Notice also the reflexive verb состояться (only perfective in meaning) which means *to be* in the sense of *to be held*:

> *There will be a meeting on*   Заседа́ние состои́тся в пя́т-
> *Friday*   ницу

SOME COMMON VERBS AND THEIR TRANSLATION

331. Act. Поступа́ть (поступи́ть) means *to act* in the sense of *to behave*: герои́чески поступи́ть в моме́нт большо́й опа́сности *to act heroically in a moment of great danger*. Вести́ себя́, держа́ть себя́ (or держа́ться), with no perfective forms, mean rather *to conduct oneself*: он де́рзко ведёт себя́ *he behaves impudently*. Де́йствовать is a more abstract word. Of armies, it means *to be in action, to operate*: пехо́та де́йствует се́вернее реки́ *the infantry is in action north of the river*; of individuals *to follow a course of action*:мы дру́жно де́йствовали *we took concerted action*. In these meanings де́йствовать has no perfective form but in the meaning *to act upon, to have an effect on* it has the perfective form поде́йствовать: о́тдых благоприя́тно поде́йствовал на его́ не́рвы *rest had a beneficial effect upon his nerves*.

Игра́ть (сыгра́ть) means *to act* on the stage: сыгра́ть роль Макбе́та (or simply сыгра́ть Макбе́та) *to act the part of Macbeth*. *To act* a play may be either игра́ть (сыгра́ть) or дава́ть (дать) пье́су.

To act as meaning *to carry out the duties of* is usually best translated by служи́ть: служи́ть перево́дчиком *to act as interpreter*. A more formal expression is исполня́ть (исполни́ть) обя́занности which, in signatures, is abbreviated to и. о.: и. о. заве́дующего (исполня́ющий обя́занности) *acting manager*.

332. Ask. Спра́шивать (спроси́ть) means, in general, *to ask for* (information), проси́ть (попроси́ть) means, in general, *to request* (to do something). Compare спроси́ть кого́-нибудь о чём-нибудь *to ask someone about something*;

попроси́ть кого́-нибудь о по́мощи *to ask someone for help* (i.e. *to give help*). Either verb may be used when the meaning is *to ask for something from someone*: спроси́ть (or попроси́ть) каранда́ш у кого́-нибудь *to ask someone for a pencil* (for the use of genitive or accusative after these verbs see para. **32** (ii)). Only спра́шивать (спроси́ть) may be used in such expressions as приди́те к нам и спроси́те меня́ *come to our house and ask for me*.

To ask for trouble is напра́шиваться (напроси́ться) на неприя́тности. *To ask a very high price* is запра́шивать (запроси́ть) о́чень высо́кую це́ну (за- here used as a prefix meaning *to do to excess*). To ask a question is задава́ть (зада́ть) вопро́с

333. Beat. Бить (поби́ть) means primarily *to drub*: он жесто́ко поби́л её *he beat her cruelly*. Notice, however, that when бить means *to hit* (one blow) its perfective form is not поби́ть but уда́рить.

Бить (поби́ть) means also *to beat* (in a sporting contest) and *to beat* (*to break*) *a record*.

Би́ться is used of the heart: его́ се́рдце сла́бо бьётся *his heart is beating feebly*.

Отбива́ть (отби́ть) means *to beat off* (ата́ку—*an attack*), also *to beat time* (отбива́ть такт).

The verb колоти́ть is somewhat colloquial in the meaning of *to drub* but may be used in the sense of *to beat upon*: колоти́ть кулака́ми по столу́ *to beat the table with one's fists*.

334. Catch. The imperfective verb лови́ть may mean simply *to chase*, *to hunt* without necessarily meaning that the pursued object is caught (see para. **226**). Лови́ть ры́бу means *to fish*, *to angle* (*to catch* only in a frequentative sense). *To catch a fish* is пойма́ть ры́бу. An alternative expression meaning *to angle* is уди́ть ры́бу.

Схва́тывать (схвати́ть) may not be used of catching fish but may be used as a synonym of лови́ть (пойма́ть) when its fundamental meaning of *to seize*, *to grab* is appropriate: схвати́ть (пойма́ть) му́ху, бегле́ца *to catch a fly, a fugitive*.

Both of the above verbs, together with a third verb улáвливать (уловúть), may translate *to catch* in various figurative meanings. Поймáть (уловúть) взгляд, схóдство, слýчай, *to catch a glance, a likeness, (to seize) an opportunity.* Поймáть (уловúть, схватúть) смысл слóва *to grasp the meaning of a word.* Улáвливать (уловúть) may only be used figuratively.

Захвáтывать (захватúть) or застигáть (застúгнуть) mean *to catch unawares, to surprise*: меня по дорóге захватúло дождём *I was caught by the rain on the way.* *To catch in the act* is застигáть (застúгнуть) or заставáть (застáть) на мéсте преступлéния. Заставáть (застáть) когó-нибудь дóма means *to catch someone in.*

Notice the verb прививáться (привúться) meaning *to catch on* of a fashion: нóвая мóда не срáзу привилáсь *the new fashion did not catch on at once.*

335. Change. The simple verb менять, which has no perfective form, is used in a wide range of meanings: менять дéньги, одéжду, мнéние, слýжбу *to change money, clothing, an opinion, one's occupation.* The reflexive verb means *to become different*: погóда меняется *the weather is changing*; with an object in the instrumental case *to exchange*: меняться кнúгами с кéм-нибудь *to exchange books with someone.*

There are several common compound verbs which, in special meanings, may be used as alternatives of менять or instead of менять when the meaning is perfective. Обмéниваться (обменяться) домáми с кéм-нибудь *to exchange houses with someone*, размéнивать (разменять) дéньги *to change money* (into smaller units or into foreign currency): емý удалóсь разменять фýнты на францýзскую валюту *he succeeded in changing pounds into French currency.* Both изменяться (изменúться) and переменяться (переменúться) may mean *to become different*: он менялся (изменúлся, переменúлся) в лицé *his expression changed.*

Certain verbs, not based on the root мен-, may translate *to change* in special meanings: переодевáться (переодéться) *to change one's clothes*; раздýмывать (раздýмать) *to change one's mind* (and do nothing); compare передýмывать (передýмать) *to change one's mind* (and do something else); пересáживаться (пересéсть) *to change trains.*

336. Fall. In all meanings in which пáдать has a perfective form, пасть may be used. Пасть only and not упáсть may be used in the following common meanings:

The fortress fell	Крéпость пáла
He fell in battle	Он пал в бúтве

Упáсть, however, may be used as an alternative perfective form in:

He slipped and fell	Он поскользнýлся и упáл (пал)
Suspicion fell on her	Подозрéние упáло (пáло) на неё
Prices fell	Цéны упáли (пáли)

An alternative verb to translate *fall* of prices is понижáться (понúзиться). Either упáсть or пасть may be used in the idiom пáдать (пасть, упáсть) дýхом *to become discouraged, to lose heart.*

Выпадáть (вы́пасть) is commonly used meaning *to fall* of snow or rain after some interval: пóсле дóлгой зáсухи наконéц вы́пал дождь *after a long drought rain has fallen at last.* Notice also the idiom емý вы́пало на дóлю *it fell to his lot to . . .*

Спадáть (спасть) is used meaning *to subside* (of a river), *to abate* (of heat): спáла водá в рекé *the river subsided.*

Попадáть (попáсть) is a very useful verb. The reflexive form попадáться (попáсться) also exists and either the reflexive or non-reflexive form may be used in the expressions попáсть (попáсться) в ловýшку *to fall into a trap*; попáсть (попáсться) на ýдочку *to fall for a bait*; попáсть (попáсться) в плен *to be taken prisoner.*

The non-reflexive verb попадáть (попáсть) often translates English *get*: как попáсть на вокзáл *how does one get to the station?* он попáл в бедý *he got into trouble.* It is also the commonest translation of *to hit* of missiles: пу́ля попа́ла ему́ в плечо́ *the bullet hit him in the shoulder*. Note also: мы не попадём *we won't get in* (of theatre or cinema).

337. Feel. Чу́вствовать (почу́вствовать) means *to feel* an emotion or a physical sensation: *to feel joy—hunger* чу́вствовать ра́дость — го́лод. It may also translate *feel* meaning *to be aware*: я чу́вствую, что он нас не лю́бит *I feel that he does not like us*, or *to appreciate*: он чу́вствует язы́к *he has a feel for the language*.

Although ощуща́ть (ощути́ть) may, like чу́вствовать (почу́вствовать), be used of both physical sensations and emotions, it is used much less frequently of emotions than sensations. The verbal noun ощуще́ние means, in fact, *sensation* and is used in the terms слуховы́е — зри́тельные — ощуще́ния *auditory—visual—sensations*. The adjective ощути́тельный means *perceptible, palpable, appreciable*: ощути́тельная поте́ря *an appreciable loss*.

Испы́тывать (испыта́ть), пережива́ть (пережи́ть) both mean *to experience, to undergo*. Пережива́ть is commonly used of unpleasant experiences: он тяжело́ пережи́л утра́ту ма́тери *he felt the loss of his mother keenly*. The verbal noun испыта́ние means *trial, ordeal*: проходи́ть (пройти́) тя́жкое испыта́ние *to undergo a severe ordeal*.

Щу́пать (пощу́пать) means *to feel, to touch* inquiringly, with the object of finding something out: он щу́пал карма́ны в по́исках спи́чек *he felt in his pocket for matches*. Note the adverb о́щупью *gropingly*: я пробира́лся о́щупью по коридо́ру *I was groping my way along the corridor*.

Notice: есть у вас охо́та танцова́ть? *do you feel like dancing?*

338. Fight. Би́ться (no perfective form in this meaning) means *to fight* in general, with fists or weapons (cf. French *se battre*). It may also mean *to struggle with* (a problem): *we struggled for a long time with this problem* мы до́лго би́лись над разреше́нием э́той пробле́мы.

Боро́ться has the special meaning *to wrestle*. It may also be used, abstractly, meaning *to wrestle with, to struggle with,*

to strive for: боро́ться с закоренéлыми предрассýдками
to struggle with deep-rooted prejudices; боро́ться за бóлее
высóкий ýровень жи́зни *to strive for a higher standard of
living*.

Дра́ться (подра́ться) is often used of fisticuffs, *to scrap*.
Notice the cognate nouns драчýн and дра́ка: он большóй
драчýн *he's always ready for a scrap*; доходи́ть (дойти́) до
дра́ки *to come to blows*.

Сража́ться (срази́ться) is a more bookish word than
those already given: он сража́лся как лев *he was fighting
like a lion*. The cognate noun сражéние means *battle* and
the verb is used most commonly of military operations:
они́ хра́бро сража́лись в защи́ту рóдины *they fought
valiantly in defence of their homeland*. Note also the verb
воева́ть which means *to wage war*: Ита́лия три гóда
воева́ла на сторонé Герма́нии *Italy fought for three years on
Germany's side*.

339. Have. When the sense is one of concrete possession,
the most natural Russian translation is y with the genitive
case: у негó большóй дом *he has a large house*. Имéть, however, may be used, as well as the construction with y, when
the object possessed is abstract. Не моё дéло. Не имéю
приказáния (Katayev) *It's not my business. I have no orders.*
When both subject and object are abstract, only имéть
may be used: смерть короля́ имéла óчень ва́жные по-
слéдствия *the king's death had very important consequences;* пьéса
имéла большóй успéх *the play had a great success*. Имéть only
is used when *have* in English is followed by an infinitive
construction: имéть мýжество отказа́ться *to have the
courage to refuse*.

340. Look. Смотрéть (посмотрéть) and глядéть (погля-
дéть), followed by на and the accusative case, are generally synonymous in the meaning of *to look at*, but смотрéть
is a more narrowly literary word, глядéть more expressive,
a fresh word (Bulakhovsky). Смотрéть is used without на
in a number of special meanings: смотрéть рýкопись *to*

glance at, *to look through a manuscript*, смотре́ть достопри-мечáтельности гóрода *to view the sights of a town*, смотрéть скáчки *to watch the races*, смотрéть пьéсу *to see a play*.

Взгля́дывать (взгляну́ть) на means *to cast a glance at*. Notice укрáдкой взгляну́ть на когó-нибудь *to steal a look at someone*.

To look after in the sense of *to care for* is ухáживать за: ухáживать за больны́м, за ребёнком *to look after an invalid, a child*. Notice also ухáживать за сáдом *to tend a garden*. The verb присмáтривать (присмотрéть) за means *to keep an eye on, to supervise*: присмáтривать за ребёнком в отсу́тствие родѝтелей *to look after a child in the parents' absence*; присмáтривать за рабóтой *to supervise work*. This verb may also mean *to look out for* in the sense of *to look for*: присмáтри-ваем дом *we are looking out for a house*. In this meaning, the perfective form means *to find*.

To look like (to resemble) may be translated in various ways. The verb вы́глядеть (cf. German *aussehen*) is imper-fective despite the stress: дом вы́глядит совсéм нóвым *the house looks quite new*. As an alternative имéть вид (cf. French *avoir l'air*) may be used: дом имéет совсéм нóвый вид.

To resemble is normally translated by походи́ть на or быть похóжим на: чертáми лицá он похóдит (похóж) на дя́дю *facially he resembles his uncle*. Notice the colloquial idioms: похóже на дождь (or похóже, что бу́дет дождь) *it looks like rain*; э́то на негó похóже *that's him all over*!; на что вы похóжи *what a sight you are!*

To look on to, to overlook may be translated by смотрéть, гляде́ть, выходи́ть, followed by the prepositions в or на, according to the substantive they govern: óкна смóтрят на (в) двор *the windows overlook the yard*; кóмната выхóдит óкнами на юг *the room looks south*; спáльня гляди́т óкнами на у́лицу *the bedroom overlooks the street*; окнó выхóдит в сад *the window opens on to the garden*.

To look forward to is often best translated by ждать с нетерпéнием (с удовóльствием).

To look up (a word in a dictionary) is искáть; if *to look up*

implies *to find*, then, of course, находи́ть (найти́) is used: я
нашёл э́то сло́во в словаре́ *I looked up this word in a dictionary.*

341. Lose. Теря́ть (потеря́ть) can be used meaning both
to mislay and *to be bereft of*: я потеря́л свою́ кни́гу *I have lost
my book*; девяти́ лет, он потеря́л отца́ *at nine, he lost his
father.* An alternative verb meaning *to be bereft of* is лиша́ть-
ся (лиши́ться) чего́-нибудь: он лиши́лся зре́ния *he lost his
sight*; он лиши́лся ре́чи *he was struck dumb.* *To lose conscious-
ness* may be either лиша́ться чувств or теря́ть созна́ние.

Утра́чивать (утра́тить) is often used with abstract qualities: он утра́тил наде́жду *he lost hope.* It may also mean *to
forfeit*: вы утра́тили права́ на насле́дство *you have forfeited
your rights to the inheritance.* Notice that neither this verb nor
лиша́ться (лиши́ться) may be used in the meaning of *to
mislay.*

The verb пропада́ть (пропа́сть) means *to be missing, to
go missing*: ключи́ всё пропада́ют *keys are always getting lost.*
The perfective form may mean *to be lost* in the sense of *to be
gone for ever*: все мои́ де́ньги пропа́ли *all my money is gone*;
его́ интере́с к ру́сской литерату́ре пропа́л *all his interest in
Russian literature has gone.*

Проигрывать (проигра́ть) means *to lose* of a sporting
contest or a lawsuit: он проигра́л суде́бный проце́сс *he lost
the case.* This verb, as well as теря́ть (потеря́ть), may also
mean *to lose* in the sense of *to suffer*: пье́са мно́го проигра́ла
(потеря́ла) от плохо́й постано́вки *the play lost a lot through
bad presentation.*

342. Make. Заставля́ть (заста́вить) means *to make* in the
sense of *to oblige* or *to compel*: дождь заста́вил нас оста́ться
до́ма *we were obliged by the rain to stay at home*; оте́ц заста́вил
его́ просиде́ть це́лый ве́чер над зада́чей *his father made
him spend the whole evening over the problem.*

To make meaning *to manufacture* may be translated by
фабрикова́ть (no perfective), although this verb is more
commonly used in the metaphorical sense of *to fabricate*
(ложь, ба́сни, &c.). In this meaning the perfective is

сфабриковáть. Synonyms of фабриковáть meaning *to manufacture*, with both imperfective and perfective forms, are вырабáтывать (вы́работать), выде́лывать (вы́делать), and изготовля́ть (изготóвить). Notice the figurative use of вырабáтывать in: егó дрýжба с Гóрьким вы́работала из негó прекрáсного писáтеля *his friendship with Gor'ky made a splendid writer of him*.

To make meaning *to cook* is готóвить or приготовля́ть (приготóвить): ктó готóвит зáвтрак? *who is making the breakfast?* Of liquids or liquid foods, however, варúть (сварúть) is used: варúть кóфе, суп, *to make coffee, soup*.

To make a speech is произносúть (произнестú) речь.

Notice the expression: из неё вы́йдет хорóшая пианúстка *she will make a good pianist*.

343. Move. Подвигáть (подвúнуть) is followed by an object in the accusative case when the meaning is *to transfer from one place to another*: подвúньте э́тот стул, пожáлуйста *move this chair, please!* If a movement in a definite direction is meant then передвигáть (передвúнуть) is preferable: роя́ль нáдо передвúнуть из э́той кóмнаты в сосе́днюю *the piano should be moved from this room into the next*.

Двúгать (двúнуть) is followed by an object in the instrumental case when the meaning is *to stir, to make a movement with*. This construction is especially common with parts of the body: он двúнул ногóй *he moved his leg*.

Сдвигáть (сдвúнуть) may mean either *to move from* or *to move together*. In the first meaning, it is often followed by the expression с мéста where English says simply *move*: э́тот стол тяжёл, не сдвúнешь с мéста *this table is heavy, you'll never move it*. Notice the use of the reflexive verb in вопрóс не сдвúнулся с мéста *the discussion made no headway*. It is usually clear from the context whether сдвигáть (сдвúнуть) means *to move from* or *to move together*: сдвúньте э́ти два столá посередúне кóмнаты *move these two tables together in the centre of the room*. Notice сдвигáть (сдвúнуть) брóви *to knit the brows*.

To move to anger, tears, laughter is usually best translated by the verb вызывáть (вы́звать) followed by y and the genitive case of the person concerned: измéна вы́звала у негó бéшенство *the betrayal moved him to furious anger.* An alternative expression meaning *to move to tears* is трóгать (трóнуть) когó-нибудь до слёз. Трóгать (трóнуть) may also mean simply *to move*: он был глубокó трóнут аплодисмéнтами *he was deeply moved by the applause.*

To move off, to draw out of a train is трóгаться (трóнуться): пóезд трóнулся *the train started.*

To move house is normally translated by переезжáть (переéхать): мы переéхали на нóвую квартúру *we have moved into a new flat.*

To move in good society is вращáться в хорóшем óбществе. Ходúть/идтú (пойтú) are used of chessmen, followed by the instrumental of the piece moved: он пошёл пéшкой *he moved his pawn.*

344. Pay. Платúть (заплатúть) is followed by the dative of the person paid and за and the accusative of the object paid for: мы заплатúли мясникý за мя́со *we have paid the butcher for the meat.* Notice платúть (заплатúть) по счёту *to settle the account.*

The verb оплáчивать (оплатúть) may be used transitively meaning *to pay for.* Being a transitive verb, it is often very useful in passive constructions: хорошó оплáчиваемая рабóта *well-paid work*; откры́тка с оплáченным отвéтом *a reply-paid postcard.* Notice also мы оплатúли убы́тки *we made good the losses*; кто оплáтит расхóды? *who will meet the expenses?*

Отплáчивать (отплатúть) means *to pay back* and is often used figuratively with an instrumental complement: емý отплатúли той же монéтой *he was paid in his own coin*; нýжно отплатúть добрóм за зло *one must return good for evil.*

Выплáчивать (вы́платить) means *to pay off debts.* *To pay off (to dismiss) workmen* is рассчúтывать (рассчитáть) рабо́чих. Notice also я наконе́ц рассчита́лся с ним *I have at last got even with him.*

To pay meaning *to be profitable* is translated by окупа́ться (окупи́ться): преступле́ние не окупа́ется *crime doesn't pay.*

345. Permit. Позволя́ть (позво́лить) кому́-нибудь сде́-лать что́-нибудь means *to permit (to allow) someone to do something.* This verb has wider meanings than simply *to give permission*: здоро́вье не позво́лило ему́ е́хать *his health did not permit him to go*; наско́лько позволя́ют обстоя́тельства *as far as circumstances permit.*

Разреша́ть (разреши́ть) is more official in tone, *to authorize, to permit*: не разреши́ли постано́вки пье́сы *the performance of the play was not authorized*; кури́ть разреша́ется *smoking permitted.* Дозволя́ть (дозво́лить) is also an official word: дозво́лено цензу́рой *authorized by the censorship.*

Допуска́ть (допусти́ть) means *to admit*, followed by до and the genitive, or к and the dative: меня́ не допуска́ли до экза́менов *I was not admitted to the examinations.* This verb may also mean *to tolerate*: э́того нельзя́ допуска́ть *that cannot be tolerated.*

346. Put/Place. Класть (положи́ть) is used meaning *to put (to lay)* in contexts where лежа́ть translates *to be (to lie)* (see para. **328** (ii)): положи́те письмо́ на стол *put the letter on the table*; положи́ли больно́го в больни́цу *they put the sick man in hospital* (cf. больно́й лежи́т в больни́це).

Класть (положи́ть) is also used of putting articles into drawers, suitcases: положи́те мои́ руба́шки в я́щик *put my shirts in the drawer.* Also of adding flavourings to food or drink: не клади́те мне са́хару в чай *do not put any sugar in my tea.* But notice, when the substance added is a liquid: нале́йте мне молока́ в чай, пожа́луйста *put some milk in my tea, please.*

Класть (положи́ть) is also used when the object is not placed in any special position, upright or horizontal: положи́те де́ньги в карма́н *put the money in your pocket.*

Notice класть (положи́ть) коне́ц чему́-нибудь *to put an end to something.*

Ста́вить (поста́вить) is used to translate *to put* in contexts where стоя́ть translates *to be* (*to stand*) (see para. **328** (i)): поста́вьте цветы́ в во́ду *put the flowers in water*; поста́вьте стака́ны на подно́с *put the glasses on the tray*. Notice that like класть (положи́ть), this verb is almost always followed by the accusative of motion although English often says *to put in* (not *into*). But contrast ста́вить (поста́вить) сло́во в вини́тельном падеже́ *to put a word in the accusative case.*

Ста́вить (поста́вить) may translate *to put* in a wider range of meaning than класть (положи́ть):

To put on a play	Ста́вить пье́су
To put to the vote	Ста́вить на голосова́ние
To put up a record	Ста́вить реко́рд
To put in a telephone	Ста́вить телефо́н

Помеща́ть (помести́ть) translates *to place* an order or an insertion in a newspaper: мы помести́ли зака́з у заграни́чной фи́рмы *we placed an order with a foreign firm*; помести́те объявле́ние в газе́ту *put an advertisement in the newspaper.*

Сажа́ть (посади́ть) has various special meanings:

To put in plants	Сажа́ть расте́ния
To put in prison	Сажа́ть в тюрьму́
To place under arrest	Сажа́ть под аре́ст

Compare сиде́ть в тюрьме́ *to be in prison*, сиде́ть под аре́стом *to be under arrest*: сажа́ть (motion) corresponds to сиде́ть (location) as класть to лежа́ть and ста́вить to стоя́ть.

Дева́ть (деть) means *to put* in the sense of *to do with*. It is mainly used with the adverbs куда́, не́куда, туда́: куда́ я дел ту кни́гу *where have I put that book?*; куда́ мне деть э́ти де́ньги? *what shall I do with this money?*.

347. Pull/drag. Дёргать (дёрнуть) means *to pull, to tug*: он дёрнул во́жжи *he tugged the reins*; он дёрнул меня́ за рука́в *he tugged me by the sleeve. To pull a tooth* is вырыва́ть (вы́рвать) зуб.

Тяну́ть (потяну́ть) means *to draw, to haul*: он тяну́л

ребёнка за рука́в к дверя́м *he was drawing the child by the sleeve to the door* (contrast он дёрнул меня́ за рука́в above). Тяну́ть (потяну́ть) на букси́ре means *to have in tow*. Notice the impersonal construction его́ тя́нет домо́й *he is home-sick*.

Таска́ть (abstract verb of motion), and the concrete form тащи́ть (потащи́ть) may mean *to carry*: куда́ вы та́щите э́ти кни́ги? *where are you carrying these books?*, but most often means *to drag*, *to lug along*: ло́шади с трудо́м тащи́ли са́ни *the horses had difficulty in dragging the sleigh*; он потащи́л ведро́ с водо́й от коло́дца к до́му *he lugged the bucket of water from the well to the house*. Notice он е́ле та́щится *he can hardly drag himself along*.

Волочи́ть means *to drag along the ground*, *to trail*, *to draggle*: волочи́ть мешо́к с карто́фелем *to drag a sack of potatoes*. The reflexive form is used intransitively: дли́нное пла́тье у неё волочи́лось по́ полу *her long dress trailed along the floor*. Notice он е́ле воло́чит но́ги *he can hardly put one foot in front of the other*.

348. Run. For бе́гать, бежа́ть (побежа́ть), see para. **284**. As well as the physical action of running, бежа́ть may mean *to escape*, *to take to flight* (in this meaning бежа́ть serves as both imperfective and perfective form): солда́ты бежа́ли *the soldiers took to flight*; он бежа́л из тюрьмы́ *he escaped from prison*. Synonymous with бежа́ть in this meaning is убега́ть (убежа́ть).

Избега́ть (избежа́ть) may mean either *to avoid* (*to escape*) or *to shun*: он избега́ет всех ста́рых друзе́й *he shuns all his old friends*; как он избежа́л наказа́ния? *how did he escape punishment?* Notice that this verb is followed by the genitive case.

Спаса́ться (спасти́сь) means *to take refuge from* (cf. French *se sauver*): мы спасли́сь от дождя́ в амба́ре *we took refuge from the rain in a barn*. Notice он едва́ спа́сся *he had a narrow escape*.

To run of a road is тяну́ться: доро́га тя́нется вдоль реки́

the road runs along the river. To wind is извива́ться: тропи́нка
извива́ется в го́ру *the path winds up the hill.*

Струи́ться means *to run in streams*: пот струи́лся по его́
щека́м *perspiration ran in streams down his cheeks*; дождь
струи́лся по стёклам *rain was streaming down the window-
panes*. Notice also ли́ться: вино́ ли́лось реко́й *wine ran like
water*.

Notice:

Our tea has run out	У нас вы́шел чай
The play ran for two years	Пье́са шла два го́да
The novel ran into five edi-tions	Рома́н вы́держал пять из-да́ний
Who runs the business?	Кто ведёт де́ло?

349. Shine. Блесте́ть (semelfactive блесну́ть) means *to
glitter* when the glitter is steady and sustained: не всё то
зо́лото, что блести́т *all that glitters is not gold*; or *to sparkle*
(of eyes, the lights of a town). This verb may be used
metaphorically and in such contexts its present-tense form
in -щешь, -щет, is the more usual: он бле́щет остроу́мием
he is brilliantly witty. The semelfactive verb may mean *to
flash*: блесну́ла мо́лния *the lightning flashed*; used metaphorically, it refers to a single occasion: в свое́й ре́чи он
блесну́л красноре́чием *his speech was brilliantly eloquent*. It
may have a pejorative meaning *to show off*: он лю́бит
блесну́ть остроу́мием *he likes to show off his wit*.

Notice the expressions: у него́ блесну́ла мысль *an idea
flashed across his mind*. The present participle active of
блесте́ть translates the English adjective *brilliant*: блестя́-
щий успе́х *a brilliant success*.

Блиста́ть is used, almost exclusively, with metaphorical
meaning: блиста́ть мо́лодостью, красото́й *to be radiant
with youth, beauty*. It may be used as a synonym of блесте́ть
in the meaning of *to be brilliant, to stand out*. Notice он
блиста́л свои́м отсу́тствием *he was conspicuous by his absence*.

Свети́ть means *to shine* of a light-giving body (sun,
moon, stars). The reflexive form свети́ться also means *to*

shine in this sense, but less brightly (moon, stars, lights in a window). Светиться is also used metaphorically of emotions expressed in the eyes: глаза́ у неё свети́лись от ра́дости *her eyes shone with joy*.

Сверка́ть (semelfactive сверкну́ть) means *to glitter* when the glitter is intermittent (cf. блесте́ть above): бриллиа́нты сверка́ли *the diamonds were glittering*; *to flash*: меч сверка́л в его́ руке́ *the sword flashed in his hand*; *to sparkle* (of water in the sunlight), *to twinkle* (of bright stars). The semelfactive verb may be used, like блесну́ть, of lightning; сверкну́ла мо́лния *the lightning flashed*. Notice also он сверкну́л глаза́ми *his eyes flashed fire*.

Сия́ть means *to shine brightly* (sun, moon, stars); notice the verbal noun in со́лнечное сия́ние *the sun's radiance*. This verb may also be used metaphorically: он сия́л от ра́дости *he was beaming with delight*.

350. Sit. Сиде́ть means *to be sitting* (на сту́ле *on the chair*). Сади́ться (сесть) means *to sit down* (на стул *on the chair*; notice the accusative of movement).

Приса́живаться (присе́сть) means *to sit down for a moment*: он почу́вствовал уста́лость и присе́л на край сту́ла *he felt tired and sat down for a moment on the edge of the chair*. Присе́сть is also the perfective form of приседа́ть which may mean either *to curtsy* or (followed by на ко́рточки) *to squat*.

Уса́живаться (усе́сться) means *to sit down to, to settle down to*: он усе́лся писа́ть пи́сьма *he settled down to write letters*.

Проси́живать (просиде́ть) means *to sit for a length of time*: мы просиде́ли це́лую ночь у посте́ли больно́го отца́ *we sat up all night with our sick father*. Notice also the transitive meaning *to wear out the seat*: я просиде́л брю́ки *I've worn the seat out of my trousers*.

Выси́живать (вы́сидеть) *to sit through*: мы с трудо́м вы́сидели до конца́ конце́рта *we had difficulty in sitting through the concert*. Notice the transitive meaning in выси́живать цыпля́т *to hatch out chicks*.

To sit an examination is сдавáть экзáмен. The perfective сдать means *to pass* (an examination). *To pass an examination* may also be вы́держать экзáмен.

Приподнимáться (приподня́ться) в постéли translates *to sit up in bed*.

351. Stand. Стоя́ть means *to be standing* (в углу́ *in the corner*). Also *to stand still*.

Time does not stand still	Врéмя не стои́т
The clock has stopped	Часы́ стоя́т

Станови́ться (стать) means *to place oneself in a standing position*: он стал на цы́почки *he stood on tiptoe*; нам пришлóсь стать в óчередь *we had to stand in a queue* (cf. the accusative here with the prepositional after стоя́ть). Notice стать на я́корь *to come to anchor* and compare стоя́ть на я́коре *to be standing at anchor*; also стать на колéни *to kneel down* and стоя́ть на колéнях *to be kneeling down*. Sometimes the past tense of стать with resultative meaning, may be used as a synonym of the present tense of стоя́ть:

The clock has stopped	Часы́ стáли
Work is held up	Рабóта стáла

Вставáть (встать) means *to stand up*, also *to get up* (i.e. *to get out of bed*), often followed by с постéли. Notice also он встáл из-за столá *he got up from table*. This verb may also mean *to take up a position* somewhere, without necessarily meaning *to stand up*: он встáл на брезéнт *he stood on the tarpaulin*. Notice also the metaphorical use of the verb in он наконéц встáл на путь и́стинный *he at last began to follow his true path in life*.

Вставáть (встать) may also mean *to rise* of mountains, obstacles, problems: пéред нáми встáли леси́стые гóры *wooded mountains rose before us*; встáл вопрóс *the question arose*.

To stand meaning *to endure* may be translated by выдéрживать (вы́держать) or выноси́ть (вы́нести): горожáне вы́держали дóлгую осáду до тогó, как сдáться *the townsfolk stood a long siege before surrendering*. Notice э́тот дом выдержал проверку временем *this house has stood the test of time*; корабль выдержал бурю *the ship weathered the storm*. Выносить (вынести) means rather *to endure* in the sense of *to bear* or *to tolerate*: он плохо выносит жару *he does not stand the heat well*; я не выношу лицемеров *I cannot stand hypocrites*. The verb терпеть may also be used to translate *to stand* in this sense.

To stand of a situation is обстоять: как обстоит дело теперь? *how do matters stand now?*

352. Stop. Останавливаться (остановиться) means *to stop* of something in motion, *to halt, to pull up*: машина остановилась *the car pulled up*. Notice the metaphorical он не остановился перед убийством *he did not stop at murder*. This verb has certain special meanings: мы остановились в лучшей гостинице *we put up at the best hotel* (cf. French *descendre*): не нужно останавливаться на трудностях *it is unnecessary to dwell on the difficulties*. The non-reflexive verb means *to bring to a stop*. Notice он остановил взгляд на стуле в углу *his gaze came to rest on the chair in the corner*.

Приостанавливаться (приостановиться) means *to pause*: она приостановилась у окна магазина *she paused for a moment at the shop window*; дело приостановилось *the matter is temporarily at a standstill*. (Cf. the meaning of the prefix при- in присаживаться (присесть).) The non-reflexive verb has a number of special meanings:

The censor held up the performance of the play	Цензор приостановил пьесу
It was impossible to check the spread of the epidemic	Нельзя было приостановить распространение эпидемии
They granted a stay of execution	Они приостановили смертную казнь

Прекращаться (прекратиться) means *to stop, to cease*, in the sense of *to break off, to come to a sudden or unexpected stop*: их дружба тут же прекратилась *their friendship ended then and there*. The non-reflexive verb means *to break off* in прекращать (прекратить) сношения *to break off relations*; прекращение военных действий means *cessation of hostilities*.

Переставать (перестать) also means *to cease* but without the sense of suddenness or unexpectedness of the verb above. Compare дождь вдруг прекратился *the rain suddenly stopped* with дождь перестал *the rain stopped* (i.e. petered out). Переставать (перестать) is the verb most commonly used before an infinitive although прекращать (прекратить) is possible: он перестал говорить *he stopped talking*.

To stop in the sense of *to prevent* is translated by мешать (помешать): это не мешало мне идти *that did not stop me going*.

353. Think. Думать о may mean *to think about* (French *penser à*) or *to think of* (French *penser de*): я часто думаю о вас *I often think of you*, что вы думаете о нём? *what do you think of him?* A special perfective form of this verb exists, подумать, meaning *to think for a while*: подумайте хорошенько *think well!* Notice also the now frequently used impersonal думается which is an alternative to кажется in the sense of *I think, it seems to me*: мне думается, ему не выздороветь *I do not think he will recover*.

The perfective verb вздумать means *to take it into one's head*: что вы вздумали сказать это? *what made you say that?* The reflexive verb is used impersonally with the same meaning: ему вздумалось бежать *he took it into his head to run away*.

Обдумывать (обдумать) means *to turn over in one's mind, to ponder*, e.g. план, решение *a plan, a decision*.

Придумывать (придумать) means *to devise, to think up* (выход из трудного положения *a way out of a difficult situation*).

Мыслить means *to think* referring to the process of abstract thought: я жить хочу, чтоб мыслить и страдать (Pushkin) *I wish to live in order to think and suffer*. Размышлять (размы́слить—rarely used) о чём-нибудь means *to reflect upon something* (notice the preposition).

Соображáть (сообрази́ть) means *to consider, to weigh up*: я до́лго соображáл, éхать ли мне и́ли нет *I considered for a long time whether I should go or not.* Notice по семéйным соображéниям *for family reasons (considerations).* The perfective form of this verb often means *to grasp*: он срáзу сообрази́л, в чём дéло *he grasped the point at once.*

Счита́ть (счесть) *to consider* may be followed either by the instrumental case or by за and the accusative case: я не счита́ю его́ у́мным человéком (за у́много человéка) *I do not consider him a clever man.*

354. Turn, spin. Вертéть means *to spin* when followed by the accusative case: вертéть колесó *to spin a wheel.* Followed by the instrumental case *to whirl, to twist*: он шёл, вертя́ трóстью *he walked along, twirling his cane.* Notice also: онá вéртит им, как хóчет *she twists him round her little finger.*

Враща́ть means *to revolve* (transitive), *to rotate*: враща́ть колесó *to rotate a wheel.* The reflexive forms of both вертéть and враща́ть translate the English intransitive verbs: волчóк вéртится *the top is spinning*; земля́ враща́ется вокру́г своéй óси *the earth rotates on its own axis.*

Notice the figurative meanings of these verbs: разговóр вертéлся вокру́г войны́ *the conversation turned on the war*; он дéсять лет враща́лся в óбществе престу́пников *for ten years he moved among criminals.*

Повора́чивать (поверну́ть), alternative imperfective form повёртывать, may mean *to turn* either transitively or intransitively: он поверну́л кран—ключ в замкé *he turned the tap—the key in the lock*; он поверну́л напра́во — за у́гол *he turned right—the corner.* The reflexive verb may translate the English intransitive verb in the sense of *to turn oneself bodily*: он поверну́лся лицóм ко мне *he turned to face me,* but not in the sense of changing direction in motion (this must be translated by the non-reflexive form as above).

To turn inside out is вывора́чивать (вы́воротить) наиз-на́нку. *To turn up* (= *to present itself*) is подвёртываться (подверну́ться): подверну́лся слу́чай пое́хать в Росси́ю *the chance to go to Russia turned up.*

To turn on—the light, the engine is включа́ть (включи́ть) свет — мото́р; *to turn off* is выключа́ть (вы́ключить). *To turn on the tap* is открыва́ть (откры́ть) кран (cf. поверну́ть кран above, simply *to turn the tap*). *To turn off the tap* is закрыва́ть (закры́ть) кран.

To turn out may be ока́зываться (оказа́ться): оказа́лось, что мы учи́лись в той же шко́ле *it turned out that we went to the same school*; or выходи́ть (вы́йти): таки́е де́ти ча́сто выхо́дят престу́пниками *such children often turn out criminals*; or выдава́ться (вы́даться): по́сле дождли́вого у́тра, день вы́дался хоро́шим *after a wet morning, it turned out a fine day.*

355. Walk. *To take a walk* is идти́ (пойти́) гуля́ть. Notice that гуля́ть may also mean simply *to be out of doors, to take fresh air*, гуля́йте бо́льше *take more fresh air.*

The reflexive verb прогу́ливаться (прогуля́ться) may mean *to stroll about*: он пошёл прогуля́ться по па́рку *he went for a stroll in the park.* The non-reflexive verb прогу́ливать (прогуля́ть) may mean *to absent oneself from work, to play truant*: меха́ник прогу́ливал уже́ четвёртый день *the mechanic had not been at work for three days.*

The verb прогу́ливать (without perfective form) means *to take for a walk*: я сего́дня у́тром прогу́ливал дете́й *I took the children for a walk this morning.*

356. Work. Рабо́тать and труди́ться are largely synonymous; both may refer to mental and/or physical work: рабо́тать (труди́ться) над кни́гой *to be working on a book.* Труди́ться, however, may be used stylistically to translate *toil*: мужи́к, трудя́сь, не ду́мает, что си́лы надорвёт (Nekrasov) *the peasant, as he toils, does not think that he will overtax his strength.*

Занима́ться may also mean *to work* especially with reference to mental or artistic work: занима́ться медици́ной *to practise medicine*; студéнты усéрдно занимáются *the students are working hard.*

Обрабáтывать (обрабóтать) means *to work up, to develop, to treat*: он три недéли обрабáтывал статью *he took three weeks to work up the article.* Notice also обрабáтывать (обрабóтать) стиль *to perfect one's style.* This verb may also mean *to work the soil*—зéмлю), *to process* (*material*—материáл).

Отрабáтывать (отрабóтать) свой проéзд means *to work one's passage.*

Разрабáтывать (разрабóтать) рудни́к means *to work a mine.* The perfective verb may mean *to work out*: рудни́к разрабóтан *the mine is worked out.* Notice also разрабóтать вопрóс *to exhaust a theme.*

Сотрýдничать с кéм-нибудь над чéм-нибудь means *to collaborate with someone on something*: сотрýдничать в журнáле *to contribute to a magazine.*

To work a miracle is твори́ть (сотвори́ть) чýдо: он сотвори́л чудесá *he worked wonders.*

IV

THE ADVERB, THE CONJUNCTION

THE FORMATION OF ADVERBS

Adverbs formed from adjectives and participles

357. The most numerous of Russian adverbs are those which coincide in form with the short neuter adjective:

Бо́йко	*Smartly*	Изли́шне	*Excessively*
Не́жно	*Tenderly*	Неуклю́же	*Awkwardly*
Ло́вко	*Skilfully*	И́скренне (or искренно)	*Sincerely*

Note that the adverbs кра́йне (*extremely*) and сре́дне (*moderately*) have no corresponding adjectival neuter short forms.

358. Russian adverbs are also formed from past participles passive and present participles active. These adverbs often correspond to English adverbs in *-edly* and *-ingly* respectively:

Взволно́ванно	*Excitedly*
Незаслу́женно	*Undeservedly*
Неожи́данно	*Unexpectedly*
Угрожа́юще	*Threateningly*
Предостерега́юще	*Warningly*
Одобря́юще	*Approvingly*

359. Also numerous are the Russian adverbs in -и́чески, -ски, and -цки, formed from adjectives in -и́ческий, -ский, and -цкий:

Логи́чески	*Logically*	Дру́жески	*Amicably*
Дура́цки	*Foolishly*		

It will be observed that the adverbs in -и́чески, like the

adjectives from which they are formed, have predominantly qualitative meaning: ритми́чески *rhythmically* (i.e. with the quality of rhythm). The adverbs in -ски and -цки, on the other hand, like their corresponding adjectives, refer predominantly to persons: бра́тски *fraternally* (i.e. like a brother). This sense of comparison may be strengthened in Russian by the addition of the prefix по-:

Like a boy, as a boy would do	По-мальчи́шески
Like a fisherman, as a fisherman would do	По-рыба́цки

The choice of the form with or without по- will, most often, be determined by stylistic rather than semantic factors, since there is almost no difference in meaning, in Russian as in English, between, e.g. дура́цки *foolishly* and по-дура́цки *like a fool*. One form or the other, in both languages, may seem preferable according to the context.

360. Adverbs in -ски, formed from adjectives of nationality, are combined with the prefix по-, to mean *in Russian* (по-ру́сски), *in English* (по-англи́йски), &c.:

He spoke in French	Он говори́л по-францу́зски

Notice that *in Latin* is по-латы́ни. These adverbs may also mean *in the Russian* (&c.) *style*:

Sturgeon à la russe	Осетри́на по-ру́сски
Turkish coffee	Ко́фе по-туре́цки

361. Adverbs are also formed with the prefix по- (forming one unhyphenated word) from adjectives denoting time, number, or sequence—English *by*:

Подённо	*By the day*	Поочерёдно	*By turns*
Поме́сячно	*By the month*	Посме́нно	*By shifts*
He is paid monthly		Ему́ пла́тят поме́сячно	

362. Adverbs, with special meanings, are formed from various (now otherwise defunct) case-forms of the short

adjectives, combined in a single word, witl prepositions:

За meaning *while yet* (short accusative form):

За́темно *Before daybreak* (i.e. *while yet dark*)
За́светло *Before dark* (i.e. *while yet light*)
За́живо *Alive* (i.e. *while yet alive*)

Buried alive Погребённый за́живо

Notice also the adverbs за́мертво and за́просто:

He fell as if dead	Он упа́л за́мертво
She dropped in on us unan-nounced	Она́ зашла́ к нам за́просто

До (short genitive form):

These adverbs in Russian often correspond to a simple
English adjective, used adverbially, in such expressions as:

To wipe dry	Вытира́ть (вы́тереть) до́суха
To rub the skin red	Натира́ть (натере́ть) ко́жу до́крас-на́
To strip naked	Раздева́ть (разде́ть) до́гола
Red (white) hot	До́красна́ (до́бела́) раскалённый

Note also

To eat one's fill	Наеда́ться (нае́сться) до́сыта
To clear one's plate	Съеда́ть (съесть) всё до́чиста

Из (short genitive form):

Useful are adverbs of colour which combine with adjectives of colour to form such compound adjectives as:

И́зжелта-кра́сные цветы́ *Yellowish-red flowers*
И́ссиня-чёрные во́лосы *Raven-black* (i.e. *blue-black*) *hair*
И́ссера-голуба́я кра́ска *Greyish-blue paint*

Note also и́скоса: смотре́ть (посмотре́ть) на кого́-нибудь
и́скоса *to throw a side-long glance at somebody*; and издалека́:
го́род ви́ден издалека́ *the town is visible from a distance*;
начина́ть (нача́ть) разгово́р издалека́ *to broach a subject
cautiously*.

C (short genitive form):

Many of these adverbs describe the reason or motive for an action:

To act in a fit of passion (in the heat of the moment)	Поступа́ть (поступи́ть) сгоряча́
To collide with the wall through short-sightedness	Ната́лкиваться (натолкну́ться) на сте́ну со́слепа
To lose one's way when drunk	Заблуди́ться спья́на

(no imperfective in this sense)

To fall into a trap unawares	Попада́ть (попа́сть) в западню́ спроста́
To act with a hidden design (disingenuously)	Де́йствовать неспроста́

The adverb слегка́ may translate *slightly*:

Slightly reddish hair	Слегка́ рыжева́тые во́лосы
With a slight smile	Слегка́ улыба́ясь

or *lightly*:

To touch lightly upon a subject	Слегка́ каса́ться (коснуться) те́мы

По (short dative form):

To divide equally	Разделя́ть (раздели́ть) по́ровну

363. (i) Russian adverbs may also be formed from a combination of prepositions and the case-forms of the long adjective. The commonest of these are made up of по- and the form of the dative singular masculine and translate the English *in (such and such) a way*:

По-но́вому	*In a new way*
По-ра́зному	*Differently*
По-зи́мнему	*In the winter style*
По-друго́му (по-ино́му)	*Differently*

To turn over a new leaf	Начина́ть (нача́ть) жить по-но́вому
Dressed in one's winter things	Оде́тый по-зи́мнему
Matters were turning out rather differently for the Germans	Не́сколько по-ино́му скла́дывались дела́ с не́мцами
Everyone would give a different answer	Ка́ждый отвеча́л по-ра́зному

По-ра́зному and по-друго́му (по-ино́му) are not interchangeable: по-ра́зному means *each differently* whereas по-друго́му means literally *otherwise, in a different way*; compare the adjectives ра́зный (ра́зного ро́да *of different kinds*) and друго́й (в друго́м ме́сте *elsewhere*).

(ii) Note the following adverbs of this group, which are unhyphenated:

As before	Попре́жнему
Apparently	Повиди́мому
To no purpose	Попусто́му

(iii) These adverbs are often found in negative constructions which may translate idiomatically the English *for* in indirect comparisons:

On a rainy morning, cold for summer . . .	Дождли́вым, не по-ле́тнему холо́дным, у́тром . . .

(iv) The dative singular of the 1st and 2nd person possessive pronouns also combines with по- to form adverbs, по-мо́ему, по-тво́ему, по-на́шему, по-ва́шему (note the stress of по-мо́ему, по-тво́ему). These adverbs have two meanings, firstly *in my—our—your opinion*, secondly *as I—we —you wish/think best*:

In my opinion, that is not true	По-мо́ему, э́то не пра́вда
I shall do as you wish	Я сде́лаю по-ва́шему
Have it your own way	Будь (пусть бу́дет) по-ва́шему

Where appropriate, по-своему is used meaning *as I—we— you wish/think best*:

> *I shall do as I think best*   Я сделаю по-своему

По-своему may also mean *in its own way*:

> *Every unhappy family is un-*   Каждая несчастливая семья
> *happy in its own way*   несчастлива   по-своему
> (L. N. Tolstoy)

364. Adverbs are also formed with по- and the nominative/accusative plural form of possessive adjectives in -ий: these adjectives refer predominantly to animals: собачий (*a dog's . . .*), волчий (*a wolf's . . .*). The adverbs thus formed may be compared with those in -ски, which refer predominantly to persons (para. **359**). Adverbs in -ьи, however, may not be used without по-:

> *He is as cunning as a fox*   Он по-лисьи лукав
> *When in Rome, do as the*   С волками жить, по-волчьи
> *Romans do*   выть

A common adverb of this group which does not refer to an animal is по-человечьи, which is synonymous with по-человечески *humanly, like a human being*:

> *I see how super-humanly*   Вижу, какой он не по-
> *clever and awesome he is*   человечьи умный и жут-
> кий (Gor'ky)

These adverbs will also be met in the dative singular form (по-собачьему) but less commonly than in the form of the nominative plural.

365. Several useful adverbs are formed with the preposition в and the feminine accusative form of the long adjective:

> *To scatter in all directions*   Бежать врассыпную
> *To deliver by hand*   Доставлять (доставить) вручную
> *To fight at close quarters*   Биться врукопашную
> *(hand-to-hand)*
> *To play chess blindfold*   Играть в шахматы вслепую

Adverbs formed from nouns

366. Some adverbs are simply the instrumental singular forms of nouns:

Да́ром	*Gratis*	Ры́сью	*At a trot*
Ря́дом	*Side by side*	Ша́гом	*At a walk*
За́лпом	*At a gulp*		

Both ры́сью and ша́гом, as nouns, may be combined with adjectives:

To move at a smart trot	Идти́ (пойти́) бо́йкой ры́сью
To walk at a leisurely pace	Идти́ (пойти́) ти́хим ша́гом

The adverb sometimes differs from the instrumental form proper in stress:

Верх	instr. Ве́рхом	but Верхо́м	*On horseback*
Бег	,, Бе́гом	,, Бего́м	*At the double*
Круг	,, Кру́гом	,, Круго́м	*Round about*

An adverb кру́гом also exists but it is used in one expression only:

(*My*) *thoughts are in a whirl*	Голова́ (у меня́) идёт кру́гом

The noun corresponding to certain adverbs of this group no longer exists:

Укра́дкой	*Stealthily*	Босико́м	*Bare-foot*
Ползко́м	*On all fours*	Пешко́м	*On foot*
Гуська́м	*In Indian file*	О́прометью	*Headlong*

367. Certain adverbial expressions consist of a preposition and the appropriate case-form of the noun:

До неузнава́емости	*Beyond recognition*
До невозмо́жности	*To the last degree*
До бо́ли	*Painfully*
Без у́держу	*Unrestrainedly*
На ре́дкость	*Exceptionally*
По о́череди	*In turn*
До безу́мия	*To distraction*

До невероятности	*Unbelievably*
С лишком	*Odd*
В одиночку	*Single-handed (alone)*
He has changed beyond re-cognition	Он изменился до неузнаваемости
A girl of exceptional beauty	На редкость красивая девушка
Thirty odd	Тридцать с лишком

368. Certain adverbs consist of preposition and noun combined in one word:

Вброд:

To ford a river	Переходить (перейти) реку вброд

Вплавь:*

To swim (across) a river	Переправляться (переправиться) через реку вплавь

Вслух *Aloud*:

Reading aloud	Чтение вслух

Впопыхах* (i) *Hastily*, (ii) *in one's haste*:

To do something hastily	Делать (сделать) что-нибудь впопыхах
In my haste I left the book at home	Впопыхах я оставил книгу дома

Взаперти* *In seclusion*:

To live a secluded life	Жить взаперти

Натощак* *On an empty stomach*:

To smoke on an empty stomach	Курить натощак

Напролёт *Through*:

The whole night through	Всю ночь напролёт

Наповал* *Outright*:

To kill outright	Убивать (убить) наповал

Наизна́нку *Inside out*:

    To turn a coat inside out   Вывора́чивать (вы́воротить and вы́вернуть) пальто́ наизна́нку

Исподтишка́* *On the quiet*:

    To laugh up one's sleeve   Смея́ться исподтишка́

Попола́м *In equal quantities*:

    Half-wine, half-water   Вино́ попола́м с водо́й

Подмы́шкой* *Under the arm*:

    To carry under the arm   Носи́ть подмы́шкой

    * means that the component noun no longer exists.

369. In the following expressions, English uses an adjective and noun or, occasionally, a compound noun, where Russian uses an adverb and noun:

Horse-riding	Езда́ верхо́м
Sweetened tea	Чай внакла́дку
A soft-boiled egg	Яйцо́ всмя́тку
A hard-boiled egg	Яйцо́ вкруту́ю
Wholesale and retail trade	Торго́вля о́птом и в ро́зницу
A daydream	Сон наяву́
Bulging eyes	Глаза́ навы́кате
Eternal friendship	Дру́жба наве́ки

370. Note сродни́ and за́мужем, which translate English predicative adjectives:

I am related to him	Я ему́ сродни́
Her daughter is married	Её дочь за́мужем

Gerunds used as adverbs

371. Certain gerunds in -а, -я, may be used adverbially: шутя́ *jokingly, in jest* (note я шутя́ мог бы сде́лать э́то *I could* *do that in my sleep*); не шутя́ *in earnest*; не спеша́ *in a leisurely manner*:

We are now working in earnest	Мы тепе́рь не шутя́ рабо́таем

Some of these gerunds have become part of adverbial expressions:

To be up and doing	Не сиде́ть сложа́ ру́ки
To run like mad	Бежа́ть очертя́ го́лову
To stand gawking	Стоя́ть рази́ня рот

372. Certain gerunds, in becoming adverbs, change their stress:

Gerund	*Adverb*
Молча́ *not speaking*	Мо́лча *silently*
Стоя́ *standing*	Сто́я *upright, on one's feet*
Не хотя́ *not wishing*	Не́хотя *reluctantly*

Contrast:

The boy was repeating his lesson, standing at the blackboard	Ма́льчик отвеча́л уро́к, стоя́ у доски́
He seemed to be asleep on his feet	Он как бу́дто сто́я спал

373. Few gerunds in -а́я, -я́я, may be used as adverbs, but the following negative expressions are useful:

To spend money recklessly	Тра́тить (истра́тить) де́ньги не счита́я
To speak without reflection	Говори́ть (сказа́ть) не ду́мая
To work like a fiend	Рабо́тать не поклада́я рук
Studies go on uninterruptedly	Заня́тия иду́т не прерыва́ясь

Note also the following adverbialized gerunds in -учи, -ючи:

Кра́дучись *Stealthily* (идти́ кра́дучись *to slink along*)

Припева́ючи *Prosperously* (жить припева́ючи *to be in clover*)

Уме́ючи *Skilfully* (обраща́ться с деньга́ми уме́ючи *to handle money skilfully*)

THE COMPARISON OF ADVERBS

374. (i) The comparative forms of adverbs in -o, -e, are the same as those of the corresponding predicative adjectives:

Лу́чше	*Better*	Я́рче	*More brightly*
Мудре́е	*More wisely*		

As with adjectives, the addition of the prefix по- to the comparative adverbs gives the sense *rather (somewhat) more*:

Повы́ше *Somewhat higher*

Certain common adverbs have dual comparative forms:

Ра́нее/ра́ньше	*Earlier*	по́зже/поздне́е	*Later*
Да́лее/да́льше	*Farther*		

По́зже and поздне́е are interchangeable. Ра́нее and да́лее are more bookish in tone than ра́ньше and да́льше. For the alternatives бо́лее/бо́льше, ме́нее/ме́ньше, see para. **435.**

(ii) The superlative degree of adverbs is formed by adding всего́ or всех to the comparative form:

Бо́льше всего́	*More than all things*
Бо́льше всех	*More than all people*

I like skating best of all	Бо́льше всего́ мне нра́вится ката́ться на конька́х
I love him best of all	Я люблю́ его́ бо́льше всех

Лу́чше всего́ may also mean *at one's best*:

I work best in the morning	Я рабо́таю лу́чше всего́ у́тром

Notice the idiomatic meaning of ме́ньше всего́ in:

You're the last person I was expecting to see	Вот кого́ я ожида́л ме́ньше всего́

ADVERBIAL CLAUSES

As   **Time**

375. (i) If the subjects of the main and subordinate clauses
are the same, and the action in the main clause interrupts
that in the subordinate clause introduced by *as*, *as* is usually
best translated into Russian by the use of the present gerund:

When Peredonov arrived home, as he was still taking off his coat, he heard sharp noises coming from the dining-room	Когда́ Передо́нов пришёл домо́й он услы́шал, ещё снима́я пальто́, доноси́вшиеся из столо́вой ре́зкие зву́ки (Sologub)

(ii) If, however, the subjects of the main and subordinate
clauses are different, the above construction becomes impossible and *as* is translated by когда́:

The line of carts stood the whole day at the riverside and moved off as the sun was setting	Обо́з весь день простоя́л у реки́ и тро́нулся с ме́ста, когда́ сади́лось со́лнце (Chekhov)

376. If the actions in both main and subordinate clauses
are momentary and simultaneous, or almost simultaneous,
как is used more commonly than когда́:

As I looked upon the steppe where we had sung so many songs . . . I could hardly hold back my tears	Я как посмотре́ла на степь, где мы сто́лько пе́сен спе́ли . . . е́ле слёзы сдержа́ла (Fadeyev)

377. When *as* means *in proportion as* (French *à mesure que*),
it is translated by по ме́ре того́, как. Usually, in such constructions, the main and subordinate clauses express two
processes, of which one is the result of the other:

His breathing became deeper and easier as his body became rested and cooler	Его́ дыха́ние станови́лось всё глу́бже и свобо́днее по ме́ре того́, как отдыха́ло и охлажда́лось его́ те́ло (Kuprin)

While

378. (i) *While*, designating either the interruption of one action by another, or coincidence over the entire period of two actions, is normally translated by покá or в то врéмя, как. A comma is placed after в то врéмя:

While I was reading, it was snowing	Покá (в то врéмя, как) я читáл, шёл снег
While I was reading, it began to snow	Покá (в то врéмя, как) я читáл, пошёл снег

(ii) When the emphasis in the subordinate clause is not upon the duration of the state, but the state is simply regarded as a stage in time, *while* is most naturally translated by когдá:

The old man died while Matvei was still a child	Старúк ýмер, когдá Матвéй был ещё ребёнком (Korolenko)

379. *While* meaning *whereas* (French *tandis que*) is also translated by в то врéмя как, but usually in this meaning no comma is placed after в то врéмя:

While Shatski's examinations began on 10th March, Kartashov's were due to begin in May	В то врéмя как у Шáцкого экзáмены началúсь с десятого мáрта, у Карташёва онú должнú бúли начáться в мáе (Garin)
One side would suddenly . . . droop while the other would, as it were, become filled with mysterious, life-giving sap	Однá сторонá вдрýг . . . обмякнет, в то врéмя как другáя слóвно нальётся живúтельной, тайнственной влáгой (Furmanov)

Note that the subordinate clause introduced by в то врéмя как may either precede or follow the main clause. There exist two other expressions meaning *while (whereas)*, между тем, как and тогда как, but the subordinate clause which they introduce must follow the main clause:

In a long barrel all the powder ignites before the discharge of the shot, whereas in a short barrel it has not time to explode	В длинной стволине порох воспламеняется весь до вылета дроби, тогда как в короткой он не успевает весь вспыхнуть (S. Aksakov)

Между тем, как (but not тогда как) may, however, like в то время, как be used with strictly temporal meaning and, when it is so used, the clause it heads may stand before or after the main clause.

When

380. (i) If the subjects of the main and subordinate clauses are the same, *when* meaning *after* is usually best translated by the use of the past gerund:

When I have washed, I go downstairs	Умывшись, я иду вниз

(ii) If, however, the subjects are different the above construction becomes impossible and когда or после того, как must be used:

Darya cheered up completely when Dunyasha arrived from the field	Дарья окончательно развеселилась после того, как Дуняша пришла с поля (Sholokhov)

381. (i) For *when* meaning *after*, in certain subordinate clauses, with frequentative meaning, see paras. **187** (ii) and **194** (ii).

(ii) When the action in the main clause is envisaged as following immediately that in the subordinate clause, как in Russian usually translates English *when* implying *as soon as*:

When we have loaded, we will set off	Как погру́зим, так и пое́дем (Katayev)
I shall never get to the fortress, but when day breaks I shall lie down in the wood	Мне не дойти́ до кре́пости, но как рассветёт, ля́гу в лесу́ (L. N. Tolstoy)

For *when* followed by present in English but future in Russian, see para. **201**.

382. *When* in English, introducing a subordinate clause, the action of which interrupts the action in the main clause, is normally translated by когда́:

Markelov's guests were still asleep when a messenger arrived bringing him a letter from his sister	Го́сти Марке́лова ещё спа́ли, когда́ к нему́ яви́лся посла́нец с письмо́м от его́ сестры́ (Turgenev)

If, however, the action in the subordinate clause happens suddenly or unexpectedly, как is used. Как вдруг *when suddenly* is almost a cliché in Russian:

They were turning to go back when suddenly they heard, no longer loud conversation but a shout (As they were turning . . . they suddenly heard . . .)	Они́ повора́чивались, что́бы идти́ наза́д, как вдруг услыха́ли уже́ не гро́мкий го́вор, а крик (L. N. Tolstoy)

383. After certain types of main clause, *when* is translated by как, with or without вдруг:

(i) After negative clauses expressing a distance or a period of time which is interrupted by the action in the subordinate clause:

Nitikin had not even covered two hundred paces when the sound of a piano was heard from the other house also	Не прошёл Ники́тин и двухсо́т шаго́в, как и из друго́го до́ма, послы́шались зву́ки роя́ля (Chekhov)

It was less than half an hour since his arrival, and he was already, with the most good-natured frankness, telling us his life-story (Not half an hour had passed . . .)	Не прошло́ и получа́са с его́ прие́зда, как уж он, с са́мой доброду́шной открове́нностью, расска́зывал свою́ жизнь (Turgenev)

Не успе́л, essentially an expression of time, is also followed by как:

I had not had time to answer when my brother spoke up	Я не успе́л отве́тить, как заговори́л брат

(ii) After main clauses expressing a wish, order, or intention which is frustrated by the action in the subordinate clause. The main clause often contains the particle бы́ло or adverbs уже́, ещё:

I was about to order the horses to be harnessed with all possible speed when suddenly a fearful snow-storm arose	Я веле́л бы́ло поскоре́е закла́дывать лошаде́й, как вдруг подняла́сь ужа́сная мете́ль (Pushkin)
Seeing no one in the cabin, Nekhlyudov was about to leave when a long drawn-out, tearful sigh betrayed the presence of the owner	Не ви́дя никого́ в избе́, Нехлю́дов хоте́л уже́ вы́йти, как протя́жный, вла́жный вздо́х изобличи́л хозя́ина (L. N. Tolstoy)

384. *Whenever, every time* is normally translated into Russian by ка́ждый (вся́кий) раз, когда́. Ка́ждый (вся́кий) раз, как is also occasionally found but, in present-day Russian, much less frequently:

Whenever Istomin was seized by one of his familiar attacks of fever	Ка́ждый раз, когда́ Исто́миным овладева́л знако́мый при́ступ лихора́дки (Kuprin)

For *whenever* with concessive sense (когда́ ни), see para. **411.**

385. In statements in which the English *when* has no antecedent defining a specific state or occasion, когда́ in Russian is preceded by тогда́:

You did not do that even when it was not yet too late	Ты не сде́лала э́того, да́же тогда́, когда́ ещё бы́ло не по́здно (Fadeyev)
A man is happy only when he is single	Челове́к сча́стлив лишь тогда́, когда́ одино́к

386. *Since when* is in Russian с како́го вре́мени or с каки́х пор. *Until when* is до како́го вре́мени, or до каки́х пор:

Until when will you stay?	До каки́х пор вы оста́нетесь?

Before

387. *Before,* introducing a subordinate clause, may be translated by до того́, как, or пре́жде чем, or пе́ред тем, как. До того́, как, and пре́жде чем mean *before* in the sense of *up to the time of, by the time of, earlier than*:

Many accidents happened here before they widened the road	Произошло́ здесь мно́го несча́стных слу́чаев до того́, как расши́рили доро́гу
She will be ready before you arrive	Она́ бу́дет гото́ва, пре́жде чем вы придёте
Why then do you go to bed before you feel sleepy?	Заче́м же вы ложи́тесь в посте́ль, пре́жде чем вам спать хо́чется (Turgenev)

Пе́ред тем, как means *just before*:

He rushed out of the house at the very last moment before the roof fell in	Он вы́скочил из до́ма в са́мый после́дний моме́нт пе́ред тем, как обру́шилась кры́ша (Ilyonkov)

If the subjects of main and subordinate clauses are the same, these conjunctions are normally followed by the infinitive:

Before leaving the house he put out the light	Пре́жде чем вы́йти из до́ма, он вы́ключил свет

After

388. When the subjects of the main and subordinate clauses are the same, *after* is often best translated by the use of the past gerund:

After passing his examinations, he left . . .	Сдав свои́ экза́мены, он уе́хал . . . (Gor'ky)

If the subordinate follows the main clause, it may be strengthened with уже́:

He wrote that after receiving my letter	Он написа́л э́то, уже́ получи́в моё письмо́

If the subjects are different, *after* must be translated by по́сле того́, как:

He went out after I telephoned him	Он вы́шел по́сле того́, как я позвони́л ему́

Since

389. (i) *Since*, introducing a subordinate clause, is normally translated by с тех пор, как:

He had gone perceptibly grey since we parted from him	Он заме́тно поседе́л с тех пор, как мы расста́лись с ним (Turgenev)

(ii) *Since then* is с тех пор or с того́ вре́мени:

A whole lifetime has passed since then	Це́лая жизнь прошла́ с тех пор (Bunin)

(iii) *Since the time that* is translated by с, used as a preposition, and как:

Since the moment when Samara found itself in Czech hands	С моме́нта, как Сама́ра очути́лась во вла́сти че́хов (Fedin)

Until

390. (i) *Until* should always be translated by пока́ не. It is colloquial and sometimes incorrect to omit не:

I cannot undertake anything until she answers me	Я не могу́ предприня́ть ничего́, пока́ она́ не отве́тит мне (L. N. Tolstoy)

Notice, however, the difference between пока́ не and когда́ in:

I waited until the door was opened (period of waiting completed)	Я ждал, пока́ не откры́ли дверь
Then he stood about two hours in the dark passage waiting for the door to be opened (period of waiting incomplete)	Пото́м он стоя́л часа́ два в тёмных сеня́х и ждал, когда́ отопру́т дверь (Chekhov)

Alternatively, the final clause of the second example might have read: пока́ отопру́т дверь or что́бы о́тперли дверь.

(ii) *Not until* is translated by то́лько (когда́):

It was not until the end of the following day that Kirill chose the moment to send Anochka a note	То́лько к концу́ сле́дующего дня Кири́лл вы́брал мину́ту, что́бы посла́ть А́ночке запи́ску (Fedin)
It was not until he turned the corner that I saw him	То́лько когда́ он поверну́л за у́гол я уви́дел его́

Just, as soon as, scarcely (hardly)

391. (i) *To have just* in Russian is то́лько что followed by the perfective past:

I have just arrived in England	Я то́лько что прие́хал в А́нглию

To be just is едва́, лишь, or то́лько, followed by the present tense:

He is just beginning to speak Russian	Он едва́ начина́ет говори́ть по-ру́сски

Occasionally то́лько что is found in this sense:

Dawn is just beginning to tinge the horizon	У́тренняя заря́ то́лько что начина́ет окра́шивать небоскло́н (L. N. Tolstoy)

То́лько, with the perfective past, may mean *just as*:

Just as he entered the room, the lights went out	То́лько он вошёл в ко́мнату, поту́х свет

With успе́л *almost before*:

. . . and then, having undressed, he fell fast asleep almost before his head touched the pillow	. . . и пото́м, разде́вшись, то́лько успе́л положи́ть го́лову на поду́шку, засну́л кре́пким сном (L. N. Tolstoy)

(ii) Placed first in the main clause, то́лько что (or лишь то́лько) means *no sooner . . .*; the subordinate clause may or may not be introduced by как:

He had no sooner entered the room than an argument started	То́лько что он вошёл в ко́мнату, (как) возни́к спор

As soon as is как то́лько (чуть то́лько), sometimes shortened to как (чуть):

As soon as he entered the room . . .	Как (чуть) то́лько он вошёл в ко́мнату . . .
In Saratov, as soon as he arrived, he began to search for the actor Tsvetukhin . . .	В Сара́тове он, как прие́хал, взя́лся разы́скивать актёра Цвету́хина . . . (Fedin)

Scarcely (hardly) is едва́ (едва́ лишь or едва́ то́лько); the subordinate clause may or may not be introduced by как:

He had scarcely come in when the telephone began to ring	Едва́ он вошёл, (как) зазвони́л телефо́н

Place
Where

392. Где is preceded by там in sentences similar to the temporal sentences in which когда is preceded by тогда (see para. **385**):

Where, in the darkness, the eye could no longer distinguish field from sky, a light was flickering	Там, где глаз не мог ужé отличи́ть в потёмках пóле от нéба, я́рко мерцáл огонёк (Chekhov)

Similarly куда́ is preceded by туда́:

I'll go where he goes	Я пойду́ туда́, куда́ и он

Cause, reason
Since

393. *Since* with causal meaning is in Russian так как. The subordinate clause introduced by так как may precede or follow the main clause; if it precedes, the main clause is often introduced by то:

Since he is a poor man, she may not marry him	Так как он бéдный человéк, то онá, быть мóжет, не вы́йдет за негó зáмуж

Why, because

394. (i) Почему́ and отчего́ mean *for what reason?* Зачéм was also used with this meaning in the early nineteenth century but now means only *with what purpose?* Почему́ и or отчего́ и may mean *therefore*:

He was not at home, therefore I left a note	Егó нé было дóма, почему́ я и остáвил запи́ску (Pushkin)

Потому́ и or оттого́ и may mean *and that is why* . . . :

She is jealous of Barbara, and that is why she is withholding the post from me for so long	Онá ревну́ет к Варвáре, потому́ мне и мéста не даёт так дóлго (Sologub)

(ii) Sometimes потому́ and оттого́ stand in the main and что in the subordinate clause. This is a stylistic device used, at need, to balance the sentence. It is often found when, in English, *because* is qualified by an adverb or adverbial phrase, e.g. *only because, perhaps because, for the further reason that* (ещё потому́, что):

The fourth detachment was composed of people, declared to be criminals, only because they were morally above the average level of society	Четвёртый разря́д составля́ли лю́ди потому́ то́лько зачи́сленные в престу́пники, что они́ стоя́ли нра́вственно вы́ше сре́днего у́ровня о́бщества (L. N. Tolstoy)

It is also found when the sentence expresses two or more reasons or consequences:

We are miserable and take a gloomy view of life, because we do not know what work is	Оттого́ нам невесе́ло и смо́трим мы на жизнь так мра́чно, что не зна́ем труда́ (Chekhov)

(iii) When alternative conjectural reasons are given for an action or state, expressed in English by *either . . . or* (*because* understood), Russian uses то ли . . . то ли:

Some gentleman, reading his newspaper and yawning the whole time, either from great weariness or from boredom, cast two or three unpleasant sidelong glances at the boy	Како́й-то господи́н, чита́вший газе́ту и всё вре́мя зева́вший, то ли от чрезме́рной уста́лости, то ли от ску́ки, ра́за два неприя́тно покоси́лся на ма́льчика (Andreyev)
The runner did not return from Remizov: either he must have been killed on the way, or Remizov could offer no help	От Ре́мизова связно́й не верну́лся: то ли он был уби́т по пути́, то ли Ре́мизов не мог ниче́м помо́чь (Simonov)

(iv) *Not that . . . but*, repudiating in English a possible cause of what precedes and giving the real cause, is translated into Russian не то, чтобы . . . но:

Not that I do not like the cinema, but I am tired	Не то, чтóбы я нé был охóтником до кинó, но я устáл

(v) *(All) the less, because, (all) the more, because* are translated into Russian тем мéнее . . . что, тем бóлее . . . что:

His death was regretted all the less because he had been a heartless skinflint	О смéрти егó тем мéнее сожалéли, что он был бессердéчным скупцóм
Spring is all the pleasanter because it follows winter	Веснá тем приятнее, что слéдует за зимóй

(vi) *In that* implying *because* is translated by тем:

He differs from the other boys in that he likes reading	Он отличáется от другúх мáльчиков тем, что любит читáть

Consequence

So that

395. (i) The English *so that*, expressing the result of a pre-stated cause (French *de sorte que* followed by the indicative) is in Russian так что:

The ice has become thin in places, so that skating is dangerous	Лёд местáми стал тóнким, так что катáться на конькáх опáсно

(ii) *So . . . that* may be translated in three ways, так . . . что, настóлько . . . что, до тогó . . . что:

The sack was so heavy that no one could lift it	Мешóк был так тяжёл, что никтó не мог поднять егó

До такóй стéпени (lit. *to such an extent that*) may also be used as a stylistic variant of the three alternatives given:

I could not help smiling, so true was all that	Я не мог не улыбнýться, до такóй стéпени всё э́то бы́ло вéрно (Rozhdestvensky)

396. The sequence of cause and effect, expressed in English by *one has only to . . . for*, is translated into Russian by сто́ит (то́лько) кому́-нибудь . . . как (что́бы):

He has only to forsake Nadezhda Fyodorovna and go to St. Petersburg to obtain all he needs	Сто́ит ему́ то́лько бро́сить Наде́жду Фёдоровну и уе́хать в Петербу́рг, как он полу́чит всё, что ему́ ну́жно (Chekhov)
He has only to open his mouth for everyone around to fall silent	Сто́ит ему́ заговори́ть, что́бы все круго́м замолка́ли (L. N. Tolstoy)

397. *. . . is enough to (make) . . .* is translated into Russian by доста́точно что́бы, with the noun designating the cause or reason in the genitive case:

The slightest rustle in the passage or cry in the yard is enough to make him raise his head and listen	Доста́точно мале́йшего шо́роха в сеня́х, и́ли кри́ка во дворе́, что́бы он по́днял го́лову и стал прислу́шиваться (Chekhov)

Purpose

To, in order to, so as to, lest

398. (i) Что́бы is often omitted after verbs of motion:

I have come to talk to you	Я пришёл поговори́ть с ва́ми

It is included, however, when the sense of purpose is strong:

Danilov went out in order to allow the couple to say goodbye	Дани́лов вы́шел, что́бы не меша́ть супру́гам прости́ться (Panova)

(ii) If the sense of purpose is particularly emphasized затем, что́бы or для того́, что́бы are used (lit. *with the object of*). These conjunctions, like потому́ что and оттого́ что, and in similar circumstances (see para. **394** (ii)), may be split up:

. . . *Gor'ky had asked me to this carriage in order to tell me of his plan for the revival of a genuine literature for children in Russia and to obtain my co-operation in this task*	. . . Го́рький зате́м и позва́л меня́ в э́тот ваго́н, что́бы рассказа́ть о своём за́мысле возрожде́ния по́длинной де́тской литерату́ры в Росси́и и привле́чь меня́ к э́той рабо́те (Chukovsky)

(iii) *So as to, in such a way as to,* are translated by так, что́бы:

If the Germans arrive, they must behave in such a way as not to arouse suspicion	Е́сли приду́т не́мцы, они́ должны́ вести́ себя́ так, что́бы не возбуди́ть подозре́ния (Fadeyev)

(iv) *Lest* is что́бы не:

He carefully undressed in the hall, lest he should awake his family	Что́бы не разбуди́ть свои́х, он осторо́жно разде́лся в пере́дней (Chekhov)

(v) Rejected purpose (*instead of*) is expressed in Russian by вме́сто того́, что́бы:

Instead of going up to him, I went and stood by the table	Вме́сто того́, что́бы подойти́ к нему́, я ста́ла к столу́ (L. N. Tolstoy)

Comparison

As . . . as, as much as

399. (i) *As . . . as*, in simple comparative statements, is translated by так (же)... как:

He is as rich as I	Он так же бога́т, как я

If two different qualities are compared, как may be strengthened by и:

He is as kind as he is rich	Он так же добр, как и бога́т

Alternatively, сто́лько же . . . ско́лько и (насто́лько . . . наско́лько) may be used in such sentences: он сто́лько же добр, ско́лько и бога́т.

(ii) *As much as* with verbs may be translated by так (же) . . .
как, сто́лько (же) . . . ско́лько, ог сто́лько (же) . . . как:

. . . *no one wished that people might become enriched with knowledge and culture as much as M. Gor'ky did . . .*	. . . никто́ так не жела́л, что́бы лю́ди обогаща́лись зна́ниями и культу́рой, как э́того жела́л М. Го́рький . . . (Maximov)
I am not so much indignant at the loss of my clothing as at the thought that I shall have to walk along stark naked	Меня́ не сто́лько возмуща́ет лише́ние оде́жды, ско́лько мысль, что мне придётся идти́ нагишо́м (Chekhov)

Just as, just like

400. Так же как may translate either *just like* or *just as* (i.e. may precede either noun or verb):

(*He*) . . . *will keep an inn just like his father*	(Он) . . . бу́дет, так же как и оте́ц, содержа́ть тракти́р (Gogol')
. . . *his son will remember this unusual day just as he himself . . . remembers his first trip in a coach*	. . . его́ сын бу́дет вспомина́ть э́тот необыкнове́нный день, так же как он сам . . . вспомина́ет своё пе́рвое путеше́ствие в дилижа́нсе (Fedin)

As if, as though

401. (i) Normally translated by бу́дто (бы) or как бу́дто (бы):

. . . *this gladness was gone in a flash, as if it had never been*	. . . э́та ра́дость так же мгнове́нно и прошла́, бу́дто её во́все не быва́ло (Gogol')

(ii) Бу́дто (бы) is used, idiomatically, after verbs of saying to give the statement the character of an allegation of doubtful truth:

He assures us he has seen it himself	Он уверяет, будто сам видел

This construction is particularly common with the verb притворяться (притвориться) *to pretend*:

He pretends never to have read this book	Он притворяется, будто он никогда не читал эту книгу

Condition

402. (i) In a conditional clause, introduced by *if*, the indicative is used *if the condition is not contrary to fact*:

If they have gone when you arrive, return at once	Если они уже ушли когда вы придёте, возвращайтесь сразу
If he is reading, I shall not disturb him	Если он читает, я не побеспокою его

Whereas in English a condition referring to future time is expressed by the present tense (disguised future), in Russian either the imperfective or perfective future is used:

If he comes before six o'clock, inform me	Если он придёт до шести часов, сообщите мне

(ii) In frequentative constructions, in which each individual action is envisaged as completed, если and other conditional conjunctions (e.g. раз *once*) may be followed by the perfective present instead of the imperfective past or present. The verb in the apodosis also appears in the perfective present:

Such people, once they begin a task, carry it through to the end	Такие, раз уж возьмутся за дело, так доведут его до конца (Chukovsky)
If he fell, then one had only to tell him that he had fallen like a horse and . . . he would jump up and gleefully run to tell everyone that he had fallen like a horse	Если он упадёт, то стоило ему сказать, что он упал как лошадь и . . . он вскочит и весело побежит объявлять всем, что упал как лошадь (Garin-Mikhailovsky)

These constructions are similar to those in which the perfective present is used as an historic present (see para. **191**). Sometimes conditional meaning is expressed in Russian with the perfective present alone, used historically, without éсли:

If he noticed a fault, he would whistle, bite his nails and climb on to the control panel to correct it	Заме́тит непола́дку, посвисти́т, покуса́ет но́гти и ле́зет на щит исправля́ть (Krymov)

(iii) Éсли, followed by the indicative, may also introduce a statement of fact or assumed fact in clauses which are not true conditional clauses:

If the first gesture expressed a threat, the second betokened irony	Éсли пе́рвый жест выража́л угро́зу, то второ́й говори́л об иро́нии (Stanislavsky)

403. If the condition is a general statement, referring not to one definite person but to a number of persons or to humanity in general, it may be expressed by éсли followed by the infinitive:

For if we think about it and look into it, he is a peasant through and through . . .	А е́сли поду́мать и разобра́ться, то мужи́к мужико́м . . . (Chekhov)

404. *Provided that* (so long as) is éсли то́лько:

He would have decided that there was no reason not to marry the girl, whoever she was, provided he loved her	Он реши́л бы, что нет никаки́х причи́н не жени́ться на де́вушке, кто бы она́ ни была́, е́сли то́лько он лю́бит её (L. N. Tolstoy)

405. *Unless* may be either éсли не or то́лько éсли with different verbal constructions:

I shall not stay unless he leaves	Я не бу́ду остава́ться, е́сли он не уйдёт, *or* Я оста́нусь, то́лько е́сли он уйдёт

Otherwise, which may express the same meaning in English as *unless*, can be rendered in four ways, а то, не то, а не то, ина́че:

Come in time, otherwise we shall go to the theatre without you (Unless you come in time . . .)	Придите во́-время, (а) не то пойдём без вас в теа́тр

406. *On condition that* при усло́вии, что:

She will marry him on condition that he leaves England	Она́ вы́йдет за́муж за него́ при усло́вии, что он уе́дет из А́нглии

Notice при про́чих ра́вных усло́виях *all other things being equal*.

407. If the condition is *contrary to fact* е́сли is followed by the subjunctive; the verb in the apodosis is placed in the conditional (in form identical with the subjunctive):

If I had fallen, I would never have got up	Е́сли бы я упа́л, то уж никогда́ бы не встал (Turgenev)
If a favourable wind were blowing, we would sail along much faster	Е́сли бы дул попу́тный ве́тер, мы плы́ли бы значи́тельно быстре́е

Note the fact that the apodosis when it follows the protasis is often introduced by то as in the first example. Sometimes also, е́сли may be omitted, verb and subject in the protasis inverted, and the apodosis introduced by так:

Had you not missed the train, I would not have made your acquaintance	Не опозда́ли бы вы к по́езду, так я не познако́мил-ся бы с ва́ми

408. The apodosis of a conditional sentence may be expressed with бы alone, unaccompanied by the past-tense form. Most often the omitted verb is бы́ло:

Ten pounds would suffice me	Мне бы дово́льно десяти́ фу́нтов

Mor is also sometimes omitted:

Who can that be so early?   Кто бы э́то так ра́но?

Notice also the use of е́сли бы не *but for*, in the protasis:

But for the rain, I would go   Е́сли бы не дождь, я пошёл
for a walk   бы гуля́ть

409. Е́сли бы is used also in polite requests:

I have finished and would be   Я ко́нчил и был бы о́чень
very happy if any of my   сча́стлив, е́сли бы кто́-
esteemed listeners wished   либо из мои́х высоко-
to ask me for explanations   уважа́емых слу́шателей
or to raise any objections   пожела́л обрати́ться ко
  мне за разъясне́ниями
  и́ли с возраже́ниями
  (Pavlov)

410. Conditions contrary to fact may be expressed by the 2nd person singular of the imperative as well as by е́сли and the subjunctive:

If I knew a trade, I would   Знай я ремесло́, жил бы в
live in the town   го́роде (Gor′ky)

Notice the expressions будь то *were it . . .* and не будь (followed by the genitive) *but for . . .*:

Were it the General himself,   Будь то сам генера́л, я не
I would not listen to him   слу́шал бы его́
But for me, he would have   Не будь меня́, он бы у́мер
died

Concession

411. (i) Concessive clauses, introduced by such expressions as *whatever, whenever, however much*, are normally translated into Russian by the use of the appropriate pronoun or adverb (что, когда́, ско́лько) with the negative particle ни alone, or with ни and the subjunctive particle бы:

Strange as it may seem   Как стра́нно ни ка́жется
Strange as it seemed   Как стра́нно ни каза́лось

Both these phrases may also be expressed: как бы стра́нно

ни каза́лось. Note that the subjunctive construction may have either past or present meaning according to the context, but if ни alone is used, the tense of the English clause must be expressed by the tense of the Russian verb.

(ii) In frequentative constructions, when each individual action is envisaged as completed, the Russian perfective present may translate an English present:

Is it not clear that whatever Lipochka does, she does from sheer immaturity?	Не я́сно ли, что Ли́почка, всё что ни сде́лает, сде́лает по соверше́нной неразви́тости? (Dobrolyubov)

412. *If not . . . then at least* is normally translated into Russian е́сли не . . . то:

One, if not fine, at least typically St. Petersburg morning . . .	Одни́м, е́сли не прекра́сным, то соверше́нно петербу́ргским у́тром . . . (Herzen)

413. *Although* is normally translated by хотя́ and when the subordinate clause introduced by хотя́ precedes the main clause, the latter may be introduced, seemingly tautologically, by но. In this way the contrast between the statements made by the main and subordinate clauses is emphasized:

Although young, he is experienced	Он, хотя́ молодо́й, но о́пытный

Хотя́ бы is a synonym of да́же е́сли *even if*:

I would not forgive him, even if he were on his knees before me	Я не прости́л бы его́, хотя́ бы (да́же е́сли бы) он стоя́л на коле́нях пе́редо мной

It may also translate *even* or *say* when the speaker is adducing an example or illustration:

His talent is evident, even in his earliest sketches	Его́ тала́нт ви́ден, хотя́ бы в пе́рвых его́ о́черках

Let us take, as an example, say Turgenev	Возьмём, в ка́честве приме́ра, хотя́ бы Турге́нева

414. The conjunction хоть has several idiomatic meanings. Note:

You can read for two hours if you like	Вы мо́жете чита́ть хоть два часа́
I will do it, if not for you, at least for your father	Я сде́лаю э́то, е́сли не для вас, хоть для ва́шего отца́

415. *It is true*, used concessively, is translated by пра́вда, often standing as first word in the sentence:

He is clever, it is true, but he does not know everything	Пра́вда, он умён, но не зна́ет всего́

416. Notice the expression (да) и то used idiomatically, meaning *and even (then)*, in such sentences as:

I have only one suit and even (then) it is very shabby	У меня́ то́лько оди́н костю́м, (да) и то о́чень поно́шенный

417. *In spite of everything* is невзира́я (несмотря́) ни на что:

In spite of everything, I shall continue to live in Russia	Невзира́я ни на что, я бу́ду продолжа́ть жить в Росси́и

THE CONJUNCTIONS 'а', 'и', AND 'же'

418. A in Russian is often merely an alternative for и (*and*) or но (*but*). Certain of its uses are, however, distinctive from the point of view either of meaning or of style:

(i) A may be used with similar meaning to в то вре́мя как—English *while*:

My mother was having something out with my father: she was making him some reproach, while he, as was his custom, walked about and remained politely silent	У ма́тушки происходи́ло объясне́ние с отцо́м: она́ в чём-то упрека́ла его́, а он, по своему́ обыкнове́нию, ходи́л и ве́жливо отма́лчивался (Turgenev)

(ii) A is commonly used in conjunction with certain adverbs, notably ещё, всё, ужé, до сих пор, мéжду тем:

The sun had not yet risen ... but, on the field-aerodrome, engines were already roaring, as they warmed up	Сóлнце ещё не поднялóсь, ... а на полевóм аэродрóме ужé ревéли прогревáемые мотóры (Polevoy)
August has passed but there is as yet no reply to this note sent by the Soviet Government	Áвгуст прошёл, а на э́то заявлéние совéтского правительства до сих пор нет отвéта (Press)
It was long past dawn, but the lamp was still burning with a feeble, smoky flame	Ужé давнó рассвелó, а лáмпа всё горéла коптящим бессильным огонькóм (Fedin)
The doctor replied: 'I, for my part, do not fear for you, but still you are very seriously wounded'	Врач отвéтил: «Я же не боюсь за вас, а мéжду тем вы óчень тяжелó рáнены» (Pavlenko)

(iii) A is found, with strong adversative sense, especially after negatives:

Already not seven but twelve years had passed	Прошлó ужé не семь, а цéлых двенáдцать лет (Turgenev)

(iv) Very common is the combination а сам(а), contrasting two different actions of the subject of the sentence:

He would bring her tickets for the theatre but would himself stay at home	Он приносил ей билéты в теáтр, а сам оставáлся дóма (Kaverin)
In his study, uncle asked the guests to sit down and make themselves at home, but he himself went out	В кабинéте, дядюшка попросил гостéй сесть и расположиться как дóма, а сам вышел (L. N. Tolstoy)

(v) A is used in slightly emphatic parentheses, which reinforce the speaker's point:

Since he settled here (and that will be five years now) he has never once left the town	С тех пор, как он посели́лся здесь (а э́тому бу́дет уже́ пять лет), он ни ра́зу не выезжа́л из го́рода (Quoted by Vinogradov)

(vi) Notice the expression а вдруг, followed by the perfective present, which may translate *but what if?*:

But what if he does not arrive in time?	А вдруг он не во́-время придёт?

419. И has several meanings in addition to simple *and*:

(i) **at all:**

They did not know what to do at all	Они́ не зна́ли, что и де́лать

(ii) **even:**

I will not even wish you good-night	Не хочу́ и до́брой но́чи жела́ть тебе́ (Gogol')
We decided that the doll would have to be taken back, all the more because Marusya would not even notice it	Мы реши́ли, что ку́клу необходи́мо унести́ обра́тно, тем бо́лее, что Мару́ся э́того и не заме́тит (Korolenko)

(iii) **indeed:**

At first our aunt would look into our room . . . but her visits became less frequent and finally ceased altogether. We only saw her indeed . . . at dinner . . .	Пе́рвые дни загля́дывала к нам в ко́мнату тётушка, . . . а пото́м ста́ла ходи́ть ре́же и наконе́ц совсе́м переста́ла. Мы то́лько и ви́делись с не́ю . . . за обе́дом . . . (S. Aksakov)

(iv) as (so) much as:

They were greatly enjoying themselves, but no one so much as looked at us	Им было очень весело, а на нас никто и не смотрел (S. Aksakov)
I thought as much	Я так и думал

(v) just, precisely:

That's just the point	В том-то и дело

With personal pronouns, this emphatic sense is translated by *it is, that is*:

I hope Victor will not forget to bring some wool, mine will soon all run out. That's him coming now	Надеюсь, Виктор не забудет привезти шерсти, а то моя скоро вся выйдет. Вот он и едет (L. N. Tolstoy)

420. И is also used idiomatically with the words да, так, and только:

(i) Да и means *and indeed*:

I made no reply—and indeed what cause had I to reply?	Я ничего не отвечал, да и зачем мне было отвечать (Turgenev)

(ii) Так и may mean *as much* (see para. **419** (iv)). Notice also:

I told him, in so many words, that he was a fool	Я так и сказал ему, что он дурак

(iii) Так и also means *literally, simply* in metaphorical expressions:

His spectacles were literally jumping up and down on his brow	На его лбу очки так и прыгали (Mamin-Sibiryak)
I don't know why, my heart was simply thumping	Не знаю отчего, сердце у меня так и билось (S. Aksakov)

(iv) То́лько и ... что translates idiomatically *nothing but*, *only*: notice the partitive genitive:

His only redeeming feature is that he works hard	То́лько и хоро́шего в нём, что усе́рдно рабо́тает
At first, I did nothing but lie with a book in my hands	Пе́рвое вре́мя, я то́лько и де́лал, что лежа́л с кни́гой в рука́х (Bunin)
People are talking of nothing else	То́лько и разгово́ров, что об э́том

421. Notice that ни the negative of и, is used to translate *nor* (French *non plus*):

He did not know her, nor did she know him	Он её не знал, ни она́ его́ не зна́ла

422. Же

(i) **however**

Tatyana Ivanovna Gardenina always spent the winter in St. Petersburg. In the summer, however, she had, for some time, lived abroad	Татья́на Ива́новна Гарде́ни́на постоя́нно проводи́ла зи́му в Петербу́рге. Ле́том же, с не́которых пор, жила́ за грани́цей (Ertel')

(ii) **also**

Children are a joy to their parents, they are also a support to them in old age	Де́ти ра́дость роди́телям, они́ же и опо́ра им в ста́рости

(iii) **for (my) part ...**

The doctor replied: 'I, for my part, do not fear for you ...'	Врач отве́тил: «Я же не бою́сь за вас... »

(iv) **after all**

Why don't you trust him? He's your brother, after all	Почему́ вы не доверя́ете ему́? Он же ваш брат

(v) **very**

We shall go this very day   Мы сего́дня же пое́дем

(vi) **else** (after и́ли)

Either I do not understand   Или я вас не понима́ю, и́ли
   you or else you do not wish   же вы не хоти́те поня́ть
   to understand me   меня́

SOME COMMON ADVERBS AND THEIR TRANSLATION

Again

423. The general word is опя́ть: неуже́ли тебе́ опя́ть есть хо́чется *surely you're not hungry again*. Сно́ва means *afresh, anew*: нача́ть жить сно́ва *to begin life anew*. Ещё раз means *once more, on one more occasion*: скажи́те э́то ещё раз и вы пожале́ете об э́том *say that once more and you'll be sorry*. *As much again* is ещё сто́лько же; *half as much again* is в полтора́ ра́за бо́льше.

Already

424. Уже́ is more often used in Russian than *already* in English (see para. **203** (i)): уже́ по́здно *it's late, it's getting late*. Ещё may be used as a synonym of уже́ meaning *as early as, as far back as*: э́то бы́ло изве́стно уже́ (ещё) в 1910 году́ *that was known as early as 1910*.

Уже́ не раз means *several times*: я уже́ не раз виде́л его́ с конца́ войны́ *I have seen him several times since the end of the war*. Уже́ давно́ means *it is a long time since*: я уже́ давно́ не ви́дел её *it's a long time since I've seen her;* note also вот уже́: мы не ви́делись вот уже́ пять лет *we haven't seen each other for five years* (*It's five years since we've seen each other*).

Altogether (Quite, At all)

425. Although the English equivalents of вполне́, совсе́м, and соверше́нно are normally given as *fully*, *altogether*, and *completely*, these three words are, in positive statements, synonymous. Вполнé may be used with adjectives, whereas *fully*, in English, may only be used with verbs and participles: вполнé достóйный человéк *an altogether worthy man*, вполнé образóванный человéк *a well-educated man*. In unemphatic negative statements не вполнé, не совсéм, and не совершéнно are, similarly, synonymous: не вполнé (совсéм, совершéнно) достóйный человéк *a not altogether worthy man*. In emphatic negative statements, however, (English *not at all, not in the least*) only совсéм не, совершéнно не and a third expression, вóвсе не, may be used; вполнé не is impossible: он вóвсе (совсéм, совершéнно) не ожидáл этого *he did not expect that at all*. Вóвсе without не is now archaic. The unity of the expression вóвсе не is demonstrated by the fact that, with the long forms of the past participle passive, не remains separate: *a completely unsolved problem* вóвсе не решённый вопрóс but совершéнно (совсéм) нерешённый вопрóс.

Целикóм and всецéло mean *wholly*: он целикóм (всецéло) поглощён своéй рабóтой *he is wholly immersed in his work*.

Always

426. Meaning *constantly, all the time, always*, is best translated by постоянно, всё врéмя, or simply всё: этот ребёнок всё плáчет *this child is always crying*.

Enough

427. With adjectives and adverbs довóльно means *enough* in the sense of *rather* or *fairly* but not in the sense of *sufficiently*: довóльно хорóшая пьéса *a fairly good play*. *Enough* meaning *sufficiently* with adjectives and adverbs is translated by достáточно: он достáточно богáт, чтóбы купить три дóма *he is rich enough to buy three houses*.

With a noun *enough* meaning *sufficient* may be translated by either довóльно or достáточно: довóльно (достáточно) у вас кирпичéй на пострóйку дóма? *have you enough bricks to build the house?*

Note that *not enough* may be idiomatically translated by

ма́ло: ма́ло купи́ть кни́гу, на́до ещё чита́ть её *it is not enough to buy a book, one must also read it.*

Even

428. *Even* meaning *as early as* is translated by ещё or уже́: ещё (уже́) ребёнком он был выдаю́щимся скрипачём *even as a child he was an outstanding violinist.*

Not even in Russian is да́же не (not не да́же): да́же он не зна́ет об э́том *not even he knows of this*; никому́, да́же Ле́нину, не́ было ска́зано об опа́сности *no one, not even Lenin, was told of the danger.*

Exactly, precisely

429. Ро́вно is used only with numbers or quantities: ро́вно в два часа́ *at precisely two o'clock*; ве́сом ро́вно в килогра́мм *exactly a kilogram in weight*; note also он ро́вно ничего́ не по́нял *he understood precisely nothing.*

То́чно may also be used with numbers but is also combined with identifying words: то́чно така́я же кни́га *precisely the same sort of book*; он так то́чно поступи́л как брат *he behaved in exactly the same way as his brother.*

Как раз is the exact equivalent of *just*: как раз то, что мне ну́жно *just what I need*; боти́нки мне как раз впо́ру *the boots are just right for me.* Note that как раз may be used as a predicate: шля́па мнс как раз *the hat is just my size.*

И́менно in positive statements is synonymous with как раз in its identifying sense: и́менно то, что мне ну́жно *just what I need*; и́менно alone, however, is used in questions and reported questions: кто и́менно сказа́л э́то? *who exactly was it who said that?*; ско́лько и́менно вам ну́жно апельси́нов *exactly how many oranges do you need?*; я спроси́л его́, куда́ и́менно он е́дет *I asked him where exactly he was going.*

Notice не то что(бы) . . . но, *not exactly . . . but*:

She did not exactly run Versilov's estate but kept a neighbourly eye on it	Она́ не то что управля́ла, но по сосе́дству надзира́ла за име́нием Верси́лова (Dostoyevsky)

First

430. Снача́ла means *first of all* or *at first*: снача́ла ду́май, пото́м говори́ *think before you speak* (*first think, then speak*); снача́ла их бесе́да шла вя́ло *at first their conversation languished*. In the meaning *from the beginning* alternative spellings are possible, снача́ла or с нача́ла: нача́ть снача́ла (с нача́ла) *to begin from the beginning*.

Пре́жде всего́ may also mean *first of all*: он до́лжен пре́жде всего́ ко́нчить э́то *he must first finish this*. Пре́жде всего́ also means *first and foremost*; Пу́шкин пре́жде всего́ поэ́т *Pushkin is first and foremost a poet*.

Впервы́е means *for the first time* (synonym of в пе́рвый раз): я впервы́е пое́хал в Ло́ндон в 1940 году́ *I first went to London in 1940*.

Во-пе́рвых *in the first place* (во-вторы́х *secondly*, в-тре́тьих *thirdly*).

Here, There

431. Тут is more colloquial than здесь meaning *in this place*. Note that *who is there?* in Russian may be, as well as кто там?, кто здесь?, or кто тут? Тут may also be used without locative meaning, corresponding to English *hereupon, with this, there, now*: тут де́ло ко́нчилось *there the matter ended*; тут он подошёл ко мне *with this, he came up to me*. Тут же may mean *there and then, on the spot*: на́ша дру́жба прекрати́лась тут же *our friendship ended there and then*. Там may mean *then*: подойди́те бли́же, там вас ви́дно бу́дет *come nearer, then I'll be able to see you*; там ви́дно бу́дет *we shall see when the time comes*.

Inside, outside

432. Внутри́ means *inside* (location) and внутрь *inside* (motion): они́ все бы́ли внутри́ *they were all inside*; они́ все вошли́ внутрь *they all went inside*. Note also внутри́ страны́ and внутрь страны́: мне нра́вится жить внутри́ страны́ *I like living inland*; они́ е́хали внутрь страны́ *they travelled inland*.

The opposites of внутри́ and внутрь are снару́жи and нару́жу respectively: обива́ть (оби́ть) дверь снару́жи во́йлоком *to cover the outside of a door with felt*; его́ преступле́ние вы́шло нару́жу *his crime came to light*; э́ти иссле́дования вы́вели ва́жные фа́кты нару́жу *these researches brought important facts to light.*

Left, right

433. Нале́во, напра́во may mean either *to the left (right) of* (location or motion), or *on the left (right) of*: повора́чивать (поверну́ть) нале́во (напра́во) *to turn to the left (right)*; нале́во от до́ма был парк *to the left of the house was a park.*

Сле́ва, спра́ва may mean either *on the left (right)* or *from the left (right)*: сле́ва от него́ *on his left*; сле́ва напра́во *from left to right.*

Long

434. До́лго means *for a long time* referring to the actual duration of a state or action (French *pendant longtemps*): я до́лго смотре́л на него́ *I looked at him for a long time.*

Давно́ means *for a long time* preceding the moment of speech (French *depuis longtemps*): я давно́ не вида́л его́ *I haven't seen him for a long time.* Compare:

I waited for you for a long time, but you did not come	Я вас до́лго ждал, а вы не пришли́
I had been waiting for you for a long time when you came	Я уже́ давно́ поджида́л вас, когда́ вы пришли́

Давно́ уже́ пора́ means *it is high time*: давно́ уже́ пора́ нам уйти́ *it is high time we went.*

Давно́ may also mean *a long time ago*: я давно́ купи́л э́тот дом *I bought this house a long time ago.*

Задо́лго до *a long time before . . .*; они́ уе́хали задо́лго до полу́ночи *they left long before midnight.*

Надо́лго means *for a long time*, referring to the completion of a state or action, as opposed to до́лго referring to
their duration; compare:

The meeting was lasting a long time and Voroshilov went home	Собра́ние продолжа́лось до́лго, и Вороши́лов уе́хал домо́й
The meeting dragged out for a long time and I missed the train	Собра́ние затяну́лось надо́лго, и я опозда́л на по́езд

In the first sentence Voroshilov went home before the end
of the meeting; in the second the speaker stayed till the end
of the meeting, with the result that he missed the train.

Надо́лго is also used with imperfective or perfective
verbs expressing intention: я е́ду в Ло́ндон надо́лго *I am
going to London for a long time;* он уе́хал надо́лго *he has gone
away for a long time.*

No longer referring to the duration of a state or action is
бо́льше не (French *ne ... plus*): я бо́льше не хочу́ рабо́тать
I don't want to work any longer; я бо́льше не бу́ду ждать его́
I shall not wait any longer for him. No longer referring to the
cessation of a state or action is бо́льше не or уже́ не: он
бо́льше (уже́) не ма́льчик *he is no longer a boy.*

Before long is ско́ро: он ско́ро придёт *he will be here before
long.* Не ско́ро ещё is used to translate *it will be a long time
before*: не ско́ро ещё мы встре́тимся опя́ть *it will be a long
time before we meet again.* Вско́ре (lit. *in a short time*) may
translate *not long*: он вско́ре отве́тил на моё письмо́ *he did
not take long to answer my letter.*

More, less, most, least

435. Бо́лее and ме́нее are bookish in tone and less used
than бо́льше and ме́ньше when both are possible.

Only бо́льше or ме́ньше may be used with nouns or as
pronouns: у меня́ бо́льше я́блок, чем у него́ *I have more
apples than he*, я бо́льше истра́тил, чем вы *I have spent more
than you.*

Only бо́лее or ме́нее may be used in combination with adjectives and adverbs: он бо́лее бога́тый челове́к, чем я *he is a richer man than I*; чита́йте кни́гу бо́лее внима́тельно *read the book more carefully*.

There are also certain fixed expressions in which only бо́лее or ме́нее may be used: бо́лее и́ли ме́нее *more or less*, тем не ме́нее *none the less*, не бо́лее и не ме́нее как *no less than* (*quite simply*): де́ло шло не бо́лее и не ме́нее как о войне́ и́ли ми́ре *the issue was, quite simply, war or peace*.

More with numerals is ещё: ещё два ра́за *twice more*.

When *more* means *rather* it should be rendered by скоре́е: он скоре́е похо́ж на отца́, чем на мать *he is more like his father than his mother*.

At most may be translated by не бо́льше (*not more than*) or by са́мое бо́льшее: у него́ не бо́льше трёх коро́в (са́мое бо́льшее три коро́вы) *he has three cows at most*. *At least* may similarly be translated by са́мое ме́ньшее, не ме́ньше, or by a third variant по кра́йней ме́ре.

Much

436. In combination with comparative adjectives or adverbs, гора́здо should be used and not мно́го, which is colloquial: гора́здо лу́чше *much better*. With verbs *much* is translated by намно́го: я намно́го предпочита́ю мя́со ры́бе *I much prefer meat to fish*.

Too (*much*) may be translated by either сли́шком or сли́шком мно́го; сли́шком indicates excessive intensity or degree, сли́шком мно́го excessive quantity. With nouns сли́шком мно́го is, naturally, always used: сли́шком мно́го ма́сла *too much butter;* note also the pronominal use of сли́шком мно́гие (*too many people*): сли́шком мно́гие ду́мают, что . . . *too many people think that . . . .* With verbs either сли́шком or сли́шком мно́го is used, according to whether excessive intensity or degree or excessive quantity is meant: не на́до сли́шком предава́ться развлече́ниям *one must not indulge too much in pleasure*; не на́до сли́шком мно́го говори́ть *one must not talk too much*. (See also *very much.*) Слишком is most often used with verbs of thinking, feeling, or wishing.

With certain words слишком may be omitted:

Twenty roubles for a ticket is too much	Двадцать рублей за билет — это много
You are too young to judge of that	Рано вам судить об этом
It is too late to think of that now	Поздно теперь думать об этом

Very much may be either очень or очень много: the difference between очень and очень много is the same as that between слишком and слишком много. Like слишком, очень is most often used with verbs of thinking, feeling, or wishing: я очень сомневаюсь *I very much doubt*, я очень боюсь *I'm very much afraid*, я очень хочу работать *I very much want to work*. Notice that with изменяться (измениться) one may say either он очень изменился or он очень сильно изменился, since the meaning may be *to a great extent* (qualitatively) or *a great deal* (quantitative physical change). One does not, however, say он очень много изменился.

Notice the difference between не очень *not very* and очень не *anything but, not in the least*: я не очень люблю вино *I don't like wine very much*; он очень не в духе *he's very much out of sorts* (*anything but in a good temper*).

Notice that the adverb сильно is very commonly used with verbs to express great intensity or great quantity and may correspond to a wide variety of English adverbs:

I was forcibly struck by his remark	Я был сильно поражён его замечанием
I am greatly in need of money	Я сильно нуждаюсь в деньгах
He drinks heavily	Он сильно пьёт
My curiosity was keenly aroused	Моё любопытство было сильно возбуждено
He was sweating profusely	Он сильно потел

| *He fell seriously ill* | Он си́льно занемо́г |
| *She is very uneasy* | Она́ си́льно беспоко́ится |

Now

437. Сейча́с may mean either *at once* (immediate future) or *just now* (immediate past): он сейча́с придёт *he will be here presently*; как вы сейча́с говори́ли *as you were just saying*.

Тепе́рь may mean *nowadays*: шахтёры тепе́рь живу́т припева́ючи *miners nowadays are in clover*.

Both сейча́с and тепе́рь may mean *at present, at the moment*: где он тепе́рь (сейча́с) живёт? *where is he living now?*

Now ... now ... is translated by то..., то...: то снег, то дождь *snow one moment, rain the next*.

From now on, henceforth is впредь: впредь я бу́ду жить в А́нглии *from now on I shall live in England*.

Now (French *or*) in narrative is expressed by а: а так как он не прие́хал, я реши́л, что он уби́т *now, as he did not come, I decided he had been killed*.

Really, surely

438. 'Ра́зве is used when the speaker expects the answer *no*, неуже́ли when the speaker hopes to receive the answer *no*' (Unbegaun, *Russian Grammar*, p. 279): ра́зве э́то случи́лось в про́шлом году́? *did that really happen last year?* неуже́ли вас оскорби́ло то, что я сказа́л? *surely you weren't offended by what I said?*

V

THE PRONOUN AND PRONOMINAL WORDS

PERSONAL

Себя

439. (i) The personal pronouns present no special difficulties, except possibly себя, the reflexive pronoun applicable to *all* persons. It will be noticed that the various cases of себя are used idiomatically in a few common expressions, such as the following:

Собой is added to хорош, дурен, and недурён (short forms) to convey the idea of *facially, externally*:

She is very good-looking   Она очень хороша собой

Very similar is the force of собой in the expression само собой разумеется *of course, it goes without saying*, i.e. the thing is obvious on the surface.

Представлять собой (followed by the accusative) is a literary synonym for быть, являться (see para. **329**).

(ii) Stressed себе is common in the possessive sense of one's own (see para. **454**), and, in combination with сам, in the same meaning:

I am my own boss   Я сам себе хозяин

Notice, too, the idiom:

He's a very crafty customer   Он очень себе на уме
    (colloq.)

Unstressed себе (sometimes with знай) is a particle used colloquially in a way which allows no direct translation, but which often suggests *keeping on despite everything*:

He just keeps on *lying there*   Он лежит себе там, и
    saying nothing   ничего не говорит

Not too bad, alright (cf. collo-   Ничего́ себе́, та́к себе́
   quial English *just* keeping
   on *living*)

440. With a few verbs себя́ is used independently (not
amalgamated as ся) in a way not suggested by the English
equivalents (see also para. **258**):

How does the patient feel?	Как себя́ чу́вствует боль- но́й?
He is behaving badly	Он ведёт себя́ пло́хо
He'll prove his worth before long	Он ско́ро себя́ пока́жет

You

441. When вы refers to one person only, it is usually followed by the *singular* number of a noun or an adjective in
the long form, and by the *plural* number of a verb or an
adjective in the short form (or оди́н):

You are not so jolly as you were yesterday	Вы сего́дня не тако́й весё- лый, каки́м вы бы́ли вчера́
You are right, I think	Вы, ка́жется, пра́вы
Do you live on your own, Anna?	Вы живёте одни́, А́нна?

For the translation of the indefinite personal pronoun *you*,
see *one* (para. **514**).

He, She

442. Э́то may replace он or она́ when reference is made
to a specific subject already mentioned or about to be mentioned (cf. French *c'est, c'était*):

At length he came up to me. He was a leisurely indi- vidual . . .	Наконе́ц он подошёл ко мне. Э́то был неторо- пли́вый челове́к . . .
She's a clever woman, our new teacher	Э́то у́мная же́нщина, на́ша но́вая преподава́тель- ница

It

443. When *it* refers to a single specific object which is masculine or feminine, it will be translated by он or она́:

How do you like my skirt?	Как вам нра́вится моя́ ю́бка? Она́ о́чень краси́ва
It is very pretty	

444. When *it* refers not to a specific object (e.g. *skirt*, para. **443**) but to a general state of affairs or set of circumstances previously mentioned or implied, it will be translated by э́то. In the following sentences the author is reminiscing about a time and an adventure just alluded to:

Yes, it was a wonderful time. It was an absolutely amazing adventure for a nine year old boy	Да, э́то бы́ло чу́дное вре́мя. Э́то бы́ло изуми́тельное приключе́ние для девяти́летнего ма́льчика (Maisky)

445. *It is, it was,* used in introducing a narrative sequence to set a scene or define the place or time of an action, may be idiomatically translated by де́ло:

It was in winter. The ground was covered in snow	Де́ло бы́ло зимо́й. Земля́ была́ покры́та сне́гом

446. *It* is not translated in Russian when it does not refer at all to any subject previously mentioned or implied (the so-called 'unspecified *it*'). This use of *it* is especially common in expressions involving the weather, time, and distance:

It is cold outside	Хо́лодно на дворе́
It is hailing	Идёт град

(Very colloquial is оно́ похо́же на дождь *it looks like rain*)

It is Friday today	Сего́дня пя́тница
Is it far to the station?	Далеко́ до вокза́ла?

447. *It* will not normally be translated in combinations of it is + adjective + infinitive (e.g. *it is good to, better to, hard to, easy to, too late to,* &c.):

It is never too late to mend	Испра́виться никогда́ не по́здно
It is easier to get into trouble than to get out of it	Ле́гче попа́сть в беду́, чем вы́путаться из неё

448. *It is, it was* are not translated in Russian in such contexts as 'it was *A* that *did B*', 'it was *in A* that *B happened*' where the English simply means *A did B, B happened in A*:

It was on just such a day that I first met him	В тако́й-же день я встре́тился с ним в пе́рвый раз (*Not* э́то бы́ло в тако́й-же день, что . . .)
It was just about that time that his new novel was published	Как раз о́коло того́ вре́мени был и́здан его́ но́вый рома́н
It was Lenin's strategy that rescued us from this impasse	Страте́гия Ле́нина вы́вела нас из э́того тупика́

449. Notice the omission of *it* in translating sentences such as:

I don't speak Chinese but I understand it	Я не говорю́ по-кита́йски, но понима́ю

where the language spoken is expressed by an adverbial construction in Russian.

POSSESSIVE

My, your, his, &c.

450. When these possessive pronouns refer to the subject of the sentence they may be omitted:

I am looking for my sister	Я ищу́ сестру́
She loves her mother	Она́ лю́бит мать

No possible ambiguity can arise from their omission, they

are not emphatic, and it is more usual to leave them out than to translate them.

451. (i) When they refer to the subject of a clause, they may also be translated *either* by мой, твой, &c., depending on the person, or by the reflexive свой, irrespective of the person:

I am looking for my sister Я ищу мою (свою) сестру

It is probably true to say that in spoken Russian nowadays мою is as common if not more common than свою in the above context, but that neither is as common as the omission of the pronoun altogether, except where emphasis is desired (*my own*). With a 2nd person singular subject свой is much more common than твой. With a subject in the 3rd person, of course, only свой can be used.

(ii) It should be added that while one has the option of using either свой or мой, твой, наш, and ваш, one does not have the option of using either себя, *or* the oblique cases of я, ты, мы, and вы. Thus:

You are only thinking of yourself Вы думаете только о себе (not вас)

But:

You are only thinking of your own safety Вы думаете только о своей (вашей) безопасности

452. Care is needed with свой in the nominative case:

(i) The use of свой is almost completely restricted to the object or prepositional complement of a sentence as above. It may not, for example, be used in the subject of a subordinate clause to translate a possessive pronoun which refers to the subject of the main clause:

John said that his sister was abroad Джон сказал, что его сестра за границей (своя would be impossible)

(ii) Свой may, however, be used in the grammatical subject of a Russian sentence in *have* constructions, where the

Russian grammatical subject corresponds to the English grammatical object:

The director had his own plan	У дире́ктора был свой план
Communism has its good and bad sides	В коммуни́зме есть своя́ хоро́шая и своя́ плоха́я сторона́

(iii) The only other instances of свой qualifying a nominative subject (or predicate) occur in a few idioms and proverbs, where the possessive sense of свой is often no longer felt:

Accounts between friends are easily settled	Свои́ лю́ди — сочтёмся
He is one of us	Он для нас свой челове́к
Charity begins at home	Своя́ руба́шка бли́же к те́лу

453. Свой has many idiomatic uses of which the following may be noted:

Opportunely	В своё вре́мя
To die a natural death	Умира́ть (умере́ть) свое́й сме́ртью
I am upset, I am not myself	Я сам не свой

As a substantive свой = *one's people, one's folk.*

454. The English possessive pronouns may also be idiomatically rendered in Russian by oblique cases of the appropriate personal pronoun, with or without prepositions. Several common examples of this construction are:

(i) Personal pronoun in the dative, with no preposition:

He wiped his brow	Он потёр себе́ лоб
He pressed my hand	Он пожа́л мне ру́ку
She broke her neck (lit. *head*)	Она́ слома́ла себе́ го́лову
Fear and malice gripped my heart	У́жас и зло́ба сти́снули мне се́рдце

The first thing that sprang to my eyes	Пе́рвое, что бро́силось мне в глаза́
It fell to my lot	Мне вы́пало на до́лю
It occurred to me (came into my head)	Мне пришло́ в го́лову

In almost all the above examples, the object mentioned is a part of the body.

(ii) Preposition and personal pronoun:

She never came into my room	Она́ никогда́ не приходи́ла ко мне в ко́мнату
I ran off into my study	Я убежа́л к себе́ в кабине́т
I lay down in my room	Я лёг у себя́ в ко́мнате
Tears were flowing from her eyes	Слёзы текли́ у неё из глаз

In these and many similar examples, motion towards, or rest in a place are expressed.

DEMONSTRATIVE

This, that

455. While э́тот and тот correspond in the main to the demonstrative *this* and *that* to indicate differing degrees of proximity, it will be noticed that э́тот, especially in its neuter form э́то, is very widely used where English says *that*. Very often in such a case it refers to something just previously mentioned or indicated:

That's true (i.e. what you have just said)	Э́то пра́вда
That depends (e.g. the answer to the question you have just asked)	Э́то зави́сит
I used to live in Paris, but that (i.e. the fact just mentioned) *was a long time ago*	Я когда́-то жил в Пари́же, но э́то бы́ло давно́
That's the kettle boiling	Э́то ча́йник кипи́т

Notice also:

Who's that? What's that?	Кто э́то тако́й? Что э́то тако́е?

456. *This is* . . . and *these are* . . . may both be translated by э́то . . . :

These are not my books	Э́то не мои́ кни́ги

But not if the pronoun is emphasized:

Those books are yours and these are mine	Те кни́ги ва́ши, а э́ти — мои́

457. Э́тот is commonly preceded colloquially by вот in order to indicate more clearly the object referred to:

Give me this book here	Да́йте мне вот э́ту кни́гу (ce livre-ci)

458. Вот meaning *here is* (*voici*) is commonly found with adverbs of time, cause, manner, &c., where in English we say *that is when, why, how*:

That is how the war began	Вот как начала́сь война́

Notice also the colloquial

That's all, that's the lot	Вот и всё

459. *That of* (*celui de*). Russian has no comparable construction:

The climate here is very like that of England	Зде́шний кли́мат о́чень похо́ж на англи́йский

460. Сей = э́тот survives independently today in a few stereotyped formulas, e.g. сию́ мину́ту *this minute*, до сих пор, по сей день *up to now*. It is also used ironically: сей ю́ноша всё зна́ет *this lad knows everything!*

461. *This and that, this or that*:

(i) Rather colloquial is и то и сё, as for example in the words of a popular Soviet song: мы приземли́мся за столо́м, поговори́м о том, о сём . . . *chat about this and that*.

(ii) *This and that* meaning *various ones* will have to be translated by some such word as ра́зный:

The sick man turned to this doctor and that, but in vain	Больно́й обраща́лся к ра́зным доктора́м (то к одному́, то к друго́му до́ктору), но напра́сно

(iii) *This one or that* is тот и́ли друго́й:

Which house do you prefer, this one or that?	Кото́рый дом вы предпочита́ете — тот и́ли друго́й?

462. It will be noticed that тот is frequently used in Russian where English has no corresponding pronoun—periphrastically, for emphasis, or to give balance to a sentence:

In order to	Для того́, что́бы; за тем, что́бы
The worst came to the worst	Чего́ боя́лись, то и случи́лось
I desired with all my heart to be what you wanted me to be	Я всей душо́й жела́л быть тем, чем вы хоте́ли, что́бы я был
He who pays the piper calls the tune	Кто пла́тит, тот и распоряжа́ется

The following example illustrates the *compressed*, idiomatic use of the pronouns:

Что кого́ весели́т, тот про то и говори́т	Literally: *What gives pleasure to a man, that man speaks about that thing*

EXCLAMATORY

Such, so, what

463. Тако́й *such, such a* is used with the full form of the adjective, and так with the short form, to translate English *so* + adjective:

He is such a stupid man! (he is so stupid)	Он тако́й глу́пый! (он так глуп!)

The predicative form таков is also used:

Such is life   Такова жизнь!

Similarly какой *what, what a* is used with the full, and как with the short form of the adjective to translate *how*:

What a stupid man he is!   Какой он глупый! (как он
(how stupid he is!)   глуп!)

Both такой and какой are, of course, also used with nouns: он такой дурак! *he is such a stupid man!* Notice the following ways of rendering the exclamatory *what!*:

What weather!   Какая погода!
                         Погода какова!
                         Что за погода!

ARTICLES

A, the

464. Although Russian has no definite or indefinite article, the translation of *a* and *the* is by no means simple. Consider these two sentences:

(i) *I hope we shall find* a *shop before long*
(ii) *I bought a few old books in* a *shop in London*

In the first sentence *a* may rightly be termed indefinite, since it means *some one or other*. The speaker does not know what shop he will find, nor does his hearer. In the second sentence, however, *a* is definite in the sense that the speaker knows which shop he bought the books at, though his hearer does not. *A* in fact means *a certain one*. Translating these sentences into Russian we have:

(i) Я надеюсь, что мы скоро найдём (какой-нибудь) магазин
(ii) Я купил несколько старых книг в *одном* магазине в Лондоне

In the second sentence *a* meaning *a certain* is idiomatically rendered by оди́н *one* (from which *a, an* derive historically). The same is true in the following common contexts:

An old friend of mine often gave me lessons	Оди́н мой ста́рый знако́мый не раз дава́л мне уро́ки
A lady wishes to see you	Одна́ да́ма хо́чет вас ви́деть
This business simply leaves an unpleasant feeling	Де́ло э́то оставля́ет одно́ то́лько неприя́тное чу́вство

(See also para. **502** *a certain*).

465. *A* is also translated by оди́н:

(i) when it is a weakly numerical *one*:

| *In a word* | Одни́м сло́вом |
| *Just a minute!* | Одну́ мину́ту! |

(ii) when it means *the same, like*:

| *Birds of a feather* | Одного́ по́ля я́года (я́годы) |

466. *A* meaning *each, every* is rendered in Russian by a prepositional construction:

| *Twice a year* | Два ра́за в год |
| *Of a Sunday* | По воскресе́ньям |

467. The weakly demonstrative *the* is frequently translated into Russian by э́тот:

| *Something of the sort* | Что́-то в э́том ро́де |

468. The more emphatic definite article may be rendered by тот (cf. *ille, le*). This is especially common where the article precedes a relative clause in the sense of *the one which*:

| *I was looking in the direction from which the boat was due to come* | Я смотре́л в ту сто́рону, отку́да должна́ была́ появи́ться ло́дка |
| *The lady who is sitting in the armchair is my wife* | Та да́ма, кото́рая сиди́т в кре́сле — моя́ жена́ |

469. With comparatives *the* meaning *by so much* is translated by an instrumental:

The more the merrier	Чем бо́льше, тем лу́чше

470. Notice how in different contexts тако́й may translate both a definite and an indefinite article:

Soviet industry has reached a level which is 5 per cent. higher than in 1951	Сове́тская промы́шленность идёт на тако́м у́ровне, кото́рый на 5 проце́нтов вы́ше 1951 го́да (Press)
I returned with the feeling that I had had a bad dream	Я верну́лся с таки́м чу́вством, как бу́дто я ви́дел плохо́й сон (Press)

INTERROGATIVE AND RELATIVE

Who (Interrogative)

471. Кто does service for both singular and plural. A verb in the predicate with кто for its subject has a singular ending even though it refers to several people. In the past tense the verb will show a masculine ending even when the subject referred to is clearly feminine:

Who has dropped a comb? (spoken to a class of girls)	Кто урони́л гребешо́к?

Which, what (Interrogative)

472. (i) Often in English *which* and *what* appear interchangeable when introducing a question. One may just as easily say *What is my best way to King Street?* as *Which is my best way to King Street?* Nevertheless, there are cases where one word is preferred to the other, and there is a certain general principle which determines this choice. The *what* question belongs to what Jespersen calls the unlimited type of question, the *which* question to the limited type. When I say, *Can I see what books you have?*, I have no idea what to expect. There is no limit to the books which may be there as far as I know. But when I say *Can I see which books you have?*, the question presupposes previous questions about books. I may know that you collect nineteenth-century Russian novels and wish to see which ones you have. A general distinction can thus be made between the unrestricted *what* and the restricted *which*.

(ii) Besides simply asking an open question, *what* may also mean *of what sort*. *What clothes was she wearing?* means *what sort of clothes*, not *which of the clothes that she has*.

(iii) In Russian какой corresponds as a rule to the unlimited *what?* and also to the question *of what sort?*; который to the limited *which?*, *which ones?*:

To what extent?	До какой степени?
What books do you like best?	Какие книги любите вы больше всего?
Which of these books do you prefer?	Которую из этих книг вы предпочитаете?

But with час, который is always used where English uses *what*:

What time is it?	Который час?
At what time?	В котором часу?

while with число Russian uses both какое and которое for the English *what*:

What is the date today?	Какое (которое) сегодня число?

(iv) Notice the Russian idiom как (*how*), for the English *what* in the following expressions:

What is your name?	Как ваша фамилия? (как вас зовут?)
What did you say? What?	Как вы сказали? Как?
What do you think?	Как вы думаете?

But:

> *What do you think about* Что вы ду́маете об э́том?
> *this?*

(v) *Which of*, of people, is кто из before a pronoun:

> *Which of you is to blame?* Кто из вас винова́т?

Before a noun both кто из and кото́рый из may be used, but кото́рый is more selective and asks *which particular one?*:

> *Which of your friends is the* Кото́рый из ва́ших друзе́й
> *cleverest?* са́мый спосо́бный?

Who, whom (Relative)

473. With a noun antecedent the normal relative pronoun is кото́рый:

> *This is the boy to whom you* Вот ма́льчик, кото́рому (not
> *gave the book* кому́) вы да́ли кни́гу

Occasionally кто is found after a noun antecedent as a stylistic alternative to кото́рый, but only in the nominative case:

> *Thereupon these people who in* Тут э́ти лю́ди, кто по нера-
> *their folly had laid down* зу́мию своему́ малоду́шно
> *their arms in cowardly* положи́ли ору́жие, узна́-
> *manner felt ashamed . . .* ли стыд . . . (Л. N.Tolstoy)

474. With a pronoun antecedent the normal relative pronoun is кто:

> *Whom the gods love die* Кого́ лю́бят бо́ги, тот ра́но
> *young* умира́ет

But when the pronoun antecedent is emphatic (*the man who, those people who*) and is used virtually as a noun, кото́рый may also be used as a relative:

> *I am the one whom you heeded* Я тот, кото́рому внима́ла
> *in the midnight silence* Ты в полуно́щной тишине́
> (Lermontov)

| *Tell me, which one is Tat-yana?* | Скажи, которая Татьяна? |
| *The one who, sad and silent like Svetlana, came in and sat by the window* | Да та, которая, грустна И молчалива как Светлана, Вошла и села у окна (Pushkin) |

Те, которые and все, которые are particularly common alternatives to те, кто and все, кто as nominative plural subjects. The verb in the relative clause after те, которые and все, которые will, of course, be in the plural. With те, кто and все, кто however, either a singular or a plural verb may be used (contrast this with the interrogative кто, which is only followed by a singular verb). Compare the following examples of singular and plural verbs after те, кто:

| *Victory will go to those who are building life* | Победа будет за теми, кто строит жизнь (A. N. Tolstoy) |
| *Those of us who read the poem were delighted with it* | Те из нас, кто читали стихотворение, были в восторге от него (Press) |

475. Какой as a relative pronoun suggests *the sort of* and often has for an antecedent такой, таков, or тот:

| *We have not got the sort of people whom we need* | У нас нет таких людей, каких нам нужно |

476. Occasionally the relative кто is found after an adjective in the predicative short form—in other words, the pronominal antecedent тот is omitted:

| *Happy he who believes . . .* | Блажен, кто верует . . . . (Griboyedov) |

Such constructions occur in poetry, or in solemn or sententious contexts generally.

Which (Relative)

477. As in the case of *who*, который is most commonly used to translate the relative *which*. Какой again is emphatic and means *the sort of . . . which* (often preceded by такой):

He has the sort of hair (which) you don't like	У него такие волосы, каких вы не любите

478. (i) The relative который, after a nominal subject, may be replaced colloquially in the nominative and accusative (in the accusative only when the antecedent is inanimate) by что in the same way as *which* may be replaced by *that*:

That is the car which (that) I saw in town this morning	Вот машина, которую (что) я видел сегодня утром в городе

But что in this sense, besides being colloquial, is felt also to be archaic, and its use is not recommended.

(ii) The relative pronoun cannot be omitted altogether as it can in English, e.g. *that is the car I saw in town this morning.*

Whoever, whatever (Interrogative)

479. Interrogative *whoever* and *whatever* are translated by кто? and что?:

Whatever made you do it?	Что заставило вас сделать это?
Whoever heard the like?	Кто слыхал подобное?

Whoever, whatever (Relative)

480. In affirmative statements where *whoever* and *whatever* mean *everyone who*, *everything that* кто and что are used, sometimes with appropriate antecedents:

Whoever says that is mistaken	Кто говорит это, ошибается
Eat whatever is on the plate	Кушайте всё, что есть на тарелке

Whose

481. Чей is used both as an interrogative and relative pronoun. Которого (которой) is used only relatively, referring back to a noun in the main clause of the sentence. It will stand second word in the subordinate relative clause:

That is the girl whose father has just died	Вот дéвушка, отéц которой (чей отéц) тóлько что ýмер

Like whom, like what

482. The following uses of какóй, какóв and their English equivalents are worth noting:

He is a common or garden impostor	Он обмáнщик, какúх мнóго
How is he today?	Какóв он сегóдня?
He used to picture the room as it would be	Он представлял себé кóмнату, какóй онá бýдет

INDEFINITE

Some

483. The misuse of the suffixes -то and -нибудь is among the most frequent mistakes made by students of Russian. There is no simple rule applying to these suffixes, which are added to the various *indicator-words*, какóй, где, когдá, кудá, кто, &c., to give an indefinite meaning (*some, somewhere, sometime, to somewhere, someone*). But the following tendencies, closely related to each other, may guide the student in his choice of suffix:

(i) The -то suffix is usually more definite, specific, restrictive than the -нибудь; то suggests something definite, although unknown; нибудь—anything at all, no matter what.

(ii) -то is commonly found in a past, fulfilled sense, -нибудь in a future, unfulfilled sense.

Compare the following examples:

(a) *Your brother called on us today and left some book for you*   Сегодня зашёл к нам ваш брат, и оставил вам какую-то книгу

(*some* means *a certain, a definite one,* although the speaker does not know what it is).

(b) *He told me something but I have forgotten what*   Он чтó-то мне сказáл, но я забы́л что

(the action has been completed in past time.)

(c) *He is looking for some job or other*   Он и́щет какóй-нибудь рабóты

(not any one in particular.)

(d) *I will write to you some day*   Я вам когдá-нибудь напишý

(some time or other in the vague future.)

After the imperative mood the -нибудь suffix is always used, a further illustration of its unfulfilled future sense:

Give me something to drink   Дáйте мне чтó-нибудь пить

It would, however, be wrong to identify -то strictly with the past and -нибудь with the future. The criterion of greater or less definition can be applied to future time as well as to past or present. An example from Forbes's *Russian Grammar* well illustrates that the first tendency (that -то is more definite than -нибудь) outweighs the second (that -то is commoner in the past than in the future), when the two do not coincide:

I shall buy you something or other (I don't know myself exactly what)   Я куплю́ вам чтó-нибудь . . .

I shall buy you something (I know what it will be, but I am not going to tell you)   Я куплю́ вам чтó-то . . .

It is interesting to note that in a recent comprehensive Russian frequency list, the -то suffixes are shown to be more common than the -нибудь with almost all indicator words.

The suffix -либо is considered rather more formal or 'bookish' than -нибудь.

Не́который and Како́й-то

484. Не́который and како́й-то are not interchangeable. Не́который means *some* in the sense of *certain ones, ones that are known*, and is most frequently found in the plural. In the singular it will be used most commonly in temporal expressions, e.g. *for some time now* с не́которого вре́мени. Како́й-то, on the other hand, cannot mean *a certain one* in the above sense of *one that is known*. One cannot, for example, translate *he was talking about some rich man known to us both* by он говори́л о како́м-то богаче́, изве́стном нам обо́им. One would say . . . об одно́м богаче́..., or in the plural ... о не́которых богача́х, изве́стных нам обо́им (. . . *some rich men known to us both*). Cf. para. **483** ii (*a*).

Ко́е-како́й

485. Ко́е-како́й means *some*, not in the sense of *a certain*, but with the plural meaning of *one or two*. It may or may not be divided by a preposition in an oblique case:

I want to put some (one or two) questions to you	Я хочу́ обрати́ться к вам с ко́е-каки́ми (or ко́е с каки́ми) вопро́сами

Не́сколько

486. Не́сколько is an indefinite numeral, meaning a relatively small number, i.e. *some = a few*. It is perhaps the most indefinite of the indefinite pronominal words:

Some years ago	Не́сколько лет наза́д
Some days later	Че́рез не́сколько дней

Here не́который would not be used in Russian, as indeed *certain* would not be used in English. Note that in oblique cases не́сколько is declined (*in some places* в не́скольких места́х) but that in the accusative/genitive case with animate objects either не́сколько or не́скольких may be used.

487. Compare the translation of *some* in the following sentences:

I read some (a few) books during the vacation, and some of them (certain ones) I liked very much	Во вре́мя кани́кул я прочита́л не́сколько книг, и не́которые из них мне о́чень понра́вились

(Не́сколько means a few lumped together indiscriminately, while не́которые singles out this one and that one from among them.)

I read some books on the subject during the vacation, but I don't remember what was in them	Во вре́мя кани́кул я прочита́л каки́е-то кни́ги на э́ту те́му, но не по́мню их содержа́ния

(Каки́е-то implies *some books or other, I don't know which ones*.)

488. Compare the following sentences which translate *some*, meaning *a little of*:

(i) *Yes, give me some, please*	Да, пожа́луйста, да́йте мне немно́жко
(ii) *Give me some bread, please*	Да́йте мне, пожа́луйста, хле́ба
(iii) *I would like to give you some good advice*	Я бы хоте́л дать вам хоро́ший сове́т

In (i) there is no noun, and немно́го or немно́жко has to be used. In (ii) the noun is concrete and divisible and *some* can be expressed by a simple partitive genitive. In (iii) the noun is abstract and *some* is not translated.

489. *Some more, any more* are both rendered simply by ещё:
Will you have some more?   Хоти́те вы ещё?

490. *Some* meaning *approximately no more than* may be idiomatically translated by како́й-нибудь (see para. **629**):

> *There were some five or six*   Оста́лось пройти́ каки́х-
> *miles to go*   нибудь пять–шесть миль

491. *Some . . . some. . . .* A common idiomatic construction is кто . . . кто . . . :

> *Some affirm it, some deny it*   Кто утвержда́ет э́то, кто от-
>   рица́ет

Some . . . others. . . . Most commonly одни́ . . . други́е . . .

492. To translate *some people*, не́которые as a noun, or не́которые лю́ди give the least definite shade of meaning; немно́гие (немно́гие лю́ди) means more specifically *a few*; ко́е-кто (with a singular verb) *one or two, people here and there*.

'Some' and 'any' questions

493. Often the word *some* is used in English without specifically denoting *a few* or *certain ones*. In such cases it may be compared with *any* and the two words may be interchanged without any apparent difference of meaning. But sometimes the use of *some* as opposed to *any* gives a particular nuance to a sentence, which has been defined by saying that *any* is negative or non-committal, whereas *some*, though indefinite, is positive in meaning. That is to say that *some* is used in questions that are really polite substitutes for commands, or to which an affirmative answer is expected; *any* in questions that ask for information, without seeming to take an affirmative or a negative answer more or less for granted. This distinction does not hold good in Russian, and the *some/any* word is not as a rule translated:

> *Have you any sisters?* (I   Есть ли у вас сёстры?
> don't know whether
> you have or not)
> *Will you give me some*   Да́йте мне, пожа́луйста,
> *sweets, please?*   конфе́т

(I see you have some; expecting the reply *what would you like?*) Notice, however, that in the second sentence, Russian uses a partitive genitive to indicate *some of a whole*—an idea which is obviously not present in the first sentence.

Something

494. For the difference between что́-то and что́-нибудь see para. **483.** The alternative forms не́что (= что́-то) and что́-либо (= что́-нибудь) are less common today:

Something like that   Что́-то в э́том ро́де

495. The pregnant *something* has no direct equivalent in Russian, except perhaps the simple form что, чего́, &c., as in the following:

You have something to be proud of   Вам есть чем горди́ться

Often the sentence must be recast or the sense paraphrased:

To think something of one-self   Быть высо́кого мне́ния о себе́

There is something in what you say   В том, что вы говори́те, есть толк (до́ля пра́вды)

Any

496. (i) *Any* is particularly common in questions and in negative statements (*not any*). It was said above (para. **493**) that the *some/any* word in open questions which simply ask for information is not usually translated in Russian (e.g. *have you any news of your aunt?* есть ли у вас но́вости о тёте?), although каки́е-нибудь *may* also be used, just as we may also say in English *have you any news at all . . . ?* But in polite requests which ask for something more tangible than information the *any* question is most frequently turned in Russian by нет ли?:

Have you any matches? (i.e. please, give me some matches)   Нет ли у вас спи́чек?

(ii) In negative questions and statements *not any* must be rendered by нет followed by the genitive of the noun, with the optional addition of никакой, with the same sense as какой-нибудь when inserted in positive questions:

There isn't any hope (at all)	Нет никакой надёжды

497. *Any = any one at all = every one* is translated by всякий or любой:

It is sold in any shop	Это продаётся в любом (во всяком) магазине
To fulfil any request I might make	Исполнить всякую мою просьбу

In the negative, всякий (любой) becomes никакой:

It is not sold in any shop	Это не продаётся ни в каком магазине

Notice that the preposition is inserted between ни and какой, which are written as separate words. In an emphatic position (and especially at the beginning of a sentence) ни один replaces никакой:

In no *shop is it sold*	Ни в одном магазине это не продаётся

Anybody at all meaning *everybody* is translated by всякий used as a noun:

Anybody will show you	Всякий вам покажет

The negative is никто:

He never spoke about his love to any one of his comrades	Он не говорил ни с кем из товарищей о своей любви

498. *Any* meaning *any one you like* (but not *every*) is любой:

Choose any three cards	Выберите любые три карты

Compare *not any* in the sense of *not any old one*:

Give me a book—not just any one, but something interesting	Дайте мне книгу, не какую-нибудь, а интересную

499. Notice the translation of *not any of* in the following sentence:

Neither on that day, nor on any of the following	Ни в тот день, ни в один из послéдующих

Anything

500. It will be noticed that что is frequently used instead of чтó-нибудь in the spoken language:

She asked him if anything unpleasant had happened (was there anything the matter)	Онá спросúла егó, нé было ли чегó неприя́тного

Compare too the following example where English may have either *anything* or *something*:

He was afraid lest anything unpleasant should happen (he was afraid some-thing unpleasant might happen)	Он боя́лся, как бы нé было чегó неприя́тного
Have you anything to say?	Есть у вас что сказáть?

In the same way кто is used for ктó-нибудь:

If anybody rings don't an-swer.	Éсли кто позвонúт, не отве-чáйте
He was afraid lest anybody should ring (he was afraid somebody might ring)	Он боя́лся, как бы кто не позвонúл

501. There are some idiomatic expressions where *anything* in English is rendered by *everything* in Russian:

She was left without any-thing	Онá остáлась без всегó
He likes swimming better than anything	Он бóльше всегó лю́бит плáвать
She was ready to do anything for her son	Онá готóва былá всё сдé-лать для своегó сы́на

OTHER INDEFINITE WORDS

Certain

502. For the uses of какóй-то and нéкоторый in the sense of *some* meaning *a certain, certain ones*, see para. **484.**

Извéстный is also commonly used in the same meaning in a few stock phrases, e.g.:

To a certain extent	До извéстной (нéкоторой) стéпени
Under certain conditions	При извéстных (нéкоторых) услóвиях
When a certain time had elapsed	Когдá прошлó извéстное (нéкоторое) врéмя

Извéстный will certainly be preferred when the emphasis is unmistakably on *one particular* . . .:

A certain type of people	Лю́ди извéстного рóда

In children's stories and fables одúн is also often found in this sense:

A certain man had a beautiful daughter	У однóго человéка былá красúвая дóчка

The translation of *a certain* by нéкий is now somewhat stilted, although common with surnames and titles:

A certain Mr. Ivanov called to see you	Нéкий г. Иванóв зашёл к вам

Whoever, whatever

503. In the indefinite sense of *it doesn't matter who* or *what*, *whoever* and *whatever* are translated by кто бы ни and что бы ни followed by the past tense of the verb:

Whoever you are, you can't do that	Кто бы вы ни бы́ли, э́того дéлать нельзя́
Whatever you do, don't go to London	Что бы вы ни дéлали, не éздите в Лóндон

A sort of

504. Како́й-то may mean *a sort of* (*rather like*), or it may mean *rather* (*a bit*):

It's a sort of novel   Э́то како́й-то рома́н
He is rather stupid (cf. col- Он како́й-то глу́пый
   loquial English *he's sort*
   of stupid)

'Such and such'

505. Тако́й-то corresponds to English *such and such* as a substitute for an unknown name or number:

On such and such a date   Тако́го-то числа́

QUANTITATIVE WORDS

Many, much

506. *Many people* may be translated in any one of the following three ways:

  (i) Мно́гие (as a noun).
  (ii) Мно́гие лю́ди.
  (iii) Мно́го люде́й.

In the nominative case it is possible to detect a difference between (i) and (ii) on the one hand, and (iii) on the other, a difference illustrated by Vinogradov as follows:

Many people think that ...   Мно́гие (лю́ди) ду́мают,
                        что ...
Many people perish in war   Мно́го люде́й ги́бнет на
                        войне́

In the first sentence мно́гие means each one of many separately; in the second, мно́го means many taken together (a collective meaning emphasized by the use of the singular verb). But in the accusative/genitive case, this distinction is not observed:

| *I knew many people there* | Там я знал мно́гих (мно́го) люде́й |

In other oblique cases мно́го is, of course, impossible.

Again with expressions of time, the same shade of difference between мно́го and мно́гие can be felt:

| *And many years slipped quietly by* | И мно́гие го́ды неслы́шно прошли́ (Lermontov) |
| *Many years have passed since I was at school* | Прошло́ мно́го лет с тех пор, как я учи́лся в шко́ле |

In the first sentence мно́гие suggests year succeeding year, each passing quietly by; in the second мно́го suggests totality of time. Two further examples may confirm the point:

| *In autumn, many days are rainy* (i.e. a certain number out of the total) | О́сенью мно́гие дни дожд-ли́вые |
| *It happened many days ago* | Э́то случи́лось мно́го дней наза́д |

507. *Many of* is always мно́гие из:

| *Many of us think differently* | Мно́гие из нас ду́мают ина́че |

508. *Much, not much*:

I have plenty of time	У меня́ мно́го вре́мени
I haven't much time	У меня́ не мно́го вре́мени
We are not devoting much attention to questions of defence	Мы уделя́ем не мно́го вни-ма́ния вопро́сам оборо́ны

But in these examples and in similar cases *not much* will also be more idiomatically translated by ма́ло (*little*).

509. Мно́гое (gen. мно́гого) may be used as a noun:

Much needs to be thought out   Мно́гое на́до обду́мать

It cannot in the singular be used as an adjective—one cannot say мы не уделя́ем мно́гого внима́ния *we are not devoting much attention*, but must say мы не уделя́ем большо́го внима́ния.

510. *Not much of a* may be rendered by нева́жный (often after a noun):

He is not much of an actor at all   Он актёр о́чень нева́жный

Few, a few

511. *A few people* may be translated by:

   (i) Немно́гие (as a noun).
  (ii) Немно́гие лю́ди.
 (iii) Не́сколько челове́к.

(i) and (ii) suggest *a few* taken individually, and (iii) *a few* collectively.

512. *A few*: see para. **486.**

Few (not many) as opposed to *a few (several)* is ма́ло. Compare:

There are a few good buildings in our town	У нас в го́роде не́сколько хоро́ших зда́ний
There are few good buildings in our town	У нас в го́роде ма́ло хоро́ших зда́ний

513. Notice the idiomatic ре́дкий (English *few* meaning *sparse*)

The tree, whose few leaves had already turned yellow . . .   Де́рево, ре́дкие ли́стья кото́рого уже́ пожелте́ли . . .

THE PRONOUN 'ONE'

514. The word *one* is a versatile word with many different uses in English:

(i) As an anaphoric pronoun it may refer back to a concrete noun already expressed:

Do you play the piano? *There's one in the study*	Игра́ете ли вы на роя́ле? В кабине́те есть роя́ль

Here the noun must be repeated in Russian. Notice, however, that as a predicative word after быть the instrumental case of the personal pronoun (им, ей) may be used instead of repeating the noun:

There is no reason at all for portraying Tolstoy as a scholarly research worker when he was not one	Соверше́нно не́зачем изобража́ть Толсто́го учёным иссле́дователем, когда́ он им не́ был (Eichenbaum)

(ii) As a 'prop-word' it is used, for example, in expressions involving the definite article or an article + adjective—*the one, the ones, a red one*, &c.:

I have lost my coat; I must buy a new one	Я потеря́л пальто́; я до́лжен купи́ть но́вое

In this context the adjective alone is translated.

(iii) It can mean *a person who*:

For one who speaks German well it is not difficult	Для челове́ка, кото́рый хорошо́ говори́т по-неме́цки, э́то не тру́дно

Here для того́, кто говори́т, &c., is a perfectly acceptable alternative.

But notice the difference in meaning when the subject of the sentence is identical with the pronominal *one* (i.e. when *one* refers to a definite person):

For one who has never been to Russia, he speaks Russian well	Для челове́ка, кото́рый никогда́ не́ был в Росси́и, он хорошо́ говори́т по-ру́сски

Here, of course, the для того, кто construction, with its indefinite sense, would be impossible.

(iv) It can mean *everyone, people generally*:

In Russian one says 'нет'; *in English one says* 'no' (spoken by an Englishman)	По-ру́сски говоря́т „нет"; по-англи́йски мы гово- ри́м „no"

When the 3rd person plural of the verb is used in this Russian equivalent of the French *on dit* construction, the personal pronoun (они́) is always omitted. Another very common way of expressing *one* in this same sense is by the 2nd person singular of the present indicative of the verb, again with the personal pronoun omitted:

One never can tell (*one never knows*)	Никогда́ не зна́ешь

515. (i) Notice the use of оди́н to mean *alone*:

I was compelled to fight alone	Я был принуждён боро́ться оди́н

The *dative singular* одному́ is used in this construction where a dative subject is implied, though not necessarily expressed:

It is always nicer to walk with somebody than by yourself	Всегда́ лу́чше ходи́ть двои́м, чем одному́

Here the sense is *it is better* for *two people to walk than* for *one person*.

She had to stand all evening. Still it was better than sitting on her own at home	Ей пришло́сь стоя́ть весь ве́чер. Но э́то бы́ло всё-таки лу́чше чем сиде́ть до́ма одно́й

(ii) Notice also оди́н, оди́н то́лько meaning *only*:

Just in one's shirt	В одно́й (то́лько) руба́шке

DEFINITIVE WORDS

Each, every

516. (i) In English *each* tends to suggest each one of a fairly small number; *every*—all members of a class or species, without dwelling on each constituent member. But there is considerable confusion of usage between the two. In Russian ка́ждый may be regarded as the equivalent of *each*, and will always in preference to вся́кий translate *each of a small number, each of two* (cf. кото́рый? which asks the question *which of two?* as compared with како́й?)

He gave each one of us a book	Он дал ка́ждому из нас по кни́ге

This example illustrates also the idiomatic use of по and the dative case to equal *each apiece*, which, as the following sentence shows, is a means of dispensing with ка́ждый altogether:

We took a tray each from the table	Мы сня́ли со сто́лика по подно́су

Ка́ждый is also used more commonly than вся́кий in the expression ка́ждый тре́тий день *every third day* and exclusively in ка́ждые три дня *every three days* where English uses *every*.

(ii) But there is as great or even greater confusion between ка́ждый and вся́кий in Russian than between *each* and *every* in English. All that can safely be said is that ка́ждый is more selective (each one out of a small number) and that вся́кий is more versatile, in that it has additional uses which ка́ждый does not have—e.g. *all sorts of, any one you like*:

All sorts of things happen in our life	В на́шей жи́зни вся́кое быва́ет

517. Что and что ни can be used idiomatically to give the sense of 'every':

Every word is a mockery	Что ни сло́во, то насме́шка

The constructions ма́ло ли кто, ма́ло ли что are used colloquially in the meaning of all sorts of people (things) and, loosely, *everyone, everything*:

Everyone knows that! — Ма́ло ли кто зна́ет э́то!

Same

518. Notice that the numeral оди́н may do service for тот же (са́мый):

They were both the same age — О́ба они́ бы́ли одного́ во́зраста

I lived in the same house as he — Я жил в одно́м до́ме с ним

The particle и is often used in Russian, with no equivalent in English, to point a comparison, *the same as . . .*:

The eldest son chose the same career as his father — Ста́рший сын вы́брал ту же карье́ру, как и оте́ц

Often *as* is translated in this context by како́й instead of как:

They are almost the same weapons as are used today — Э́то почти́ то же са́мое ору́жие, како́е и сего́дня употребля́ется

Self, the very

519. Сам, сама́ (accusative самоё), само́, and са́мый, са́мая, са́мое, are often confused:

(i) *The king himself told me* — Сам коро́ль мне сказа́л

(ii) *He showed it to me myself* — Он мне самому́ э́то показа́л

(iii) *In the very heart of London* (= *right in*) — В са́мом це́нтре Ло́ндона

(iv) *On the very top of the hill* (= *right on*) — На са́мом верху́ горы́

(v) *This train goes right to* Э́тот по́езд идёт до са́мой
    Moscow   Москвы́

Сам (i, ii) most frequently translates *self* and defines persons—by emphasizing one, it eliminates others. Its chief use is with nouns and *personal* pronouns. Са́мый (iii, iv, v) frequently defines time, place, and objects in space. Its chief use is with nouns (when it often translates *right in, right on, right to*, &c.), and with *demonstrative* pronouns (*this very one, that very one*).

520. Notice that сам is used with себя́, себе́, and собо́й to strengthen the reflexive pronoun:

She is altogether absorbed in Она́ сама́ себя́ забыва́ет в
  housework   дома́шней рабо́те

It may also mean *by oneself*, i.e. *without help*:

The wounded man got up by Ра́неный сам встал
  himself (*unaided*)

The combination сам по себе́ means *by itself*, i.e. *independently, in its own right*:

Convictions by themselves Убежде́ния са́ми по себе́ —
  mean nothing (i.e. not   ничто́
  backed by actions)

NEGATIVE WORDS
Nothing

521. The genitive ничего́ is much more common than ничто́ even where at first sight a nominative might be expected:

A. *What's the matter with* Что с ва́ми (sc. случи́лось)?
  you?

B. *Nothing*   Ничего́ (sc. не случи́лось)

Here, although a negative verb is not expressed, it is implied, and thus explains the genitive.

But ничто́ remains in the nominative when it is the subject of a verb which directly governs an object, whether in the accusative case or in an oblique case, without a preposition:

Nothing worries him	Ничто́ не забо́тит его́
Nothing pleases him	Ничто́ не нра́вится ему́

But:

Nothing ever happens to him	С ним ничего́ не случа́ется

522. When *nothing* is followed by an infinitive (e.g. *to have nothing to . . . '*), it is always translated by не́чего or an oblique case of не́чего, with or without preposition. (The nominative and accusative pronoun не́что has the positive meaning of что́-то, although not common.) See para. **300**:

There is nothing to be done there	Там не́чего де́лать

But compare:

There is nothing there	Там ничего́ нет

All cases of both ничто́ and не́чего when used with prepositions other than из (see para. **617**) are divided by the preposition into negative particle, preposition, and pronoun:

I have nothing to think about	Мне не́ о чем ду́мать
What are you thinking about?—Nothing at all.	О чём вы ду́маете? — Я ни о чём не ду́маю

The same construction is found with a variety of negative compound words, e.g. не́куда *there is nowhere to* (*go*) (cf. никуда́ не *nowhere*); не́когда *there is no time to* (cf. никогда́ не *never*)'. See para. **301.**

VI

THE PREPOSITION

TIME

At, during, in, on

At

523. В (accusative case):

   (i) The time, except *half-past*:

At five o'clock	В пять часо́в
At a quarter past five	В че́тверть шесто́го
At a quarter to six	Без че́тверти в шесть (more commonly just без че́тверти шесть)
At midday	В по́лдень
At midnight	В по́лночь

Either час or вре́мя may mean *time*:

At that time you will always find him at home	В э́тот час (в э́то вре́мя) вы всегда́ заста́нете его́ до́ма

Half-past with в takes the prepositional case:

At half-past six	В полови́не седьмо́го

but may also be expressed in the nominative case, without в: полови́на седьмо́го

   (ii) A stage in time:

At this time of the year	В э́то вре́мя го́да
At the present time	В настоя́щее вре́мя

(cf. also в после́днее вре́мя *recently*). Notice в ра́зное вре́мя *at different* times.

(iii) The age of a person:

He married at twenty-five	Он жени́лся в два́дцать пять лет (or он жени́лся двадцати́ пяти́ лет)
At my time of life	В мои́ го́ды

524. B (prepositional case):

(i) In the interrogative expression *at what time?* (cf. expressions of time with accusative case para. **523**):

At what time did he arrive?	В кото́ром часу́ он прие́хал?
(ii) *At twilight*	В су́мерках

(cf. *at dawn*, &c., para. **526**.)

(iii) With *beginning, middle, end*:

At the beginning—middle— end of July	В нача́ле — середи́не — конце́ ию́ля

Notice also, however, *at mid-summer* среди́ ле́та, *in the middle of the week* среди́ неде́ли

525. На (accusative case):

Religious feasts:

At Easter	На па́сху	*At Christmas*	На рождество́
At Shrovetide	На ма́сленицу		

The prepositional case is also found in these expressions but the accusative is more usual.

526. На (prepositional case):

At dawn	На заре́, на рассве́те
At sunset	На зака́те со́лнца

527. При (prepositional case):

When *at*, followed by a noun, corresponds to a verbal construction with *as*:

. . . *that dark mass from which I recoiled at landing (as I landed)*	. . . та тёмная ма́сса от кото́рой я шара́хнулся при поса́дке (Kaverin)

They wept at parting	Они плакали при расставании
Everyone trembled at the mention of his name	Все трепетали при упоминании его имени

528. По (dative case):

When *at* means *upon, following*:

At his signal they would begin the sowing	По его сигналу начинали сев (Musatov)

529. С (genitive case):

When *at* means *from*:

I shall begin at the beginning	Я начну с начала
. . . many people turned out to be quite different from what they seemed to be at first sight	. . . многие люди выходили совсем не такими, какими они казались с первого взгляда (M. Prishvin)
He fell in love with her at first sight	Он влюбился в неё с первого взгляда

In (during)—a point in time

530. В (prepositional case):

(i) Times of life:

In childhood—youth—old age	В детстве — юности — старости

But compare в дни молодости *in the days of one's youth.*

(ii) Months:

In February—March, &c.	В феврале — марте —

(iii) Year, decade, century:

In the year 1900	В тысяча девятисотом году
During the first decade of the nineteenth century	В первом десятилетии девятнадцатого века
In the nineteenth century	В девятнадцатом веке

Note that with десятилéтие the accusative after в is also possible with no difference in meaning. *During that year* may be either в том годý or в тот год and *during that period* в том перйоде or в тот перйод. When, however, the year is named, only the prepositional is possible. With век (сто-лéтие) only the prepositional is possible.

531. Во врéмя (genitive case):

During the First World War	Во врéмя пéрвой мировóй войны́
During the thunderstorm	Во врéмя грозы́
During the lecture	Во врéмя лéкции

Во врéмя is used predominantly with historical events, natural phenomena, activities, and not normally with periods of time. In these examples the meaning of *during* is *at some stage in*. See para. **535** for во врéмя meaning *throughout*.

532. На (prepositional case):

(i) Designates a minute, hour, year as one in a series from a definite starting point:

He scored in the fifth minute	Он забúл гол на пя́той минýте игры́
A child begins to speak during its second year	Ребёнок начинáет говорúть на вторóм годý от рож-дéния

Compare para. **541** (i) where день following на is placed in the accusative case.

(ii) Weeks:

Last—this—next week	На прóшлой — э́той — бý-дущей недéле

(iii) Certain expressions which combine a sense of time and the manner in which the time is spent:

On the way back (during the return journey)	На обрáтном путú
In the holidays	На канúкулах

(iv) Notice the idiom на ста́рости лет *in old age* and compare with the use of в in all other similar expressions (see para. **530** (i)). Notice also the idiom на моём веку́ *in my lifetime.*

In (during)—duration of time

533. В (accusative case):

    (i) The period taken to complete an action:

I shall write this story in three weeks	Я напишу́ э́тот расска́з в три неде́ли

    (ii) Meaning 'in the course of':

I go to the cinema three times a week	Я хожу́ в кино́ три ра́за в неде́лю

    (iii) Duration of a state, an action, an age, an historical event:

During his absence	В его́ отсу́тствие

(Cf. в его́ прису́тствии *in his presence* which is a prepositional expression of place.)

In the revolution of July 1830, the French bourgeoisie seized power	В ию́льскую револю́цию 1830 го́да францу́зская буржуази́я захвати́ла власть

Here the revolution is envisaged as a whole and its result described.

During the Middle Ages	В сре́дние века́

Also в ка́менный век *in the Stone Age*; в эпо́ху просвеще́ния *during the Age of Enlightenment*; в ры́царские века́ *during the Age of Chivalry.*

    (iv) In expressions which combine a sense of time and the manner in which the time is spent. Especially common are:

During the whole journey	Во весь путь (во всю доро́гу)
During all the rest of the journey, the Major did not say a word	Майо́р во весь остально́й путь не произнёс ни сло́ва (Fadeyev)

(Contrast на обра́тном пути́ para. **532** (iii))

534. За (accusative case):

(i) Synonymous with в in the meaning of *period of completion of an action* (para. **533** (i)):

I shall write this story in three weeks	Я напишу́ э́тот расска́з за три неде́ли

(ii) Meaning *over a certain period*:

Vas'ka . . . undertook to count how many wounded would come to the dressing station in one day	Ва́ська . . . взя́лся счита́ть ско́лько ра́неных за день придёт на перевя́зку (Panova)

535. Во вре́мя (genitive case):

To take notes during a lecture	Записа́ть во вре́мя ле́кции

Here the meaning of во вре́мя is *during the whole of, throughout* (cf. para. **531** where it means *at some point in*).

536. В тече́ние; на протяже́нии (genitive case):

During the nineteenth century	В тече́ние (на протяже́нии) девятна́дцатого ве́ка
During many decades	В тече́ние (на протяже́нии) мно́гих десятиле́тий

These expressions are used predominantly with nouns with temporal meaning (cf. во вре́мя para. **531**). Compare the meaning of the above examples (*during the course of*) with that of the examples with в and the prepositional case in para. **530.**

537. В продолже́ние (genitive case):

The majority, during the course, do not work at their subjects	Большинство́, в продолже́ние ку́рса, не занима́ются свои́ми предме́тами

В продолже́ние, as well as with expressions of time, is commonly used with nouns denoting a process or activity.

In—other meanings

538. Че́рез (accusative case):

After a certain interval:

I shall finish this book in three days' time	Я ко́нчу э́ту кни́гу че́рез три дня

Че́рез meaning after a certain interval is used to designate actions which occur at regular intervals:

The buses run every ten minutes	Авто́бусы хо́дят че́рез ка́ждые де́сять мину́т
Every ten steps Mitrofan Il'ich stopped	Че́рез ка́ждый деся́ток шаго́в Митрофа́н Ильи́ч остана́вливался (Polevoy)

Че́рез may also be used as a strengthening word, followed by по́сле *after*:

Three years after his marriage, he obtained the post of shipping-office manager	Че́рез три го́да по́сле жени́тьбы, он получи́л до́лжность управля́ющего парохо́дной конто́рой

The exact opposite of че́рез — по́сле in such constructions is за — до *before*:

Three years before his marriage, &c.	За три го́да до жени́тьбы и т. д.

539. При (prepositional case):

(i) Meaning *in the reign of*:

But life was easier for Radishchev in Catherine's reign	А Ради́щеву при Екатери́не ле́гче жило́сь (Musatov)

(ii) In constructions similar to those translated by *at* in para. **527**:

The documents found in the search were too revealing	Докуме́нты на́йденные при о́быске бы́ли сли́шком красноречи́вы (Ignatov)

With this sense of concomitance при is used in numerous expressions which are temporal in that they denote attendant circumstance:

In (when) crossing the street . . .	При перехо́де че́рез у́ли-цу . . .
When in doubt lead trumps	При сомне́нии ходи́ть с ко́зырей
He made his speech in complete silence	Он произнёс свою́ речь при по́лном молча́нии

Note also при си́льном ве́тре *in a strong wind*.

On—sometimes understood but not expressed in English:

540. В (accusative case):

(i) Morning and evening:

(On) that same morning	В то же у́тро
One fine evening	В оди́н прекра́сный ве́чер

(or тем же у́тром: одни́м прекра́сным ве́чером)

(ii) Days of the week:

On Monday, Tuesday, &c.	В понеде́льник, во вто́р-ник, и т. д.
On that same day	В тот же день

541. На (accusative case):

(i) With *next day* (сле́дующий день, друго́й день, за́втра) and when *day* is accompanied by an ordinal number. The sense is often but not always one of comparison with what happened the previous day:

The next day he went away	На за́втра он уе́хал
The next morning he was well again	На у́тро он уже́ был здоро́в

> *Lar'ka spent only two days*   Ла́рька сиде́л не бо́лее двух
> *in prison, on the third day*   дней, на тре́тий день его́
> *he was released*   вы́пустили (Ertel')

(ii) *On this occasion* is normally translated by на э́тот раз:

> *On this occasion sleep was*   Сон на э́тот раз заста́вил
> *longer than usual in com-*   себя́ ждать бо́лее обык-
> *ing*   нове́нного (Kuprin)

Compare such expressions as во второ́й раз of which the
sense is one of enumeration:

> *This is the second time I*   Я во второ́й раз в Пари́же
> *have been in Paris*

542. По (dative plural):

Used to describe repeated actions and the intervals at
which they occur. These constructions are similar to those
with по given in para. **551** but do not indicate the duration
of each repeated action:

> *On holidays we used to sleep*   По пра́здникам мы спа́ли
> *till about ten o'clock*   часо́в до десяти́ (Gor'ky)
> *We go to the theatre on*   Мы хо́дим в теа́тр по чет-
> *Thursdays*   верга́м

По, of course, may correspond in these constructions to
English prepositions other than *on*, depending on the
English noun used:

> *I read in the mornings*   Я чита́ю по утра́м

543. По (prepositional case):

When *on* replaces *when* and a verbal construction in
expressions such as the English *on his return* (*when he returned*):

> *On his father's death, he*   По сме́рти отца́ он уе́хал
> *went abroad*   заграни́цу

Notice also по его́ возвраще́нии *on his return*, по осмо́тре
on examination, по прие́зде *on arrival*.

Other prepositions of time

After

544. После (genitive case):

After the ball	После ба́ла

545. За (instrumental and accusative case):

Following in succession (instrumental):

Day after day	День за днём

Beyond (accusative):

After midday (midnight)	За по́лдень (по́лночь)

Compare по́сле полу́дня (полу́ночи):

After midday she began to feel the pangs of thirst	После полу́дня она́ начала́ томи́ться жа́ждой (Lermontov)

The use of по́сле means simply *at some moment after midday*. The use of за followed by the accusative case gives the sense of the movement of time beyond midday:

It was already long after midday when they arrived	Бы́ло уже́ далеко́ за по́лдень когда́ они́ прие́хали

За is used in the same way in such expressions as ему́ за со́рок *he is over forty*.

546. Вслед за (instrumental case):

Immediately following:

These words were followed immediately by a fearful noise	Стра́шный шум подня́лся вслед за э́тими слова́ми (Kaverin)

Before

547. До (genitive case):

Before the war	До войны́
Before Christ	До рождества́ христо́ва

548. Перед (instrumental case):

To work before an examination	Занима́ться пе́ред экза́меном
It is difficult to describe the excitement which I and the other actors felt before the dress rehearsal	Тру́дно описа́ть то волне́ние, кото́рое я и други́е актёры испы́тывали пе́ред генера́льной репети́цией (Stanislavsky)

Compare the difference between до того́, как and пе́ред тем, как in para. **387.** До means simply *anterior to*: пе́ред means *immediately before, on the eve of*. The common Russian expressions сра́зу пе́ред *immediately before* and задо́лго до *long before* illustrate the difference between the two prepositions.

By

549. К (dative case):

He will arrive by the end of next week	Он прие́дет к концу́ бу́дущей неде́ли

For

550. На (accusative case):

Denoting time subsequent to the action of the main verb:

I shall lend you the book for six days	Я вам одолжу́ кни́гу на шесть дней

551. По (dative case):

(i) Denoting repeated actions and the period of time which they occupy, English *for . . . on end.* The nouns denoting the period of time (час, день, неде́ля, &c.) are almost always accompanied by the adjective це́лый and are always in the plural:

I used to sit at my books for days on end	По це́лым дням я сиде́л за кни́гами (Kaverin)

(ii) As an alternative to по and the dative plural, the instrumental plural without a preposition is also possible in such expressions:

Alexei would gaze at the commissar for days on end	Алексей це́лыми дня́ми пригля́дывался к комисса́ру (Polevoy)

The instrumental plural may also translate English *for* in expressions which denote a protracted action without the notion of repetition:

... we shall not have to wait for weeks	... нам не придётся дожида́ться неде́лями (Panova)

From ... To

552. с ... до, от ... до (genitive case):

(i) С is used in combination with до when the starting-point in time is not strictly defined:

From spring to late autumn	С весны́ до по́здней о́сени
From morning to evening	С утра́ до ве́чера
From childhood to old age	С де́тства до ста́рых лет

От ... до is used when the starting-point is strictly defined:

From the second of June to the fifth of August	От второ́го ию́ня до пя́того а́вгуста
From two o'clock to a quarter to four	От двух часо́в до без че́тверти четы́ре
From twenty to thirty years of age	От двадцати́ до тридцати́ лет

In certain expressions either с or от may be used:

From February to October	С (от) февраля́ до октября́
From ancient times to the present day	С (от) дре́вних времён до на́ших дней
From cradle to grave	С (от) колыбе́ли до моги́лы

(ii) When in English *from* is not followed by *to*, c and not от is used in Russian:

I shall live here from the fif-teenth of August	Я бу́ду жить здесь с пятна́дцатого а́вгуста

(iii) C may be followed by по (and the accusative case) with a different meaning from до. C... до means *from... up to* (but not including) whereas c... по means *from... up to* (and including):

From the sixth of May to the tenth of June inclusive	С шесто́го ма́я по деся́тое ию́ня

Notice the expression по сей день *to this very day*.

(iv) C is followed by на in the expression откла́дывать со дня́ на́ день *to put off from day to day*, and in откла́дывать (отложи́ть) с ве́чера на у́тро *to put off from the evening until the next morning*.

553. Compare the following expressions:

(i) Со дня́ на́ день *from day to day, from one day to the next*:

We were expecting the de-claration of war daily	Мы ожида́ли со дня́ на́ день объявле́ния войны́
We get along from one day to the next	Мы перебива́емся со дня на́ день

(ii) Де́нь ото дня́ *gradually, day by day*, normally found with comparatives:

My life is becoming emptier day by day	Жизнь моя́ стано́вится пусте́е де́нь ото дня́ (Lermontov)

(iii) Изо дня́ в де́нь *day after day, day in day out*:

The factory exceeds the pro-gramme day after day	Заво́д перевыполня́ет програ́мму изо дня́ в де́нь (Polevoy)

These expressions are also possible, of course, with other periods of time as e.g., час, ме́сяц, год, *hour, month, year*; час о́т часу не ле́гче *things are going from bad to worse*.

Since

554. С (genitive case):

With an imperfective verb с is used in the same way as French *depuis* which, with the present tense, denotes that an action begun in the past is still in progress:

I have been waiting for you since three o'clock   Я вас жду с трёх часо́в

With a perfective verb, however, с does not mean *since* but simply states the moment at which the action was performed as in с утра́ *in the morning*, с ве́чера *in the evening*:

Katya in the morning put on her black dress and smoothly combed her fair hair   Ка́тя с утра́ наде́ла чёрное пла́тье, гла́дко причеса́ла све́тлые во́лосы (Paustovsky)

Often such constructions have the sense of the action beginning at the time stated:

It began to rain in the morning   Пошёл дождь с утра́

Towards

555. Под (accusative case):

They arrived towards evening   Они́ прие́хали под ве́чер

Alternatively this may be expressed пе́ред ве́чером

Until

556. До (genitive case):

Stay with us until Tuesday   Остава́йтесь у нас до вто́рника

Not until may be neatly translated by то́лько:

I shall not see you until Friday   Я вас то́лько в пя́тницу уви́жу

PLACE

At, in, on, translated by в and на

At

557. В (prepositional case):

The essential function of в as a preposition of place is to define location inside an encompassed space. It is used to translate *at* predominantly with the names of buildings encompassed by four walls:

Public places

At the theatre	В теа́тре
At a hotel	В гости́нице
At the cinema	В кино́
At church	В це́ркви

Places of study

At school	В шко́ле
At the University	В университе́те
At the technical school	В те́хникуме

Notice also в санато́рии *at a sanatorium*. The English expressions *at church* and *at school* have lost the definite article and become almost adverbial expressions. Russian, however, retains with these words the concrete preposition в.

558. На (prepositional case):

(i) The most typical use of на, translating *at*, is to define location combined with a sense of activity, when the noun concerned describes an occasion rather than a place:

At the concert	На конце́рте
At the play	На пье́се
At the exhibition	На вы́ставке
At the wedding	На сва́дьбе

At the funeral	На похоронáх
At the lecture	На лéкции
At the lesson	На урóке
At the war	На войнé
At the front	На фрóнте
At the military council	На воéнном совéте
At the party	На вечерúнке
At work	На рабóте
At the meeting	На собрáнии

(ii) На is also used to translate *at* with the majority of places of work:

At the post office	На пóчте
At the factory	На фáбрике
At the works	На завóде
At the market	На рúнке
At the mine	На шáхте
At the station	На вокзáле (стáнции)

Notice also на курóрте *at the health resort*. The reason for the use of на with these words is that none of them is linked with the notion of a single building or a strictly encompassed space. Завóд, фáбрика, and шáхта may all occupy an extensive space and consist of numerous buildings, housing many different forms of activity. In addition, на with шáхта may convey, more narrowly, the sense of location among the surface workings, as opposed to в шáхте which means *inside the mine* (i.e. down the mine). It is suggested by some Russian grammarians that both пóчта and стáнция are linked with the old term почтóвая стáнция *post station*, where not only was post handled but coachmen and horses were kept for the convenience of travellers. Вокзáл takes на probably because the original вокзáл was simply an open platform (called дебаркадéр, cf. French *débarcadère*) and even now designates both the station building and platforms (cf. на платфóрме below). A market consists of many stalls and covers a wide area.

(iii) Ha also translates *at* when the object or place concerned is regarded as a flat surface:

At platform No. 3	На платфо́рме No. 3
Curtains at the windows	Гарди́ны на о́кнах
At the corner	На углу́

(Cf. стол стои́т в углу́ *the table stands in the corner*). Note American English *on the corner*.

In

559. В (prepositional case):

В is used meaning *in* with the names of towns, territories, and countries, encompassed by boundaries or frontiers:

In London	В Ло́ндоне
In the Crimea	В Крыму́
In Georgia	В Гру́зии
In France	Во Фра́нции
In Siberia	В Сиби́ри
In the Donets Basin	В Донба́ссе

Notice, however, the exception на Украи́не *in the Ukraine* which is probably a Ukrainianism. Notice also на ро́дине and на чужби́не which are abstract expressions and mean *at home* and *abroad*. (For *in Alaska* see para. **562**.)

560. Ha (prepositional case):

(i) Ha translates *in* with nouns which designate activities or occasions rather than places (cf. *at* para. **558**):

In a duel	На поеди́нке
In the medical faculty	На медици́нском факульте́те
In the war	На войне́

Compare быть уби́тым на войне́ but в би́тве *to be killed in the war, in a battle.* Compare also учи́ться в университе́те, на медици́нском факульте́те *to study at the University, in the medical faculty.*

(ii) Also with places regarded as flat surfaces:

In the street	На у́лице
In the square	На пло́щади

(iii) With all points of the compass:

In the North, South, East, West	На се́вере, ю́ге, восто́ке, за́паде

(iv) With mountainous regions inside Russia which do not possess strictly defined borders:

In the Caucasus, in the Urals	На Кавка́зе, на Ура́ле

but в А́льпах, в Пирене́ях, в Карпа́тах *in the Alps, in the Pyrenees, in the Carpathians.*

(v) With natural phenomena which are not tangible:

In the sun	На со́лнце
In the fresh air	На све́жем во́здухе
In a draught	На сквозняке́

Contrast *in the rain* под дождём.)

561. Notice that with certain nouns either в or на may be used to translate *in*:

In the kitchen	В (на) ку́хне
In the sky	В (на) не́бе
In the eyes	В (на) глаза́х
In the yard	В (на) дворе́
In the fields	В (на) поля́х
In the saddle	В (на) седле́

Also в (на) мо́ре *at sea* but only в откры́том мо́ре *in the open sea.* Notice that the adverbial expression на дворе́ (*outside*), takes only на, similarly the metaphorical expression на седьмо́м не́бе (*in the seventh heaven*). В in general is a more concrete preposition of place than на, which accordingly lends itself more easily to use in adverbialized expressions. This difference between в and на comes out clearly when they are used with forms of transport. На in such contexts expresses the method of travel in principle rather than the actual journey, whereas в expresses a definite journey inside a conveyance. Compare:

Travel by car is more convenient than by train	Удобнее éхать на маши́не, чем на по́езде
Three boys and their father were travelling in the car	Три ма́льчика с отцо́м éхали в маши́не

On

562. На (prepositional case):

Used with islands and peninsulas:

On the island of Malta	На о́строве Ма́льте
On the Scandinavian peninsula	На скандина́вском полу́острове

Notice also на Аля́ске *in Alaska* (Alaska is a peninsula).

At, in, on, translated by prepositions other than в **and** на

At

563. У (genitive case):

(i) Corresponding to French *chez*:

I shall live at my aunt's	Я бу́ду жить у тётки
I am having a suit made at the best tailor's	Я шью себé костю́м у лу́чшего портно́го

(ii) Denoting close proximity:

She is sitting at the piano	Она́ сиди́т у роя́ля
The car stopped at the prison gates	Маши́на останови́лась у тюре́мных воро́т

Certain expressions used with у in this meaning have an implied temporal meaning:

At the fork in the road he was the first to turn right	У развилки доро́ги, он пéрвый поверну́л напра́во (Erenburg)

564. При (prepositional case):

(i) May be used as a synonym of у as given in the preceding paragraph (ii):

A house with two lighted windows stood at the entrance to the village	Дом с двумя́ освещёнными о́кнами стоя́л при въе́зде в село́ (A. Tolstoy)

При however may, in addition, give a sense not only of nearness but of actual attachment:

The doctor 'lives in' at the hospital	До́ктор живёт при больни́це
At court	При дворе́

При may also be used in the abstract expression при сме́рти *at death's door* in which у may not be used.

(ii) При also means *present at*:

Pet'ka was present at this scene	Пе́тька был при э́той сце́не (Kaverin)

565. За (accusative and instrumental case):

(i) In contrast to у (first example para. **563** (ii)) за means that the person near an object is also engaged in some activity connected with it:

She was sitting at the piano playing a waltz	Она́ сиде́ла за роя́лем, игра́ла вальс

We can appreciate this meaning of за if we bear in mind such English expressions as *behind a desk, behind the plough* which have the same connotation of activity connected with the object in question as за, of which, of course, the basic meaning is *behind*.

(ii) Like в and на, за is followed by the accusative case when motion is expressed:

The princess seated her daughter at the piano	Княги́ня усади́ла дочь за роя́ль

566. К (dative case):

He fell at the king's feet	Он упа́л к нога́м короля́

In

567. У (genitive case):

Churchill was then in power У вла́сти тогда́ был Че́рчиль

On

568. С (genitive case):

Used with сторона́ (*side*) followed by от and the genitive case to indicate relative position:

On the right (to the right) of С пра́вой стороны́ от до-
the road is a wood ро́ги нахо́дится ро́ща

But N.B. the translation of 'on the wrong side' in the idiom:

He got out of bed on the Он сего́дня у́тром вста́л с
wrong side this morning посте́ли с ле́вой ноги́

569. По (accusative case):

Used with сторона́ (and рука́) to denote place where, in a more concrete sense than с пра́вой стороны́ от above (position relative to):

He was walking on the Он шёл по ту сто́рону
other side of the road доро́ги

На with the prepositional case may be used as a synonym of по and the accusative in this locative sense.

570. По (dative case):

Used with the verb ударя́ть (уда́рить) *to hit*:

He hit me on the head Он уда́рил меня́ по голове́

Notice the idiom ударя́ть (уда́рить) по рука́м *to strike a bargain*.

To, into, translated by в, на **and** к

To

571. В, на (accusative case):

(i) Those nouns which take в or на with the prepositional case meaning location take the same preposition with the accusative case meaning motion:

| *To go to the theatre* | Идти (пойти) в театр |
| *To go to the play* | Идти (пойти) на пьесу |

(ii) With islands and peninsulas *to* is translated by на:

| *Lenin went to Capri to con-* | Ленин поехал на Капри |
| *fer with Gor'ky* | советоваться с Горьким |

572. К (dative case):

(i) К is always used to translate *to* with persons:

| *He returned to his parents* | Он вернулся к родителям |
| *I am going to the doctor's* | Я иду к врачу |

Compare он вернулся в отцовский дом *he returned to his father's house.*

(ii) The noun following к meaning *to* always represents the ultimate point of the movement expressed:

| *The ship reached (came to)* | Корабль приплыл к берегу |
| *the shore* | |

К is especially common after verbs with the prefixes при- and под- meaning *up to*:

| *Come up to the table* | Подойдите к столу |

Into

573. В (accusative case):

Except with nouns which must take на translating *at* and *in*, *into* is almost always translated into Russian by в. (Note, however, эта улица упирается в площадь *this street abuts on to [comes out into] the square.*) With the meaning of *into*, в is usually preceded by a verb strengthened with the prefix в-. Compare:

| *I was going to the theatre* | Я шёл в театр |
| *I was going into the theatre* | Я входил в театр |

In certain constructions в may be used after a noun, without a verb, when motion is implied:

| *The door into the side room* | Дверь в боковую комнату |

From, out of, off, translated by из, с, and от

574. There are three main Russian prepositions which designate movement away from. These prepositions, из, с, and от, form pairs with в, на, and к respectively. Almost invariably when в, на, and к are used with a noun to mean motion to or motion towards, из, с, and от are used with the same noun to mean motion away from:

We came out of the theatre	Мы вышли из теа́тра
The guests from the Ukraine arrived today	Го́сти с Украи́ны прие́хали сего́дня
The ship left (sailed away from) the shore	Кора́бль отплы́л от бе́рега

Notice, however, *to get into bed* ложи́ться (лечь) в посте́ль, but *to get out of bed* встава́ть (встать) с посте́ли; *to sit down in an armchair* сади́ться (сесть) в кре́сло, but *to rise from an armchair* встава́ть (встать) с кре́сла. Compare сади́ться (сесть) на стул and встава́ть (встать) со сту́ла. If, however, a verb with the prefix вы- is used with посте́ль and кре́сло, it is followed by из: он вы́скочил из посте́ли *he leapt out of bed.*

575. The concrete meaning of из is *out of*, of с *from the surface of* or *down from*, of от *away from.*

The combination от . . . до means essentially the distance from one point to another:

It is 450 miles from Glasgow to London	От Гла́зго до Ло́ндона 450 миль

The combination из . . . в envisages the place of departure and the place of arrival, and the emphasis is on the journey between the places, not on the distance between them:

I was travelling from Birmingham to Cambridge via London	Я е́хал из Бирминга́ма в Ке́мбридж че́рез Ло́ндон

The train was making for Moscow from Leningrad	Поезд направля́лся из Ленингра́да в Москву́

This last sentence, however, may be expressed by по́езд направля́лся из Ленингра́да на Москву́, in which case it has the further meaning that the train will not necessarily end its journey at Moscow, but may go farther.

The combination от . . . к also envisages the place of departure and the place of arrival, and may be synonymous with из . . . в:

The steamer was sailing up the Volga from Astrakhan to Saratov	Парохо́д поднима́лся по Во́лге от А́страхани к Сара́тову

This combination is especially common when the verb of motion is itself prefixed by от:

The ship left one shore in the morning and reached the other in the evening	Кора́бль отплы́л от одного́ бе́рега у́тром и приплы́л к друго́му ве́чером

576. The combination с . . . на means *down from—on to*:

The book fell from the table on to the floor	Кни́га упа́ла со стола́ на́ пол

Notice расска́з о прибы́тии с Ма́рса *the story of the arrival from Mars*. С also, of course, often translates *off*:

At the first turning off the square	При пе́рвом поворо́те с пло́щади

Into, translated by other prepositions than в **and** на

577. За (accusative case):

Used with по́яс (*belt*) and голени́ще (*boot-top*) when the literal meaning is *behind*:

I thrust my pistol into my belt and went out	Я заткну́л за́ пояс пистоле́т и вы́шел (Lermontov)

... the snow which had got into his boot-tops   ... снег, который ему забился за голенища (L. N. Tolstoy)

За may also, of course, be used with these words in the instrumental case meaning location, *in*: за поясом *in one's belt*. Note also the word пазуха which means the space between the breast and the clothing and is used with за meaning *in, into*: он засунул руку за пазуху *he thrust his hand inside his jacket*.

578. Внутрь (genitive case):

Used in the expression внутрь страны meaning *inland* (lit. *into the country*):

We were travelling inland   Мы éхали внутрь страны

The corresponding expression describing location is внутри страны:

We live inland   Мы живём внутри страны

From, out of, translated by other prepositions than из, с, and от

579. Russian prepositions usually define position or movement with great precision. Two prepositions which offer excellent examples of this precision are из-под and из-за, both followed by the genitive case:

A series of articles came from his pen (lit. *from under*)   Ряд статей вышел из-под его пера

The soldiers came out of the firing line   Солдаты вышли из-под огня

She rose from the piano without playing (lit. *from behind*)   Она встала из-за рояля, не игра́в

580. Под (accusative and instrumental case):

This preposition may also define motion or location with great precision:

| She hung the lamp from the ceiling | Онá повéсила лáмпу под потолóк |
| The lamp was hanging from the ceiling (lit. *under*) | Лáмпа висéла под потолкóм |

Other English prepositions of place

About

581. По (dative case):

When the meaning is *from one part to another of the surface of an object* or *in one part and another of*, i.e. whether there is movement or not:

| It is pleasant to wander about the streets of London | Приятно бродить по улицам Лóндона |
| Scattered about the floor lay books on all sorts of subjects | Разбрóсанные пó полу лежáли книги сáмого разнообрáзного содержáния |

По in this meaning is often found in combination with a verb with the prefix раз- meaning *in different directions* or *in separate places*:

| They hung the pictures about the walls | Они развéсили картины по стенáм |

582. Óколо, вокрýг, кругóм (genitive case):

When *about* means *around*:

| He looked anxiously about him | Он смотрéл опáсливо вокрýг (óколо, кругóм) себя |
| To beat about the bush | Ходить кругóм да óколо |

Above

583. Над (instrumental case):

| Above sea level | Над ýровнем мóря |
| He raised the chair above his head | Он пóднял стул над головóй |

Notice that над takes the instrumental case whether motion is present or not.

584. Вы́ше (genitive case):

With rivers (lit. *higher than*):

Saratov stands on the Volga above Astrakhan	Сара́тов лежи́т на Во́лге вы́ше А́страхани

Along

585. Вдоль (genitive case):

Meaning *along the length of, alongside*:

He was walking along the shore	Он шёл вдоль бе́рега
Bonfires burned along the shore	Костры́ горе́ли вдоль бе́рега

Вдоль may be followed by по and the dative case: он шёл вдоль по бе́регу.

586. По (dative case):

По, used alone, means *along the line of* or *over the surface of*:

The airman was flying along the frontier when he was shot down	Лётчик лете́л по грани́це, когда́ его́ сби́ли
He is walking along the street	Он идёт по у́лице
Pink along the edges	Ро́зовый по края́м

Before

587. Пе́ред (instrumental case):

In front of:

He stood before the king with bowed head	Он стоя́л пе́ред королём, поту́пив го́лову

588. При (prepositional case):

In the presence of:

Be careful not to say that before witnesses	Смотри́те, не скажи́те э́того при свиде́телях

589. На (prepositional case):

He struck her before my eyes	Он ударил её на моих глазах

Behind

590. За (instrumental and accusative case):

The instrumental is used for location, the accusative for motion:

There is a statue behind the house	За домом стоит статуя
He placed his hands behind his back	Он заложил руки за спину

591. Сзади, позади (genitive case):

These are stronger words than за for denoting location:

The lorry brought up the rear	Позади (сзади) всего шёл грузовик
There is a large garden at the back of the house	Позади (сзади) дома большой сад

Below, beneath

592. Под (instrumental and accusative case):

The instrumental case is used for location, the accusative for motion:

He lives below us	Он живёт под нами
The duck dived beneath the boat	Утка нырнула под лодку

593. Ниже (genitive case):

With rivers (cf. выше, para. **584**):

Astrakhan stands on the Volga below Saratov	Астрахань лежит на Волге ниже Саратова

Beside

594. У (genitive case):

Meaning *near to, at*:

He was sitting beside the river watching the movements of the fish	Он сидéл у рекú, следя́ за движéниями рыб

Beyond

595. За (instrumental and accusative case):

Instrumental case with location, accusative with motion:

Beyond the swamp stands an old house	За болóтом стоúт стáрый дом
This goes beyond the bounds of legitimate competition	Это выхóдит за предéлы закóнной конкурéнции

By

596. У (genitive case):

Meaning *at*

They were sitting by the fireside chatting	Сúдя у камúна, онú бесéдовали

597. Чéрез (accusative case):

Meaning *via*:

We travelled to Paris by London	Мы éхали в Парúж чéрез Лóндон

598. Мúмо (genitive case):

Meaning *past*:

I was going by (passing) the house when I heard a shot	Я шёл мúмо дóма, когдá услы́шал вы́стрел

Down

599. С (genitive case):

We walked down the hill	Мы шли с горы́ пешкóм

Alternatively *down the hill* in this sentence may be translated под гору. Note, however, that whereas идти (пойти) с горы can only have the concrete and specific meaning *to come down a hill*, идти (пойти) под гору has acquired adverbial meaning—*downhill*:

I feel dizzy when I travel downhill	У меня кружится голова, когда еду под гору

Идти (пойти) под гору may also have the metaphorical meaning *to go downhill* and has as its opposite идти (пойти) в гору *to rise in the world*.

600. По (dative case):

Meaning *over the surface of in a downwards direction*:

Tears were rolling down her cheeks	Слёзы катались у неё по щекам

601. Вниз по (dative case):

With rivers:

The steamer was sailing down river	Пароход плыл вниз по течению реки
We were sailing down the Volga	Мы плыли вниз по (спускались по) Волге

Near

602. Около (genitive case):

Meaning *somewhere near*:

Near the town stands a factory	Около города стоит фабрика

603. Под (instrumental and accusative case):

Instrumental with location, accusative with motion. Под is really short for под стенами *under the walls* and means therefore *very near*:

Peter moved his forces near (up to) Poltava	Пётр двинул полки под Полтаву
We live in a villa near (on the outskirts of) Moscow	Мы живём в даче под Москвой

The close proximity designated by под is well illustrated by the fact that *the battle of Stalingrad* is translated into Russian би́тва под Сталингра́дом; similarly *the victory at Stalingrad* побе́да под Сталингра́дом. Alternatively, би́тва при Сталингра́де is possible although при is more commonly used of battles which took place not in the vicinity of (i.e. not under the walls of) a town:

The battle of Borodino (a village)	Би́тва при Бородине́
The battle of Thermopylae (a pass)	Би́тва при Фермопи́лах
The battle of Tsusima (a sea-battle)	Би́тва при Цуси́ме

Of

604. На (accusative case):

With вид (*view*) when *of* means *on to*:

A wonderful view of the river	Великоле́пный вид на ре́ку

605. С (genitive case):

With ко́пия (*copy*) when *of* means *from*:

Make a copy of this letter	Сними́те ко́пию с э́того письма́

These two examples show once again the precision of Russian prepositions.

Over

606. Че́рез (accusative case):

Like *over*, че́рез may mean either *from one side to the other*, (*across*), or *over the top of*:

The bridge over the river	Мост че́рез ре́ку
The ladies were exchanging remarks over the table	Да́мы перегова́ривались че́рез стол (Pushkin)
To fly over a range of mountains	Перелета́ть (перелете́ть) че́рез го́рный хребе́т

He was . . . talking to me,	Он ... устáвив глазá кудá-
. . . with his gaze directed	то чéрез мою́ гóлову ...
somewhere over my head	разговáривал со мной
	(Gor'ky)

Notice also нести́ (понести́) чéрез плечó *to carry over one's shoulder*. A synonym of чéрез in the meaning of *over the top of* is повéрх (genitive case). This preposition should be used when the meaning of чéрез is ambiguous:

| *He was looking at the child* | Он смотрéл на ребёнка |
| *over his spectacles* | повéрх очкóв |

Чéрез here could mean either *through* or *over*.

607. За (accusative and instrumental case):

(i) Used with the word борт:

| *To throw overboard* | Выки́дывать (вы́кинуть) зá борт |
| *Man overboard!* | Человéк за бóртом! |

Note, however, *to fall over a cliff* пáдать (пасть, упáсть) со скалы́ (lit. *to fall off a cliff*).

(ii) За is often a synonym of чéрез meaning motion from one side to the other of:

| *To cross the Volga* | Переезжáть (переéхать) за Вóлгу |
| *To cross one's threshold* (i.e. to travel over, to step over) | Переходи́ть (перейти́) за порóг |

Also зá море *over the sea*, зá горы *over the hills*. Note that a verb with the prefix пере- may be used in such contexts without чéрез or за (cf. English *to cross*): переезжáть (переéхать) Вóлгу *to cross the Volga*. When *over* in English means location and not motion, then, of course, only за (instrumental case), and not чéрез, may be used:

| *Over the hills* | За горáми |
| *Overseas* | Зá морем |

608. Над (instrumental case):

Meaning *above, overhead*:

A brown storm-cloud was stationary over the farm	Над ху́тором ста́ла бу́рая ту́ча (Sholokhov)
A shell flew overhead	Снаря́д пролете́л над на́ми

609. По (dative case):

Meaning *over the surface of*:

A flush spread over his face	Румя́нец разли́лся по его́ лицу́

Round

610. По (dative case):

Meaning *from one to the other*:

It is pleasant in summer to travel round one's friends	Прия́тно ле́том е́здить по друзья́м

611. За (accusative and instrumental case):

Used with у́гол (*corner*) and поворо́т (*turn*). The accusative for motion, the instrumental for location:

The car turned the corner into the square	Маши́на поверну́ла за́ угол на пло́щадь
The church is round the corner	Це́рковь за угло́м

612. О́коло, вокру́г, круго́м (genitive case):

Meaning *round about*:

The fields round the town	Поля́ о́коло (вокру́г, круго́м) го́рода

When, however, *round* means precisely *in a circle round* only вокру́г or круго́м may be used.

The earth revolves round the sun	Земля́ враща́ется вокру́г (круго́м) со́лнца
To travel round the world	Путеше́ствовать вокру́г (круго́м) све́та

Through

613. Сквозь, че́рез (accusative case):

(i) In many common uses of *through* сквозь and че́рез are interchangeable:

Through a sieve—opening—slit—keyhole	Сквозь (че́рез) си́то —отве́рстие — щель — замо́чную сква́жину

(ii) Сквозь is more common than че́рез when the passage through is obstructed or difficult:

He pushed his way through the crowd	Он продра́лся сквозь толпу́

Сквозь is also more common when the meaning is *visible through*:

Visible through smoke—mist—dust	Ви́дно сквозь дым — тума́н — пыль

Сквозь and not че́рез is used in a number of idioms:

To shut one's eyes to something	Смотре́ть (посмотре́ть) сквозь па́льцы на что́-нибудь
To look through rose-coloured spectacles	Смотре́ть (посмотре́ть) сквозь ро́зовые очки́
To fall through the floor with shame	Прова́ливаться (провали́ться) сквозь зе́млю от стыда́

(iii) Че́рез has two special meanings in which сквозь may not be used:

We shall go east through (via) Edinburgh	Мы прое́дем на восто́к че́рез Эдинбу́рг
We were travelling through Georgia	Мы е́хали че́рез Гру́зию

614. По (dative case):

(i) Meaning *over the area of*:

The good news quickly spread through the town	Ра́достная весть бы́стро распространи́лась по го́роду

(ii) Used with воздух:

The stone flew through the air   Камешек летел по воздуху

Under

615. Под (accusative and instrumental):

Accusative for motion, instrumental for location:

Under the water   Под водой
The seal dived under the water   Тюлень нырнул под воду

Notice под ружьём было сто тысяч человек *there were a hundred thousand men under arms* and брата призвали под ружьё *my brother has been called to the colours.*

CAUSE

About

616. От (genitive case):

She is mad about him   Она без ума от него

617. Из (genitive case):

Much Ado about Nothing   Много шума из ничего

After

618. С (genitive case):

Used with дорога (*journey*) when *after* means *from, as a result of*:

I am very tired after my journey   Я очень устал с дороги

Because of

619. Из-за (genitive case):

Used when, as often happens in English, *because of* is followed by a concrete, physical reason:

She refused because of a headache   Она отказалась из-за головной боли

We did not go because of the rain — Мы не пошли из-за дождя

For

620. По (dative case):

(i) Used with причина (*reason*):

For some reason or other — По той или иной причине
For what reason? — По какой причине?

(ii) In the expression жениться по любви (*to marry for love*):

They married for love — Они женились по любви

Opposite жениться по расчёту *to make a calculated marriage*.

621. Ради (genitive case):

For the sake of:

He risked his life for your sake — Он ради вас рискнул жизнью

Ради is found most frequently in fixed expressions such as ради смеха *for a laugh*, ради шутки *for a joke*.

From, out of

622. От, с, из (genitive case):

Of these three common prepositions of cause, от is the most common since it can refer to both physical and emotional reasons and is used in both literary and everyday speech:

Her eyes were red from weeping — Её глаза были красны от слёз
He drinks from boredom — Он пьёт от скуки

For the difference between the verbs страдать and болеть, followed by от and the genitive and by the instrumental without preposition, see para. **50**. С, in causal expressions, has a colloquial flavour and should, in writing, be used only in a number of fixed expressions predominantly emotional in meaning. Common expressions of this kind are:

From grief	С го́ря	*From anguish*	С тоски́
From joy	С ра́дости	*From fear*	Со стра́ху
From annoyance	С доса́ды	*From shame*	Со стыда́
From boredom	Со ску́ки		

These expressions are almost clichés but will often be found with от instead of c. In doubt, it is almost always safe to use от. Из like с designates predominantly emotional reasons but, unlike с, is a strictly literary word:

Out of respect for	Из уваже́ния к
Out of hatred for	Из не́нависти к
Out of love for	Из любви́ к
Out of curiosity	Из любопы́тства

Of

623. От (genitive case):

Used to define the cause of death:

He died of consumption	Он у́мер от чахо́тки

Through

624. Благодаря́ (dative case):

Thanks to:

He was rescued only through your intervention	Он спа́сся то́лько благодаря́ ва́шему вмеша́тельству

625. Из-за (genitive case):

(i) *Through the fault of*:

It was through you that I caught cold	Из-за вас я простуди́лся

(ii) Used when the reason is a quality of character:

Through laziness	Из-за ле́ни
Through carelessness	Из-за невнима́тельности

626. По (dative case):

A synonym of из-за in meaning (ii) above. Elsewhere по is used predominantly when the reason is an abstract one:

Through stupidity	По глупости
Through the fault of the General	По вине генерала
Through a happy combination of circumstances	По счастливому стечению обстоятельств

With

627. От (genitive case):

Her eyes are wet with tears	Её глаза мокры от слёз
The apple-tree branches are heavy with fruit	Ветви у яблонь тяжелы от плодов
I am delighted with (at) your progress	Я в восторге от ваших успехов

PREPOSITIONS OTHER THAN THOSE OF TIME, PLACE, AND CAUSE

About

628. О (об, обо) (prepositional case), про (accusative case) относительно, насчёт (genitive case):
по поводу (genitive case):
в (prepositional case):

(i) All these prepositions may be used, in different contexts, to translate *about* meaning *concerning, on the subject of.* О (об, обо) is used predominantly after verbs of saying, thinking, knowing and hearing, and their cognate nouns:

Tell us about the accident	Расскажите нам о несчастном случае
I try not to think about him	Я стараюсь не думать о нём
The rumour about the king's death	Слух о смерти короля

Notice that Russian makes the same distinction as English

between expressions such as *to remember, to forget, to remind* and *to remember about, to forget about, to remind about*, the former having general and the latter specific meaning:

I have forgotten his surname	Я забы́л его́ фами́лию
I reminded him about (of) his promise	Я напо́мнил ему́ о его́ обеща́нии

(ii) Про is occasionally found as a synonym of о (об, о́бо) in the meanings given above but is much less common.

(iii) Относи́тельно, насчёт may be used in Russian where English, with certain nouns, uses *concerning* to define a broader, more abstract relationship than *about*:

Our suspicions concerning him were justified	На́ши подозре́ния относи́тельно него́ оправда́лись
Fears concerning the submarine proved groundless	Опасе́ния насчёт подво́дной ло́дки оказа́лись неоснова́тельными

(iv) По по́воду means *in connexion with* (по́вод *occasion, motive*):

I have come to see you about the money you owe me	Я к вам по по́воду де́нег, кото́рые вы мне должны́
'Romanticism springs from fear of looking the truth in the face', said he yesterday evening concerning Bal'-mont's poetry	,,Романти́зм — э́то от стра́ха взгляну́ть пра́вде в глаза́'' — сказа́л он вчера́ ве́чером по по́воду стихо́в Ба́льмонта (Gor'ky)

The following sentence shows clearly the difference between о and по по́воду:

... critics will again reproach us on the grounds that our article is written not about Oblomov but apropos of Oblomov	... кри́тики упрекну́т нас опя́ть, что статья́ на́ша напи́сана не об Обло́мове но по по́воду Обло́мова (Dobrolyubov)

(v) B is used in the expression знать (понима́ть) толк в чём-нибудь *to know a lot about something*:

He is well up in mathematics   Он зна́ет толк в матема́тике
(knows a lot about)

629. О́коло (genitive case):
        с (accusative case):

(i) These prepositions are used to translate *about* meaning *approximately*. Other ways of expressing *about* with this meaning are by inversion of substantive and numeral or by the use of the adverbs приблизи́тельно and приме́рно.

(ii) In quantitative expressions consisting simply of noun and numeral, any of the above methods of translation may be used:

About fifty miles   (*a*) О́коло пяти́десяти миль
                       (*b*) С пятьдеся́т миль
                       (*c*) Миль пятьдеся́т
                       (*d*) Приблизи́тельно (при-
                            ме́рно) пятьдеся́т миль

The indefinite pronoun каки́е-нибудь (каки́х-нибудь) may also mean *about* (some) but with a nuance of *only, no more than*:

Only some fifty miles   Каки́е-нибудь (каки́х-ни-
                          будь) пятьдеся́т миль

(iii) An approximate time is normally expressed with о́коло or by inversion:

About two hours ago   О́коло двух часо́в наза́д
                        (часа́ два наза́д)

With the words по́лдень, по́лночь (*midday, midnight*), inversion is, of course, impossible:

About midnight   О́коло полу́ночи

С can express only an approximate duration of time. Compare the two parts of the sentence:

The concert lasted about two hours and finished about two hours ago	Концéрт продолжáлся с два часá и кóнчился часá два назáд

(iv) With inverted noun and numeral any prepositions present are placed between them, and the presence of such prepositions makes the use of óколо or с impossible:

In the direction of the Volga, about two versts away, was situated the village of Pseki and, about four versts farther into the steppe, a small Cossack settlement	По направлéнию к Вóлге, вёрстах в двух, былá расположена дерéвня Псéки а версты́ на четы́ре в степь, небольшáя казáцкая станúца (Gor'ky)

When no other preposition is present óколо and с may stand either before the numeral or between the inverted noun and numeral, the latter if it is wished especially to emphasize the indefiniteness of the expression:

They arrived somewhere about two in the afternoon	Онú приéхали часóв óколо двух пополу́дни

(v) С is used most commonly to express quantity, or to compare size or weight:

About a kilogram in weight	Вéсом с килогрáмм
A man about my height	Человéк рóстом с меня́

Notice that whereas с, in such expressions, designates approximation, the preposition в is used to express exact amount:

A ton in weight	Вéсом в тóнну
A room twenty feet in length	Кóмната длинóй в двáдцать фу́тов

(vi) When such single-word expressions as полчасá (half an hour) are used, accompanied by a preposition, the adverbs приблизúтельно, примéрно, or the indefinite pronoun какúе-нибудь (какúх-нибудь) must be used:

In about half an hour	Приблизúтельно (примéрно) чéрез полчасá

In about half an hour, not more	Чéрез какие-нибудь (каких-нибудь) полчасá

Above

630. Свéрх, свы́ше (genitive case):

These prepositions mean *above* in the sense of greater in quantity. Свы́ше is commonly found with numerals corresponding to English *upwards of*:

Above a thousand people	Свы́ше ты́сячи человéк

Сверх means *in excess of, over and above*:

Above establishment	Свéрх штáта

631. Вы́ше (genitive case):

Morally above:

He is above such base actions	Он вы́ше таки́х пóдлостей

Notice also вне подозрéния *above (beyond) suspicion*.

After

632. Пóсле (genitive case):

Meaning *next to* in achievement:

After Tolstoy, Turgenev is the best Russian writer	Пóсле Толстóго лýчший рýсский писáтель — Тургéнев

633. По (dative case):

Meaning *according to, like*:

He is a man after my own heart	Он человéк мне по душé
The child was christened after its father	Ребёнка окрести́ли по отцý

634. Вслед (dative case):
за (instrumental case):

These prepositions, in different contexts, mean *after* in the sense of *in pursuit of*. Вслед means *in pursuit of* as a person is departing, за means *in pursuit of* with the object of catching:

They shouted something after him, but he did not stop	Они́ крича́ли ему́ что́-то вслед, но он не останови́лся
He was running breathlessly after the bus	Он бежа́л задыха́ясь за авто́бусом

Вслед за (instrumental case) is also used meaning *after, following,* but not necessarily in pursuit of:

Morozka . . . climbed down from the hayloft after Varya	Моро́зка . . . вслед за Ва́рей поле́з с сенова́ла (Fadeyev)

Against

635. Про́тив (genitive case):
с (instrumental case):

Meaning *in opposition to,* про́тив is the generally used word:

I have nothing to say against such a proposal	Не́чего мне сказа́ть про́тив тако́го предложе́ния

Notice the idiom е́сли вы ничего́ не име́ете про́тив *if you have no objection.* С is used with reflexive verbs of mutual action: би́ться с *to fight against,* боро́ться с *to struggle against.*

636. О (accusative case):

Meaning *contact with*:

The bottom of the boat scraped against something	Дни́ще ло́дки цара́пало обо что́-то
The ship struck (ran against) a rock	Кора́бль уда́рился о скалу́

Notice that the preposition translating *against* in the sense of *contact with* is not always о but may vary according to the prefix of the verb:

The old man leant against the wall	Стари́к прислони́лся к стене́

| *They ran up against difficul-ties* | Они наткну́лись на тру́дности |

637. На слу́чай (genitive case):

Meaning *against the eventuality of*, *in case of*:

| *We are taking measures against a possible shortage of water* | Мы принима́ем ме́ры на слу́чай недоста́тка воды́ |

Notice the idiom сберега́ть (сбере́чь) де́ньги на чёрный день *to save money for a rainy day*.

638. На фо́не (genitive case):

Against the background of:

| *The bright colours of the picture stand out against the dark wall* | Я́ркие цвета́ карти́ны выделя́ются на фо́не тёмной стены́ |

Among

639. Среди́ (genitive case):
   ме́жду (instrumental case):

Среди́ means fundamentally *in the middle of*; ме́жду *between*:

We found the mushrooms among some dry leaves	Мы нашли́ грибы́ среди́ сухи́х ли́стьев
Gor'ky in our midst	Го́рький среди́ нас (Fedin)
The lion stands out among animals for its strength	Лев выделя́ется среди́ живо́тных свое́й си́лой
They divided the booty equally among themselves	Они́ раздели́ли добы́чу по́ровну ме́жду собо́й
They reached complete agreement among themselves	Они́ договори́лись обо всём ме́жду собо́й

Notice that ме́жду takes the genitive case in the metaphorical expression ме́жду двух огне́й *between two fires*.

At

640. В (prepositional case):
    за (accusative case):

Both prepositions may be used meaning *at* with expressions of distance (*at* often understood in English):

At about three versts from Kislovodsk	Вёрстах в трёх от Кисловодска (Lermontov)
In the steppe, about sixty versts from the fortress	В степи, вёрст за шестьдесят от крепости (Pushkin)

But notice *at what distance?*

At what distance from London did the accident happen?	На каком расстоянии от Лондона произошла катастрофа?

641. По (dative case):

In expressions of price and value:

At a reduced price	По пониженной цене
At any rate, at least	По крайней мере

642. Под (accusative case):

(i) In the expression под диктовку *at the dictation* (*of*):

She wrote the letter at her father's dictation	Она писала письмо под диктовку отца
The decision was taken at the manager's dictation	Решение было принято под диктовку заведующего

(ii) In the expression под большие проценты *at a high rate of interest*:

He has invested his money at a high rate of interest	Он поместил деньги под большие проценты

Beneath (below)

643. Ниже (genitive case):

Meaning *lower than, shorter than*:

He is below average height	Он ниже среднего роста

Also morally:

He is beneath contempt	Он ни́же презре́ния

Beside

644. Пе́ред (instrumental case):

Meaning *compared with*:

Beside Tolstoy, all novelists are insignificant	Пе́ред Толсты́м, все рома́нисты ничто́жны

645. Вне (genitive case):

In the expression вне себя́ (от) *beside oneself (with)*:

He was beside himself with joy	Он был вне себя́ от ра́дости

Beyond

646. Вне (genitive case):

In the expression вне спо́ра *beyond dispute*:

His talent is beyond dispute	Его́ тала́нт вне спо́ра

647. Сверх (genitive case):

Exceeding:

The play was successful beyond the author's expectations	Пье́са име́ла успе́х сверх ожида́ний а́втора

By

648. По (dative case):

c (instrumental case and genitive case):

путём, посре́дством (genitive case):

(i) These prepositions translate, in different contexts, *by* describing means or method. Both по and c are used to describe means of communication and travel but c is more specific in this use than по: посыла́ть (посла́ть) по по́чте *to send by post*, but получа́ть (получи́ть) письмо́ с у́тренней (вече́рней) по́чтой *to receive a letter by the morning (evening) post* (notice that both prepositions may be replaced by an instrumental construction without a preposition: по́чтой, у́тренней по́чтой, *by post*, *by the morning post*, also по возду́шной по́чте, возду́шной по́чтой *by air mail*). *To travel by rail* is е́хать (пое́хать) по желе́зной доро́ге, but *to arrive by the one o'clock train* is приезжа́ть (прие́хать) с часовы́м по́ездом (or часовы́м по́ездом). *To inform by telephone* is сообща́ть (сообщи́ть) кому́-нибудь по телефо́ну.

(ii) Notice:

He pulled up the weeds by the roots (by meaning *with)*	Он вы́рвал со́рные тра́вы с ко́рнем

(iii) С with the genitive case describes method in a restricted number of expressions in which English says *by* but Russian *from*. The commonest of these expressions are брать (взять) с бо́я *to take by force, by storm* and продава́ть (прода́ть) с торго́в (с молотка́) *to sell by auction*:

The infantry took the town by storm	Пехо́та взяла́ го́род с бо́я
The house was sold by auction	Дом был про́дан с торго́в (с молотка́)

(iv) Путём and посре́дством mean *by means of*:

He cured himself of rheumatism by means of physical exercises	Он излечи́лся от ревмати́зма путём (посре́дством) физи́ческих упражне́ний

649. В, на (prepositional case):

For these prepositions used with means of travel see para. **561.**

650. На (accusative case):

(i) Used when *by* denotes the difference between two quantities, two amounts, two points in time:

By what amount do your expenses exceed your income?	На каку́ю су́мму ва́ши расхо́ды превыша́ют дохо́ды?

Bread has come down in price by five copecks	Хлеб подешевéл на пять копéек
We missed the train by five minutes	Мы опоздáли к пóезду на пять минýт

Note also, in expressions of distance where actual units of measurement are not used:

He missed death by a hair's breadth	Он был на волосóк от смéрти
We were already a rifle-shot from him (lit. *separated from him by a rifle-shot*)	Мы бы́ли ужé от негó на ружéйный вы́стрел (Lermontov)

(Cf. он в туз из пистолéта в пяти́ сажéнях попадáл (Pushkin) *he could hit the ace from a pistol at thirty-six feet*.)

(ii) Expressing multiplication, division, dimensions:

If you divide (multiply) thirty by five . . .	Éсли вы разделя́ете (умножáете) три́дцать на пять . . .
A room thirteen feet by twelve	Кóмната тринáдцать фýтов на двенáдцать

(iii) Unit or method of sale:

Tomatoes are sold by the pound (by weight)	Помидóры продаю́тся на фунт (на вес)

651. По (dative case):

(i) Used when *by* describes personal qualities (*by nature, by character*) or personal standing (*by profession*):

He is gay by nature	Он весёлый по приро́де
He is a lawyer by profession	Он юри́ст по профéссии

Note that with qualities of character по приро́де is generally synonymous with от приро́ды (*naturally lazy* лени́вый по приро́де or лени́вый от приро́ды). When, however, the quality referred to is a congenital physical defect, only от приро́ды (which means fundamentally *from birth, congenitally*) can be used, e.g. слепóй от приро́ды *blind from birth.* По приро́де cannot be used in such constructions any more than *by nature* can be used in English.

(ii) When *by* means *by looking at* or *according to*:

I knew by his eyes that he was suffering	Я знал по его́ глаза́м, что он страда́ет
It is twelve o'clock by my watch	По мои́м часа́м двена́дцать

(iii) *One by one*:

Copeck by copeck he amassed a huge sum	Он по копе́йке накопи́л огро́мную су́мму

But notice *one after the other* оди́н за други́м:

They were killed one by one	Они́ бы́ли уби́ты оди́н за други́м

(iv) *By invitation*:

I am here by invitation	Я здесь по приглаше́нию

652. За (accusative case):

Used with verbs meaning *to hold, to seize, to take, &c.,* referring to the object taken or held:

He led his sister by the hand	Он вёл сестру́ за́-руку
He pulled the door by the handle	Он дёрнул дверь за ру́чку

But notice держа́ть ло́шадь под уздцы́ *to hold a horse by the bridle*.

653. Под (instrumental case):

Used in expressions of naming or defining:

What is meant by the word 'Romanticism'?	Что разуме́ется под сло́вом «романти́зм»?
He goes by the name of Nezhdanov	Он изве́стен под и́менем Нежда́нов

For

654. Для (genitive case):
на (accusative case):
по (dative case):
под (accusative case):
к (dative case):

These prepositions translate, in different contexts, *for* meaning *for the purpose of, meant for, intended for*:

(i) Для means primarily *for the sake of*:

Everything for victory	Всё для побе́ды

It is also used when *for* expresses close personal interest:

A present for grandmother	Пода́рок для ба́бушки

Для also describes a function when the connexion between the nouns preceding and following it is particularly close, so that the English equivalent is often a hyphenated word:

Spectacle-lenses	Стёкла для очко́в
A document-file	Па́пка для бума́г

(ii) На is used when *for* implies intention in making or doing something:

This money can be used for repairing the factory	Э́ти де́ньги мо́жно употребля́ть на ремо́нт фа́брики
They have gone for a walk	Они́ отпра́вились на прогу́лку

Notice дава́ть (дать) на во́дку *to tip* (i.e. *to give for vodka*).

(iii) По means *to do with, for dealing with*:

The committee for the raising of the standard of living	Коми́ссия по повыше́нию у́ровня жи́зни
Syllabuses for political education	Конспе́кты по политучёбе

(iv) Под is used meaning *for* when the meaning is *for use as, for the cultivation of, for containing*:

They need premises for a school	Им ну́жно помеще́ние под шко́лу
We have prepared this field for cabbage	Мы пригото́вили э́то по́ле под капу́сту
This barrel is meant for wine	Э́та бо́чка предназна́чена под вино́

Note that when a field or building is already in use in some function, it is followed by под and the instrumental:

A cabbage-field	По́ле под капу́стой
Premises in use as a school	Помеще́ние под шко́лой

(v) К is used when *for* means intended for an occasion, often a meal:

I have ordered meat for Thursday	Я заказа́л мя́со к четвергу́
We shall keep the eggs for breakfast	Мы сбережём я́йца к за́втраку

655. На, за (accusative case):

These prepositions translate *for* meaning *in exchange for, as a reward (punishment) for*. На translates *worth* in мя́со на́ пять рубле́й *five roubles worth of meat* and is used in a similar function in:

How many books can I buy for that pile of money?	Ско́лько книг я куплю́ на ту ку́чу де́нег?

За does not imply financial value but merit or shortcoming:

He was awarded a Stalin prize for that novel	Ему́ за тот рома́н была́ присуждена́ ста́линская пре́мия
He was reduced to the ranks for drunkenness	Он был разжа́лован в солда́ты за пья́нство

656. Ha (accusative case):

Ha has a number of special uses translated into English by *for*. It may mean:

(i) *For the maintenance of* :

He took Russian prisoners from a camp and made them work for him	Он взял из лагеря и заставил на себя работать русских военнопленных (Grin)

(ii) *On the occasion of* :

I gave him a book for his birthday	Я дал ему книгу на день рождения

(iii) *Provision for* :

We have laid in food for the winter	Мы запаслись пищей на зиму

(iv) *As against* :

For every good apple in the barrel there were five bad ones	На каждое хорошее яблоко в бочке было пять плохих

(v) *Sufficient for* :

A dinner for ten people	Обед на десять человек

(vi) *Quest for* :

Prospecting for oil	Разведка на нефть

(vii) *Distance from a centre* :

He is the most brilliant man for miles around	Он самый блестящий человек на мили кругом

657. За (accusative case):

(i) *Covering the period* :

He is compiling a weather report for the past week	Он составляет сводку погоды за прошлую неделю

(ii) *On behalf of* :

My brother will sign for me	Мой брат подпишет за меня

658. Для (genitive case):

(i) Personal interest:

This is an important business for him	Это ва́жное де́ло для него́

(ii) Comparison, *taking into account*:

He is too thoughtful for his age	Он сли́шком заду́мчив для свои́х лет

Note that не по (dative case) may be used as an alternative for сли́шком . . . для: он заду́мчив не по лета́м. Notice also по на́шим времена́м *as times go, for these times*:

It was not a magnificent meal but, as times go, a plentiful one	Это был обе́д не роско́шный, но оби́льный по на́шим времена́м

659. В (accusative case):

Meaning *to be a member of*:

He proposed a new candidate for the presidium	Он предложи́л но́вого кандида́та в прези́диум

From, out of, off

660. Из, с, от, у (genitive case):

(i) In different contexts из, с, от, and у translate *from, out of, off*, referring to source or origin. As a general rule, with places or localities, when в or на is used to describe location, из and с respectively are used to describe origin: в Гру́зии *in Georgia* and апельси́ны из Гру́зии *oranges from Georgia*, на ле́вом берегу́ реки́ *on the left bank of the river* and залп с ле́вого бе́рега *a volley from the left bank.*

(ii) In non-locational contexts из is used when *from* means *a member of, one out of*:

She is from a good family	Она́ из хоро́шей семьи́

Also meaning *from the contents of*:

Extracts from a novel	Отры́вки из рома́на

I understood from his allusions that . . .	Я по́нял из его́ намёков, что . . .

(but cf. '*to take the hint*' понима́ть (поня́ть) с полусло́ва).
Из also means *made of* or *consisting of*:

A stone house	Дом из ка́мня
A team made up of Scottish and English footballers	Кома́нда из шотла́ндских и англи́йских футболи́стов

(iii) С is not commonly found meaning origin but is used when the origin is clearly from the surface of:

Bark from a tree	Кора́ с де́рева

Note the expressions брать (взять) приме́р с кого́-нибудь *to take an example from someone* and снима́ть (снять) ко́пию с карти́ны *to make a copy of a picture*.

(iv) От is used generally with persons:

I learned of that from my uncle	Я узна́л об э́том от дя́ди

Also with objects which give rise to phenomena perceptible to the senses:

The light from the street-lamp	Свет от фонаря́
The smell from the flowers	За́пах от цвето́в

(v) У is also used with persons but expresses a sense of possession on the part of the person concerned whereas от simply expresses taking away from:

I borrowed two roubles from him	Я за́нял у него́ два рубля́
I took my book from the boy	Я отобра́л свою́ кни́гу от ма́льчика

У is also used with an object from which a component part is taken or broken:

I have broken the spout off the tea-pot	Я отби́л но́сик у ча́йника

And when the meaning is one of personal service (cf.
French *chez*):

I am taking treatment from a famous doctor	Я лечу́сь у знамени́того врача́

661. (i) Из, от, and с are also used to translate *from* referring to remainder. Из refers to one or several out of many:

One soldier out of a hundred was left	Оста́лся оди́н солда́т из ста

(ii) От refers to a quantity left from a whole:

Two cutlets are left over from lunch	От за́втрака оста́лись две котле́ты

(but *two cutlets out of ten* две котле́ты из десяти́).

(iii) С is used in expressions with сда́ча *change*:

Change from a rouble	Сда́ча с рубля́

662. По (dative case):

По translates *from* meaning *according to* or *from the contents of*:

A costume made from a pattern	Костю́м сши́тый по образцу́
We all learned from the same books	Мы все учи́лись по тем же кни́гам

663. Не в (accusative case):

He was singing out of tune (out of time)	Он пел не в тон (не в такт)

In

664. На (prepositional and accusative case):

(i) With the prepositional case на translates *in* in expressions describing culinary processes:

We roasted the meat in but-   Мы жа́рили мя́со на ма́сле
ter

(ii) With the accusative case на translates *in* meaning
as to with physical characteristics:

He is young in appearance   Он молодо́й на вид
He is blind in the right eye Он слеп на пра́вый глаз
He is lame in the left leg   Он хром на ле́вую но́гу

(Note also он туг на у́хо *he is hard of hearing.*)

На is also used, as an alternative to the instrumental case
without preposition with конча́ться (*to end*) when applied
to words:

This word ends in a con-   Э́то сло́во конча́ется на
sonant   согла́сную (согла́сной)
Verbs ending in -ать   Глаго́лы конча́ющиеся на
                                -ать

665. По (dative case):

(i) Meaning *according to*:

They are similar in size   Они́ одина́ковы по вели-
                                чине́

The senior in rank was   Пе́рвый по ра́нгу был
General Ivanov   генера́л Ивано́в

(ii) *On the subject of*:

Problems in geometry   Зада́чник по геоме́трии
I am doing research in   Я занима́юсь исслѐдова-
physics   ниями по фи́зике

(iii) Distributively:

We counted the eggs in   Мы счита́ли я́йца по дю́жи-
dozens   нам (or дю́жинами)

666. От (genitive case):

In the name of:

I am speaking in my father's Я говорю́ от и́мени отца́
name

Of

667. В (accusative and prepositional case):

(i) Used with the accusative case in expressions of amount or quantity (see para. **629** (v)):

A loan of twenty pounds	Заём в два́дцать фу́нтов
An army of forty thousand men	А́рмия в со́рок ты́сяч челове́к
A two-storied house (house of two stories)	Дом в два этажа́

(Notice also *the string was almost as long as the whole room* верёвка была́ длино́ю почти́ во всю ко́мнату).

(ii) With the prepositional case в expresses discrepancy or mistake in amount:

A miscalculation of twenty pounds	Просчёт в двадцати́ фу́нтах
An error of ten roubles	Оши́бка в десяти́ рубля́х

668. От (genitive case):

(i) *Of the nature or character* :

There is something of the bureaucrat about him	В нём есть что́-то от бюрокра́та

(ii) *Originating on*:

The order of 15th April	Прика́з от пятна́дцатого апре́ля

669. С (instrumental case):

(i) *Containing*:

A letter of complaint	Письмо́ с жа́лобой

(ii) *To do with*:

One of Gor'ky's best stories is 'The Affair of the Clasps'	Оди́н из лу́чших расска́зов Го́рького — „Де́ло с застёжками“

670. Ha (accusative case):

On the night of the 30 April–   В ночь на пе́рвое ма́я
    1 May

On

671. Ha (accusative and prepositional case):

(i) Object or purpose (accusative case):

On what has he spent his   На что он потра́тил де́нь-
    money?   ги?

(ii) With the accusative of quantity на is used in the expression жить на *to live on* meaning to manage on a certain sum of money:

They are living on slender   Они́   живу́т   на   ску́дные
    means   сре́дства

When, however, the meaning is *to live on* (*a diet*) the verb пита́ться is used, followed by the instrumental case:

They live on vegetables   Они́ пита́ются овоща́ми

672. По (dative case):

(i) *To do with*:

Work on the draining of the   Идёт   рабо́та   по   осу́шке
    swamps is under way   боло́т
Decisions on reparations   Реше́ния по репара́циям

(ii) The combination по слу́чаю *on the occasion of*:

I expressed my sympathy with   Я вы́разил ему́ сочу́вствие
    him on the loss of his   по слу́чаю утра́ты ма́тери
    mother

(iii) The expression по ра́дио *on the wireless*:

I like to listen to music on   Я люблю́ слу́шать му́зыку
    the wireless   по ра́дио

673. О (accusative case):

Meaning *against*:

I have cut my hand on a knife	Я обре́зал себе́ ру́ку о нож

674. Под (instrumental case):

He was forbidden, on pain of death, to leave the capital (cf. English *under the threat of*)	Ему́ бы́ло запрещено́, под стра́хом сме́рти, уе́хать из столи́цы
He went home early on the pretext of tiredness	Под предло́гом уста́лости он ра́но пошёл домо́й

675. С (genitive case):

Used in a number of idioms with the word сторона́ (*side*):

My uncle on my father's side	Мой дя́дя со стороны́ отца́
Very kind of you (i.e. *on your part*)	О́чень любе́зно с ва́шей стороны́
On the one hand . . . on the other	С одно́й стороны́ . . . с друго́й

Over

676. За (instrumental case):

While drinking (eating):

To chat over a glass of beer (a meal)	Бесе́довать за стака́ном пи́ва (едо́й)

Through

677. Че́рез (accusative case):

Through the medium of:

The order to retreat was passed through the liaison officer	Прика́з об отступле́нии был пе́редан че́рез связно́го офице́ра
We notified him of his father's death through the newspaper	Мы извести́ли его́ о сме́рти отца́ че́рез газе́ту

To

678. К (dative case):

| *The preface to a book* | Предисло́вие к кни́ге |

679. По (accusative case):

Up to the level of :

| *I was standing up to the knees in water* | Я стоя́л по коле́ни в воде́ |
| *I am full up* | Я сыт по го́рло |

(Cf. para. **552** (iii) for по in a similar meaning in temporal phrases.)

680. До (genitive case):

As far as:

| *I am soaked to the skin* | Я промо́к до косте́й |

681. Под (accusative case):

To the accompaniment of :

| *He usually sings to (the accompaniment of) the piano* | Он обыкнове́нно поёт под роя́ль |
| *I fell asleep to the sound of animated conversation* | Я засну́л под оживлённый разгово́р |

682. На (accusative case):

| *Who set these lines to music ?* | Кто положи́л э́ти стихи́ на му́зыку ? |

Towards

683. Пе́ред (instrumental case):

Meaning *vis-à-vis* in a moral sense:

| *He is guided by a strong sense of responsibility towards his family* | Он руково́дится си́льным чу́вством отве́тственности пе́ред семьёй |
| *He is oppressed by a sense of guilt towards his father* | Его́ угнета́ет чу́вство вины́ пе́ред отцо́м |

684. Ha (accusative case):

Purpose:

We are saving money towards our children's education	Мы сберегáем дéньги на образовáние детéй

With

685. С (genitive case):

(i) Used in the expression *to begin with*:

This word begins with a capital letter	Это слóво начинáется с прописнóй бýквы

But notice *this word is written with a hyphen* (*with* 'ы') это слóво пúшется чéрез чёрточку (чéрез „ы") [no sense of beginning].

(ii) Used also in the sense of to take action from the moment consent or approval is given:

She married with her father's consent	Онá вы́шла зáмуж с соглáсия отцá
I went abroad with my uncle's approval	Я поéхал за-границу с одобрéния дя́ди

Notice also *by common consent* с óбщего соглáсия, *with your permission* с вáшего разрешéния.

686. Ha (prepositional case):

(i) After би́ться *to fight* and similar verbs, describing the means of combat:

They fought with their fists	Они́ дрáлись на кулакáх,

бой на штыкáх *bayonet-fighting*.

(ii) When *with* means literally *on*, notably with the word подклáдка (*lining*):

A dressing-gown with a blue lining	Халáт на голубóй подклáдке

687. В (accusative and prepositional case):

Dotted with:

A red tie with blue spots	Крáсный гáлстук в си́них крáпинках

But notice:

> *A black suit with grey stripes* — Чёрный костюм в се́рую поло́ску

The accusative is used because the stripe runs the whole length of the suit whereas the spots on the tie are all over it (cf. *a freckled face* лицо́ в весну́шках).

688. При (prepositional case):

(i) *Taking into account, in view of* :

With his wealth and intelligence he need fear no one — При его́ бога́тстве и уме́, не́кого ему́ боя́ться

(ii) *Despite, for all*:

With all his abilities, he does not prosper — При всех его́ спосо́бностях, он не преуспева́ет

With the aid of при по́мощи (кого́-нибудь), *with the co-operation of* при соде́йствии (кого́-нибудь).

689. К (dative case):

I have no urgent business with him — Нет у меня́ спе́шного де́ла к нему́

RUSSIAN PREPOSITIONS USED WITH CERTAIN NOUNS, VERBS, AND ADJECTIVES

Nouns

About

690. В (prepositional case):

There is no doubt about his reliability — Нет сомне́ния в его́ надёжности

At

691. К (dative case):

My disgust at this action — Моё отвраще́ние к э́тому посту́пку

For

692. К (dative case):

A passion for reading	Страсть к чтéнию
Greed for money	Áлчность к деньгáм
Love for one's father	Любóвь к отцý
Contempt for money	Презрéние к деньгáм
Respect for culture	Уважéние к культýре
A weakness for oranges	Слáбость к апельсúнам

693. По (dative case):

Longing for home	Тоскá по рóдине

694. По (prepositional case):

To wear mourning for some- one	Носúть трáур по кóм- нибудь

695. На (accusative case):

A fiend for work	Зверь на рабóту
Demand for coal	Спрос на ýголь

696. В (prepositional case):

There's no need for this	В э́том нет никакóй нáдоб- ности

697. О (prepositional case):

The order for retreat	Прикáз об отступлéнии
A proposal for the construc- tion of a school	Предложéние о пострóйке шкóлы

In

698. К (dative case):

Trust in a friend	Довéрие к дрýгу
Interest in aeroplanes	Интерéс к самолётам

Of

699. В (prepositional case):

An accusation of theft	Обвинéние в крáже
Reproaches of laziness	Упрёки в лéни

Suspicion of arson	Подозрéние в поджóге
A vow of friendship	Кля́тва в дрýжбе

700. На (accusative case):

The last hope of victory	Послéдняя надéжда на побéду

701. К (dative case):

Envy of one's brother	Зáвисть к брáту

702. О (prepositional case):

News of the battle	Весть о би́тве

To

703. К (dative case):

Attention to detail	Внимáние к подрóбностям

Verbs

At

704. На (accusative case):

He was angry at this suggestion (see para. **718**)	Он серди́лся на э́то предложéние

705. Над (instrumental case):

Why do you laugh at him?	Почемý вы смеётесь над ним?

706. В (accusative case):
по (dative case):

To fire at a target	Стреля́ть (вы́стрелить) в цель
To fire at the retreating enemy forces	Стреля́ть (вы́стрелить) по отступáющим врáжеским войскáм

В means to fire at a fixed point, по (lit. *after*) at a moving target.

For

707. За (accusative case):

How much did you pay for this house?	Ско́лько вы заплати́ли за э́тот дом?
We are interceding for him with the General	Мы хлопо́чем за него́ у генера́ла

In

708. В (accusative case):

To believe in God	Ве́рить в Бо́га
She often dresses in bright colours	Она́ ча́сто одева́ется в я́ркие цвета́

Into

709. На (accusative case):

Translate this into French	Переведи́те э́то на францу́зский язы́к

710. В (accusative case):

He turned into a drunkard	Он преврати́лся в пья́ницу

Of

711. Из (prepositional case):

This house consists of five rooms	Э́тот дом состои́т из пяти́ ко́мнат

But notice *a five-act play* (consisting of five acts) пье́са в пяти́ де́йствиях; and compare the different meaning of *to consist of* in the following example:

His duties consist of translating German novels	Его́ обя́занности состоя́т в перево́де неме́цких рома́нов

On

712. На (accusative case):

I am relying on you	Я наде́юсь (полага́юсь) на вас

713. На (prepositional case):

I insist on the return of my book	Я настáиваю на возвращéнии своéй кнѝги

Notice настáивать (настоя́ть) на своём *to insist on having one's own way, to carry one's point.*

714. Над (instrumental case):

He is working on a translation of 'War and Peace'	Он рабóтает над перевóдом „Войнѝ и мѝра"
They took pity on him	Онѝ сжáлились над ним

To

715. На (accusative case):

He agreed to my proposal	Он согласѝлся на моё предложéние
They have not replied to my letter	Онѝ не отвéтили на моё письмó
He has been appointed to a new post	Егó назнáчили на нóвое мéсто

716. В (accusative case):

We have appointed him to the council	Мы егó назнáчили в совéт

В here means *to be one of the members of*, на above means simply *to a single post*.

With

717. По (dative case):

She is busy with household tasks	Онá хлопóчет по хозя́йству

718. На (accusative case):

He was angry with his brother (see para. **704**)	Он сердѝлся на брáта

Adjectives

At

719. К (dative case):

Good at languages   Спосо́бный к языка́м

For

720. За (accusative case):

Grateful for help   Благода́рный за по́мощь

721. К (dative case):

Ready for departure   Гото́вый к отъе́зду

Notice that гото́вый may take either к or на (accusative case) with slightly different meanings (see para. **137** (iii) (*b*)).

Of

722. На (accusative case):

Capable of murder   Спосо́бный на уби́йство

Compare спосо́бный к *good at* above.

Sparing of words   Скупо́й на слова́

723. Для (genitive case):

Typical of him   Типи́чный   (характе́рный)
                           для него́

To

724. К (dative case):

Good to the poor   До́брый к бе́дным
Inclined to laziness   Скло́нный к ле́ни

725. С (instrumental case):

The room adjacent to mine   Ко́мната сосе́дняя (сме́ж-
                                       ная) с мое́й

726. На (accusative case):

Similar to (like) his father   Похо́жий на отца́
Susceptible to flattery   Па́дкий на лесть
Sensitive to injustice   Чу́ткий   на   несправедли́-
                                   вость

727. Для (genitive case):

Changes common to all Slavonic languages	Изменéния óбщие для всех славя́нских языкóв
Detrimental to the health	Врéдный для здорóвья

728. От (genitive case):

Near (to) the station	Блúзкий от вокзáла

With

729. От (genitive case):

Eyes wet with tears	Мóкрые от слёз глазá
Apple-trees heavy with fruit	Тяжёлые от плодóв я́блони

(Notice the order of words.)

730. К (dative case):

He is very strict with his son	Он óчень строг к сы́ну

(Alternatively строг с сы́ном.)

RUSSIAN PREPOSITIONAL EXPRESSIONS CORRESPONDING TO ENGLISH COMPOUND NOUNS

731. Для (genitive case):

A flour bin	Ларь для мукú
A milk jug	Кувшúн для молокá
A watchman's cabin	Бýдка для стóрожа
Spectacle lenses	Стёкла для очкóв

732. Из-под (genitive case):

A milk bottle	Буты́лка из-под молокá
A jam jar	Бáнка из-под варéнья

733. На (prepositional case):

A bath chair	Крéсло на колёсах
A spring mattress	Матрáс на пружúнах
Honey cakes	Пря́ники на медý
A fur-lined coat	Пальтó на мехý

734. О (prepositional case):

A three-legged table	Стол о трёх нóжках
Satire is a double-edged weapon	Сатúра — пáлка о двух концáх

735. От (genitive case):

A door-knob	Рýчка от двéри
The library key	Ключ от библиотéки

(Compare ключ к библиотéке *the key to the library*.)

An insecticide	Срéдство от насекóмых
A headache powder	Порошóк от головнóй бóли

736. Под (accusative case):

Imitation mahogany furniture	Мéбель под крáсное дéрево

737. У (genitive case):

The station square	Плóщадь у вокзáла

VII

THE NUMERAL AND NUMERAL WORDS

738. We shall draw attention in this chapter mainly to morphological difficulties concerned with numerals and numeral words, and, in addition, to constructions involving them. Stress peculiarities will be noted, as will trends discernible in current Russian speech, modifying traditional usage.

CARDINALS

Half

739. The variety of Russian nouns prefixed by пол- or полу- and the declension of such nouns can cause much confusion. We can distinguish between the following:

(i) Compound nouns which in the nominative case combine пол- with a noun in the genitive:

Common examples are: Полчаса́   *Half an hour*
Полмину́ты *Half a minute*
Полдю́жины *Half a dozen*

Such nouns express measurement of time, weight, distance, &c. When they are used in the nominative or accusative singular, adjectives qualifying them normally go in the nominative plural:

Every half-hour	Ка́ждые полчаса́
For the last six months	За после́дние полго́да

In oblique cases, both parts of the noun may be declined, with пол- changing to полу- throughout, and the second part following the regular declension of the noun concerned (час, минута). Thus:

Half an hour	Полчаса
Half an hour's walk (drive) from here	В получасе ходьбы (езды) отсюда
He arrived half an hour later than he expected	Он пришёл получасом позже, чем думал

But frequently (especially colloquially) the пол- is left unchanged:

In half a glass of water	В полстакане воды
Half-way	На полпути

When these nouns are used in any other case except the nominative and accusative singular, adjectives qualifying them agree in gender and number with the second half of the compound:

After the first half-hour	После первого получаса
After the first half-minute	После первой полуминуты

(ii) Compound nouns which in the nominative case combine пол- with a noun in the nominative: e.g. полдень *midday*; полночь *midnight*. Here the meaning is clearly not *half of*, but *the middle of*: compare полдень *midday* with полдня *half a day*. Полдень and полночь follow the same declensional pattern as the nouns in section (i), but полу is stressed:

Up to midday	До полудня
Towards midday	К полудню

Notice the adverbial expression пополудни *in the afternoon*.

(iii) Compound nouns which in the nominative case combine полу- with a noun in the nominative: e.g.

Half-moon	Полумесяц
Semicircle	Полукруг
Demigod	Полубог

Such nouns which correspond to English half-, semi-, demi-, are declined regularly, полу- remaining unchanged.

740. The following idioms should be noted:

In two, half and half	Пополáм
To cut in half	Рéзать (разрéзать) пополáм
I bought the book half-price	Я купи́л кни́гу за полцены́
Children under 5 half-price (official notice)	Дéти в вóзрасте до пяти́ лет плáтят полови́ну

Notice too:

We met half-way from the station	Мы встрéтились на пол-пути́ от вокзáла
We had to turn back half-way	Мы должны́ бы́ли верну́ться с полпути́
It was half raining, half snowing	Пáдал не то дождь, не то снег

Colloquially *half* with expressions of time by the clock may be rendered by пол instead of полови́на:

Half-past one	Пол вторóго

(cf. colloquial English *half one* for '*half-past one*').

One

741. (i) Оди́н is commonly used as a pronoun to mean *alone, only* (see para. **515**).

(ii) Notice that *one o'clock* is simply час (without оди́н). Similarly *one inch wide* ширинóй в дюйм.

(iii) In counting *one, two, three* . . . a Russian says раз, два, три, . . . (i.e. *once, two, three* . . .). A variation of this, once heard by us in Moscow, was раз, два, Стáлин!

(iv) Notice the agreement with compound numerals ending in оди́н:

21 big houses	Двáдцать оди́н большóй дом

Have you met the 21 Hungarian refugees who arrived last week?	Встрéтили вы двáдцать одногó венгéрского бéженца, котóрые прибыли на прóшлой недéле?

One and a half

742. (i) Полторá (i.e. пол and вторá = вторóго), feminine полторы (like два, три, четыре) is followed by the genitive singular of the noun. Полýтора does service for all the oblique cases and genders, the feminine полýторы being now archaic:

It is impossible to make do with a mere 1,500	Одними полýтора тысячами невозмóжно обойтись

This word is particularly common in combination with сýток, but then the stress is on the *first syllable*:

36 hours	Пóлтора сýток

Adjectives qualifying полторá may be in both nominative and genitive plural cases:

She waited a good hour and a half	Онá ждалá дóбрые (дóбрых) полторá часá

(ii) There is also a special word in Russian for *one and a half hundred* — полторáста, which gives полýтораста in all oblique cases.

Two, Three, Four, Both

743. 2, 3, 4, and *both* combined with nouns qualified by adjectives:

(i) In nominative and accusative: with masculine and neuter nouns the qualifying adjective normally goes in the *genitive plural*:

Two large tables	Два больших столá
My two old friends	Мои два стáрых дрýга (and два моих стáрых дрýга)

But it may be noticed that certain adjectives and pronominal adjectives (which commonly *precede* numerals),
notably пе́рвый, после́дний, ка́ждый, and друго́й, are
usually found in the *nominative plural* in this context:

The first two hours	Пе́рвые два часа́
During the last three years	За после́дние три го́да

There is in fact a clear tendency for all adjectives *preceding*
numerals to stand in the nominative plural with nouns of
all genders.

(ii) In nominative and accusative: with feminine nouns,
the tendency in nineteenth-century literature was for
adjectives to go in the nominative plural. Nowadays, however, there is such widespread use of the nominative *and*
the genitive plural that both must be considered permissible alternatives:

Two big rooms	Две больши́е (or больши́х) ко́мнаты

It should be added that the adjective commonly goes in the
genitive plural with nouns which have a different stress in
the nominative plural from that in the genitive singular:

Three high mountains rose above the town	Над го́родом поднима́лись три высо́ких горы́ (gen. sing.)

The reason for this may be that if the nominative plural
высо́кие were used, the natural tendency would be to follow
it by the *nominative* plural го́ры because of the combination
high mountains высо́кие го́ры.

(iii) In oblique cases: the numeral, adjective, and noun
are all in agreement:

With two new ties	С двумя́ но́выми га́лстуками

744. 2, 3, 4, and *both* combined with adjectives used as
nouns:

(i) If the adjective-noun is masculine or neuter, it will
go in the genitive plural:

Three icecreams	Три моро́женых

(ii) If it is feminine, the tendency is for it to go in the nominative plural if the numeral is itself nominative:

Two drawing-rooms　　　Две гости́ные

745. 2, 3, 4, and *both* when combined with nouns used in the plural only must, in the nominative and accusative, be translated by the collective forms, дво́е, тро́е, &c.:

Two watches　　　Дво́е часо́в

In oblique cases the use of the appropriate form of the collective numeral is optional:

With two watches　　　С двумя́ (дво́йми) часа́ми

746. 2, 3, 4, and *both* when combined with the nouns час, шаг, ряд, шар, cause the stress of these nouns to shift from the stem to the ending:

Till one p.m.　　　До ча́са дня
Two p.m.　　　Два часа́ дня

747. Attention is drawn to the following peculiarity in compound numbers ending in 2, 3, and 4, when used with animate objects:

I counted 24 soldiers　　　Я сосчита́л два́дцать четы́ре
　　　　　　　　　　　　солда́та
I counted 24 cows　　　Я сосчита́л два́дцать четы́ре
　　　　　　　　　　　　коро́вы

Contrast this with the grammatical norm:

I counted 4 soldiers　　　Я сосчита́л четырёх солда́т
I counted 4 cows　　　Я сосчита́л четырёх коро́в

However, the effect of the former construction on the latter has produced a departure from the grammatical norm, so that it is now usual to say я сосчита́л четы́ре коро́вы (or in the masculine четы́ре вола́) when the noun refers to an animal. When the noun refers to a person one may say either я сосчита́л четы́ре солда́та, or я сосчита́л четырёх солда́т.

Five and upwards

748. (i) These numbers present no syntactical difficulties, being followed invariably, in the nominative and accusative, by the genitive plural of adjective and noun, and in oblique cases agreeing with adjective and noun.

(ii) The following points of morphology and stress should be noted:

(*a*) *5 to 10, 20 and 30* decline like feminine nouns ending in a soft sign, but the stress shifts from the stem to the ending in all oblique cases.

(*b*) But in the combinations пя́тью пять, шéстью шесть, &c. ('*5 times 5*', '*6 times 6*') the stress of the numeral in the instrumental case is on the *stem*.

(iii) *11 to 19* decline in the same way, but the stress remains throughout on the same syllable as in the nominative.

(iv) *21 to 29, 31 to 39*, &c.: both parts decline, e.g. *up to 25* до двадцати́ пяти́.

(v) *40* has only one oblique form сорока́ for all cases.

(vi) *50, 60, 70, and 80*: both parts decline, the second like a feminine noun ending in a soft sign, despite the fact that it ends in a *hard* consonant десят. In the instrumental, пяти́десятью will be found as well as the grammatically more conventional пятью́десятью. Notice the stresses пятьдеся́т, шестьдеся́т, but се́мьдесят, во́семьдесят. In oblique cases the stress always falls on the ending of the first part.

(vii) *90 and 100* have the one oblique form девяно́ста and ста for all cases. Сту is now archaic, although colloquially one still hears по́ сту.

(viii) *200, 300*, &c., *to 900*: both parts decline, with сто in the plural (-со́т, -ста́м, &c.). The stress of 200, 300, and 400 in the nominative and accusative is on the first part; in oblique cases on the ending (e.g. две́сти, двухсо́т, двуста́м, &c.). The stress of 500, 600, 700, 800, and 900 is on the ending in all cases.

One thousand, one million

749. (i) In the nominative and accusative тысяча is always followed by the genitive plural.

(ii) In oblique cases when *unqualified* by a pronoun, numeral, &c., two constructions are possible. Either тысяча is treated as a numeral and followed by a noun in the same case (but in the plural), or it is treated as a noun and followed by a noun in the genitive plural (cf. *mille francs* and *un milliard de francs*):

Not to mention the 1,000 roubles he owed her	Не говоря о тысяче рублях (рублей), которые он был должен ей

Notice that in the instrumental case there are two distinct spellings: тысячью when used as a numeral (e.g. тысячью рублями) and тысячей when used as a noun (e.g. тысячей рублей):

He was walking along the street with 1,000 roubles in his pocket	Он шёл по улице с тысячей рублей (тысячью рублями) в кармане

(iii) In oblique cases when *qualified* by a pronoun, numeral, &c., тысяча is always treated as a noun and therefore followed by the genitive plural:

With a mere 1,000 roubles in the bank	С одной только тысячей рублей (not рублями) в банке

(iv) Миллион is a noun and always requires nouns following it to be in the genitive plural, irrespective of its own case.

General observations

750. (i) The 20's, the 30's, &c., when referring to historical decades, are translated by the *ordinal* forms of the numerals:

In the 20's of the last century	В двадцатых годах прошлого века
In the 1900's	В девятисотых годах

This is not the case when they refer to people's ages:

He is in his twenties   Ему́ два́дцать с чём-то (лет)

or

He is in his 'teens'   Он подро́сток (ему́ ещё нет двадцати́ лет)

(ii) *People* in the genitive plural case is translated by челове́к not люде́й, after the numerals 5 and upwards (see para. **103**).

(iii) *Years* in the genitive plural is translated by лет, not годо́в, except in combination with ordinal numbers denoting decades:

30 years   Три́дцать лет

In the course of the 30's   В тече́ние тридца́тых годо́в

(iv) Inversion of numerals suggests approximation:

She is about 30   Ей лет три́дцать

(v) Approximation of age:

She's getting on for three   Ей идёт тре́тий год

Approximation of time:

It's getting on for four o'clock   Уже́ почти́ четы́ре часа́ (идёт к четырём часа́м)

It's just gone four   Уже́ бо́льше четырёх (пошёл пя́тый час)

(vi) Adjectives compounded from numerals are prefixed as follows: *one-* одно-: *one-storied* одноэта́жный; *unilateral* односторо́нний. Adjectives with the едино- prefix are classified as *bookish.*

Two-, three-, four-; двух-, трёх-, четырёх-: *three-year-old* трёхле́тний. Adjectives with the дву- prefix are generally archaic or technical: *bi-syllabic* двусло́жный.

Five-, &c.; the prefix is again the genitive of the numeral: *fifty years old* пятидесятиле́тний.

Ninety-, hundred-; the prefix is the same as the nominative, девяно́сто-, сто-: *hundred-gramme* стогра́ммовый.

Thousand-; the prefix is тысяче-: *thousandth anniversary* тысячеле́тняя годовщи́на.

ORDINALS

751. (i) Compound ordinals have only the last number in the ordinal form: *131st* сто тридцать пе́рвый.

(ii) Notice the idioms:

In the first (second) place	Во-пе́рвых (во-вторы́х)
The day before yesterday	Тре́тьего дня (позавчера́)
The year before last	В тре́тьем году́ (в поза-про́шлом году́)

(iii) Пе́рвый is more commonly used to mean *best* than *first* is in English, e.g. пе́рвый учени́к *best pupil*, пе́рвый сорт *best quality*. Notice too мой пе́рвый враг *my worst enemy*.

COLLECTIVE NUMERALS

752. (i) The only *obligatory* use of the collective, instead of the cardinal, numeral to translate 2, 3, and 4 in conjunction with a noun, is in the case of a noun existing in the plural only. Thus *two sledges* must be translated by дво́е сане́й.

(ii) The collective numeral *may* be used with a masculine or common noun denoting a person of the male sex, as an alternative to the cardinal. Thus *two brothers* дво́е бра́тьев *or* два бра́та. It may not be used with feminine nouns or with nouns denoting animals.

(iii) With the pronouns мы, вы, and они́, the following uses of the collective numeral may be noted:

There were two of us in the boat	Нас бы́ло дво́е в ло́дке, or Нас бы́ло два челове́ка в ло́дке

But in the nominative:

We two	Мы о́ба, мы дво́е (not мы два)

(iv) The collective numerals пя́теро and upwards are seldom used today and are tending to become obsolete.

NOUNS EXPRESSING NUMBER

753. The nouns двóйка, трóйка, &c., denote the figures 2, 3, &c., and their use nowadays is chiefly colloquial (as четвёрка, for a *number 4 bus*) or else technical, e.g. the number of a playing card: семёрка червéй (черв) *7 of hearts*; the number of a crew: четвёрка *a rowing four*; the number of a team of horses: трóйка *a team of three*.

The nouns пятóк, десятóк (5, 10 individual things) are used colloquially in association with items purchased in these quantities and especially with eggs: *5 eggs* пятóк яйц (cf. *half a dozen eggs*).

Similar in use are сóтня (100 of a thing) and more rarely полсóтни (50 of a thing).

DISTRIBUTIVE EXPRESSIONS

754. Most grammars observe a distinction between the construction after по with the numerals 2, 3, 4, 200, 300, and 400 (i.e. the accusative case of the numeral: *200 roubles each* по двéсти рублéй; *three magazines each* по три журнáла, and after по with all other numerals (i.e. the dative case of the numeral: *five roubles each* по пяти рублéй—note that numeral and noun, although in oblique cases, are not in agreement).

But the tendency in *spoken* Russian is for по to be followed by the accusative case after all numerals in this distributive sense. По пять рублéй is probably as common as по пяти рублéй (*five roubles each*). *Two forty's*, i.e. two tickets at 40 copecks each, is invariably два по сóрок in current speech. In literary Russian this tendency is being resisted.

ADVERBS

755. *Once, twice, &c.*: the normal forms раз, два рáза, &c., are replaced by special forms for multiplication purposes:

Once three is three   Одúножды три—три (cf. одˉнáжды *once upon a time*)

Twice three are six	Два́жды три — шесть (alternatively два на три — шесть)

and similarly with три́жды, четы́режды.

With numerals 5 and upwards the multiplicative adverb is spelt in the same way as the instrumental case of the numeral *but* has initial, instead of final, stress.

Nine nines are eighty-one	Де́вятью де́вять — во́семьдесят оди́н

756. *Twice as, three times as, &c.*: to denote comparisons of quantity the forms вдво́е, втро́е, вче́тверо (i.e. the collective numerals prefixed by в) are used, with a comparative adverb:

Twice as loud	Вдво́е гро́мче
We outnumber them exactly three to one	Мы ро́вно втро́е превосхо́дим их по числу́

Forms exist for adverbs from the numerals 5 to 10, i.e. впя́теро, вше́стеро, &c., but like the collective numerals пя́теро, ше́стеро from which they derive, they are seldom used in comparison with в пять раз, в шесть раз:

Ten times as fast	В де́сять раз скоре́е

757. *Twice as* much (i.e. вдво́е бо́льше) can be expressed by вдвойне́, *doubly, in double quantity*:

To pay double	Плати́ть вдвойне́

Similarly втройне́ *three times as much* (втро́е бо́льше).

758. *Two together, in twos*: вдвоём. Втроём and вчетверо́м are also used, but the higher adverbs are seldom found:

The two of us painted the house	Мы вдвоём с ним покра́сили дом
When she and I are on our own	Когда́ мы вдвоём с ней

759. *In two, in three, in four,* after verbs of dividing, cutting, &c., are translated by на́двое, на́трое, на́четверо. По́ двое, по́ трое translate *in twos* (*two by two*) and *in threes* respectively.

ADJECTIVES

760. Single: usually оди́н (*not a single* ни оди́н). Еди́нственный suggests *only one.* Еди́ный has both the meaning of *single* and *only one,* but tends to have a more literary or rhetorical flavour than either оди́н or еди́нственный. It also means *united, inseparable* as in the words of the Soviet national anthem . . . еди́ный, могу́чий Сове́тский Сою́з. Едини́чный generally means *individual* as opposed to *collective* (де́ятельность едини́чных люде́й *the activity of individual people*), or *isolated* in the sense of *exceptional, rare* (едини́чный слу́чай *an isolated case*). Одино́кий means *solitary, lonely.* Notice:

A single bed	Односпа́льная крова́ть
He (she) is single	Он хо́лост, нежена́т (она́ незаму́жняя)
In single file	Гусько́м
A single ticket	Биле́т в оди́н коне́ц

761. Double: Двойно́й means *twice as much* (двойно́й паёк *double ration*) or *consisting of two parts.* Дво́йственный is essentially figurative (*two-sided, two-faced*). In a grammatical context it translates *dual* number (дво́йственное число́). The basic meaning of двоя́кий is *containing two possibilities* (двоя́кое значе́ние *double meaning*). Notice:

A double bed	Двуспа́льная крова́ть

762. Triple: Тройно́й means *three times as much, treble the quantity,* or *consisting of three parts.* Тро́йственный is most frequently applied to treaties and alliances (Тро́йственный Сою́з *Triple Alliance*). Троя́кий means *threefold, containing three possibilities* (троя́кое толкова́ние *threefold interpretation*).

AGREEMENT OF NUMERAL AND PREDICATE

763. The following should be treated as guiding principles, not hard-and-fast rules. There is considerable freedom in the matter of agreement of numeral and predicate both in written and spoken Russian.

764. (i) When the subject is a cardinal numeral, the verb is normally in the singular, and, in the past tense, neuter:

Of the 12 chairs, 3 were left   Из двена́дцати сту́льев оста́лось три

But when the numeral clearly refers to animate objects, the plural is used:

Of the three sisters, one died and two got married   Из трёх сестёр одна́ умерла́, а две вы́шли за́муж

(ii) When the subject is a collective numeral, the verb may be commonly in either the singular or the plural, though there is a preference for the plural if the numeral precedes the verb, and for the singular if the verb precedes the numeral:

2 arrived   Дво́е пришли́; пришло́ дво́е

(iii) If the numeral (whether cardinal or collective) is qualified by an adjective or clause, the verb is in the plural:

All 26 are singing   Все 26 пою́т (Gor'ky)

765. When the subject is a numeral-noun combination:

(i) If the noun refers to an inanimate object or animal, the verb is normally singular, and, in the past tense, neuter:

98 per cent. of the harvest was gathered in by the collective farms   98 проце́нтов урожа́я бы́ло со́брано колхо́зами

33 schools have already been built this year   В э́том году́ уже́ постро́ено 33 шко́лы

When a plural verb is found, it is often because the noun in the genitive is qualified by an adjective:

Those wonderful 5 years passed almost unnoticed — Те замеча́тельные пять лет почти́ незаме́тно прошли́

By November 123 major and 506 minor pits had been restored — К ноябрю́ бы́ли восстано́влены 123 кру́пные ша́хты (gen. sing.) и 506 ме́лких шахт (Press)

(ii) If the noun refers to a person, the verb is normally plural:

3 farmers arrived — Прие́хали три колхо́зника

148 generals surrendered to the Soviet forces — 148 генера́лов сда́лись в плен сове́тским войска́м (Press)

But the singular is found:

(*a*) with words expressing approximation, e.g. бо́лее, ме́нее, свы́ше, почти́, &c.:

More than 600 workers were arrested — Бо́лее 600 рабо́чих бы́ло аресто́вано

(*b*) with the words всего́, то́лько:

43 delegates in all attended the congress — Всего́ съе́халось на съезд 43 делега́та

Compare:

The 43 delegates had 51 votes — 43 делега́та име́ли 51 го́лос

(*c*) with a few verbs of existence, such as быть, име́ться:

He had 3 sons — У него́ бы́ло три сы́на

(*d*) often in statistical lists where attention is drawn to the strikingly large number of people in the mass, or to people as a united whole:

90 million electors voted — Голосова́ло 90 миллио́нов избира́телей

50,000 workers were on strike — Бастова́ло 50 ты́сяч рабо́чих

766. Nouns expressing a definite number (e.g. двойка, тройка, &c., дюжина, сотня, тысяча, миллион) generally have verbs in agreement with them in gender and number, in written, though not always in spoken Russian:

1,000 soldiers escaped to Germany	Тысяча солдат убежала в Германию

767. Nouns expressing an indefinite number:

(i) With куча and масса only a singular verb is used.

(ii) With большинство, меньшинство, множество, and ряд the following points should be observed:

(*a*) if they are used absolutely, the verb will be in the singular:

The majority voted for war	Большинство голосовало за войну

(*b*) if they govern a noun in the genitive singular, the verb will also be in the singular:

The majority of the group declared itself in favour of the new proposal	Большинство группы высказалось за новое предложение

(*c*) if they govern a noun in the genitive plural, the verb is commonly found in both singular and plural. When the noun in the genitive plural refers to persons, a plural verb is common if the persons appear as *active* agents:

The majority of the students arrived late	Большинство студентов приехали поздно

On the other hand in *passive* constructions involving persons (and also in those active constructions where the verb is of a non-dynamic nature—e.g. *to die*), a singular verb is normal:

The majority of the soldiers were sent to Moscow for the winter	Большинство солдат было отправлено на зиму в Москву

768. Indefinite *numeral-words*:

(i) A singular verb is normally used with ма́ло, мно́го, немно́го, сто́лько, and ско́лько regardless of the nouns they govern:

There were few people there   Там бы́ло ма́ло люде́й

(ii) With не́сколько, both singular and plural verbs are used, and the principles laid down in para. **767** concerning active and passive constructions apply also to не́сколько.

769. Numeral and noun combinations in which the noun expresses duration of time (*minute, hour, day, year, &c.*) have verbs in the singular number and (in the past tense) the neuter gender:

40 years passed   Прошло́ со́рок лет

This applies also to fractions (e.g. полови́на, треть, че́тверть) which are grammatically feminine nouns:

It struck half-past six	Проби́ло полови́на седьмо́го
A third of the day remained	Оста́лось треть дня
A quarter of an hour went by	Прошло́ че́тверть часа́

VIII

SOME REMARKS ON WORD-ORDER AND OMITTED WORDS

770. The order of words in Russian, a highly inflected language, is much freer than in English which, like other relatively uninflected languages, can often show the grammatical relationship between words only by their position in the sentence. The freedom of Russian word-order may be exploited to express varied shades of meaning and emphasis which are expressed in English by methods less neat than the transposition of words or may even be incapable of expression. In addition, certain syntactical deficiencies of Russian may be offset by the manner in which the various parts of the sentence are arranged. The very freedom of Russian word-order often makes it possible to translate an English passage into Russian without changing at all the English order of words. At the same time, this freedom is part of the idiomatic structure of the language and an adequate translation from English into Russian may be transformed into a good translation by making, where appropriate, changes in the order of words. In this chapter we indicate some of the salient idiomatic characteristics of Russian word-order.

The position of the subject

771. The subject in Russian may stand at the end of its sentence or clause, if the writer wishes to emphasize it, or especially to bring it to the reader's attention:

Her guests at dinner that day were Strakun and the Englishwoman	Обéдали у неё в э́тот день Стракýн и англича́нка (Bunin)

(Notice how the same balance of emphasis is achieved in the Russian sentence as in the English, by different syntactical means.) This arrangement of words is especially common at the beginning of a narrative or a critical study, when the author, by placing the subject at the end of the introductory sentence, draws to it the attention of the reader:

In the mist and half-light of dawn, while everyone in Sinope was still asleep, a pirate ship approached the town	На рассвéте, в тумáне и сýмраке, когдá все ещё спáли в гóроде Синóпе, подошёл к Синóпу разбóйничий корáбль (Bunin)
The poet Alexander Trifonovich Tvardovski worked with great energy and success during the Great Patriotic War	Óчень актѝвно и успéшно рабóтал во врéмя Велѝкой Отéчественной войнь́ı поэ́т Алексáндр Трифóнович Твардóвский (Soviet History of Literature for Schools)

The inversion of subject and verb

772. The inversion of subject and verb is much more frequent in Russian than in English. It occurs commonly at the beginning of a story when the author is setting the scene or bringing the reader into the course of events:

The river flows to the sea, year follows year. Every year, with the approach of spring, the grey forest above the Dniester and Reuth grows green	Течёт рекá к мóрю, идёт год за гóдом. Кáждый год зеленéет к веснé сéрый лес над Днéстром и Реýтом (Bunin)

Notice the frequency of inversion, in such contexts, even

after adverbial expressions of time, which are not normally followed by inverted subject and verb:

One evening, in the spring of 1916, I was sitting alone in the chalky twilight	Как-то вечером, весной 1916 года, сидел я один в белёсых сумерках (Rozhdestvensky)
One early spring day, we were travelling to Batum from Port Said	Однажды, ранней весной, шли мы в Батум из Порт-Саида (Bunin)

The author does not, however, invert subject and verb if he wishes to begin his story without preamble. Such a beginning in Russian often corresponds to the beginning of an English story with the definite article, when the author does not trouble to proceed from the unknown to the known:

The guests had long since departed	Гости давно разъехались (Turgenev)
The restaurant was empty. Only Leonid Antonovich and I remained	Ресторан опустел. Остались только я и Леонид Антонович (Kuprin)

773. Subject and verb are also usually inverted when the verb is one which denotes coming into existence, existing or passing. The Russian verbs most commonly found in such constructions are наступать (наступить), наставать (настать) *to come*, быть, бывать *to be*, проходить (пройти) *to pass*. The subject in English is normally accompanied by the indefinite article or no article:

A time will come when I shall no longer be your slave	Настанет время, я вам больше не буду рабом
Autumn came	Наступила осень (Katayev)
Strange things happen	Бывают странные случаи
But war soon came	Но вскоре стала война (Erenburg)

The subject usually only precedes these verbs when it is strongly individualized (English definite article, possessive pronoun, demonstrative adjective):

... they (his comrades) kept on repeating: 'Till we meet again soon, till we meet again soon'.... And now the meeting had come	... они́ (това́рищи) тверди́ли: до ско́рой встре́чи, до ско́рой встре́чи... и вот встре́ча наступи́ла (Fedin)
Her childhood and youth, and that of her two brothers, passed in Pyatnitsky Street	Де́тство и ю́ность её и двух бра́тьев прошли́ на Пятни́цкой у́лице (Chekhov)
The whole of that day passed in the best way possible	Весь э́тот день прошёл как нельзя́ лу́чше (Turgenev)

774. Semantically similar to the verbs in the preceding paragraph are a larger number of verbs which mean *to begin, to arise, to exist* in more specific contexts and which also often precede their subject. The commonest of these verbs is идти́ (пойти́) in its meaning of *to be going on* (imperfective), *to begin* (perfective): иду́т перегово́ры *negotiations are going on*, ему́ шёл два́дцать пе́рвый год *he was in his twenty-first year*, идёт дождь *it is raining*, пошёл снег *it began to snow*. Идти́ (пойти́) with inverted subject is very common in expressions describing the weather. Inversion is also common with other verbs in expressions describing weather conditions, e.g. стои́т си́льный моро́з *it is freezing hard*, поду́л ве́тер с се́вера *a wind blew up from the north*, загреме́л гром *it began to thunder*. Less frequently, such expressions will be found with non-inverted subject and verb and since weather conditions do not easily lend themselves to individualization there is almost no difference in sense between inverted and non-inverted order. There is, for example, as little difference between дождь шёл с ра́ннего утра́ and шёл дождь с ра́ннего утра́ as in English between *rain had been falling since early morning* and *it had been raining since early morning*. Notice, however, the more appreciable difference in the degree of individualization between:

The thunderstorm broke as we were walking home	Гроза́ разрази́лась, когда́ мы шли домо́й

and

It began to thunder	Загреме́л гром

Inverted order may also express the indefiniteness of future time, compared with the definiteness of past time, expressed by non-inverted order:

When the wind blew up from the north...	Когда́ ве́тер поду́л с се́вера ...
If a wind blows up from the north...	Е́сли поду́ет ве́тер с се́вера ...

In the past tense the speaker is referring to a definite wind of which he had experience.

775. There are several other verbs which mean *to arise, to begin* in special senses and are commonly accompanied by an inverted subject. Common among these are:

Случа́ться (случи́ться), происходи́ть (произойти́) *to happen*:

An accident happened	Произошёл несча́стный слу́чай

Вспы́хивать (вспы́хнуть) *to flare up, to break out* :

War broke out	Вспы́хнула война́
A fire broke out	Вспы́хнул пожа́р

Слы́шаться (послы́шаться) *to be heard, to echo*:

Steps were heard	Послы́шались шаги́

Возника́ть (возни́кнуть) *to spring up, to appear*:

A brilliant idea came to him	Возни́кла у него́ блестя́щая мысль

and a number of verbs with the prefix раз-, e.g. разгора́ться (разгоре́ться) *to flame up, to flare up*, раздава́ться (разда́ться) *to be heard, to ring out*, разы́грываться (разыгра́ться) *to rise* (of the wind), *to burst forth* (of a storm). The subject, if it precedes these verbs, is usually strongly individualized:

At midnight a storm arose, but by early morning the ship had already passed the Lido. During the day the storm burst forth with fearsome violence . . .	С полу́ночи подняла́сь бу́ря, но поутру́ ра́но кора́бль уже́ минова́л Ли́до. В тече́ние дня бу́ря разыгра́лась с стра́шной си́лой. . . (Turgenev)

This passage offers a very good example of the author proceeding from the unknown to the known, from inverted subject and verb (English indefinite article) to non-inverted subject and verb (English definite article).

776. Inversion of subject and verb is common in Russian when the subject is an anaphoric pronoun referring back to a noun in the preceding clause or sentence. The inversion draws the reader's attention to the pronoun and through the pronoun back to the original noun:

Before us stretches only one road and it is like an endless bridge. They are taking this road and cannot turn aside	Пе́ред на́ми одна́ то́лько доро́га и похо́жа она́ на бесконе́чный мост. Иду́т они́ э́той доро́гой и никуда́ сверну́ть не мо́гут (Press)
In this public house wine is probably sold at not less than the fixed price but it is patronized much more assiduously than all similar neighbouring establishments	В э́том кабаке́ вино́ продаётся вероя́тно не деше́вле поло́женной цены́, но посеща́ется он гора́здо приле́жнее, чем все окре́стные заведе́ния тако́го же ро́да (G. Uspensky)
They brought out horses. I did not like them	Вы́вели лошаде́й. Не понра́вились они́ мне (Turgenev)

777. Inversion of subject and verb is also common to balance a relative or comparative clause which includes an auxiliary verb and infinitive:

Historical events are accompanied by . . . sufferings and hardships which men cannot avert	Истори́ческие собы́тия сопровожда́ются…страда́ниями и лише́ниями, кото́рых не мо́жет отврати́ть челове́к (Fedin)
Sufferings do not cease to exist, just as pain does not cease to be felt because it is known by what illness it is caused	Страда́ния не перестаю́т существова́ть, как не перестаёт ощуща́ться боль оттого́, что изве́стно, како́й боле́знью она́ порождена́ (Fedin)

778. Indicative of the greater freedom of Russian, compared with English word-order, is the fact that after negative adverbial expressions in English (*never before, never again, nor, nowhere*) or expressions positive in form but negative in meaning (*scarcely, only, only once, seldom*) inversion is compulsory, whereas in Russian both inverted and non-inverted order are possible, the choice being often purely stylistic:

But never, since the day of his father's death, had Louis Roux gone near the completed cafés and not once had he tried the ruby brandies	Но никогда́ Луи́ Ру, со дня сме́рти своего́ отца́, не подходи́л бли́зко к достро́енным кофе́йням, и ни ра́зу он не про́бовал руби́новых настоек (Erenburg)
Never before had Rodion's foot trod on foreign soil	Никогда́ до сих пор не ступа́ла нога́ Родио́на на чужу́ю зе́млю (Katayev)
Scarcely had the scarlet fever passed when pneumonia set in	Едва́ ко́нчилась скарлати́на, начало́сь воспале́ние лёгких (Katayev)

| *But scarcely had the boy taken a running dive into the sea . . .* | Но едва́ ма́льчик, разбежа́вшись, бултыхну́лся в мо́ре . . . (Katayev) |

Position of subject and complement

779. In Russian sentences containing verbs meaning *to be, to become, to be considered, to turn out, to seem*, different shades of meaning and emphasis may be expressed by changing the positions of subject and complement. If the complement in Russian follows the verb, it will normally be translated into English with the indefinite article:

| *The colonel turned out to be a traitor* | Полко́вник оказа́лся изме́нником |

The subject preceding the verb is usually to be translated with a definite article in English but may correspond to an emphatic indefinite article:

| *Even a colonel may turn out to be a traitor* | И полко́вник мо́жет оказа́ться изме́нником |

The complement preceding the verb in Russian is usually to be translated with a definite article in English:

| *The traitor turned out to be the colonel* | Изме́нником оказа́лся полко́вник |

It may, however, correspond to an emphatic indefinite article:

| *The colonel may be a coward but he will never become a traitor* | Полко́вник, быть мо́жет, трус, но изме́нником он никогда́ не ста́нет |

The subject following the verb may correspond to either the definite or indefinite article in English:

| *The traitor turned out to be a colonel* | Изме́нником оказа́лся полко́вник |

(Cf. with example above.)

The position of the object

780. Just as the subject may in Russian be brought into prominence by being placed at the end of its sentence or clause, so the object may be emphasized by being placed at the beginning. This may be paralleled in English, as in:

His threats he took pleasure in carrying out . . .	Свой угрозы он с удовольствием приводил в действие. . . (Fedin)

Or the Russian order of words may have to be changed in English as in:

(I) would have given anything in the world just for these charming little fingers to have patted me also on the brow	(Я) бы отдал всё на свете, чтобы только и меня эти прелестные пальчики хлопнули по лбу (Turgenev)

Notice that the emphasis upon the object in this position is often strengthened in Russian by such words as и (*also, even*) всего, только (*only*).

781. The object in Russian is often placed first in the first sentence of a story when it is uppermost in the author's mind and he wishes to bring it first to the reader's attention. The same effect may be achieved in English by the use of a passive construction:

This little story was told by the saddler nicknamed 'The Cricket'	Эту небольшую историю рассказал шорник „Сверчок“ (Bunin)
I was awakened by a strident noise	Меня разбудил жестокий шум (Erenburg)

782. The object in initial position is very common in Russian when the indefinite third person plural or an impersonal construction translates an English passive. The order of words in Russian achieves the same balance of emphasis as the passive in English:

He was detained in hospital for a week	Его подержа́ли неде́лю в го́спитале (Fedin)
Pavlik, exhausted by the oppressive heat and the journey, began to nod. He had to be put to bed in a black, oil-skin hammock	Па́влик, размо́рённый духото́й и доро́гой, стал клева́ть но́сом. Его́ пришло́сь уложи́ть спать на чёрную клеёнчатую ко́йку (Katayev)

783. The object may, for emphasis, stand between subject and verb:

Surely you loved your own son	Неуже́ли ты своего́ сы́на не люби́ла (Turgenev)

Pronoun objects, however, with or without prepositions, often precede the verb simply as a stylistic alternative, without emphasis:

She whispered something	Она́ что́-то шепта́ла (Fedin)
The better I knew him the more attached to him I became. I soon understood him	Чем бо́льше я узнава́л его́, тем сильне́е я к нему́ привяза́лся. Я ско́ро его́ по́нял (Turgenev)

784. If a verb governs a direct object and an indirect pronominal object (but not an indirect nominal object) the indirect object with or without·preposition usually immediately follows the verb:

The police-officer, without looking at the man with the moustache, stretched out his hand to him	При́став, не гля́дя на уса́того, протяну́л к нему́ ру́ку (Katayev)
'Are you busy at present?' she said, without taking her eyes off me	Вы тепе́рь за́няты? — промо́лвила она́, не спуска́я с меня́ глаз (Turgenev)
(She) . . . carefully unwound the ball (of wool) and placed it over my hands	[Она́]... стара́тельно развяза́ла свя́зку [ше́рсти] и положи́ла мне её на́ руки (Turgenev)

The position of the adjective and adjectival expression

785. The normal position of the attributive adjective in Russian is immediately before the noun it qualifies. For emphasis, however, it may be placed at the beginning of the sentence:

You have chosen fine apartments, I said	Отлѝчную вы вы́брали кварти́ру, промо́лвил я (Turgenev)
Our life is out of the ordinary, said Lidya Nikolayevna to Shtrem	Необыкнове́нная у нас жизнь, сказа́ла Ли́дя Никола́евна Штре́му (Erenburg)

This construction is particularly common with nouns which designate persons:

She is a charming woman	Очарова́тельная она́ же́нщина (Bunin)

786. As well as at the beginning of the sentence, but more rarely, an adjective may be placed for emphasis at the end of the sentence ('Lighter elements can be placed near the centre while heavier ones are relegated to more peripheral places'—Jespersen on word-order in English, equally true of Russian):

He was an uncommonly good story-teller	Расска́зчик он был необыкнове́нный (Pavlenko)
He had a phenomenal memory for people	Па́мять на люде́й у него́ была́ феномена́льная (Pavlenko)

787. An attributive adjective may acquire slight emphasis by being placed before a demonstrative or possessive adjective:

I remember my first morning in barracks	Я по́мню пе́рвое моё у́тро в каза́рме (Kuprin)
This short conversation was heard by Aloysha	Коро́ткий э́тот разгово́р слы́шал Алёша (Fedin)

By placing the attributive adjective first, the writer brings it first to the reader's attention and it becomes therefore the weightiest word of its phrase.

788. Sometimes in English the noun in a complement or object is simply an indicator-word and the adjective or adjectives accompanying it bear the logical stress. This logical stress may be expressed in Russian by placing the attributive adjective or adjectives after the noun:

My father was a thoroughly kind, clever, cultured, and unhappy man	Отéц мой был человéк весьмá дóбрый, ýмный, образóванный и несчáстный (Turgenev)
The steamer 'Turgenev' was considered even for those days a fairly antiquated craft	Парохóд „Тургéнев" считáлся дáже и по томý врéмени сýдном порядочно устарéвшим (Katayev)
His face wore a pleasant enough but roguish expression	Лицó егó имéло выражéние довóльно приятное но плутовскóе (Pushkin)

789. A predicative adjective may for emphasis stand at the beginning of the sentence:

Only her father was close to Parasha	Блúзок был Парáше лишь отéц (Bunin)
I have known few people kinder, gentler, milder	Добрéе, крóтче, мягче я мáло встречáл людéй (Gor'ky)

790. Qualifying adjectival expressions consisting of a pronoun or noun in an oblique case, with or without a preposition, normally precede the noun when another single adjective is present:

It was a painful evening for him	Это был тяжёлый для негó вéчер (Erenburg)
The house next door	Рядом с нáми дом
I have similar tastes to his	У меня схóдные с ним вкýсы
. . . swinging freely his thin legs in blue Austrian puttees	. . . свéсив на вóлю тóнкие в австрúйских голубых обмóтках нóги (Fedin)

Frequently in such constructions, a participle is found instead of an adjective. The participle may be modified by an adverb:

. . . in heated goods-wagons, crammed with people, which happened to be there	... в случа́йно подверну́вших- ся заби́тых наро́дом ваго́- нах-теплу́шках (Fedin)
The events described in this book . . .	Опи́сываемые в э́той кни́ге собы́тия . . . (Katayev)

Omitted words

791. The verb is often omitted in Russian, especially in narrative, when the meaning is clear without it. The omitted verb may be a verb of motion:

'Sh! Hello! Don't open the door, I'll come through the window', whispered Grigori	„Ти́ше! Здра́вствуй! Не отпира́й дверь, я — че́рез окно́", шо́потом сказа́л Григо́рий (Sholokhov)

Or a verb of saying:

'Vera, what does this mean?', he asked impatiently. Vera said not a word, only her chin quivered	„Ве́ра, что э́то зна́чит?" с нетерпе́нием спроси́л он. Ве́ра — ни сло́ва, то́лько подборо́док у неё дрожа́л (Goncharov)

792. Often, where in English two verbs or verbal clauses are joined by *and*, Russian may omit the conjunction и. This may happen:

(i) When the verbs describe actions which rapidly follow each other:

Two gendarmes took Nikolai by the arms and roughly led him into the kitchen	Дво́е жанда́рмов взя́ли Ни- кола́я под руки, гру́бо повели́ в ку́хню (Gor'ky)

(ii) When the verbs describe habitual actions, closely connected with each other:

| *I used to get up every day before sun-rise and go to bed early* | Встава́л я ка́ждый день до восхо́да со́лнца, ложи́лся ра́но (Chekhov) |

(iii) When the verbs describe simultaneous actions, closely connected with each other:

| *The child was crying and struggling* | Ребёнок пла́кал, би́лся (Gor'ky) |
| *Everyone was tired and in a bad humour* | Все уста́ли, обозли́лись (Gor'ky) |

793. When the subjects of the main and subordinate clauses are the same, the personal pronoun which in English heads the subordinate clause, is normally omitted in Russian:

| *He was firmly convinced that he had a complete right to rest* | Он был твёрдо уве́рен, что име́ет по́лное пра́во на о́тдых (Bunin) |
| *She never knew, one day, whether she would have enough to eat the next* | Она́ никогда́ не зна́ла накану́не, бу́дет ли сыта́ за́втра (Gor'ky) |

The personal pronoun may occur, in Russian, for emphasis or precision:

| *Finishing her course in the boarding-school, Sosnovskaya at once informed her mother that she had decided to devote herself to art* | Ко́нчив курс в пансио́не, Сосно́вская то́тчас же заяви́ла ма́тери, что она́ реши́ла посвяти́ть себя́ иску́сству (Bunin) |

The personal pronoun is normally expressed in both clauses when the main clause follows the subordinate:

| *I have not kept the magazines and papers in which my writings appeared* | Журна́лов и газе́т, в кото́рых я печа́тался, я не сохраня́л (Chekhov) |

794. In Russian, a pronoun object is often omitted in the second clause of a sentence when it is clear to which noun or pronoun in the first clause it would refer:

Gerasim motioned him towards him with his finger and took him into the coach-house	Гера́сим подозва́л его́ к себе́ па́льцем, отвёл в каре́тный сара́й (Turgenev)

This may also occur in the second of two successive sentences:

You will learn the order of march in ten minutes from Korsakov. He is just making it out	Поря́док движе́ния узна́ете че́рез де́сять мину́т у Корса́кова. Он сейча́с составля́ет (V. Nekrasov)

795. The answer to a question is often given in Russian by repeating the word which bears the logical stress in the question:

'But does she love him?', he asked.	,,А она́ его́ лю́бит?'' спроси́л он.
'Yes'	,,Лю́бит'' (Turgenev)
'And is Denisov a good fellow?', she asked.	,,А что, Дени́сов хоро́ший?'' спроси́ла она́.
'Yes, he is'	,,Хоро́ший'' (L. N. Tolstoy)

If the answer is negative then, of course, the negative particle is added. Negative answers to the above questions would have been expressed by не лю́бит and нехоро́ший.

796. Before nouns or pronouns in apposition, a preposition is repeated in Russian where it is not repeated in English:

I am speaking of literature as one of the thermometers of spiritual health	Я говорю́ о литерату́ре, как об одно́м из термоме́тров духо́вного состоя́ния (Gor'ky)
They look upon him as a hero	Они́ смо́трят на него́, как на геро́я

When the pronoun все in an oblique case follows a personal pronoun governed by a preposition, the preposition may for emphasis be repeated before the appropriate case of все:

And so, when enough tractors have been built, there will be evening clothes for all of us	Ита́к, когда́ настро́ят доста́точно тра́кторов, у нас у всех бу́дут вече́рние туале́ты (Press)

RUSSIAN WORDS

All numbers refer to paragraphs. Words occurring in the vocabulary sections at the ends of the chapters on the Noun, Adjective, Verb, and Adverb are not included. Where lists occur in Russian, the whole list is not included in the index, but a representative word has been selected, e.g. за́лпом *at a gulp* illustrates the adverbial use of the instrumental singular of a noun, but a separate entry is not given in the index for the other Russian words да́ром, ря́дом, ры́сью, ша́гом mentioned in the same paragraph.

рад, 45, 136 (i).
ра́ди, 621.
ра́доваться, 42.
разма́хивать, 51.
ра́зный, 461 (ii).
ра́неный (ра́ненный), 156 (ii).
располага́ть, 47 (i).
располо́жен, 327 (ii).
расстава́ться, 52 (iii).
ре́дкий, 513.
рискова́ть, 47 (ii).
роди́ться, 52 (iii).
ро́знь, 44 (iii).
руководи́ть, 47 (i).
ряд, 56 (vii), 57 (ii).

с, 529, 554, 568, 574, 575, 576,
  599, 605, 618, 622, 629, 635,
  648, 660, 661, 669, 675, 685,
  725.
с . . . до, 552.
со дня на́ день, 553 (i).
с тех пор, как, 389 (i).
сад, 56 (ii), 57 (i).
сам, 519, 520.
сам по себе́, 520.
са́мый, 519.
сверх, 630, 647.
свой, 451, 452, 453.
свы́ше, 630.
себе, себе́, 439 (ii).
себя́, 439 (i), 440.
сего́дня, 38.
сей, 460.
се́стрин, 147 (ii).
сза́ди, 591.
сиде́ть, 328.
сирота́, 6.
сквозь, 613.
скрежета́ть, 51.
следи́ть, 263.
слуга́, служа́нка, 8 (iii).
служи́ть, 41 (i), 52 (iii).
слыть, 52 (ii).
слы́шать, 198 (iii), 204 (ii).

слы́шно, 303.
смея́ться, 42.
смотре́ть, 263.
смотри́те, 213.
снег, 56 (iii).
соба́чий, 149 (i).
сове́товать, 41 (ii).
совсе́м бы́ло, 206.
согла́сен (с and на), 137 (iii).
сомнева́ться, 266.
состоя́ть, 52 (i), 330.
состоя́ться, 330.
со́тня, 753.
сочу́вствовать, 42.
спра́шивать, 32 (ii).
спья́на, 362.
среди́, 639.
сродни́, 370.
станови́ться, 52 (i).
ста́рший, 145 (iv).
стать, 302.
стесня́ться, 33.
сто́ить, 34.
сто́ит то́лько, 396.
сто́лик, 60.
столо́вая, 153 (i).
сторони́ться, 33.
стоя́ and сто́я, 372.
стоя́ть, 328.
страда́ть, 50.
студе́нтка, 8.
ступа́йте, 213.
стыди́ться, 33.
суди́ть, 311.
судья́, 5.
су́мочка, 60.
суть, 325 (i).
сходи́ть, 287 (ii).
счита́ться, 52 (ii).
сын, 17 (iii).

так как, 393.
так(же) ... как, 399 (i), (ii), 400.
так что, 395 (i).
так, что́бы, 398 (iii).

ENGLISH—RUSSIAN INDEX

All numbers refer to paragraphs. This index does not include words listed alphabetically in the vocabulary sections at the end of the chapters on the Noun, Adjective, Verb, and Adverb.

Enough to, is, 397.
Even, 419 (ii); *even if,* 413; *even then,* 416.
Every, 516–17.
Everyone, 517.

Few (a few), 486, 511–13.
For, 550–1 (time); 620–1 (cause); *plan for,* 29 (i); 654–9; see also 692–7, 707, 720–1.
For (my) part, 422 (iii).
Four, 743–7.
From, out of, off, 574–6, 579–80 (place); 622 (cause); 660–3.
From . . . to, 552–3.

Gender: masculine nouns ending in -a, 5; nouns denoting animals, 10; nouns denoting persons, 8, 9; nouns of common gender, 6.
Genitive case: after negatives, 37; after verbs, 32–36; in -y (-ю), 31; to express the date, 38.
Gerunds: in -a, -я from imperfective verbs, 318; in -a, -я from perfective verbs, 319; in -ши, -в, -вши, 320, 322–3; used to translate *when* and *after,* 380, 388.

Half, 739–40.
Have only to . . . for, 396.
Have something done, to, 259.
He, 442.
His, 450–4.
However, 422 (i).
However much, 411.

If, 402–10.
If not . . . then, 412.
If you like, 414.
Imperative: in conditional sentences, 410; modal use of, 281–3.

Imperfective past used stylistically instead of perfective past, 198.
Impersonal constructions: expressing disinclination or incapacity, 310; expressing English passives, 311–12; expressing physical or emotional states, 308–9; *it is necessary, it is fitting, one has to,* 304; *it is possible, impossible,* 305–6; *one must, ought to,* 307; *there is, there are,* 298; *there is someone (no one) to,* 299; *there is something (nothing) to,* 300; *there is somewhere (nowhere) to,* 301; *there is enough (not enough),* 302.
In, 530–2 (point in time); 533–7 (duration of time); 538–9 (other temporal meanings); 559–61, 567 (place); 664–6; see also 698, 708.
In order to, 398.
Indeed, 419 (iii).
Infinitive: expressing desirability, with бы, 272; desirability without бы, 274 (i); warning or apprehension (negative infinitive with бы), 273; a command, 274 (iii); *should, ought to,* 275; *have to, must,* 276; *shall, should, will, are to, can,* 277 (i); incredulity or disinclination, 277 (ii); impossibility or inevitability, 278.
Instrumental case: after verbs, 47–52; after adjectives, 53; as a limiting accusative, 54; expressing extent or measurement, 46 (iv), manner, 46 (ii), route, 46 (iii), time, 46 (i); of predicate adjectives, 140; of predicate nouns, 21; used adverbially, 366.
Into, 573, 577–8; see also 709–10.

PRINTED IN GREAT BRITAIN
AT THE UNIVERSITY PRESS, OXFORD
BY VIVIAN RIDLER
PRINTER TO THE UNIVERSITY